THE GIRL IN THE
WOODS

JAMES WHALEY

iUniverse, Inc.
Bloomington

THE GIRL IN THE WOODS

iUniverse books may be ordered through booksellers or by contacting:

iUniverse
1663 Liberty Drive
Bloomington, IN 47403
www.iuniverse.com
1-800-Authors (1-800-288-4677)

ISBN: 978-1-4759-4422-8 (sc)
ISBN: 978-1-4759-4423-5 (ebk)

Printed in the United States of America

iUniverse rev. date: 08/21/2012

CONTENTS

DEDICATION

I am delighted to be able to dedicate this work to my family. Elinor, Kristi, Roger, Jimmy, Nisha, Madison, I love you all. May God bless you.

ACKNOWLEDGEMENTS

So many people have assisted me in reaching the level of writing I am involved with at this time. I appreciate the efforts made by so many to teach me the skills and techniques of story telling. A special and grateful thanks to Dorothy Hush for pain-stakingly proof-reading each and every page to correct my punctuation, sentence structure, and her patience on my repeated grammatical errors. Thanks to the writing group: Joanne, Dorothy, and Marvin, for their continued support and encouragement, and for being part of the writing group for so many years. And finally but certainly not the least, to those who have read some of my work and expressed an appreciation of it. Your encouragement is what urged me on.

PROLOGUE

The car's headlights bit into the darkness as it slowly pulled to the edge of the clearing and came to a stop. The driver punched the headlight button, switched off the radio, and killed the motor. The driver sat starring into the void of the night for several minutes, as if contemplating the next move. From the backseat of the sedan came the soft whimpering of the girl. "Your father brought this upon you himself, young lady, so there's no point in crying over it. Time to pay the piper, as they say," he said over his shoulder. Getting out of the vehicle, the driver popped the trunk lid and removed a short handled spade, then opened the rear door. "Let's go." There was no movement from the backseat. As if expecting as much, the driver reached into the car, grabbed the upper arm of the girl, and pulled her out. "Now listen, we can do this the easy way or the hard way, that's your choice. You understand me?" There was no response from the girl, except for the quiet sobbing. Leaning the shovel against the door of the car, the figure unsnapped the flashlight from the waist belt, switched it on and grabbed the shovel with the same hand. Carefully, the girl was guided into the trees and across the footbridge. The pair were quickly swallowed up by the darkness. When they reached the spot that had been selected the night before, the girl was shoved to a kneeling position. With one swift motion the flashlight dropped to the ground, the shovel raised high in the air and came down on the head of the girl with a thud. The girl crumbled into a heap and lay still. Quickly jamming the shovel into the soft soil the figure scooped out a shallow grave. Using the shovel, the girl's body was rolled into the depression and the soil replaced. Selecting a bough of a nearby bush, it was easily broken and used to brush the ground leaving no bootprints as the figure backed away from the girl's resting place in the woods. The driver, in an orderly manner, collected the tools used and headed back to the car. The night's work was finished.

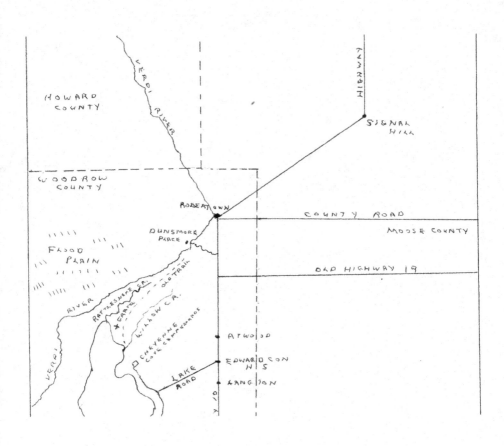

CHAPTER 1
WANDA KELLAM

"Happy Birthday to you, happy birthday to you, happy birthday, dear Ralph, happy birthday to you." The singing stopped, then "And many more!" came a lone voice from the midst of the small group. As usually happened, his sister, Jonie, had the last word. Ralph smiled his thank you to the small gathering in the back yard of the home of Wanda and Delbert Kellam. Ralph stood six feet tall, with hazel colored eyes and short blond hair. Broad-shouldered, he looked every bit the part of the defensive back he played on the high school football team. In fact, after the party, he would have to scurry around and head for the football field to be ready for the 7:00 kickoff between Robertown and Allisonville, Missouri, in a non-conference game. The home team was an odds on favorite to win by a large margin.

The day was October 15, 2010, and sixteen-year-old Ralph Kellam was enjoying a late Friday afternoon. School was out for the week and his birthday party was just beginning. The fall day had been pleasant, with the temperature hovering around 68 degrees. His home town of Robertown, Kansas, had a population of about 20,000 people and probably twice that many cats and dogs. Robertown, named after its founder William Roberts, who led a train consisting of eight family wagons to the high side of the bend in the Verdi River. The eight families had applied for a post office in 1872 under the name Robertstown, to honor their leader, but through a clerical error the approval of the post office came back as Robertown. The town representatives, rather than fight it, allowed the name to stick. The Verdi River ran through Woodrow County, where a vast portion of the county located on the western side of the river had been identified as a flood plain. The river ran from the northwest, entered the county and continued to Robertown, where it changed direction and meandered to the southwest through the county. The county population ran around 30,000, of that 90 percent existed on the eastern side of the Verdi River. Even at that, there were only two other towns in the county, both relatively small and lacking any real industry in either of them. Robertown, fortunate in having two glass producers, a cement producing plant and a large trade area to draw from, teemed with small town business. Ralph enjoyed the "laid-back" atmosphere, as his father described it, because it fit his style of living. Ralph had no ambition to leave his hometown and head for the metropolitan area around Topeka, as many of his classmates planned to do.

"Here you go Ralph, enjoy it." His mother handed him a huge piece of German Chocolate cake.

"Thanks mom, did you leave any for the others?"

"Don't worry, there's plenty more where that came from." She smiled at her son. "I hope you're happy with the small crowd, I kept the invitations at a minimum as you asked."

"It's perfect, Mom quit worrying. I told you I didn't want a large party and you did fine. I am glad that you asked Sarah Muncie, though, she's a nice girl but doesn't get invited to many parties."

"Well, she is in your class and she's always so quiet and so very polite, I like her."

"Don't tell Jonie, but so do I," Ralph said quietly so only his mother could hear.

"I'm happy for you, Ralph, but about the party, we could have had some live music of some sort. I did pass on bringing in the magician and his donkey, as Jonie suggested."

"You know I'm not into the music fad like Jonie, and I do appreciate your not going along with her idea of a magic show. She'd have found some way to embarrass me with that donkey."

"You should know that's her way of showing she admires you. The more she teases, the more you should appreciate her attention to you.

One of these days she will grow up and then take a more mature attitude toward you."

Almost as if on cue, his sister came bounding up. "When do we pin the tail on the donkey, bro?" Jonie announced loudly, as she reached up and mussed his hair with her hand and was off without waiting for a comment from either her brother or mother. Ralph tried to smooth down his hair. He glared after his sister as she turned and gave him a big grin.

"I'll wait for that day with great delight."

"Just remember what I said. She and I will have another talk, though my talks only seem to last a short time with her." His mother smiled, as she patted his arm and moved away to help serve cake to someone.

Watching as Jonie did the same thing to Mike Mitchell's hair, Ralph admired the patience Mike showed. He was a good friend and fellow classmate in school, A quiet kid with a similar build as Ralph, but would never hurt a fly. He accepted Jonie's antics without so much as a disparaging comment. Ralph also noticed that Jonie, still considered a little girl by some, looked the spitting image of her mother. Her long full hair the color of cherry wood swung in a pair of pig tails behind her, and those big brown eyes missed nothing. Her oval face did not have a blemish, but now shown with perspiration on her dark-toned skin. Many of the seniors in Robertown High School had noticed the young, gangly eighth grader, before she even reached the arbitrary age of a high school student. "She will break many a heart," her father was known to say on several occasions

Ralph had heard people describe his mother as a pretty woman, with a full head of auburn hair and brown eyes on a classic oval face, she looked the part of a celebrity. Every one had been surprised that she had said yes when Delbert Kellam had asked her to marry him. No one was more amazed than "Del" himself. Wanda Vanderson displayed the image of strength. But Wanda Kellam's real strength came as a result of her morbid and long suffering childhood. Less than six months ago, Ralph's father had told him the story of her early childhood.

According to Ralph's father, when Wanda was only a little girl her mother passed away from cancer of the liver. She watched her mother as she struggled with the pain and agony of abdominal cancer. The child, at the age of eight, experienced the slow deterioration of her mother's body heard the moans and groans during the day and cries of a woman in great pain during the night. The sounds were horrific and continuous. Then came the silence of death. Her mother's death created a great void that nothing or no one could fill. While she was still suffering from the loss of her mother, her father, Ralph Vanderson, sustained a fatal fall from a water tower he had contracted to paint. It proved to be too much for the child, she went into severe depression and began to have nightmares dealing with zombies and vampires. Her dreams were extremely graphic and stayed with her during her waking hours. Doctors prescribed every thing from anti depressants to sleeping pills for the child.

Shortly afterward, a judge declared her a ward of the court and placed her in the custody of her mother's brother, Tony Winstead and his wife, Wilma. Tony lived about five miles east of Robertown, He or his wife drove the child to school, whenever she felt secure enough to attend, due to fears she developed about the big yellow school bus. The dreams continued well into her teens and young adulthood. It was only after Ralph and Jonie came along, that the dreams begin to subside into a manageable state and now the episodes were few and far between. She was still plagued with flash backs of seeing her mother's ravaged body being devoured by a ghastly creature.

Ralph watched his mother move in and out of the crowd. He knew it wasn't easy for her. For that was another gruesome and painful experience she had suffered through. He had heard the story numerous times. She was about his age now, and had gone duck hunting with her uncle Tony and one of her classmates. When the classmate got restless and decided to leave the duck blind to go to the truck for a snack, she carelessly dragged her shotgun along the top of the blind. Suddenly, the trigger caught on a nail head causing the gun to discharge. The blast from the gun hit Wanda in the knee cap and exploded the leg. At the emergency room of the hospital the surgeons decided nothing could repair all the damage and they removed the leg just above the knee.

Afterward, the teen suffered from self-consciousness that led to a new phase of nightmares. These dreams dealt with deformed people and animals who ran in packs attacking people without warning or sense of purpose. About six months after her recovery, she was fitted with a prosthesis. It was an inexpensive model and a poor fit. To make it work properly the teen developed a habit of swinging her leg in a circular motion in order to take a step. It was an ungraceful move and one that caused people to stare at her. Soon she refused to go to school because of the attention received from her classmates.

Her uncle and aunt eventually convinced her to try a new prosthesis service and they were fortunate enough to find one that fit the girl in a fashion more useful and would function properly. No longer did she have to do the swing motion. However, when she relaxed, and did not concentrate on what she was doing, the swing would return to embarrass her once again. Over the years she had learned to accept the attention and deal with it simply by ignoring it. Jonie now served as a coach and would subtly let her mother know when her concentration would stray.

But Wanda Vanderson Kellam's out-look on life drastically changed when Ralph was born. She and her husband had tried for almost two years to conceive a child, without success. Her family doctor, a Doctor Morrison, ran some tests on both her and Del. His conclusion was that on a scale of one to ten, their chances for conceiving was near zero. Both wanted a child. They decided to pursue the possibility of adopting. They applied with the American Adoption Associates Inc,. and were placed on the approved list, with little difficultly. On October 15, 1994, they got the call they had been waiting for. A 16-year-old girl had given birth to a healthy, robust baby boy. "We can't tell you any more details other than the girl is destitute, and has no way to support herself, let alone a baby. "Are you interested?" the caseworker asked.

Neither of the Kellams hesitated, their answer was a resounding "Yes!" The Kellams had been married for four years. Wanda was 24 years old, her husband Del five years older. They were ready and willing to become parents. The excitement of a baby in the house seemed like a shot in the arm for their marriage and would prove to be a great benefit to them both. The new born baby boy became Ralph Delbert Kellam, named after his grandfather and father.

Del's income was sufficient to allow Wanda to be a stay at home mother. This continued until Jonie was three the couple felt the need for Wanda to work outside the home. She was able to work for the same company where she had been employed, she filled her old position of secretary and receptionist at Wardsell and Fuller, a locally owned financial planning firm that had been in business in Robertown since 1888.

CHAPTER 2

DEL

D elbert Kellam became Del Kellam at an early age. In the household he grew up in, neither of the parents showed warmth to one another and certainly none for Del. As an only child he spent considerable time by himself. His mother had given him birth and as far as she was concerned, she had fulfilled her obligation to the family. What care Del got came from his father, who was ill equipped in the art of raising and caring for his child. "I spent weeks on end by my self, fixing my own meals and doing whatever I wanted to do." Del was lonely most of his life, continuing well into his college days.

When Del was fifteen his mother left the family and skipped town with a neighbor who was an over-the-road truck driver. The neighbor, who also had a wife and two children of high school age, had been a good personal friend of the family. His father became so upset that he left Del in the hands of a friend and went looking for his wife. He returned a week later, after finding no trace of her. Del's father was so ashamed that his wife "run off," he retired well before he planned. He left the tax accounting firm he had built over the past forty-six years, to his son. Ralph had been only about three and knew nothing of the story until his father had confided in him. Ralph had more respect for his father after learning what the conditions had been for him during his teenage years.

Late that evening, after the football team had succeeded in proving the odds makers correct with a 34 to 3 victory over the Missouri team, and with nearly everything put back in its place after the afternoon party, Ralph and his dad were sitting in the family rec room. Ralph had always enjoyed the room since the remodeling project a year ago. Complete with a pecan-colored wood floor, a Native American rug covering the floor space in front of the leather couch large enough to easily seat four people. His dad sat in a matching over-stuffed chair located nearer the limestone fireplace that graced the north wall of the room. In the far corner sat a TV where Jonie usually had her Wii program set up. At other times his dad used it to watch an old western on a VHS tape or CD.

On two sides of the twenty by fifteen foot room were solid wood mahogany cabinets which were produced in a local cabinetry shop. Above the waist high cabinets on one wall were a row of windows facing three clumps of rose bushes that peeked into the room from the outside. One section of the cabinets contained a large selection of games of all sorts: board games, card games, and activity games that the family enjoyed playing. Ralph grimaced at the thought of playing **Clue** with Jonie. She always came up with the first correct guess on who did it, in what room, and with what weapon, to win the game.

Another section of the wood cabinets housed the collection of genealogy records his dad was always working with on lazy Sunday afternoons. In all the hours he spent looking, his father had traced back only four generations. "It's difficult when you start with so many blanks that can't seem to be filled in," was his dad's excuse, and Ralph never challenged him on it. The wall across from the fire place contained a full built-in book case which housed some of the family heirlooms, pictures, artifacts, and even a shelf or two of books. Jonie in particular enjoyed looking at the family mementos her mother had so carefully arranged on the shelves. The room was lit with recessed lighting and decorative floor lamps situated at the ends of the couch. A table lamp sat on the small end table beside his dad's chair. Above the arched doorway leading to the dinning room was a shelf of trophies that Jonie won in competition for skeet shooting and tennis.

It was a comfortable room, one Ralph suspected his dad also enjoyed, as he spent many weekends, and evening hours studying papers he brought home from work, or reading a book in the peace and quiet of the room. Ralph's mind wandered to the story his father had told him just last year about his own childhood. Ralph admired his father's honesty and the way he faced difficulty. Physically he and Del were much different His father was a man slight of build, with thinning dark hair that laid straight and flat on his head. He had somewhat of a hook nose, as if it had been broken at some time in the past. Del had a weak chin with a deep cleft in the center of it, his eyes were deeply set and dark, almost black. He had the look of a man much older than his forty-five years, a man quite different than what his occupation would suggest, an independent tax accountant who had taken over the family business set up by his father. Both father and son considered it best to stay independent rather than join into a partnership with anyone else, or join another established firm. He had often said that he felt better about himself and his career by running the family business. Even if it meant less income, and called for more of a demand of his time. But he had a loyal and substantial clients who provided all the business he could handle by himself. Del had not tried to find anyone to fill the void after his own father had retired. He implied, when asked, that he would be proud if Ralph joined the firm after college, and it became a father and son company.

Ralph returned his thoughts to the present. "Dad, I want to ask you something."

His father looked up from the papers he was studying, removed his reading glasses, and said, "Yes?"

"The fishing trip you and mom promised me for my birthday. You know , the one to Lake Lawson, I . . . would like to go alone. Just by myself. Can I? please Dad?"

Del studied his sons face and saw the sincerity in it. "May I ask why?"

"Dad, you and I have gone on many fishing trips and I have enjoyed them, but I think I would like to go on this one by myself. It will give me time to think about things like the direction I want my life to go. It's time that I started thinking about that, don't you agree?"

"Your reasoning, makes sense, but is it a good idea for you to go off on your own though? There wouldn't be anyone around if you should need help. I'm sure that will never fly with your mother."

But that is just the point, I want the opportunity to depend on myself, and as far as mom is concerned, she will agree if you talk to her. Please, dad?"

"But a whole week without knowing if you are okay, that's a lot to ask of a parent, particularly a mother."

"You said yourself that you spent weeks on your own when you were much younger than I am. Dad, I want to do this."

"Okay, son, if you promise to take care of yourself and don't make me regret this later. I will talk to your mother."

Ralph let out the breath of air he had been holding. "Thanks, Dad, you're the greatest. I'll be okay." Ralph stood, held out his hand. Ralph was smiling, but Del was not.

"I have quite a job cut out for myself, don't I?" He knew convincing his wife of the deal would not be easy.

CHAPTER 3

JONIE

The month of October passed quickly for Ralph. His plan was to leave for Lake Lawson right after school on the 24th of November and return on the evening of the 28$^{th.}$ He would miss no school because of Thanksgiving vacation, and still have five full days on his own. The lake was only a thirty mile drive southwest of Robertown, so there would be plenty of time for him to arrive at the lake and have his camp set up well before nightfall.

"Ralph, I know we promised a fishing trip for your birthday, but are you sure you don't want dad to go along? It will be so lonely, up there by yourself." His mother fussed. She had not given in entirely on the idea of his going alone.

"Yeah, bro, the boogie man might get you." Jonie quipped. Ignoring her, Ralph smiled at his mother.

He put his arm around Wanda, "Mom, come on, I can take care of myself, I am not some silly little thirteen-year-old, like some I know," he said, grinning at Jonie who made a weird face at him, stuck out her tongue and grinned back at him.

"You want me to go with him and see that nobody tries to harm your little boy, Mom? I could be his baby sitter, and tuck him in at night." Jonie was on a roll and she knew it. But her mother was in no mood to be placed into one of Jonie's attempts to get her brother's goat.

"Shush, Jonie, I'm serious. I don't like the idea, not one bit." She started to remind him that he would also miss the Thanksgiving dinner, but at the Kellam house that was really just another meal. The only guests was Uncle Tony and Aunt Wilma, both of whom they saw almost daily.

Del, who had been hoping to stay out of the discussion chimed in, "You must cut the apron strings, Wanda, the boy is right, he can take care of himself."

"I'm just saying . . ."

"We've discussed this several times, Wanda." Del glanced at Jonie, who was about to say something, and added, "You too, young lady."

Wanda knew her husband was right. She had reluctantly agreed if Ralph promised to take his cell phone with him and call home regularly. Neither Ralph nor his father bothered to tell her that the cell phone reception around Lake Lawson was iffy at best.

For the next two weeks, Ralph spent much of his spare time getting his camping and fishing gear in order. Camping and fishing were two of his three leisure activities, hunting came in third. He enjoyed the outdoors and the excitement of exploring nature's beauty always thrilled him. And he enjoyed the exhilaration of the hunt, but the shooting of birds and animals usually left him regretting his actions. His sister, Jonie, had found a way to enjoy the firing of a gun and the excitement of hitting the target, without the destruction of nature. She had become a very adept student of skeet shooting, getting better with each passing tournament she entered.

"Hey, bro, what cha' doing?"

"Speak of the devil, and she shall appear."

"Hey, I'm trying to be nice here. Don't get me started. I just wanted to let you know that I think it's a great idea to go by yourself on this trip. I wish I were going with you though. I think it would be fun."

"Yeah, but you would have to promise not to open your yap and we know that couldn't happen for more than a few minutes."

"You think I talk too much? Ralph looked at his sister and saw a serious side that rarely came to the surface.

"Sometimes."

"That's what a couple of girls at my school said today. They said I'm always talking, and I never shut up."

"Oh, Jonie, don't pay any attention to what they say. They don't know you well enough to be your judge. You just like to interact with people and that's no crime. Ignore them and be yourself. Just don't annoy your big brother, you may need him some day," Ralph said, grinning.

"Maybe I should be more like Sarah Muncie, she doesn't talk much at all. She came to the school today with a group of kids from the high school FTA. I can't see her as a future teacher. She doesn't say much."

"No," Ralph said, "but when she does, what she says is important and people listen."

"Whoa, bro, I think you got a thing for her," Jonie said. "You like her, don't you?"

"She's nice and I think you could take a lesson or two from her," he answered.

"Okay," she chirped, as she reached to muss his hair, but he was too quick and ducked out of the way. Then she was off, to who knows where.

Later, when Ralph related the conversation to his mother he said, "I hope she doesn't say anything to Sarah,"

"That's like hoping that the wind doesn't blow," said his mother.

Ralph had been a two-year-old when Jonie was born, so he didn't remember her birth, but he and Jonie had both heard the story more than once from their mother.

Wanda and Del had tried for almost two years to have a child, when they were told that it was not likely to happen, they adopted Ralph. Almost two years later, when Wanda felt poorly and nauseous around food, she made an appointment to visit Dr. Morrison, the same doctor who told her it was doubtful she would ever conceive a child. He ran a battery of tests before making his diagnoses.

"Wanda I don't know how it happened but it did, you're with child. It's a one in a million shot and you are going to need to take good care of yourself. You may never have this opportunity again. Do you understand?" Wanda nodded. She was speechless, a child of her body, it truly was a miracle.

The pregnancy progressed without flaw or complication, and on September 17, 1997, the surprise package was born. Joanna Beth Kellam became a reality. The parents were ecstatic and two-year-old Ralph had a baby sister. He adored her as the rest of the family did, and played with her as often as he was allowed. As Joanna began to develop a personality it became obvious that the formal name of Joanna did not fit the rambunctious tomboy of a girl. It seemed she never met a stranger, and had a daredevil attitude toward trying new experiences with a mind of her own. Ralph was the first to refer to her as Jonie. "Mom, Jonie ruined my fort." "Mom, Jonie is bothering Mike and me. She keeps bombing our trucks from the tree."

When her father also picked up the nickname, it naturally followed that her mother did also. "Jonie quit that." "Jonie, stop pestering your brother, and get down out of that tree before you fall out." Joanna soon became the outgoing, and buoyant Jonie. One of her first real attempts to tease her brother came when she started school. That September, when the 17th rolled around, she made it a point to remind her brother that he was only two years older than she.

Ralph disagreed. "I am three years older than you."

Her grown up response amounted to a question. "How old are you right now?"

"I am eight, I will be nine next month."

"You are eight and I am six. That makes me only two years younger than you."

"But you will be six for one whole year, I will be nine in less than a month."

"Yeah, but for that month you will be only two years older than I am." Every year she reminded him of this fact. And every year Ralph had to ignore her taunts for twenty eight days. On October 15, he could finally tell her that he was three years older than she.

Last June, Ralph and his dad had gone out by the mall on the west side of town to the Kansas Department Of Transportation complex to the driver testing station. They applied for a learner's permit so Ralph could enroll in the driver's education training class that summer.

He completed the course, received his learner's certificate and since he had turned sixteen was qualified for taking the Kansas driver's license test. The test was scheduled for Tuesday morning on the 19th of October. He had studied the driver's manual and felt confident he could pass the written part of the test, it was the driving part that worried him.

"It's quite simple, Ralph, if you fail the driving part of the test, then you wait two months and retake it," his father said.

"Yeah, but that would mean that I couldn't drive myself on the fishing trip. I was planning on asking Mom if I could borrow her car to go to the lake."

"Hey, Mom needs a car to take me to the skeet tournament. I can't miss the Verdi Valley Rendezvous Shoot. It's the biggest one of the year. And Mom will need a car to take me." Jonie was near tears as she had been listening from the hallway.

"That's Thanksgiving weekend. The Kellam Tax Office will be closed for the four day weekend. If your mother needs a car she can use mine. I don't plan on going anywhere except to my easy chair." With that, Del Kellam thought he had dispensed with the problem.

"Mom won't like it if you wreck her car. You better be careful, bro," Jonie said smiling again, and with a mischievous look in her eye. "You won't pass the test anyway, I bet you won't, not the way you parallel park."

"Okay, Let's concentrate on the issues that are at the table now. Then we can worry about those that might occur, or might not," Del broke in, "nothing need be decided until after the 19th. Then if the test goes well, AND we ALL hope that it does." Del placed the emphasis on two words while looking at Jonie sternly as he did. "Any questions Jonie?"

In a rare show of forgiveness, she bowed her head and walked over to her brother and gave him a hug. "I know you will pass the test, bro, I was just trying to rile you a little. Sorry."

As Jonie predicted, all did indeed go well. Ralph passed both the written exam and the driving section of the test without difficulty. When the evaluator pointed to a slot marked with traffic cones and told Ralph to park the car between the cones, he took a nervous glance at the evaluator. "Don't get nervous son, just pretend your little sister is fast asleep in the back seat, and if you wake her she is going to start giving you directions on how to do it." Ralph laughed and relaxed sufficiently to do what was asked of him with no problem.

During the next three weeks, he drove his mother everywhere she needed to go, just to show her what a careful driver he was. And it worked, she was so impressed that she agreed to let him use her car to go on his fishing trip.

CHAPTER 4
THE FISHING TRIP

When the 24th of November finally arrived, Ralph had everything in prime working order, packed and ready to go. The plan called for him to drive the thirty miles to Lake Lawson, select a campsite in the Cheyenne Cove Camping Grounds, and set up his tent. He hoped to fish the small Willow Creek, which was one of several small rivers that fed the lake. That is, provided, it wasn't already being fished by others.

Things started to go wrong from the very beginning. At the beginning of the season, the coach of the football team had announced the practice schedule. There would be no practice the week of Thanksgiving. The week before Thanksgiving he changed his mind and scheduled a practice on the 24th and on the Saturday after Thanksgiving on the 27th. Ralph told the coach that he would be out of town on the 27th but didn't want to press his luck and ask to be excused on the 24th also. So it was after six o'clock by the time he got home and the car packed. This would put him in a rush to set up camp before sundown. Because he was in a hurry, he forgot to grab his fresh food supply. He started backing out of the drive when Jonie came running out with a satchel. Recognizing the food satchel he slammed on the brakes. Jonie opened the car door and tossed it in. "Thanks Sis," he said, "I owe you one."

"Gotta take care of my bro," she replied. And with a final wave he headed south of town. The drive to the lake went without incident. He

15

found the entrance to the campgrounds with no problem. As he turned into Cheyenne Cove, he noticed, to his surprise that there were only two other campers. Apparently the lateness of the season and the holiday had discouraged others from enjoying the pleasant weather.

He parked the car, checked the campgrounds and picked a site near the back which was rather isolated. It was also near the restrooms and showers provided for campers. They would be open until the first of December at which time the State would shut off the water to prevent freezing of pipes. Ralph filled out the required papers and stuffed them in the camp box, then started setting up his tent. Next, he cleaned the fire pit which had been left in disarray by previous campers.

The sun had all but disappeared by the time he had everything in place, leaving just enough light with which to fix his evening meal. He choose a packet containing the makings of spaghetti and a sauce. He topped the meal off with a piece of apple pie his mother had stuffed into the food satchel. After finishing his meal and cleaning the utensils, he sat by the small fire for some time. Not really thinking about anything in particular, he let his eyes take in the flames and enjoyed the peace and quiet of the evening. Suddenly the cry of a screech owl made him jump. He grinned at himself and decided to turn in. Within a matter of minutes he was fast asleep. He slept so soundly that the family of raccoons who came to visit did not awaken him, as they quarreled and chirped among themselves rattling the pots and pans he had hung on sticks in the ground to dry.

Ralph awakened at daybreak because he faced his tent to the east and the sun peeking over the open horizon had shone its rays directly into the tent, and into his eyes. *A good alarm clock,* thought Ralph. *I'll have to remember that.*

The campground was situated with an open plain to the east, and wooded area on the other three sides. From previous visits, he knew that Willow Creek was just to his right about a hundred yards through the woods. He decided to fore go breakfast and try the river for a chance of catching an early rising large mouth bass. He grabbed his fishing gear and headed into the woods.

He arrived at the river just about where it emptied into the lake. He attached his favorite green lure to his fishing line and made a perfect cast into the shallows of the river. Expertly, letting the lure drift with the current of the water, he waited. When the lure dropped into the deeper water along the near side of the river, a fish struck the line. Setting the hook, Ralph began reeling in the line. Twice the big bass came out of the water in a glorious leap in an attempt to shake free. After a time Ralph worked the fish close enough to see it was a big one. Landing the fish proved to be difficult because the dip net had been neglected in his hurry to get to the river. Slowly working the exhausted fish to the edge of the water where it flopped on the grass near his feet. Ralph was excited, he estimated the fish to be about six pounds, Ralph could hear Uncle Tony in his head: "You always throw the first fish back for good luck."

"But this would make a great breakfast, with some fried potatoes to go with it," he argued with his thoughts. After staring at the fish that had given him a good battle, the teenager gave in and released the bass back into the water. "Add a few more pounds and someone someday will be thrilled to snag you again." Ralph spoke to the fish. "It might be me."

Jonie would have something to say about talking to fish, I'm sure, he thought, *but that is why I came alone so I wouldn't have to worry what someone else might say or do.* Ralph started whistling as his stomach started rumbling. *Time for a breakfast of sausage and biscuits, then maybe some freshly caught bass for a mid afternoon lunch,* Ralph thought, as he gathered up his gear and started back to the campground.

After a fine breakfast, Ralph took a walk around the campground. As he passed the only other occupied site in the area, he waved at a young boy and a man that Ralph assumed to be his dad. It appeared they were packing up. As Ralph approached the man said, "We were just camping overnight. Have to get back, got to take the boy to his mothers' for Thanksgiving." They both watched the young boy sprinkle water on the almost dead fire.

"I bet he likes camping out," Ralph said. "I certainly did when I was his age. Still do."

The man nodded, "I have a big pile of twigs that he gathered for the fire. If you need any help yourself. Well, we best be going, I promised him one more walk to the river before we go. You here for a few days?"

Ralph nodded. "Last camp out this year I expect. Take care." Moving on, he took another look back as the two headed the same direction Ralph had taken the night before. *I better give them time at the river before going back myself.* Wandering through the rest of the campground, he eventually ended up back at his campsite. Deciding to do some housework, he washed up the breakfast utensils and shook out his sleeping bag, hanging it over a nearby bush to air out. When he saw the man and his boy back at their campsite, Ralph quickly grabbed his fishing gear, this time remembering to take the dip net, and headed back to Willow River. The temperature stayed cool and it proved to be a good time to fish. In the first hour, Ralph caught four nice bass, and kept one of them for his lunch. After a leisurely lunch, he decided to hike the shore line of the lake.

He spent most of the afternoon walking around the eastern shore of the lake. He found two nice clam shell specimens for Jonie's shell collection, but he saw much more human debris, than natural waste. Noticing the sun getting low in the western sky, Ralph hurried back to camp. He wanted to fish the Creek in the hour or two just before sunset. That was a good time to go after the feeding Big Mouth Bass. He stopped at the campground and grabbed his fishing gear. Fishing at the same spot as before, he had numerous strikes, but landed only two small bass. By the time he returned to the campgrounds without a fish for his dinner, it was dusk. He settled for a can of Dinty's Beef Stew for his evening meal.

He awoke the next morning to a cold rainy day. His breakfast consisted of a bowl of Honey Nut Cheerios, with powdered milk, and a banana, which he ate in his tent. He spent the morning reading *To Kill a Mocking Bird*. The skies didn't clear, but the drizzle-like rain stopped about noon. At least, it was dry enough that he could get out of the tent and fix a real meal. After bacon, scrambled eggs, and three pancakes, Ralph felt more like a true camper. The grass was still wet, but the cool air felt invigorating, so off to Willow Creek he went. This time he had better luck, he returned with two large bass for his nighttime meal. After cleaning the fish, he wrapped them in aluminum foil and baked them in the coals of an open fire. They tasted delicious to Ralph. He slept well that night. The next morning dawned with a bright warm sun. After breakfast, Ralph decided that this would be a good day to explore the Rattlesnake Creek hiking trail. He made sure everything in the campsite was secure, and headed north past the showers, then through the woods to the Rattlesnake trail head which started about a hundred yards from Cheyenne Cove. It had been a year, or so, since his last visit to the trail head with his dad. This would be the first time attempting to find it himself. Arriving at the spot where he expected to find the trail, Ralph remembered the foot bridge across Willow Creek. After a few minutes searching the trail sign, the foot bridge came into view. Rattlesnake Trail ran between the Rattlesnake Creek and Willow Creek, both of which emptied into Lake Lawson. Ralph seemed to recall that the trail took about an hour to walk. He also remembered Rattlesnake Creek was aptly named. Where it ran through a pocket of shale rock, the rock outcrops on both sides of the river were notorious for harboring rattlesnakes. *They shouldn't be a problem this time of the year as cool as it is,* he thought. *If I stay on the trail, there should be even less of a chance of encountering one of the creatures.*

Ralph explored the trail for almost an hour, figuring that he must have traveled a mile maybe two. The rumble in his stomach told him it was time to turn back. Retracing his route, he neared a bend in the trail, and stopped to look around. Ralph noticed that the lake could be seen through the trees to the west. *I know where I am,* he realized, *I could cut through the woods and end up just north of the Cheyenne Cove campgrounds. Wouldn't that be a challenge, to blaze a new trail?* Excited at the prospect of covering unexplored territory, he left the trail and started though the woods. Without paying attention to the change in the topography of the land, he soon lost sight of the lake. *No problem,* he thought, *I just need to keep going west. When I hit the high ground, the lake will re-appear.*

Soon, finding himself in a deep ravine, he glanced at the sun, and with it almost directly overhead, realized he did not know which direction was west. *All I need to do is climb to the top of that ridge and then I can see the lake again,* Ralph mumbled. As he traversed the ravine and started up the other side, the underbrush thinned. With travel now easier, he stopped to take a drink from his canteen. As he stood looking around for a better way up the hill, he noticed some one had recently been digging between two bushes. The dirt was freshly turned. Walking over to the spot, an uneasiness came over him. *This looks like a grave. My God! I believe something is buried here!*

Curious as to what it could be, Ralph began to carefully dig through the soft, damp, soil. Suddenly his hand hit something solid. Ever so lightly he brushed away the dirt. *It's a plaid shirt or jacket,* he thought, as he dug a little deeper. His fingers hooked on an edge of cloth and instinctively he reacted by jerking his hand away. Out from the dirt, fell a plaid sleeve with a dainty little hand protruding from the cuff opening.

Ralph jumped back and landed in one of the bushes. Numb, and unable to immediately comprehend what he had found, he froze. It was several minutes before he gained the courage to continue digging, He uncovered a clump of long, dark, matted hair. He brushed away more dirt, a face! *A girl, a young girl.* Again the realization of what he had uncovered caused him to stop as if frozen.

His mind raced. *What to do? Where to go? Who to tell?* It took time for him to gain control of himself. *First, I have to mark the spot. I need to find out where I am so that I can lead someone back here.* Slowly he placed fallen tree branches around the body. Then he marked the spot by stacking several rocks into a pile in the open area near the bushes. Climbing up the side of the ravine, he soon located the lake. At that point he again piled several large stones together so that they could be seen from a distance. Then he headed for the lake. Once at the shore of Lake Lawson, he again made a large stack of stones and added several large tree limbs to them so that the spot could be seen from both on the water and from a distance on the shore.

Satisfied that he could find the marker, Ralph headed around the lake to the point where he would leave it and retraced his route back to the campground. It took less than an hour for him to reach his tent. After a few minutes of rummaging through his pack, he located the cell phone his mother had insisted be with him at all times. Not knowing who else to call, he called home. Punching in the number, he waited, Nothing. Glancing at the cell phone and seeing the words flash on the message center, "No Signal" Ralph realized at once that the phone would be no help. Grabbing his car keys from the pack, Ralph bolted for the car. Backing out of the park area, the teen realized he didn't know where to go. Not wanting to waste time getting help, he decided to drive to the highway and try the cell again. Reaching the junction of the highway, he stopped and punched redial. This time to his relief, a "dialing" message appeared.

"Hello, Ralph?" his dad said. Excitedly, Ralph told his father about the body he had found. Del calmly commanded Ralph to stay right there at the junction and wait for the Woodrow County Sheriff to appear. "I will call the sheriff, Ralph," his father said.

Ralph spent an anxious eternity waiting for the authorities to arrive. About ten minutes later his cell phone rang. "Yes?" he answered, "Dad, is that you. I can barely hear you."

His dad's voice though recognizable, was garbled. Finally, giving it up as a lost cause, Ralph closed the phone. A half hour later, a Sheriff's car with two officers inside pulled up beside him. Ralph explained what he had found. "Let's go take a look," one of the officers said, "park your car on the shoulder and come with me." Ralph did as he was told. *So much for time by myself, I guess my fishing trip alone has just ended.* The boy's thoughts proved to be right on.

CHAPTER 5
THE GIRL IN THE WOODS

"Mighty fine marking of a trail," Deputy Randy Simmons said complimenting Ralph upon seeing the marker on Lake Lawson shoreline, "You say it's about a quarter of a mile into the trees?"

"Yes, it's in the first deep ravine almost due east of here," Ralph replied nervously.

"Well, let's go take a look." Deputy Simmons gestured for Ralph to lead the way, the other officer right on his heels. At the top of a rise in the topography, Ralph pointed out the pile of rocks down below. The Deputy nodded, motioned to the other officer and headed toward the depression without a word. Ralph followed at a distance. His anxiety increased with each step. He wondered if he had imagined the whole thing. Was the body of a girl really there?

"Well, you spoke the truth, alright. I want you to back away and be careful where you step. We have a crime scene, and we don't want to mess it up. You wait there at the rock pile, if you would please. Officer Stevens and I need tape off the area, and call it in to headquarters on the radio."

The Deputies marked off the area with yellow security tape, wrapping it around trees, Ralph took another look at the grave site. It struck him as strange that the ground around the grave did not appear to be disturbed. Someone must have spent a lot of time and effort to clean up the site after the girl was buried. Ralph didn't think much about it at the time, he was more curious than anything. Deputy Simmons and his partner finished with the tape and made their call, Then Simmons turned to his partner and said, "Marlon, go back to the unit and wait on the medical personnel. They'll need you to lead then to the site." When Officer Stevens left, Deputy Simmons turned to Ralph and said, "There will be a lot of people here in about twenty minutes, son, so why don't I take your statement while we wait? That be okay with you?"

"What do you mean, statement, Officer" Ralph asked, puzzled.

"My name is Randy, why don't you tell me how you came to be here, what led you to the body, and what you did once you found it? Go slow, I will be writing down what you say."

Ralph nodded and began telling the Deputy exactly why he was at the lake and why he was there. Relating the story made Ralph thirsty and he stopped once and took a sip from his canteen.

The break allowed Simmons to ask a question. "Why are you alone? why did you come here by yourself? I would have guessed a boy your age might bring a friend, either male or female, for company. You came alone, that's strange."

At first, Ralph didn't catch the implication the Officer was making, but when it hit him, it landed like a ton of bricks. "Hey, wait a minute, I told you the truth, I didn't lie to you."

"Well, you have to admit it is strange, now what are you so nervous about anyway."

"Wouldn't you be nervous if you had just discovered a body buried in the ground?" Ralph said defensively.

"Well son, I just did and, no, I am not nervous, not at all like you are."

Ralph couldn't believe it, *what is this guy implying? Does he really believe that I would do such a thing? And . . . and then lead the Sheriff's office to the place where it must have happened?* The teen could only stare at the Deputy.'

Almost as if Simmons heard what Ralph had thought, he said, "More than one guy has thought of being the one to discover a crime that they committed themselves, so you wouldn't be the first to think they could get away with something by doing just what you did. How did you get all that dirt on you? And under your fingernails? You think I wouldn't notice that? Now, do you want to tell me what really happened between you and this girl?"

"I already told you, I . . . ," Ralph stammered. Officer Simmons attention was drawn to the top of the ridge of the ravine. An older fellow was picking his way down the side of the valley with ease. Dressed in a suit and tie, he stood out. Ralph immediately recognized the man. In fact, everyone over the age of ten probably knew him. Standing somewhere around six feet tall with dark sunglasses and wearing a western hat, the man appeared to be about thirty pounds over the recommended weight level. Ralph also became aware of a pair of very impressive cowboy boots the man was wearing. It was the Woodrow County Sheriff, Mike "Snuffy" Smith, a man who had held the same office for twenty-eight years. So many people in the county owed him a favor that no one dared vote against him, let alone run against him. One, or the other, of the local political groups would sponsor his re-election every four years. He wore a gray light weight civilian type suit with black tie. That was his uniform. He went directly to the grave site and examined it. Then he walked over to where Simmons and Ralph stood a little way off. At that moment the quiet around them erupted into a den of noise as almost a dozen people came over the ridge and down into the ravine like a herd of elephants. Some loaded down with large containers that looked like industrial suitcases. Others appeared to be medical and rescue personal. They were led by Officer Stevens, who stopped them about fifty feet away from the grave site. Only the medical team continued to proceed. Deputy Stevens went back up the ravine. Ralph guessed that he was returning to lead more people to the grave site.

Sheriff Smith watched for a moment, then faced Deputy Simmons. "Who discovered the body, Randy?"

"The boy here. Tell the Sheriff your name, son."

Ralph gulped a mouth full of air. "Ralph Kellam, I live in Robertown."

"You Del's boy?"

"Yes sir," the teen replied.

"You do a good job at defensive back. You guys slaughtered that Missouri team, but things will get a little tougher now that league play has begun. Think you can take Osage Center this year?" Before Ralph had a chance to answer, the Sheriff turned to the crowd and visited with some of them. Then he moved through the crowd and approached the grave site. Ralph was able to get a clear view of the site. Nothing appeared to have changed as far as the body was concerned. Only the face and one arm with a hand lay exposed. It appeared just as Ralph had left it. *That's what I need to get across to Deputy Simmons, I got dirt on me and under the nails on my hands, when I opened the grave and found the girl.*

About that time, a second wave of people, with Officer Stevens in the lead, stood at the rise overlooking the ravine. They were dressed in street clothes, and not in any sort of uniform.

Deputy Simmons stopped the group from advancing, "I don't want anyone going any further unless I give the okay. You folks get out your ID's, if they say PRESS on them, you might as well find a place to park yourself, because you're not going any closer than you are right now." By the time he had processed the group, most of them were left standing near the rock pile Ralph had constructed to mark the grave site, which lie about fifty yards into the brush.

One of the "Press" crowd, a man in a Detroit Lions baseball cap, worked his way over to Ralph. "How did you get involved in this, son?" Ralph turned to answer the man, then noticed the pad and pencil in his hand. Ralph shook his head, moved away and stepped closer to the deputy. Simmons reached out and laid a hand on Ralph's shoulder. "We still have a statement to complete, so don't you go anywhere, or talk to anyone, until I say it's okay. You got that kid?" Ralph nodded, and stood quietly as the deputy gave the reporter in the ball cap a stern look. Ralph watched as Sheriff Smith nodded to another of his Deputies standing beside the grave and the officer began to finish the job Ralph had started. When the girls body was cleared of soil, more pictures were taken. Eventually the body was lifted out of the shallow grave and laid out on top of the ground. Ralph realized he did not know the girl nor did he think she attended his school. The teen assumed the girl was of high school age, at least she appeared to be. There were only two high schools in Robertown, one was the public high school, and the other, Trinity Academy, was operated by one of the churches of the community. Robertown's enrollment was about 800 students and the Academy had another 30 or more students. The only other high school in the area was Edwards Consolidated School located about half way between the towns of Atwood and Langton in the southeastern corner of Woodrow County. The enrollment of the Consolidated School located about 18 miles south of Robertown barely managed to maintain more than 100 students in the four year school.

Ralph's thought's were jarred back to the present when officers at the grave site placed the body of the girl in a large black bag and zipped it up tight. Four men carried it out of the ravine, as members of the press continued to snap pictures of the action, black bag and all. Within minutes, most of the assembled group of officials had also disappeared. The Sheriff and Deputy Simmons stood near Ralph until the others had all left the area.

When the sheriff became satisfied no one else could overhear, he said,. "Now, son, I want you to start at the beginning and tell me your story. Don't leave any thing out, and remember I want the truth and nothing else. If you lie to me and I find you out, it will go rough on you. Now let's hear your story."

Ralph related the morning's events including seeing the man and boy at the campground when he first arrived. Then of his decision to hike the trail to the lake, including the shortcut to the lake which led him to find the grave. He finished with his attempts to contact somebody, and finally getting in contact with his Dad, and the meeting of Deputy Simmons at the junction. "I have been in sight of Deputy Simmons ever since," he added.

Sheriff Smith asked some of the same questions Simmons had asked. "How did you get so dirty." "Are you sure you came to the lake alone?" Then he asked, "Did you know the girl?"

Ralph replied, "I didn't recognize her, I don't know. I didn't see her face that well."

Sheriff Smith studied Ralph for a minute, as if trying to decide something, and then said. "We may have more questions for you, don't talk to the press, and don't plan on leaving the County'" You got that, boy?"

"I understand, but there is a problem, the football team plays Signal Hill a week from Friday, and that's an away game."

"So what's the problem?"

"Signal Hill is in Apache County."

"You're not getting smart with me, are you, boy?" The sheriff studied the boy again, this time with a much sterner look on his face.

"No sir."

"Don't worry, if you're on school business, I'll forgive the 'leaving the county' part."

Deputy Simmons motioned Ralph to follow him. "Come on kid, I'll take you back to your car. Then I suggest you go home and stay there." Ralph nodded. the three started for the lake shore and down to the Deputies car. Ralph's weekend fishing trip was apparently over.

CHAPTER 6

JONIE

When Ralph arrived home, he was bombarded with a barrage of questions. The first onslaught came from his parents, who were concerned for his well-being and safety. After explaining how he handled the necessary act of reporting his discovery and the interview with the sheriff and his deputy, Ralph's father congratulated Ralph for following a good procedure and doing the right thing in cooperating with the law. However, to make sure all the bases were covered, Del insisted on calling a lawyer friend and retaining him on Ralph's behalf. "You never know how the mind of an investigator will think and I want to make sure your rights are protected." Ralph's mother agreed, "we need someone who knows the legal process and how it works," she added.

But, it was Jonie who asked the really tough questions about his experience. After Ralph had begged off eating anything and said he wanted to go to his room and unpack, Jonie quickly followed and hit him with a series of questions. "How did it feel, to touch the body? Were you scared when the Sheriff showed up? How do you think the girl died? Was she killed? Do you think she is someone we know? Come on, Bro, out with the good stuff."

"Jonie, you know that if I tell you anything, you will tell all your friends, and rumors will get started, and I will end up in trouble with the sheriff."

"No I won't, I won't tell a soul, I promise."

"Yes, you will, you're a girl, and girls tell each other everything. What they don't know, they make up."

"No, we don't, come on, bro, you got to give me something. I have to have something to tell my friends when they ask, and they're going to ask. So at least, tell me what it was like to find a dead person."

"It was yukky, okay, Jonie? It was scary and yukky. Every time I glanced at her, I thought I saw her move. Once when I caught my hand on the sleeve of her jacket, I thought I saw her move. But then I watched for a while and I knew she was dead."

How did you know, Ralph, how did you know she was dead?"

Ralph looked at his sister and hesitated. From Jonie's facial expression it was obvious she thought he wasn't going to answer her. "Come on, tell me," pleaded Jonie.

"Because of the smell, okay, Jonie, because of the smell, I knew she had been dead for some time." Ralph blurted it out before thinking how his sister might react. But Jonie looked fine, it was Ralph who didn't feel so well, He headed for the bathroom down the hall.

Later that evening, as Ralph lay on his bed going over the day's events, he thought about his sister. In many ways, Jonie was still a little girl, and in other ways she could handle things better than himself. Like today, she never blinked an eye when he told her about the smell from the body of the girl. Ralph also knew that his sister had a ton of friends. It would not be possible for her to keep from telling what she knew about the girl's death, when the story came out. It would take all of five minutes for it to be all over her school. Within a day it would be the talk among the high school students, as well. Ralph didn't need that but he knew Jonie needed something to tell her friends.

One of Ralph's earliest recollection of Jonie occurred when he started school and Jonie wanted to go too. His mother had her hands full trying to explain to Jonie that there were laws governing who could and could not attend school. She stomped her feet and demanded that her mother take it to court because the idea of any law keeping her from going school with her brother certainly had to be an unfair law.

The second incident Ralph recalled had to do with tennis. Ralph didn't play tennis on a organized team at school, but he did participate in the tournament sponsored by the City Recreational Program. When Jonie was five she decided she would play too. The ages for the program started at 8 years of age and continued through adulthood. Jonie had been so determined that her mother got the program director to allow her to play with the eight to ten age group. Everyone had been surprised when she qualified for the tournament by winning most of her individual matches. She made it to the quarter finals that first year. The next year she won the tournament.

When she entered the middle school in the sixth grade she immediately informed the tennis coach at the high school her intentions to play on his team since the middle school did not field a team. The Coach in turn, talked the athletic director at the middle school to get her some matches so that she would leave him alone. That year the middle school had a tennis team of two. Jonie talked one of her friends into playing with her so they could play in the doubles matches. The team won the league tournament in both singles and doubles that year. This year the middle school had a paid coach and a team of 12 players with a full schedule of matches. Jonie was the player-coach for the team.

The other sport Jonie participated in was skeet shooting. She took up skeet shooting at the age of ten. Again the cause of her interest in skeet shooting involved Ralph. When her brother enrolled in the hunter safety class sponsored by the local Kansas Wildlife Commission, Jonie enrolled too. Ralph was fourteen at the time and Jonie eleven. In Kansas, a person could hunt legally without a license until the age of sixteen. Ralph wanted to take the course early so that if he failed, there would be time to take it again before the age of sixteen. Jonie did not hunt, but wanted to learn about guns so she would know as much as her brother. To take the course one had to be at least eleven. Jonie made it just under the wire. Jonie's mother did not approve of Jonie handling a gun, any kind of gun. She didn't even like the idea of Ralph shooting a gun, but her husband told her "many boy's dream about hunting for food, it's in their blood to hunt for food."

"I can find all the food he needs at the store. There is no need to shoot anything." She would argue. But the men won out, and Ralph enrolled in the class. Jonie, over her mother's sincere and adamant objections, was right behind him. Jonie found she didn't enjoy the thought of shooting a bird or animal, but heard about shooting "clay pigeons" and was intrigued with the idea. During the course, a section dealt with the proper methods of shooting a shotgun.

Two sections in particular excited her. One dealt with the concept of a person's dominate eye. One of the teachers of the class explained it to them. "Just as a person has a dominate hand, they have a dominate eye, the one that should be used to aim with. To find your dominate eye, form a triangular opening with your thumbs and fingers by crossing them. Stretch your arms in front of you and focus on an object in the distance as you look through the triangle, keeping both eyes open. Bring them forward keeping your eyes on the distant object. The opening in the hands will come to the dominate eye. The weak eye will end up behind the hand." When Jonie did the activity it showed that though she was right-handed, her dominate eye was the left one. So that eye would be used to sight with when she aimed a gun.

The other section she found interesting had to do with shooting at a moving target. She never considered the concept of "leading the target." She thought "see the target, shoot the target" and that would do it. The course explained several methods of aiming at a moving target, "if it is moving and you shoot where it is, by the time the shot gets to the target, it is already someplace ahead of where you shot," explained the instructor. One method that the course described was the "swing through" approach. With this method the gun is pointed at the target and the shooter swings with it. As the muzzle of the gun passes the target, the gun is fired at a blank space in front of the target. This method proved to be the best for beginning students.

Then, as Jonie's skill developed, she could try the "Sustained Lead" method, where she would point the muzzle of the gun at a point ahead of the target and move with the target at the same pace maintaining that point in front of the target. Jonie would fire the gun when she thought she had the speed of the target matched. Both of these techniques could be used when she started skeet shooting. The course opened a whole new world to her and she grabbed it by the horns and never let loose. By a stroke of luck she met Sammy Smead, who happened to be an accomplished skeet shooter and saw great promise in Jonie's ability at such a young age. He worked with her simply for the thrill of watching her develop her skills and rapidly master the art of skeet shooting.

In skeet shooting there were several different positions one had to shoot from so the targets were moving at different angles from the shooter. Skeet is a clay disc target about four inches in diameter that is launched from a tower to simulate the flushing of a bird. Jonie enjoyed everything about it because no birds were killed, yet she got the thrill of knocking down the target. However, it took a lot of practice time and dedication to the sport. That developed into the only thing Jonie wasn't prepared to give to the challenge, her time. Tennis was already taking a lot of that away from her and skeet would demand as much if not more. As a result, she never really gained a level of competency that got her noticed in the sport of competitive skeet shooting.

"Maybe some day," she would say, "I will give it what it takes, but not now." Now, she practiced when she had time and desire, which wasn't often enough to keep Sammy interested. So he moved on to a boy with half the talent but a lot more drive to achieve.

Jonie did not mind, she felt a great contentment in her life and enjoyed playing tennis and hanging out with her friends. By the age of thirteen she had accomplished much.

As Ralph recalled his sister's exploits, he had to accept the fact that, although at times she got in his way and became a nuisance to him, he was proud of her and would never want her to end up like the girl he found today. "No one deserves to be treated that way, how could anyone do that to another person?" As Ralph thought about the day's events, he slowly drifted into a restless sleep.

CHAPTER 7
THE ACCUSATION

R alph had a reasonably routine day at school on Monday following the Thanksgiving break. The Robertown Gazette, published five days a week, and normally it reached the newsstands and paper carriers about three in the afternoon, Monday thru Friday. This coincided with the time that Robertown schools were dismissed. Because of the holiday, the news of the discovery of the body of a girl at Lawson Lake by a local teen, did not make it to the Gazette until Monday afternoon. Ralph's identity was withheld by the newspaper, but the rumor persisted that he was the teen referred to in the news item. Ralph was at football practice when one of the caretakers of the combination track and football stadium came running out to the defensive coach with a copy of the afternoon's paper. After perusing the front page, the defensive coach walked over to the head coach Dwayne Zaraman, and handed him the paper. Coach Z, as his players and students affectionately called him, was in his fifteenth season with the Robertown Grizzlies. Coach Z then blew his whistle, and shouted, "All Grizzlies in, on the double." Within seconds all the players were gathered around him.

"It seems we have a celebrity among us." He held up the copy of the Robertown Gazette "Ralph Kellam, what can you tell us about the story on the front page in today's paper?" Ralph had not seen a copy of the paper, but he could guess what it probably said.

"I went on a fishing trip, and I found a body." Some of the players snickered at the announcement, thinking it was a joke. But Coach Z, in no mood for jokes, had only one interest: to make a point for his football squad.

"Men, we have our toughest challenge of the season coming up this Friday, and Mr Kellam finds it more important to go on a fishing trip than to attend practice. Isn't that right Mr. Kellam?" Ralph suddenly realized the coach wasn't interested in the story, he only wanted to use to it show that Ralph had missed the Saturday practice to go on a fishing trip. He didn't answer the coach's question, because he knew there would be no correct answer.

"What I want to know, is are we a team or not? Are we in this season together as one, or are we just a group of individuals who go our own direction when it suits us? Can you answer that question, Mr Kellam?" Ralph dropped his head. "I'm waiting Mr. Kellam, and so is the rest of the team."

"No, sir," Ralph replied meekly.

"Then I suggest you hit the showers and report for practice tomorrow only if you want to be part of the team, and not an individual, who practices when he wants. Good day, Mr. Kellam."

Ralph went to the locker room, took a shower, and went directly home. Jonie had been told in no uncertain terms to leave him alone and Ralph, still in his room when his father arrived, stayed there. Only after his mother came to his door and asked him to come to the kitchen, did he appear. He sat at the kitchen table with his dad, while his mother started dinner. He sat with his head down, not saying a word. Jonie stood in the kitchen doorway not knowing if she was allowed to stay and hear what Ralph had to say or not.

"We heard you got kicked off the football team, you want to talk about it, Ralph?" his mother asked.

"I didn't get kicked off the team, but I might as well have. I probably lost my starting position at defensive back."

"Why don't you start at the beginning and tell us the story? Jonie come on in, you may as well know Ralph's side of things, so you will know the truth, when you go to school tomorrow. Go ahead, son." Del nodded to Ralph.

Ralph related the story as he knew it. He still had not seen the evenings paper, so did not know what it said. "But I don't think that is what Coach is mad about. When I asked him to be excused from practice, I said I would be out of town, as if it was a family thing. I didn't tell him it was a fishing trip. And I think that is what set him off."

"So bro, are you going to practice tomorrow?"

"Jonie! You're here to listen," her mother admonished.

"That's okay, Mom, I'll answer her question. Yes, dear sister, I am. And if I have to run extra laps and apologize to the team, I'll do that. I made a mistake and I'll admit it. But I am not a quitter. Coach will have to kick me off the team before I will quit."

"That's my boy, I'm proud of you, son." Del reached across the table and clutched his son's shoulder. "Now let's see what the infamous Robertown News Herald has to add to today's events."

"I guess I'll finish getting dinner on the table. Jonie, you can help by setting the table, please."

Jonie made a face at that, but did as her mother said. Ralph and his dad headed for the den and the day's paper.

As Ralph and his dad perused the front page, Del noticed a puzzling line in the article. "Ralph, listen to this: *According to a source close to the Sheriff's office there is a question of how and when the girl's body was located.* What do you suppose they mean by that? Didn't you tell them you found the body?"

"Yes." Ralph thought about what his father had read. Then he remembered the questions Deputy Simmons had asked about his coming to the lake alone, and how he got so much dirt on himself. Did they still think he had something to do with the girl's death?

Tuesday morning between 10:05 and 11:00, Ralph's school schedule called for him to be in Chemistry Class. At ten-fifteen Vice-Principal Royce Jefferson walked into the classroom and quietly spoke to Mr. Greeley the teacher. He then walked over to where Ralph sat beside his lab partner. "Ralph will you come with me, please?" The class turned in unison to watch Ralph leave with the vice-principal. A man stood outside the office door. As Ralph neared he saw it was Woodrow County Sheriff Mike "Snuffy" Smith. Ralph's heart leaped to his throat.

"Come with me, son," the Sheriff said tersely.

As they exited the building, Ralph remembered what his father had said. "Shouldn't I have an adult with me, Sheriff?"

The sheriff turned to Ralph and said sternly, "We are just going to have a friendly talk. No one needs to muddy the waters with lawyers or such. When they reached the sheriff's patrol car, the sheriff opened the rear door and motioned for Ralph to get in, Ralph did, and with the Sheriff right behind him. The driver pulled away from the curb.

The sheriff turned to Ralph and said. "Son, now just between the two of us, tell me what you were doing at the lake last Thursday."

"I already did, I was on a fishing trip."

"Fishing?"

"Fishing."

"Fishing on Thanksgiving day?"

"Yes."

"By yourself?"

"By myself."

"Fishing by yourself on Thanksgiving day! Boy, don't you hear how lame that is?"

"It's the truth." Ralph didn't like the way this was going and he became a little nervous.

"The truth, let me give you a truth." The sheriff' leaned into Ralph's face. "The truth is that you took that girl with you supposedly on a fishing trip and you made advances on her. She rejected you. You got irate and your temper got the best of you and you hit her on the head with . . . with a skillet perhaps. Then you carried her to that location and buried her. Then you decided to cover your tracks by being the one to find her. How's that for the truth, boy!"

Ralph couldn't believe what he was hearing. His hands begin to shake, and he felt as though he might lose his breakfast, right there in the car. "What's the matter, boy, you scared? You didn't think I would catch on to your little game, did you? You're going to jail, so you might as well admit what you done to that girl. So tell me, boy, tell the truth, tell me how she told you to back off and how you decided to teach her a lesson. Tell me, boy, and maybe the judge will go easy on you. Tell me now!"

Ralph was so sick that he couldn't talk. He wanted to make the sheriff understand how he could never do what the sheriff said he did. At that point they pulled up in front of the Woodrow County Courthouse where the sheriff's office was located. As the driver got out and opened the door beside Ralph, the teenager's stomach could hold out no more. Just as the door opened, so did Ralph's mouth and up came his undigested breakfast, And right on to the pant legs of the driver.

"Oh no, no, tell me this did not just happen. The kid puked all over me. And my last clean uniform." Sheriff Smith ignored the whole affair as he exited the vehicle, turned to the officer and simply said, "Bring him inside." Then he entered the outer door to his office.

Deputy Sheriff, Randy Simmons, stood in the path of the sheriff. "Mike, you can't do this. You're violating the legal rights of the boy. He's under 18, we can't interrogate him without parental consent or council present. You have to release him or get his parents or lawyer down here, before we can talk to him."

"Out of my way, Deputy, I've got a homicide to solve and I'm going to question a suspect in the case. So watch how it's done."

"I'm calling his parents. Don't ask him any questions until they get here." Randy knew he walked on shaky ground. He was very near the act of insubordination, and he could be relieved of duty. "Sheriff, if you're right and you may well be, don't lose the evidence you have. If you interrogate him and the judge throws out the information because the method it was illegally obtained, then we have no case."

Sheriff Smith stopped, looked at Randy, "of course you are correct. Okay, make your call."

CHAPTER 8
MELVIN CRANKSTONE

W hen Ralph's father got the phone call from the sheriff's office, his son was being held for questioning, he grabbed his hat, stopped at his desk only long enough to dial the number of Melvin Crankstone, an attorney with the firm of Hall, Hall, and Crankstone, Attorneys-At-Law, which was also one of Del's tax firm's clients. They often traded work for pay. Melvin was the complete opposite of Delbert. He stood over six feet, six inches in height and weighing in at two-hundred-forty pounds, to say he was a big man would be putting it mildly. He carried himself with a sense of purpose and his broad shoulders and short cropped blond hair gave him an air of confidence. Even at the age of forty-five he still played a mean game of half court basketball in the adult recreation program which played every Wednesday evening at the middle school gym.

Melvin and Del were home town boys, both having been born and raised in Robertown and attended the same school having been in the same class together. Both were married. Melvin and his wife had twin girls, three years younger than Jonie. On Sunday, they attended the same church they had when young, but now they attended with their families. The only separation between the two came when they were of college age. Del enrolled in the local Woodrow Community College and then transferred to Williamsburg State University. Melvin went to Washington Law School in Kansas City, and after graduating, served two years in the United States Army. Both men returned to their hometown to set themselves up in business. Mel and Del where as close as brothers. When Del called him, Mel immediately left and arrived at the courthouse before Del.

As soon as Del walked in the door, Mel rushed to meet him. "I talked to Sheriff Smith and he assured me that no charges have been brought against Ralph. He maintains that all they want from him is a statement. I advised Snuffy that Ralph was underage and my client, that no interview be conducted without you and I present. He said that no interview would take place at the courthouse without parental approval. "To be honest with you, I think he had already talked to Ralph before they arrived at his office. If I find out that he interrogated Ralph, who is a minor, without the knowledge of his lawyer and his parents, we will have him in a bind. We'll know more on that subject when we talk to Ralph."

"Thank you, Melvin, for being here on such short notice. Any idea when we can see my son?"

"I told Snuffy to book him, or release him, and do it now. So we'll see how much clout I have around here in a bit."

They waited all of five minutes before seeing Ralph, looking disheveled and confused, walk down the hallway toward them. "Son, are you alright?" Del said, concern imprinted on his face.

"I've felt better, dad, I got sick and lost my breakfast when I puked all over a guy. I just want to get out of here, can we go now?" Del looked at Mel, who nodded his head.

"We'll let the Sheriff come to us," Mel said. They started to exit the doors leading to the street.

"Just a minute there," called Sheriff Smith, "I want to remind the suspect he is not to leave this county unless on school business. Is that clear with everybody?"

"Suspect? Suspect of what?" said Mel.

"Poor choice of words, Counselor, how about person of interest. Does that make it all better?"

"You were elected to serve the public, Sheriff, not to play games with them. If my client is not under any court order, and I haven't been presented with one, he is free to travel wherever he wishes, whether you like it or not."

Observing Mel in action made Del glad he was not only a class act lawyer but also a good friend who would be on their side. Aware that Mel knew his law and legal proceedings, and that it would cost a pretty penny to have him represent his son, Del still felt comfortable with a lawyer like Mel on the front lines, firing at the enemy. With no response forthcoming from Sheriff Smith, the three continued their exit from the building.

Once outside, Melvin had some advice for Ralph. "Keep a low profile for the next few days, Ralph, and don't drive around town any more than you have to. When you do drive, try to have Wanda, er, your mother or your father, in the car with you. And one other thing, I know this may hurt a bit, but try to have your sister or a trusted family friend around, when you go to school, or run around town.

"I will do some nosing around and see if they have any kind of evidence that they might use against you." Mel shook hands with the two of them and left to go to another part of the courthouse. Del and his son walked to the car. "I'm glad we have him on our side," Ralph confided to his father.

"Yes, he's a good man and a good friend, they don't come any better than Melvin." His father's voice was full of pride.

CHAPTER 9
THE FOOTBALL GAME

On the way home, Ralph told his dad what the sheriff had said about the death of the girl and how he thought Ralph had been involved. "I can't wait til Melvin gets word of that conversation between you and the sheriff. He will go ballistic on Smith for accusing you of a crime while basically kidnapping you from school." It was 1:30, when Ralph and his dad arrived back at home.

"Dad, I have to be at football practice by two forty five. If I am not there, Coach will think I quit the team. I don't want to give him any excuse like that to use against me. I'm in enough trouble with him as it is. I'll have time to eat something and then you will need to take me to school so I can make the practice. Can you do that?"

"I need to get back to the office myself, I have some work that I promised would be finished before five. I think I saw your mother put some ham in the fridge yesterday when she came in. Let's fix ourselves a ham sandwich with cheese and I will get some fruit. Since you lost your breakfast, you will need something in your stomach if you are going to last through the practice."

With both of them working together the sandwiches were soon on the table. Ralph poured a glass of V-8 Juice for each of them. Meanwhile Del washed and sliced two large Johnathon apples and placed them on the table.

While they worked, Ralph asked, "Dad, you don't believe any of that stuff the sheriff said about me do you?"

"Of course not, son, he is just anxious to pin the crime on someone and get the case solved quickly. He doesn't want an unsolved case on his hands, that's all." They made quick work of devouring the sandwiches and apples, each lost in their own thoughts. Ralph went to the kitchen sink to wash up the dishes. "Leave them in the sink, son, I'll explain to your mother that we were pressed for time. You better grab a jacket and we will get on the road." They scurried around and left the house. As Del backed out of the drive, he noticed a sheriff's patrol car parked three houses down the street. Aware that Ralph had not noticed, he said nothing. As he drove away, the patrol car followed. It was still with them when Del pulled into the stadium parking lot. Ralph said good bye to his dad and headed for the locker room, it was 2:45. When he entered the room, many of the team were already changing for practice. He quickly went to his locker and changed clothes. As the other team members got ready and prepared to leave the locker room, they each walked past him and gave a pat on his shoulder without saying a word. Some nodded and some smiled at him. When he was finally ready, he took a deep breath, left the locker room and ran out on the practice field. Taking his place in the pre-practice drills, Ralph started warming up, trying to loosen the muscles that had been so tight most of the day. Coach Z walked over to where Ralph was exercising. "So, you ready to play some football, Mr. Kellam?"

"Yes sir," Ralph answered, with as much gusto as he could muster.

"Good, then you won't mind giving me three laps around the track, will you?"

"No sir, I don't mind." And with that he started toward the running track which circled the outside of the practice field, happy that it was only three laps. He had expected more.

"Oh and Mr. Kellam," Coach said, stopping him, "when you finish those three laps give me three more in the opposite direction to erase them, understood?"

"Yes sir." Ralph took off as the rest of the team clapped and cheered him on. The coach ignored them. He had a tough practice lined out and three new plays for the offense to learn. The defense worked on a new pass rush formation since Signal Hill was known for its passing game. After the team finished their practice and headed to the lockers to shower, all the players were exhausted because of the tough drills Coach had given them. As the crowd thinned in the locker room, Coach Z came out of his office and approached Ralph.

"Son, I want you to know that I am proud of the way you handled yourself today. You helped make a bunch of guys a team. They will pull together better now because of your perseverance. I want to thank you for that."

"Thanks, Coach, and I am sorry I wasn't more honest with you, but I really wanted that fishing trip."

"Were they biting?"

"Yes sir."

"Then it was worth six laps?"

"Yes sir, it was." And for the first time Ralph smiled that day. The coach turned and walked back into his office. Ralph, unable to see the face of Coach Z did not notice his smile, as he entered the office.

On a cold wet October night the football team traveled to Signal Hill Consolidated School, located some twenty miles northeast of Robertown. Riding in the yellow activities bus, which smelled like it hadn't been cleaned since last season's games, proved to be a challenge in itself. No arm rests, nothing soft to lean one's head on, with forty-five teenage boys, who were excitedly nervous, with pent up energy and no outlet. The interior of the bus could aptly be compared to the inside of a cell block at the State prison. In addition, the yellow beetle-like machine zipped down the road at ten miles an hour slower than the speed limit, stopping at every railroad crossing and bouncing over rough road. It covered the thirty miles in less than one hour. Nice job, for a fifteen year old bus with over 150,000 miles on it, and historically the oldest bus in the school's fleet of yellow bugs.

Pulling into the Signal Hill Stadium area could be compared to pulling into soup kitchen at one of Kansas City's flop houses. No frills here thought Ralph, as he departed from the rear of the yellow beetle. Coach Z held up the first to dismount until all were free of the yellow beast. Then they entered the visitors dressing room as a unit. The inside of the structure matched the exterior, it showed its age.

The first half of the game proved to be miserable for both squads, as both teams fumbled and dropped passes with ease. The half ended with Signal Hill leading seven to six, Robertown had managed to score two field goals. No one spoke in the visitor's locker room at the stadium.

Coach Z , so upset that the veins in his neck stood out like worms on the ground, calmly told the team he expected more from them in the second half.

The starting players knew Coach Zaraman, some of them believed his amazing act of courage ever to be seen by a high school football team. Some of the Juniors and Seniors had seen the act before, but still didn't believe it. The coach picked up a cooler and unlatched it. Tipping it slightly showed it to be full of crushed glass. He dumped the contents in an empty foot powder box, making a bed of glass two inches deep and three feet by three feet square. The team members were so engrossed in what the coach was doing they were startled when Coach Z's voice, suddenly exploded like a hand grenade. He berated everyone around him who had played in the first half, expending all his frustrations. Any spectator would have assumed they were watching a crazed person.

Calming somewhat, he started telling each of them what went wrong in the first half. As he ranted, the players watched as he removed first one shoe, then another, first one sock then another. Barefooted he walked over to the powder box and stepped into the scattered broken glass. Gingerly, but without hesitation the man danced on the bed of broken glass. It proved too painful to watch for some of the younger players, and at the same time it proved to be legendary.

Ralph glanced over at Larry Handily, a senior who also knew Coach Z had a secret. It was a bit of information Larry and Ralph had gained from a discussion with Melvin Crankstone, one evening at a Robertown Boosters Club meeting. Melvin had revealed the fact that Zaraman learned the technique one season when he traveled with a circus sideshow.

"It's all show," Melvin told the boys. "A display he puts on for the newer members of the team."

"If I can do this, why can't you, as a team score a touchdown?" Knowing what Coach Z wanted, the starting team members, along with a number of non-starting seniors roared and clapped their hands and stomped their feet. "Now let's get out there, not to walk on glass, but to score a touchdown." The team roared out of the locker room, some as if possessed.

Whatever trick the Signal Hill coach used in his locker room worked as well for his squad. The two teams played to a higher level of determination and desire. But they also were two very evenly matched competitive opponents. Everything changed on the field in the level of play, but nothing changed on the scoreboard. With four minutes left in the game, the Signal Hill Hornets put together a drive that started on their own eight-yard line. Six plays later they were on the Grizzlies ten-yard line and had momentum going their way.

Fifty-nine seconds remained on the clock when the Hornets came to the line. Ralph, in his usual position of inside line backer, saw a flicker in the eye of the tight end. *Pass*, Ralph suddenly realized what the end had just unintentionally told him, pass, *they are running a pass play to the tight end.* Ralph took a couple of nonchalant steps to the outside, hoping not to draw attention to himself. It worked, as soon as the ball was hiked by the center, Ralph ran full speed toward the end. He was there when the ball arrived and made the interception. With a clear field ahead, his legs churning, the turf disappeared under his feet as he flew some 90 yards down the sideline, to the end zone. Touchdown!

Half the crowd sat in stunned silence as the other half went berserk with joy. The Grizzly kicker made the point after, but no one really cared. The Hornets had only twelve seconds left on the clock, insufficient in light of a perfect squib kick. Good coverage by the Robertown squad, all proved too much for the home team. The final score: Robertown Grizzlies 13 and the Signal Hill Hornets 7. The score didn't begin to tell the whole story of just how easily the game could have gone the other way. Ralph, happy about the win, celebrated with his teammates, but in his heart and mind he was greatly disappointed.

Ralph believed one thing, the carnival trick that Coach Z used at half time might as well have taken place out on the field and been the halftime show for the crowd. That's how valuable it was to the football victory. Unhappy about the leadership it showed, right then, Ralph vowed that at the end of the season, he never wanted to play for Zaraman again. For Ralph, the man showed no class; the man showed no values for Ralph to look up to as a leader or teacher. As he said to his father later, "I should have seen it when I reported to that practice. He used me as a chess player uses a pawn, I was nothing but a prop. I would quit right now on this spot, but I started the season and I'll finish it, but I'll not play another one. Besides, the only game we have left is Osage Center, and they have a great running game. That should be fun for an inside linebacker."

"Well, if it's going to be your last game, then it should be fun. Right, son?"

"Right, Dad."

CHAPTER 10

WANDA

"I love my job, why would I ever give it up." Wanda slammed a cabinet door in her attempt to punctuate her words, She was upset at her husband. Her position on the subject appeared in her posture, as she stood with hands on hips and feet set apart. If that wasn't enough, the tone of voice told the rest of the family that they were close to having a cold dinner if she were pushed any further.

"I didn't mean for you to take it this way, dear, I simply thought if it is bothering you so, that we could survive on my salary." As soon as Del uttered the words he knew they should be retracted, but it was too late.

"So now my income isn't important, is that it? I work hard for my salary and it contributes to the family welfare," she shouted. Again a cabinet door took a beating as it closed sharply. "I'll have you know, my income paid for Jonie's new braces and the dentist bill." Now a kitchen drawer took her wrath as she slammed it shut.

"Mom, what in the world are you looking for anyway?" Jonie asked, from a safe distance.

Exasperated, Jonie's mother stopped in the process of opening another cabinet drawer. She looked at Jonie, as if she did not have a clue as to the answer. "I forget."

The Kellam family were in the kitchen on a December evening filled with refreshingly chilled air. The tranquility of the weather was opposed by the turmoil now taking place between the woman and her cabinets.

Wanda had center stage, with Del standing safely away near the living room doorway. Jonie also safely out of reach of her mother, which left Ralph, setting at the kitchen table, much nearer his mother than most of the cabinet doors, presently under attack.

"Wanda, let's back up. When you came into the kitchen, you said, 'I think I will have to quit my job.' End quote."

"I meant because of conditions at work, not quit my job, like, you know, quit for real." Wanda's exasperation seemed a bit confused even to her. "What I mean is that some of the conversation at work is very difficult to hear and even more difficult not to respond the way I want to."

"You mean they don't have cabinet doors at the office." Del beamed at his joke and Jonie and Ralph laughed in unison.

She glared at Ralph. "It's not a laughing matter, and since you are the center of the discussion, you particularly should not laugh." As soon as she finished her statement, she knew the door was now open for Ralph. Her determination not to reveal the content of the office talk had been foremost in her mind.

"What do you mean Mom?"

Trying to restore some order in the chaos, Del offered, "Suppose we back out and start over from the beginning. Wanda, why don't you tell us about your day and we will just listen, okay?"

Wanda blew a puff of air out in a display of a pent up exhale. "I didn't want to talk about me, I just am so put out with some of the talk at the office. For example, there I am minding my own business when Blanche comes prancing in and asks, 'what's this I hear about Ralph? He spent the day in jail? What's going on Wanda?' As I live and breath. I'll never understand the gall of that woman."

"What did you say, how did you answer such a direct question, dear?"

"Well, I told her she had been misinformed. I told her what really happened, Ralph was basically kidnapped from school and the County Sheriff held him without cause for a few hours."

"Sounds to me you handled it pretty well, dear, didn't that satisfy her curiosity?"

"Not at all, for then she asked me if the sheriff thought Ralph had anything to do with that girl's death. Now who would ask a mother a question like that? I tell you, I wanted to punch . . ." Wanda glanced at her grinning daughter and stopped. The veins on Wanda's neck were beginning to stand out again, along with the grit of her teeth, and the clinching of her fists. Jonie giggled at the thought of her mother punching someone.

"Now, dear, relax, did that satisfy the busybody? It still sounds like you handled it well, dear," he said, calmly.

"Oh, I handled it alright, I told her the next time she passes along stories, she ought to make sure they are true."

"Good for you, dear, now what's this talk about your job?" Del, the peace maker, thought to calm his upset wife, it might be better to move on in her frustrations.

"Well, you know how close Blanche is to Mr Fuller. One word from her and I could be history."

"I know Sam Fuller, he isn't about to lose the best receptionist his firm ever had. And every one knows what a gossip Blanche Davis is, besides Sam knows it too. He probably thinks you did his business a service by reminding her not to pass on gossip at the office."

Calming somewhat, Wanda looked at her husband, "You really think so, dear? Or are you just pacifying me?"

"Well, maybe a little of both, dear, but let's not hear any more about your being fired. That won't happen as long as Sam Fuller is making the decisions for the company he owns."

"But where does that leave me?" Ralph spoke up, "I still have these rumors floating around town about being guilty of something that I didn't do." Ralph had a pained expression on his face.

"Yes dear, and that is what irritated me the most about the office talk. How many other offices across town is having the same gossip passed around the office desk, or the work room?"

"Just remember Ralph, you know the truth, and eventually the sheriff will see it too. In the mean time, we will just go about our normal routines and hold our heads up. There is nothing to be ashamed of, right, son?"

"Right dad."

"Hey bro, besides look at it this way, you're the talk of the town. You're a celebrity!" The laugh that Jonie gave them seemed to be handicapped somewhat by a nervous fear that went through them all.

Later that evening, as Wanda passed the den, she saw a light on. Stopping to investigate, she found Ralph reading the evening paper. "Anything of importance in the paper tonight?" she inquired.

"There is an editorial that caught my attention. It is about the girl at the lake. It seems the sheriff is catching some flak about not doing enough to solve the case. I think there must be a lot of pressure on him to find out what happened. There must be more people like Blanche at your office who want answers."

"That's the very thing I am most afraid of, the more pressure, the more reason to try to find some link between you and the girl. I don't trust him, it may not be justice he is after. It may be a quick solution is all that is important to him. That makes him dangerous in my mind."

"Remember, Mom, in this country you are considered innocent until proven guilty. We learned that in seventh grade civics."

"I hope you're right, Ralph, but I also know that if the sheriff believes you guilty, he will find something to imply that he is right. Then it becomes your responsibility to prove your innocence."

"Well, there is nothing for him to find."

"What if he creates something?" Ralph looked at his mother, she looked tired and worried. He thought about what she just said. He saw the fear on his mother's face.

"Don't worry so much, Mom. Everything will work out okay." Ralph wished he felt as confident as his words implied. He also felt guilty for being the source of the anguish his mother was experiencing.

CHAPTER 11
THE GIRL IN THE WOODS

"I don't care what kind of back log you have. Get me some answers and get them now." The sheriff spun around and slammed the phone down on its cradle. "McReynolds, get in here now!" Mike Smith shouted through the open office door. Almost immediately a short plump lady in a sheriff's department uniform scurried into the room panting like she just finished a mile run. She was of dark complexion and coal black hair hanging to her shoulders, straight as an arrow. Taking two or three deep breaths, she finally found enough air to speak.

"Yes, sir, I'm here." Those words apparently used up all the air in her lungs for she needed three deep breaths after uttering them.

"When are you going to lose some weight, McReynolds? I told you if you don't, you're out of here. Understand?"

"Yes, sir, is that all, sir?"

"No, that is not all. Have you finished going through the missing person files for Apache County yet?"

"Not quite all of them yet, sir, I'm working on it now."

"How about Lincoln County?"

"I was going to start on those as soon as I finished Apache County, sir." Clara McReynolds was running out of oxygen again.

"What is taking so long, McReynolds, this should have been completed days ago. Now get with it and don't eat anything until you find out who the girl is, got it?"

50

"Yes, sir. Is that all, sir?"

"Yes, that's all, get out of here." Clara turned and left the office as quick as her short legs would carry her. Once at her desk, and several deep breaths later, she grabbed a file, flipped it open and compared the photograph of the girl found in the woods at Lake Lawson and the photograph in the file. Shaking her head, she reached for another file. She had been doing this for three days now and the pictures were all beginning to look alike. Reaching for the bottom drawer of her desk, she pulled out a dollar-size Payday candy bar, unwrapped it and took a half-dollar bite. Chewing with authority, she reached for another file.

While Clara chewed, and flipped through files, Sheriff Smith already had another clerk at his desk. Marlon Stevens, a former part-time 911 operator who proved to be inept at guiding people through difficult times, now served part time on the Woodrow County Sheriff Reserve Force; which actually contained a group of men and women who served the sheriff as part time deputies and part time office help. They were expected to work twenty hours a week for which they were paid minimum wage for ten hours a week. Take home pay wasn't great but they did gain experience in law enforcement.

"Stevens, any thing yet on the state online wanted files?"

"No, sir, not yet."

"How far are you, about finished?"

Stevens began to fidget some. "I am down to the L's sir."

"L's, what in blue blazes have you been doing? That's only about halfway. What have you been doing?"

"Well, remember there was a power failure last Friday, and I had to boot up the program from the beginning. Sir."

"Couldn't you fast forward to where you left off?" The sheriff's face started turning a crimson shade of red, Stevens backed away from the desk.

"The computer program doesn't work that way, sir," he replied. "You have to do it . . ."

Smith shouted, "I don't want to know about a computer, I want information. Now, get out of here and get busy, I want those files gone over by the end of the day, do you understand, Stevens?" By the time he finished his statement, the sheriff was on his feet, pointing to the door and looked as if he would jump over the desk at any moment. Stevens disappeared immediately.

Slumping into his chair, Smith muttered, "Those darn computers, they just get in the way." *Give me the old ledger books and mug-shot three-ring binders any day, and I will find what I am looking for in no time.* "Incompetence, I am surrounded by incompetence."

Putting his head in his hands, the sheriff was about to call the crime lab in Topeka back and see if they had any results yet on the condition of the body, but it had been only about fifteen minutes since his last call. He heard a tap on the door sill. Deputy Randy Simmons stood in the doorway. "Come in Randy, good news, I hope?"

"I'm not sure. I followed him to school this morning. He spent the whole day there as expected. Then football practice and home. However, he did stop at Hall, Hall, and Crankstone on his way home. I don't know who he saw there, or what was discussed. But the question still remains, if he is innocent then why visit a law firm?"

"I can answer that, it has to do with the interview I had with him in a patrol car. His father called in a friend who happens to be a lawyer too. Did he meet with anyone else like some girlfriend, or fellow student?"

"Not unless it was at school. It's sort of difficult to shadow someone in there. I have a patrol car at the house now, in case he goes out later tonight."

"If there is any thing to be discovered, we need to find it quickly. The media is starting to get on my back about nothing new for them to report. They want action and lots of press to write. If they don't have anything new, they start writing about me not doing anything. That's not good for this office. We've got our killer, we just have to find the evidence."

"Well, I'm going to grab a bite to eat. You want to come along?"

The sheriff shook his head. "I'm going to stick around here for a while yet. Maybe try placing another call to the crime lab. They're dragging their feet again."

The clock on the wall read 5 o'clock. Sheriff Smith noticed reserve officer Stevens getting ready to leave for the day. Smith stepped to the doorway of his office. "Stevens, where do you think you are going?"

"It's quitting time, I have an appointment to keep."

The Sheriff took a few steps into the open area outside his office. "I thought I made it clear earlier that we were going to stay on this until the end."

"But that will take a couple more hours at least. I have an appointment."

"You can re-schedule the appointment. Get back to that machine."
Reluctantly, Stevens did as he was told.

Smith walked back into his office and had just sat down at his desk
when he heard a ruckus in the outer office area. He rose from his chair,
becoming aware that Clara McReynolds was making her way through
the maze of machines and desks in the outer office. Her great hulk was
knocking telephones, books, pencil holders, and anything that got in her
way, off desks and tables. As she neared the sheriff's office, she became
stuck between a copying machine and the corner of a desk. There she
stayed, holding out both hands in front of her body. In her one hand she
held a file and in the other a photograph. Sheriff Smith could also see
that her jaw was chomping down on something in her mouth.

"McReynolds, what in the world is going on now."

"I found it, Sheriff, I think I found it. The girl in the photograph, I
think I found who she is." The outburst left her speechless. She could
not get enough air to utter another word.

Launching himself across the office space, Snuffy Smith ripped
the file and photograph from her chubby little hands. Ignoring Clara's
predicament and spreading the file on his desk, he first examined Randy's
on-the-scene report, and then the coroner's preliminary report.

Name; Lois Lucille Newman, Address; 113 East 6th St. Atwood,
Kansas. Age; 13, height; 5 ft., weight; 100 pounds, description; white,
single, brown eyes, brunette, no tattoos, no identifying marks. Reported
missing 11-22-2010. Last seen; wearing plaid jacket, blue jeans, in
vicinity of the Amber Skating Arena, in Atwood, Woodrow County,
Kansas. Attends the Edwards Consolidated School in Woodrow County.
Parents; Abigail "Abby" Newman of Atwood and Fred Newman,
Hutchinson Correctional Facility, Hutchinson Ks. Parents Separated.
Birth date December 20, 1997.

Sheriff Mike "Snuffy" Smith leaned back in his chair with a
photograph in each hand. *Yep, that's her alright. I got you now. All I have
to do is connect her with Ralph Kellam and this case is closed.* With the
thought of having a suspect and solving the case still in his head, he
looked up. Smith's gaze fell on Clara struggling to free herself from the
copier and desk.

Clara ripped herself free, and waddled back to her desk, unaware of the sheriff's thoughts, she disapproved of his look and the broad smile on his face. *Not even a thank you for a job well done, not around this place, no sir.* As Clara grumbled in her thoughts, she reached for the bottom drawer of her desk.

CHAPTER 12

THE SEARCH

Later that evening. Sheriff Mike "Snuffy" Smith pulled up in front of the most admired homes in Robertown. Climbing out of the squad car, he almost stepped right into the path of the senior Woodrow County Court officer, Judge Janis Martindale. "Snuffy, why don't you watch were you're going?" Judge Janis was one of the chosen few who would call him Snuffy to his face. She got a quizzical look in return.

Sheriff Mike, his preferred title, other than Sheriff Smith, did not read the comic pages of the newspaper and was unaware of Snuffy Smith of comic fame. Therefore, he missed the joke, but suspected the nickname made him sound incompetent at least, if not downright foolish at most. But he was aware that Judge Janis was something of the talk of the town herself. A small framed lady of mid 50's living in a twelve-room home, not counting a three port garage. She loved slipping out of state and visiting nearby casinos to play a little black jack, or Keno, and to make the purchase of items she didn't want the local wags of Robertown talking about. Her only living relatives were a niece Sarah Muncie, who lived with her and a nephew who happened to be the Robertown High School Principal, Harold Hendrix. Judge Janis herself had never married, and as far as anyone knew, had no vices, except maybe a nip or two of the hard stuff, Austin Nichols Wild Turkey to be precise, which she purchased on her return trip from the casinos.

"I'm sorry, Judge, didn't see you. Out for a stroll are you?"

"Just getting some air, what brings you to my neighborhood?"

"Need a warrant, for one Ralph Kellam, of here in town."

"I know Ralph's family, good people. What kind of warrant? What's he done?"

"Just the standard search and seizure, Not sure what he's done, but I aim to find out."

"Sounds like pretty flimsy evidence of having committed a crime to me."

"You mean I need solid evidence, like photographs of the senior judicial official of the district court coming out of Big Ron's liquor's with a bottle of Wild Turkey in each hand and then crossing a state line with those same untaxed bottles of liquor. Sort of defeats purpose of tax laws doesn't it?"

"You must be in a hurry, you pulled out the big guns quick tonight. I assume you have the warrant all ready for me to sign?"

"Right here, and a pen." Handing the Judge the papers, she placed them on the car and signed her name.

"Thanks, Judge, now you have a good evening. I certainly plan to. And I'll be working."

The Sheriff climbed back in his car and squealed the tires as he pulled away. Judge Janis stared after the car and muttered, "One of these days, Snuffy, it will be payback time, mark my words."

Speeding down Broadway, Smith grabbed the radio mike. "Clara, get me Randy on the line."

In less than a minute, a voice came over the radio, "Randy here, what's up Sheriff?"

Smith answered, "I'm on my way to the Kellam house, where are you?"

"Same destination, on my way to relieve the patrol car for dinner break. Arrival in five, what is your desire?"

"Go in mute, keep patrol with you, I'll join up, we all go in together. Search and Seizure warrant. Signed by Judge Janis. All legal and within guidelines. Possible murder suspect. Okay?"

"Roger, I am on location, will inform patrol car, await your arrival."

Rolling up quietly, Sheriff Smith pulled up at the curb in front of Ralph's home. Across the street at the opposite curb sat two county patrol cars. Randy Simmons exited one and walked across the empty street. Opening his door, the Sheriff stood with one foot on the car door sill. Randy spoke first. "Did you notify the Robertown PD we were here?"

"Not a requirement on a Search and Seizure warrant."

"Okay, just hope they don't come busting in here after receiving a call from a scared neighbor."

"Have your patrol officer stationed here at the curb, just in case. You and I will serve the warrant. We are looking for evidence of knowledge of a murder suspect. Seize anything relevant to knowledge to commit a capital crime. Okay, let's go in."

After stationing Officer Marlon Stevens, the patrol driver, to watch the front of the house, the two officers approached the front door and knocked loudly.

Del Kellam could hear the clatter of dishes coming from the kitchen where Jonie and her mother were finishing the routine of stuffing dishes back into the kitchen cabinets. Ralph, usually an assistant to his mother, had been replaced by Jonie as his sister owed him "one," and it was payday. Instead he worked on an English assignment by reading a chapter in his textbook. Del had just picked up the evening newspaper when the door bell sounded. Though a photo finish, he beat Jonie to the door. Opening it, he faced Sheriff Smith. Taken aback somewhat, he quickly regained his composure and spoke. "Good evening Sheriff, I have to admit, I am surprised to see you this time of day."

"Sorry for the intrusion, Delbert, but this is not a social call, I'm here to serve you with a warrant, to search your house and premises." The sheriff held out a copy of the warrant, signed by Judge Janis Martindale. As Del took the paper and started to look at it. The Sheriff and his deputy stepped into the house and around Del and his daughter.

"Would you kindly show us to your son's room?" Randy asked firmly. Then took it upon himself to start up the hallway stairs to the second floor of the home.

"Hey, you can't go up there!" Jonie protested loudly. "My room's up there also, and nobody goes in my room."

Wanda heard the loud talk, and came rushing out of the kitchen as quickly as her legs would carry her. Not clear on what was taking place, she shushed Jonie. "What's going on here?" she asked.

"They have a search warrant, Wanda, call Melvin at home and get him over here, now, please!" Wanda returned to the kitchen to do as her husband asked.

By then Simmons had explored the upstairs rooms. He called out. "Up here Sheriff, I've located the room." Smith rushed up the stairs with Jonie hot on his heels. Del hurried after them as quickly as he could. Wanda came out of the kitchen with a cordless phone still in her hand. She started to work her way up the stairs, which wasn't easy for her. Using the railing with the one free hand and trying to manage the phone in the other, proved difficult.

Suddenly, seeing his mother struggling, Ralph who had been a spectator, came to life. "Here, Mom, let me have the phone. Hello? Hello? Mom there's no one on the phone."

"I know dear, I couldn't remember the number for Melvin, I hoped your dad knew it." Ralph slipped around his mother and bounded up the stairs. In a flash he stood beside his father.

"Dad, what's Mel's number?"

"What? Oh, it's in memory. Scroll down till you find it." Ralph followed his dad's directions.

Punching a couple of buttons on the phone, he heard the ring on the other end. Then an answering machine picked up. Ralph left a message for Mel to call ASAP. When Ralph finished with the phone, his attention fell on his room. As he, his dad, Jonie, and by now, Wanda, watched, the two uniforms in the room were wrecking it. They had already unplugged the computer tower, and had it setting in the center of the room. Now they were going at the room separately, one rummaging through his closet, and one pulling things off first the bookcase then the desk. Within minutes the room looked like a tornado had gone through it.

"I assume you're going to put everything back in it's place?" Wanda offered. They never glanced her way, and continued their search. Within a matter of minutes, they were finished. Randy Simmons jotted some words on a piece of paper, handed it to the Sheriff, who signed it, and handed it to Del. Then Randy disconnected the tower and picked it up. He also grabbed a few note books and papers that he found in the search, and marched down the stairs and out the open front door, with the sheriff leading the way. They apparently were finished carrying out the law. As the family stood on the upstairs landing. They stared in stunned in silence at the open door. The phone, still in Ralph's hand, begin to ring. Del reached for it and punched a button. He knew it would be Mel, to whom he replayed the event. Del listened for a minute, said okay, and hung up.

He turned to Jonie, "Jonie, please get your camera, and take pictures of the mess they left behind. Don't be stingy with the camera, take all the pictures you want. Mel's orders. He'll be by shortly to pick them up. He also wants to see this." Del held up the search warrant.

Jonie jumped up and disappeared into her room and in a flash returned and started snapping photographs. Ralph went down the stairs and closed the front door.

Hours later, they were gathered in the den when the door bell sounded.

"That'll be Mel, Ralph, please let him in." Ralph went to the door and soon returned with Mel beside him.

"I understand you folks are having quite a night." When no one responded, he continued. "I stopped by the sheriff's office, They have identified the girl. They got Judge Martindale to sign off on a search warrant; they have high hopes of laying this on Ralph and solve the case within hours of identifying the body. If they find anything on that computer hard drive or in those papers, they'll be back, you can count on it. So if you don't mind, I'll stick around for a while, okay Del?"

"Okay, Mel, and thanks."

"I guess I might as well go up and put my room back in order."

"Ralph, why don't you hold off on that for a bit? If they don't find what they are looking for, it wouldn't surprise me if a couple of them showed up later to do that very thing. When I visited their office, I suggested it might save them a law suit. Let's see if they take the bait. You willing to wait?"

"All night, Mr. Crankstone, sure."

"Not me," Jonie yawned. "I think the show's over for the night. I'm going to bed, 'nite all." And up the stairs she went.

CHAPTER 13
THE NEWMANS

Sheriff Smith bellowed at everyone who spoke to him the next day after the raid on the Kellam household. The analysis of the hard drive in Ralph's computer provided no evidence to his ever having had contact with anyone named Newman. The notebooks and papers confiscated during the search proved to be all school related. Randy Simmons summed it up, "We came up empty."

Sheriff Smith was not happy. Not only did the warrant provide no leads, he had to succumb to the humbling act of sending two patrol cars back to the Kellam house to restore the room left in disarray by the search. Melvin Crankstone had promised a public display of the results of the search.

"That's all the media would need, is for this office to get hit with a writ for harassment. That would make the front page for sure. So now, we go at it from a different direction, we will check for connections between the two teens from the Newman side. We'll turn up something, I'm sure. Randy, you make a visit to Hutchinson and interview Fred Newman, not that we can believe anything he says, but be sure to take some photos of the Kellam family with you. I will check with Abigail Newman and see what she knows. Maybe we missed something at the Kellam house. I may ask the judge to let us look again. Let's get after it, I want to wrap this up as fast as possible!"

As soon as he secured photographs of the Kellam family, Randy rushed home, threw a change of clothes in his overnight bag he started out of town. Glancing at the fuel gauge of the patrol car, he made one quick stop for gas, snacks, and a large drink. His route would take him first to Wichita and then to Hutchinson. Once on the road, he called dispatch on his radio. Clara, manning the dispatch switchboard, answered his call. "Clara, find me a telephone number for the liaison officer at the Hutchinson Correctional Facility. I think his name is Amherst, I worked with him in Topeka once."

After a few minutes of silence, the radio came to life. "Randy, this is Clara, I have a listing at the facility for a Henry Amherst, is that him?"

"Yeah, that's him, what's the number?" Clara relayed the number. "Thanks, Clara, see you tomorrow, or the next." Randy turned the radio off, he wouldn't be needing it for the trip.

Encountering light traffic, Randy made the trip in little over two and a half hours. After leaving the Wichita area, he dialed the number Clara gave him.

"Hey, Henry, this is Randy Simmons, long time no see. Yeah, I'm with the Woodrow County Sheriffs Department now. So how are you doing? Good, good. Say, Henry, I am headed your way. Yes, I need to talk to a fellow who's staying at your facility. A Fred Newman, no I don't have his ID number. I hoped you could arrange a meeting this afternoon. Yes, it's official business, Henry. Great. I'll see you in an hour or so . . . fine, you take care, Henry. Okay, bye."

Officer Simmons glanced at the clock on the dash, 1:15, "I ought to be there by two thirty anyway," he announced to the world.

To entertain himself, Randy pulled up the facilities site, that he had earlier saved on the patrol car computer. Keeping one eye on the road, he read out loud: "Hutchinson Correctional Facility, a state prison based in Reno County. Originally known as Kansas State Industrial Reformatory, and designed to house younger offenders, it's construction began in 1885, but because of problems did not begin to house prisoners until 1895.

"The name change took place in 1990, and today houses an average of 1,830 inmates. Many of the low security prisoners have the chance to work on such projects as a highway crew, or work at the annual state fairgrounds, on public works projects in the City of Hutchinson, and in maintaining the nearby Cheney Lake and State Park. The facility also offers the Kansas Wild Horse Program, which trains horses taken from land operated by the Bureau of Land Management."

Randy could imagine what Sheriff Smith would have to say: "They coddle to those who are in prison to be punished; some of these guys are living the life of Riley at government expense."

At 2:18 he pulled up to the prison gate on East "A" street in Hutchinson. Answering the guard's inquiry, and handing over his ID, he said. "I have an appointment with Henry Amherst."

Checking his clipboard, and finding the appointment listed, he handed Randy his ID back, and pointing said, "First door on your left. You can park over there," he added, changing locations with his hand still pointing.

Henry Amherst met with Randy, and after a short visit, Henry took his guest to meet Captain Ludlow, who paved the way for him to interview Fred Newman.

"Thanks, Henry, I owe you one."

"If I recall correctly, you owe me two. Remember Irene?"

"Oh yeah, you're right, I owe you two. See you later?" Henry nodded. Randy had no idea about Irene. *Who's Irene*?

Later, setting at a table, the chair facing toward the interior wall of a room he suspected was normally used by lawyers to meet with their clients, the atmosphere seemed cold and bare, as were the fixtures of the room. It made Randy nervous and he fidgeted with the photos sent with him. He heard a door clang twice that sounded as if it came from somewhere in the hallway from which he had been escorted through just minutes ago. Suddenly the hair on the back of his neck stood. He knew someone was behind him. Turning slightly he saw a guard in uniform at the barred door of the room. With him was a man in prison garb. The guard nodded down the hallway and the door opened. He looked at Randy, himself dressed in his deputy uniform, and acknowledged him with a nod, and said, "The cuffs stay on as long as he is out of his cell block, understand? And I stay with him, acceptable?" Since he had little choice in the matter, Randy nodded his head. Knowing that visitors always loaded up on snacks from the vending machines, Randy offered the man two fist fulls of goodies he had purchased. The man didn't move, and Randy tossed the packages on the table, then offered the prisoner his chair.

"I'll stand."

"Are you Fred Newman, formerly from Atwood, in southeastern Kansas?"

"I am."

"Fred, my name is Randy Simmons, I'm with the Woodrow County Sheriff's office. I drove all the way here to ask you a few questions. Do you have any objections?

"Depends on the questions."

"Fair enough, how long have you been away from Woodrow County?"

"About three years this January."

"Have you ever seen any of the people in these photographs?" Randy spread the photos out on the table in front of Fred. The prisoner studied the pictures carefully.

"I don't believe so, at least I don't think I have. I didn't live in Woodrow County long."

"How long?"

"I lived there while working on the new school, for about a year. Then left and came back here about four years ago.

"Take another look at these photos, you sure you never saw any of the people in them?"

"Like I said, I don't think I ever saw them before."

"Are you acquainted with the name Kellam?"

"Don't believe so." Randy wasn't getting anywhere, and he knew the sheriff wouldn't be too happy with him.

"What are you in for, Fred?"

"Who's asking?

"Why, would that make a difference?"

"Are you asking, or is Snuffy Smith asking? 'Cause if Smith is asking I'm not answering."

"What do you have against Sheriff Smith?"

"Only that the little weasel lied to me, he lied to the jury, and he lied to the judge."

"Mind if I ask for myself, what you're in for?"

"Makes no difference, you can find out easy enough anyway. They got me for burglary, I'm doing ten to twenty because it's my second offense."

"Who's 'they,' Fred?"

"That lying weasel Smith."

"How did he lie, Fred, would you tell me the story? I might be able to help you."

"How can you help?"

"I work for the guy, I know how he operates. Tell me your story and we'll see if I can help. What have you got to lose, Fred?" Randy looked the man in the eye and neither blinked.

Fred looked at the guard behind him reached for a couple of packages of the snacks still on the table and moved to the chair and sat. Randy moved to a chair on the opposite side of the narrow table.

"Smith told me if I admitted to breaking into this store and fingered the other guy, he would get me off because I helped him solve a crime. We met at this hotel room in Robertown and I gave him a signed confession and an affidavit telling what I knew, and then he reneged on his promise. He lied to the judge when he told her that the confession was a voluntary act on my part. And the judge overruled my attorney when he asked that my confession be thrown out on grounds of duress. I think she knew the Sheriff had probably made a deal with me, but she wanted a conviction. Then the sheriff lied to the jury during the trial when he told them I had a gun in my pocket when I broke into the store. But I didn't take it lying down."

"What do you mean by that?" Randy asked.

"I told him that I had a recording of our first meeting at the hotel and it was set to be mailed to the newspaper. I never seen anybody as mad as he got when I said that."

"Did you have a recording?"

"No, I wished I did. I don't think he believed me either. So because of the gun the charge was upped to burglary with a deadly weapon. which carries a greater penalty. The gun charge and my prior got me 10 to 20."

"How can I know you are telling me the truth?"

"Talk to the other guy, he'll tell you."

"And how am I supposed to find this other guy?'

"Look him up. He's over in Cell Block D."

"You mean he's here?"

"Yeah, they did him pretty much the same way."

"Are you still telling me you never heard of the Kellam family and never saw any of these people in the photos?" Fred took a bite of a Mars Bar and shook his head.

"Thanks for talking to me, Fred, now I'm afraid I have some bad news for you. You knew Lois had been reported missing?" Fred nodded his head again. "We found her body. I'm sorry Fred, she's dead."

"Yeah, I got the word, you gonna try to find who did it?"

Randy nodded, then motioned to the guard, who walked over to the chair where Fred sat and helped him to his feet. Fred scooped up the rest of the snacks from the table. They moved to the door, and the guard tapped on one bar with a key. The door opened.

As Fred left he turned back to Randy. "You going to talk to the other guy, or was that a lie also?"

"No, Fred, I plan on talking to him right now, if I can. What's his name?"

"Jesse Jennings. Over in 'D', I don't know his number."

"Don't worry, I'll find him," Randy replied.

Fred turned and shuffled up the hallway.

Randy contacted Henry, found out the number Jesse Jennings and set up a meeting with him, but by then it was near chow time for Jesse. The interview with him was short, but Randy thought he had heard enough to form an opinion on the situation. after visiting with Jennings, Randy went to see Henry again, I believe their story Henry ," Randy told him.

"I did too. I decided to do some investigating of my own into the alleged complaints by Fred and Jennings." Henry told him. "The court records, agreed with their story. I would encourage you to check it out yourself Randy, particularly if you have any doubts."

Randy knew something that Henry did not. He knew the Judge involved was Janis Martindale, a setting Judge. *This is serious business,* Randy thought, *I don't know if I want to be the whistle blower or not. My proof would have to be air tight, and above reproach by many boards and oversight commissions that might become involved.* Randy did have doubts that he could put it all together in a package that would hold up in an Attorney General's investigation. The afternoon's activities of talking with Jennings and Henry, had used up the rest of the day. Not interested in driving at night, Randy decided to check into the Sun Dome Motel and return to Robertown the next day. Besides which, he had some serious thinking to do.

*   *   *

With speeds reaching 80 miles per hour, Sheriff Smith, patrol car lights flashing and the siren blaring, raced down the road to Atwood. His "emergency," which would call for the use of lights and siren meant little to him. Even if Simmons came up empty in his mission, Smith had no plans to do the same. Somehow he would find a connection between the Kellam boy, and the dead girl, or else. And he wasn't used to leaving things to chance. As he neared the Atwood turnoff, he shut down both his speed and his emergency signals. Then he changed his mind on the speed and continued to break the speed limit on the old highway. Atwood soon came into view and the squad car squealed to a halt in front of a trailer house located at 113 East 6th. He hesitated for a minute, observing the area. He wanted speed but not recklessness. His training told him to go slow from this point. Only after first calling Clara at dispatch, and acknowledging his location, did he exit the car. *2:30 in the afternoon,* he thought, checking his watch, *not a good time to catch someone at home.* But he walked determinedly to the trailer door and knocked loudly. Smith announced his presence. "Sheriff's Office, open up."

He knocked again and called louder the second time.

From somewhere behind him came a voice, "She's not home, she's at work."

Spinning around, in a half crouch, his right hand going to his gun, the sheriff was ready for action. To his surprise, there stood a little old lady who must have been in her 80's and weighing all of 90 pounds, within five feet of him. If she had intended him harm, he would have been a dead man. Instead, she was grinning from ear to ear.

Quickly recovering his composure, he straightened himself and asked, "Do you know where she works?"

"Over at the school, but it's not out for 'nother half hour. Then she usually stops at the fillin' station, for a cold one, 'fore coming on home."

The sheriff, recognizing a source of information when he hears one, asked another question, "Does Abigail work every school day?"

"Yeah, pretty much, she's sickly, and stays home occasionally, but she works most school days."

"Have they lived here long?"

"No, moved here from somewhere back east, somewhere in Illinois, I believe."

"You know why they moved here?"

"The husband worked on the building of the new school, and lived here then. Guess he came back. Atwood's a nice place to live, I say."

"She ever have more than one cold one?"

The little old lady spread a big grin on her face. "Don't most people?" When the sheriff didn't respond, she continued, "Only on some weekends. Rarely on a school night." After a second hesitation, she added, "She invites me over for a beer on paydays, and we sometimes have more than one."

"Any boyfriends around?"

The grin disappeared, "Hey, she's a married lady, her husband is up north, or out west, I'm not sure which, but she don't fool around on him, she's a nice girl."

"What do you know about her daughter?"

"She's a worry that one. Done skipped out of the country, I hear."

"She have any boyfriends?"

"She had several sniffing around from time to time. But only one that was a bother to her and her mother." Sheriff Smith's ears perked up. Now we're getting somewhere.

"Did you ever meet him, the one who was a bother?"

"I don't mind saying, I threatened to call the cops on him once. And I would have, except he left."

"What was his name? Do you remember?"

"Of course I remember. What do you take me for? You think I'm senile or something?"

"No, no, I don't, but do you know his name? The boy who was a bother?"

"He was so much older than she, in his twenties, he was and she only a 13 year old. My, what could she have been thinking? Just because he was nice looking, I suppose. Girls these days, they don't think for themselves anymore."

"What's his name?"

"Bobby, Bobby . . . Now what was the name . . ."

"You sure? Maybe it was Ralph? You sure his name wasn't Ralph, Ralph Kellam?"

"No, it was Bobby cause he had the same name as my cat. Bobbie is my cat."

"This Bobby, what did he look like? Can you describe him?"

"Oh that's an easy one. But why don't you just go visit him? He lives just down the road a ways. Up toward Robertown."

"Can you tell me how I would recognize him?"

"He has a scar just above the left eye, where his father took after him with a broken beer bottle, once."

Sheriff Smith started to leave when the old lady clapped her hands and pointed. "Here she comes now. I guess you can ask her your questions. She's real smart, that Abigail."

The old lady introduced Sheriff Smith to Abigail Newman then went back to her own trailer when the sheriff glared at her.

Abigail looked up and down the street, checking the other three houses on the nearly empty street. She was antsy about the sheriff parked in front of her place. *If one of the kids sees that squad car parked here, there will be a dozen stories going around the school tomorrow. And I don't even know. What is going on here?*

The sheriff hoped the accusation he made to Ralph would still hold up, but first he needed to talk to Abigail and confirm what the neighbor had told him. After a lengthy discussion with Abigail, he knew no more than before.

Suddenly the sheriff heard a siren going off, and saw two pre-school age kids playing in his squad car.

"Get away, get out of there, right now" The two kids ran to one of the houses on the block.

"I'll talk to you again sometime. Mrs. Newman, but for now we only need the last name of a guy who tall man who hung around your daughter. The old lady said he was twice her age. Said his name was Bobby?"

"You mean Bobby Dunsmore? That loser? If he never shows up it will be too soon. He's a creep."

The Sheriff pulled away from the curb and made an u-turn, while muttering to himself, "I wanted to get that Kellam boy. But I better check out this other kid." He reached for the radio mike.

"Dispatch."

"Dispatch here, what do you need, Sheriff?" Clara asked politely.

"I need a location of the home of a Bobby Dunsmore. Believed to live somewhere south of town. See what 911 has on him."

"Will do, is that all? Clara asked pleasantly.

"ASAP," the sheriff shouted.

Clara did not respond, instead she made a weird face and said to herself, "ASAP my foot, we'll just dangle you on the line for a while. You're in my hands now, Mr. Sheriff. Let's see how you like being made the fool." Clara smiled as she reached for the bottom drawer of her desk.

CHAPTER 14

JONIE

"Come on, Ralph, we're burning daylight," Jonie yelled. "You need to hurry it up, bro." Jonie sat in her mother's car. She tooted the car's horn once quickly. Ralph came rushing out of the family home.

"Lay off the horn, Jonie, you'll have the neighbors calling the cops about the noise, I'm coming."

"It's about time, I've been waiting like forever. I still need a couple of hours practice this week and the day is perfect tennis weather." With the driver's side car door already opened, Ralph hopped in the driver's seat before Jonie finished making her plea.

"Which court did you want to go to again?" Ralph asked as he backed out of the drive.

"The one over at Mullhalland Park. Nobody is likely to be there."

"But I thought you didn't like to go there. You always gripe about playing on those courts."

"Yeah, and that's why the tennis coach wants me to practice more there. I do my worst playing on those courts."

A half hour later, they were warming up at the courts in question. Jonie stumbled on a return to Ralph, "Dang it," she groaned, 'these courts are so uneven. It's a shame the City can't fix them up"

"You just need to pick your feet up, it isn't always the court, you know," Ralph countered Jonie caught up with the ball and gave him a hard return.

"That's more like it," He said. The comment infuriated her, and on the next fore hand, she gave it a little extra effort. The ball sped past Ralph's outstretched racket.

"Nice passing shot." Jonie and Ralph both stopped and looked over at a young man standing at the net of a neighboring court. Neither sibling had noticed anyone else at the courts when they arrived.

Jonie recovered first. "Thanks, you play?"

"I did a little in school, but not much lately. Just thought it was a nice day to get out. We don't get many days like this in December."

Ralph took a second look at the man, *It is difficult to tell his age, he looks older than me but at the same time he looks like he should be in high school. Where have I seen him? I know I've seen him before.* Ralph felt uneasy, there was something about the man that left him anxious.

"Let's go, Jonie, we need to finish our practice," Ralph said concerned.

"Okay, bro, I'm ready for your best serve." Ralph gave her a better than average serve, Jonie slammed it back at his feet, where he dropped his racket trying to pick it up. "That all you got?" she teased.

"Okay, I admit, you're too good for me."

"Mind if I try?" It was the stranger again.

Ralph hesitated, but Jonie chirped, "Sure, why not?"

The man stepped onto Ralph's side of the court, and picked up Ralph's racket. "I haven't played for a while, so take it easy on me." As Ralph watched the two, he had to acknowledge that the guy played better than he did. Jonie had to struggle to stay with him. After a short time, the stranger held up the racket, "I surrender, I'm out of shape and out of breath. You're pretty good at the game . . . er . . ."

"Jonie, my name's Jonie, and this is my brother Ralph." They all exchanged nods. Then Jonie, never lost for words, asked, "You from around here?"

"I live a few miles out of town, I don't make it in very often. You play a good game of tennis, do you play competitively somewhere?"

"I play for the team at school. You should come watch some of our matches. We have one this Saturday. I play the first round here at eight."

"Jonie, I don't think . . ." Ralph started to object to Jonie's invitation.

"Eight a m on a Saturday, that's sorta early for me. But I'll see what I can do," the stranger ignored Ralph.

Ralph's instincts alerted him again. "Jonie, we have to go. It's dinner time."

Jonie, oblivious to Ralph's concern, and how her friendliness might be perceived, replied,

'Okay Bro, I'm ready." Hopping into the car, she turned and waved to the stranger, as Ralph started the engine. Pulling out of the park, he said, "Jonie, I had a bad feeling about that guy. Please don't be so friendly to him. There's something about him that tells me he's bad news."

"Hey Bro, you're not jealous are you? Besides, he's too old for me, so I'm still yours, Bro."

"Just remember to be careful, okay, sis?"

"Okay, but I got to tell you something, Bro, you act more like Dad every day. That you do!"

That Saturday morning found the entire Kellam family at the Mullhalland Park. Jonie had finished her first round of play and ran to where the family were seated in lawn chairs. "What did you think?" she asked no one in particular, but her father answered, "Your play was superb, but you have to admit, it was a pretty easy match."

"But you still looked great, dear," her mother chimed in.

"No contest," Ralph added.

"I have a doubles match next, then the second round of singles. The second round of singles is played at the high school courts."

"How soon does the doubles match start, dear?" Wanda asked.

"In about a half hour, I'm going to find Heather and see how she is, she hurt her toe yesterday. I hope it's okay today. See you later." She was off at a run.

"I wish I had that energy," Del said whimsically.

"I wish I could **run** like that," his wife added, with a laugh.

After a short search, Jonie found Heather Wilkes, her doubles partner, near the park play ground for toddlers. "What are you doing way over here, Heather? How's your toe?"

"The toe is fine. I was waiting for . . ."

"Hi, Heather, Oh, hello Jonie, Sorry I missed the first round. I just got here." Jonie was surprised to see the man from last night's encounter standing nearby.

"You know Jonie?" asked Heather curiously.

"We met briefly last night. How did your first matches go for you guys?"

"We both won," Heather said. "Both of us in straight sets."

"That's terrific, when do you play again?"

"We're in a doubles match next. We better get over there now, right, Jonie?"

Jonie had been observing with an uncharacteristic quietness. "Yeah, we better go."

As they parted, the man put an arm around the shoulders of her friend, and gave her a hug. "Good luck to you guys," he said as he glanced at Jonie.

After they were out of ear shot of the man, Jonie asked, "Do you know that guy, I mean who is he, anyway?"

"That's Bobby Dunsmore, he lives out in the country. We're . . . friends."

"I think I've heard the name. Is he your boyfriend?"

"We're not dating, or anything like that but . . . yeah, I guess you could say that."

"Heather, isn't he a little . . . old for you?"

"He's not so old, he's 18, that's not so old."

"Well, he looks older than that. But whatever blows your whistle, I guess."

The girls reached the court and started warming up for their game. By the time the first set started, Bobby Dunsmore sat in the portable bleachers as part of the crowd. But he did not go unnoticed by Ralph. Jonie stole a glance her brother's way, and recognized the intense, disapproving, stare her brother gave the man.

The match proved to be a difficult one, as both girls seemed to have trouble concentrating on their game. They surrendered several points and had too many unforced errors. Fortunately, they were able to put their skills together sufficiently to win the match after losing the first set.

Afterward, her brother greeted her with, "You weren't there mentally, what was going on, Jonie?" She wasn't sure how Ralph would take it, and at first didn't want to say anything. But it came out anyway. "That guy, the one from last night, he was with Heather earlier. I think he is trying to get her to go out with him. But after the doubles match he asked me if I had a boyfriend. Like he wanted to be my boyfriend."

I told you I had seen him before. Well while I was watching him in the bleachers, it came to me. He was at football practice before school started. The cheerleaders were there also practicing for try outs. He was hitting on the cheerleaders and Henry Carson got mad, and called him a name. The guy went ballistic. Threatened Henry's life. Said Henry would end up in the Verdi River. One of the coaches sent him on his way."

"What did he call him? What did he call Henry?" Jonie asked, but knew her brother would not repeat the name.

"Jonie, you've got to stay away from that creep, I noticed him in the crowd, he was watching much too intently. He even talked to one of your opponents after your match. I think he's playing all of you. Besides, he's way too old for any of you."

"Heather says he told her that he is only eighteen, do you believe that?"

"Not at all, and that's not the first lie he's probably told her. I tell you, sis, he's up to no good. He's a weirdo."

"Okay, Bro, I'll have a talk with Heather, maybe I can convince her to stay away from him."

CHAPTER 15
RALPH AND SARAH

"Hi, Sarah, you ready for the geometry test?" Ralph knew it was a redundant question because Sarah Muncie maintained a straight "A" average in all her classes except physical education. She could do neither the required push-ups nor the rope climbing that was required for an "A" in the class.

"I think so," the sixteen-year-old said. With her head down the brown eyed brunette did not look at Ralph. She appeared to be looking at some spot on the floor, but Ralph knew she was terribly shy and did not have the personality of a Jonie. He hoped to get her to talk to him, so he continued to try to engage her in conversation.

"Did you get the paper finished for Sophomore English? It's due tomorrow."

"I turned mine in on Monday." The girl's eyes flicked up to glance at Ralph. "I had it done so I didn't want to take a chance to lose it." What did you write about?" she asked. Then her face turned red and the blush made Ralph feel as though he had done something wrong and caused her embarrassment.

"Sorry, I shouldn't have been so forward," Ralph said.

"No, that's all right, I don't mind telling you what my subject is, it's about my uncle who served in Iraq during 'Desert Storm."

"Sounds interesting, I would like to read it sometime."

"I have a lot of free time at home," Sarah said, glancing at Ralph again. This time their eyes met and Ralph was warmed by the softness of the look she gave him.

"Sure, any time. Speaking of home, where is that? I don't know where you live or who your parents are, what does your father do? Where does he work?" Ralph asked.

"I don't know my father, My mother is dead, I live with my aunt. We live over on Wilson street near the Methodist church."

"I know where that is. Maybe we could go to a movie or something sometime?" Ralph blurted out the invitation without thinking about it, but he was anxious to hear Sarah's answer.

"I would have to get permission from my aunt, and she would want to know who you were first." Sarah seemed to have lost some of her shyness.

Maybe, Ralph thought, *she likes me and she feels comfortable with me. I think I would like to get to know her better.*

Sarah's blush had returned and she turned to leave. "See you in English," She called to him over her shoulder. As Ralph watched her walk away he noticed that she walked with a little bounce in her step. What he didn't realize was that he did the same thing on the way to his Phys Ed class.

CHAPTER 16

BOBBY

The Dunsmore homestead, for what it amounted to, consisted of a run down house and two out buildings. One of the buildings served as a bathroom, the other housed animal traps, pelt boards and other fur trapping paraphernalia. It was located about three miles southwest of Robertown on the opposite side of the Verdi River, in the flood plain that covered much of northwestern Woodrow County. Access to the home could be gained only by way of a poorly maintained county road which lead to an old wooden bridge over the river. Then about two hundred yards west by way of a foot path to the homestead. Rarely, if ever, did a motorized vehicle with four wheels travel the route. No mail route designated a postal address for the site, because the wooden bridge had been condemned by the county. However the county never officially closed the road, due to requests of local fishermen who used the road to gain access to the Verdi River.

The office of the county clerk identified the owner of the homestead as one Alfred Dunsmore. The taxes on the property had not been paid for a number of years. No one had any interest in the small track of land, even for back taxes. Additionally, at any time the county, fearing a liability suit, could decide to make the place inaccessible by placing a barricade on the bridge.

The Dunsmore family moved into the house in the fall of 1994, when the boy was eight years old. The mother disappeared one month later. When asked, Al Dunsmore would simply say, "She just up and left." No one questioned him that she did indeed do just that. The few times a church group, or a social worker would visit the home, they found the place littered with liquor bottles and moonshine jugs. Often being cursed at by Dunsmore, few paid a second visit. Once a month, on the second Wednesday of the month, he appeared at the Robertown Post Office and received the only mail the family ever claimed, a Social Security Disability check, which he immediately took to Don's IGA and cashed. Then he walked two blocks to Lillie's Liquors and purchased an arm load of goods.

Several times a sheriff's patrol would pick him up on Highway 10 intoxicated and he would spend the night, or a few days, in jail. No one seemed concerned about the boy during these occasions.

When the boy was about 16, he walked to a neighbor's house and told the owner that his father had passed out after drinking, and wouldn't wake up. The sheriff, who answered the call, found the man dead. For some reason the county coroner never ordered an autopsy, and the county paid for a burial with no service. The boy refused to leave the home and no county, or state agency, took any action. The teen had been taking care of himself the last eight or more years. No one, it seemed, wanted to get involved with the boy. And, being 16, he had passed the requirement age for attending school, so everyone quietly ignored the boy, even the church groups in Robertown and Atwood.

Bobby Dunsmore, now twenty-four years of age, stood about six foot tall. He had dark hair, hazel colored eyes, with a scar about an inch long above his left eye brow. When asked, his answer was that he tangled with some barbed wire once. Other folks remembered him saying that his dad came after him with a broken bottle. That story came out three days after the sheriff found his father dead in the shed housing the fur trapping supplies. No one remembered him ever having attended school. Considering his upbringing happened by circumstance, chance, and self motivation, Bobby was surprisingly physically strong. He had broad shoulders, a square cut face, and looked ever bit the part of a man with some body building training.

The local wags all had stories that were told and re-told, about what went on at the house. Particularly on weekends. Most of the tales centered around parties that included underage drinkers, and teenagers as young as middle school age. Most of the cars were parked on the east side of the bridge, and the passengers walked across the condemned bridge. Since there were no other homes in the immediate area, few people paid the activities any mind and people along Highway 10 certainly didn't bother to call the sheriff. Especially if a patrol car were already cruising the area between Old Highway 19 and Robertown along Highway 10, and seemed to be aware of the situation. The patrol was even spotted stopping some of the cars as they pulled onto the highway. So the word was that the sheriff's office had things under control.

Bobby's income came from his dad's Social Security check which he continued to receive, and accept, plus whatever cash money he made from the trapping of animals during the fall and winter months. Usually, to get to and from Robertown or Atwood, the two places he enjoyed visiting, he would hitch hike. Often he would con a ride from some teenager he had met during one of his parties. Most of the Robertown students had heard of him, even if they had never seen him, or visited his place.

The one characteristic that Bobby had, that no one wanted to witness, was pride, particularly if he had been drinking. Like his dad, he could not hold his liquor, and became very belligerent when drunk. Though no formal charges were ever made, teens often accused him of becoming nasty when when he had been drinking. Particularly if someone made fun of him. Once when he got angry, he lost all control and beat a person severely.

* * *

Sheriff Smith often worked alone when on a case or on patrol. The phrase; "no witnesses, no paper work" was attributed to him. Now standing impatiently at the open door of his car, he glanced once again at the ruined tire on the back of the squad car. He double clicked the radio mike. "Come on, come on, where are you at?" Frustrated at the unacceptable delay, he yelled into the mike, "Dispatch, come in Dispatch, Clara where are you. Clara?" The radio remained silent. Grabbing his cell phone, he punched in a number. The phone flashed the word "dialing" across the face of the screen. Still nothing. When the icon "Leave a message," lit up he flipped the phone shut and tossed it back on the driver's seat of the squad car. When he realized the radio mike was still in his hand, he tossed it too. He slammed the car door shut and walked back to the auto's trunk compartment and pulled out the car jack. Changing a flat tire was the last thing the Sheriff of Woodrow County should have to do. "I am not a tire monkey!" he announced to the world. Looking first to the north and then south, he resigned himself to the fact there was absolutely no traffic on Highway 10 this afternoon. He opened the driver's car door, leaned in and picked up the radio mike. Clicking the talk button, he tried it again, "Dispatch, Dispatch, come in Dispatch."

"Dispatch here, what can I do for you, sheriff?" Clara said, in her normal, everything as it should be, voice.

"Where have you been you Imbecile? I've tried to raise you for the last half hour. What's going on there?" Sheriff Smith yelled.

"Sorry, Sheriff, but I just answered you on your first call in. You haven't called this office since you left Atwood, an hour ago. Now what can I do for you?"

"Get me the tire shop, Glen's Tires, get Glen's Tires on the line."

"Will do, Sheriff," Clara said cheerfully. The line went dead again. *Imbecile? You haven't learned yet, Sheriff?* Clara thought, smiling.

"Dispatch, Come in Dispatch. Dispatch?" Nothing, the line had gone dead again.

Mike Smith started fuming again. *This can't be happening. Not to me, I'm the sheriff. I'll be danged if I will change that flat tire. No matter how long it takes.*

About 15 minutes later the radio zipped to life. "Sheriff, I have Glen's Tires on the line. Go ahead." Clara's voice seemed pleasant, as if nothing was amiss.

Sheriff Smith explained he needed a repair truck at the four mile marker south of town on Highway 10. The shop acknowledged the call and would be there shortly. Only after the sheriff felt comfortable with the fact that indeed help would soon arrive, did he take radio time to berate Clara about the lack of communication with dispatch.

"Dispatch," he began, "what is going on there, I want a full report on the break down of radio service from you. Do you copy?" No response, "Dispatch, do you copy?" Still no response. He realized he had been talking into a dead radio. Sheriff Smith's frustration level climbed several degrees. "Clara, where are you?" he yelled into the radio microphone. The radio remained silent.

Suddenly the radio popped to life. "Sheriff, this is Randy, did you call my unit? What can I do for you?"

"No, I did not call you, I am trying to clear up what is going on with radio dispatch. I can't seem to maintain radio contact with Clara. What is your location?" No response. "Randy, come in, Dispatch come in, ANY BODY COME IN!" The sheriff's patience disappeared, spinning around with the microphone still in his hand, the cord reached its maximum and his movement ripped the cord from the dash unit. Dumbfounded, he looked at the frayed end of the cord dangling from the mike in his hand. He double clicked the mike, then threw it into the car. It hit the passengers side door and shattered. Sheriff Smith would be without radio communications until the tire truck arrived and they could radio in for assistance.

CHAPTER 17

CLARA

The 5th Avenue candy bar wrapper floated down to the rim of the wastebasket beside her desk. Another identical wrapper already covered the top layer of the papers in the plastic container. Clara McReynolds, at age thirty-five probably tipped the scales at three hundred pounds, which at least doubled the scale shown on her doctor's chart of weight for a woman her age and height. Her eating habits were not so much from desire for food, as a release from stress. Her job could be demanding but her situation at home had been one of constant fear. Clara's skin was dark, like her father, but her mother was white and she lived with her mother.

The neighborhood consisted of low to middle class whites, there were a few Latinos at the flood plain edge of her part of town, but she was the only black in the area. When she drove down Larson Street between Seventh and Fourteenth, some of the whites gave her the look that said, "What are you doing in this part of town?" Her mother maintained that she read more into their looks than what was there. But, Clara, already synthesized from the teasing she had taken at school years ago, wouldn't accept her mother's complacent attitude toward some of her neighbors.

Already under pressure by societies view of her weight, the added stress of the racial attitude of her neighbors caused her to reach the limit of her patience. To relieve stress she ate. And when she ate, she put on weight. It became a vicious cycle.

All her woes were coupled with the stress at work. She took pride in the position she held. She was the Sheriff's Office dispatcher, an official title and position. She got to wear a uniform, (though it had to be specially tailored by her aunt) and had the responsibility of routing all squad cars for the county, she even took 911 calls when that service came up short handed. However, her pride was overshadowed by the attitude of the current sheriff. Mike Smith became her target for revenge to all those who did her wrong. Being aware of the power she held, as dispatcher, she decided to use that power. She knew the sheriff and his entire patrol force were dependent upon the dispatch center. That meant her. The switchboard, or dispatch, controlled the communication between units on patrol and the sheriff's office, also between units and between the citizens of the county and the county sheriff.

The key to the sheriff's effectiveness centered around her responding to their communications. In her hands lay the power of the office, and whether it proved to be successful or a failure, she controlled the power to make it work or not. She had chosen to get even.

Through Clara's head set came a familiar voice, "Dispatch, Dispatch, come in, Clara answer, you idiot!" Clara smiled as she unwrapped a Twink i. A few minutes later, the same voice came on the line again. "Dispatch, Sheriff Smith here, come in Dispatch." Clara flipped a switch on her console and in an official tone, said. "Dispatch here, go ahead, sheriff."

"Where in blazes have you been? At the vending machines again? I have . . ."

"Go ahead, sheriff, come in sheriff, Sheriff Smith? Come in, this is dispatch."

"I am, numbskull, I'm on the radio now, I . . . can you hear me, dispatch? Clara are you there?"

Clara flipped the switchboard toggle again. The sheriff spoke into dead air.

Two hours later, the sheriff stormed into his office. Clara, busy communicating with a patrol car, ignored him as he slammed a fist down on her desk. "Unit three clear, dispatch out." She looked up at the fuming face of her boss. "Something wrong, sheriff?" she asked politely.

"Don't give me that sugar coated mouth of yours," he snapped, slapping the desk with his hat. "I want some answers, and I want to know what is going on with you." The sheriff was so irate he had to stop to get his breath. Clara used the opportunity.

"Whatever are you talking about, sheriff? What is your problem?"

"You, you are my problem," he hissed. "My car is without a radio because of you."

"Me, I haven't been near your radio." It took all her self control not to laugh."

"You know what I mean. You've been playing with the switchboard again, haven't you?"

"Sheriff, what are you accusing me of?" At that time Deputy Simmons entered the office. Sheriff Smith rushed to the deputy, and pointing an outstretched finger at Clara, he shouted, "Tell her, tell me how she's been deliberately fouling up dispatch, tell me."

Officer Simmons looked at the sheriff with a puzzled expression, "I'd be glad to sheriff, If I knew what you were talking about, my radio is working fine, and no problems with dispatch, except that one call when you were screaming in my receiver." The Sheriff's face said it all. Angrily, he turned to Clara and huffed in her face,

"I'll catch you, fatso, and when I do, you are history, you hear? History!" He stormed into his private office, slamming the door behind him. Deputy Simmons shrugged his shoulders, and turned to his desk. Clara, smiling broadly, and reached for the bottom drawer of her desk.

CHAPTER 18
A PERSON OF INTEREST

With Sheriff Smith's car in the shop for radio repair, there were no problems with dispatch. And the night shift experienced no difficulties. But when Sheriff Smith came in at noon the next day, the potential for problems increased when he ordered Clara to stay away from the food vending machines. "I forbid you to go anywhere near them, just keep your fat butt glued to your chair. I'm going to visit with the Dunsmore boy, I'll be using car 4, and I don't want any trouble with the radio. Understood?"

"I'll do my best," replied Clara sweetly. Ten minutes later Sheriff Smith left Robertown, and headed south on Highway 10. When he came to Old Highway 19 he knew he had missed the Dunsmore turn off. He made a three point u-turn on the narrow highway. Creeping along at less than twenty miles per hour, he almost missed it again. Just in time, he caught sight of the seldom used one-lane road and made a sharp turn west toward the river. After traveling a mile, he cautiously approached the river bridge. A few yards shy of the bridge, he stopped and got out of the car, and gently put one foot onto the bridge. *Wow, this thing is shot. The county commissioners need to see this. A person would take a chance walking across it, driving across would be suicide.* As he stood with one foot on the bridge, he looked south, along the river, and noticed a deer trail as it followed the river for a few yards and then turned toward the woods. It reminded him of the stories told by the old bench warmers in front of Klinger's Drug Store, about an old trail that followed a railroad right-of-way no longer in existence. The folklore told by the old timers was that the trail once ran all the way through the Lawson Lake area. Startled, he turned sharply when a sudden squawk sounded from the radio. The sheriff returned to the car and without getting in picked up the radio's mike. "Dispatch, Sheriff Smith here." Silence. "Clara, Smith here, come in." He waited, nothing came over the radio. "Darn that woman, I'll bet she's at the vending machines again, and after I told her . . ." He stopped, realizing he was talking to himself. The sheriff stared at the bridge once more. *I want to talk to that boy and that's not going to happen unless I cross that bridge.* After retrieving the keys, he closed the car door and locked it. Back at the bridge, the officer gingerly placed one foot in front of the other and slowly stepped across the bridge. The lane now became a foot path. Sheriff Smith followed the path. He checked the thick underbrush on both sides. *I hope I don't run into any poison ivy, the last time . . .* The old homestead appeared in front of him about one-hundred yards. The underbrush had given away to tall gamma grass with several animal trails meandering through it. He studied the house and out buildings. There were no signs to indicate human presence. He approached the house to within fifty feet, and stopped to study it again. Nothing.

"What you want here, sheriff?" a voice boomed into Smith's ear and startled him and he literally jumped. The young man beside the tree let go with a loud laugh. "Gosh, Sheriff, you scare easy, and in broad daylight too." He laughed again. Sheriff Smith, still shaking from the scare, studied the man. He had broad shoulders and dark eyes, in his early to middle twenties, with a scar in his left eyebrow.

"You Bobby Dunsmore?" the sheriff asked. The man seemed surprised. Sheriff Smith couldn't tell if he was surprised the lawman knew him, or surprised the law knew where to find him.

He quickly regained his composure and replied, "Yeah, but didn't you already know that?"

"You know a Lois Newman?" The flinch was slight but the sheriff noticed. Then the eyes flickered just before the man said, "Who?"

Sheriff Smith recognized the stall. "Lois Newman, a girl about half your age."

"Can't say that I do, who is she?"

"She's the girl you been messing with in Atwood, the one whose mother told you to get lost."

"Don't recall that, what's her name again?"

"Don't get smart with me, Bobby, we can do this here or at the office. Maybe a couple of days in the bull pen at the county jail would soften you up some. You mouth off to some of those guys, they'll take you down a notch. Now when did you see the girl last? And give me a straight answer, you hear?" The sheriff glared at Bobby to make sure he got the message.

Bobby shrugged. "It's been about two weeks or more, when her mother got after me."

"You're saying you haven't seen her since that day in Atwood?" The Sheriff pressed Bobby for an answer. He suspected the story would change.

"Yeah, that's what I'm saying."

"You ever go to the lake much Bobby?"

"What lake?" Answering, with a smirk on his face.

"Remember what I said about the bull pen, Dunsmore, now you want to try that again?"

"Naw, I don't go to the lake much."

"You ever take Lois out here?"

"Who? Oh, no, she's never been here."

"Mind if I look around the place some, Bobby?"

"You got a warrant, sheriff?"

"Do I need a warrant, Bobby? The search becomes official if I do."

"Naw, go ahead, nothing here to find."

Sheriff Smith moved past the house and stepped through the doorway of a large shed. Even in the mid-afternoon light the interior of the shed looked dreary and dark. It contained a haphazard array of trapping material. The stench was over-powering. It seemed to be a mixture of a musk and decay. He changed directions to avoid the odor. Some fresh pelts stretched over pelt boards were covered with hoards of black flies. Most of the shed was stacked almost to the ceiling with junk that appeared to have been there since the shed was built. Seeing nothing of interest, the sheriff wandered over to the out-house. As he neared it, the stench forced him away. He veered away again and as he did he noticed an old water well that could easily have gone undetected earlier. Walking over to the well, he spied a shoe lying beside a chunk of wood, but practically hidden by small bush nearby. Obviously, it was much too small for Bobby. Sheriff Smith reached out and picked up a stick then used it to raise the shoe off the ground. "One of yours?" he asked, holding the shoe up for Bobby to examine. "Looks like a girls' shoe, see the pink border around the white canvas, humm . . . no shoelace. About a size six I'd say, that about right, Bobby?"

Dunsmore never blinked, and said, "I haven't the foggiest, Kids come snooping around here all the time. No telling how long that's been laying there."

"Yeah, there is, Bobby, See; it hasn't yellowed from moisture, nor faded from the sunlight. And it hasn't become soil encrusted from wind and dust. Yep, I'd say it's not been here more than a month."

"Like I said, lots of trespassers around here all the time." Bobby showed no facial movement.

Smith pulled a plastic bag from his pocket and dropped the shoe in it. "Well if it isn't yours, then you won't mind if I take it with me." The sheriff examined the rest of the area, but did not go into the house for fear of tainting his search of the premisses. He would need a warrant to enter a house , although there were times that he didn't bother with a warrant. When he was ready, he could come back with a search warrant and go through the house. Finding no additional items of interest, he decided to leave. "Before I go, Bobby, you're not planning any trips out of the county now, are you?"

"I don't know why you'd be interested in my plans, but to answer your question; no, I ain't going anyplace."

"That's good, 'cause if I were to come out here and find you gone, I might wonder if you had something to hide." Sheriff Smith retraced his steps across the bridge and back to the car. He unlocked the doors and dropped the plastic bag in the back seat. He climbed in behind the steering wheel and picked up the radio mike. "Dispatch, Smith here, any calls?" He got no response. "Dispatch, you there Clara? come in." Nothing. Tossing the mike in the passenger seat, he muttered, "dang woman, probably looking though the garbage for something to eat." He started the car and after several times in reverse, he turned the car around in the narrow lane and slowly drove to the highway and back to town.

When Sheriff Smith entered the outer area of his Woodrow County office, his first thought was of Clara. However, when he approached the dispatcher's desk, he found instead Officer Bailey manning the switchboard. Jerry Bailey started his career in law enforcement at an early age. After graduating from Blue Valley North High School in Johnson County, he attended Rockhurst College, majoring in law enforcement. When he completed that program, he participated in an internship program in Shawnee County with the Topeka Police Department. As the program began to run its course, he applied for a vacancy in the Woodrow County Sheriff's Department and won the position primarily on his educational background. Sheriff Smith said of Bailey, "We need the balance between the 'gut feeling' type of officer and the 'by the book' type." Jerry Bailey had been with the county four years now, and had not been assigned to any investigation during his years of service.

"Where's Clara?" he asked roughly.

"She had a two o'clock dental appointment, it's on the board, Sheriff," Bailey responded.

Ignoring Bailey's reference to the "on duty" board, he asked, "Has the switchboard been working okay since you took over?"

"There hasn't been any traffic since I got here."

"What do you mean, I called in not more than fifteen minutes ago." the Sheriff's yelled, frustrated.

"Didn't hear a thing at this end." Bailey, hid a grin with his hand over his mouth, as the Sheriff stormed off to his private office. Shutting the door with a bang, he tossed the shoe bag in a chair. He rummaged through the clutter on his desk as he looked for the file on the dead girl. After finding the file, he read Randy's description of the scene. Under the victim's clothing, Randy had written: *victim dressed in flannel jacket, blue blouse, and Levi jeans. Undergarments in place, no socks, and only one shoe, white canvass with pink border, no shoelace.*

Grinning, the Sheriff punched a button on his desk console. "Bailey here," came a voice over the intercom.

"Bailey, get me Simmons."

"Officer Simmons is on break, Sir, won't be back to his unit for another ten minutes."

"Darn, ask him to call me on his phone when he checks in."

"Will do, sheriff." Came Bailey's reply. The sheriff pushed another button.

Shortly another voice came on the intercom. "What can I do for you, sheriff?"

"Nancy, get me Howard at the newspaper, would you please? Tell him we need to talk, and like now."

"I'm on it sheriff." Nancy Miller, did good work. She was Hispanic and married to Ronnie Miller, who worked at J C Penney. They had one child, a ten-year-old daughter. Nancy was an efficient, reliable, receptionist, with a pleasant personality. At the age of thirty-six, she was also slim and trim, not at all like Clara. Sheriff Smith admired her. The console on his desk beeped and the sheriff picked up the phone. It was Howard Ericson. "Howard, how are you this afternoon? Got the paper to bed for today? Good, good, say Howard, I think I may have a story for you tomorrow. Yeah, got to do with the girl found in the woods down at Lake Lawson, Yeah, I think we got a break. Okay, about eight o'clock tomorrow morning? Sounds great, see you here at the office then. Okay, you're welcome, Howard, good bye." Sheriff Mike, Snuffy, Smith leaned back in his chair and smiled. He could see the headline now: *SHERIFF'S OFFICE INVESTIGATES PERSON OF INTEREST IN DEATH OF GIRL,* and he loved it.

CHAPTER 19
JONIE AND DAVID

"Thirty-Love," announced Jonie, as she prepared to serve. David rocked side-to-side trying to determine where she would try to place the ball. Jonie tossed the ball high into the air, her racket meeting it on its way down. Whoop! The ball just caught the service line and skipped beyond the reach of David's outstretched racket. "Ace, gotcha on that one, Forty-Love. Here comes another one." Jonie grinned at David, and let go a vicious serve. David managed to get his racket on the ball and got his return in, but Jonie caught it with a forehand passing shot and slammed it home. "Match point. She called.

David groaned. "Give me a break, will ya? I deserve at least one point for suffering this humiliation, don't you think?" David Masters and Jonie had been friends since their first encounter in kindergarten. When a boy accused David of shoving him first while the class stood in line for the water fountain, Jonie defended David by politely telling the teacher that the boy tried to push David out of line and David stood his ground. The teacher asked the boy if Jonie was correct and he admitted to starting the disturbance. David and Jonie were pals from that point on. They had never considered their relationship in a romantic way, but others had. However, their deep friendship wouldn't let that bother either of them.

The relationship which the two shared did not go without its problems. David was an only child and his parents were very permissive.

Allowing David to leave the house without asking for permission or explaining where he was going or when he would return. He often visited at Jonie's home, but Jonie had been to David's only once or twice. There weren't many kids in David's part of town. In fact the only other kid that David inter-acted with was Jeremy Hicks who lived in the next block over from David. Jeremy was two years older than David and even had his own car and his driver's permit. David often went to Jeremy's to get a ride to high school activities. Jeremy felt sorry for David and knew that he didn't have many friends. Jeremy felt sorry for David and considered him a friend.

David lived in a remote part of town. Not remote in the sense of no other homes around but remote in manner. Jonie lived in a upper middle class neighborhood, where the streets were wide and empty, and most of the cars were parked in the garage attached to the house. In David's neighborhood, the cars never left the street, there were few garages, and few with alley parking.

However, one of the greatest differences was in the lay of the land. Located in the flood plain, David learned of the power of the river at an early age. David's family had to worry about flooding each spring and occasionally in the fall. Jonie never feared water from the river flooding her house.

At the age of ten his parents obtained a Jon boat that they kept on the river. David often went out on the river in the boat to fish and explore. In fact, as he grew older, the more attached to the river his life became. A few of his classmates referred to him as "river rat" but seldom to his face. He didn't like the connotation that the term implied. When David and Jonie needed a place to crash after school, or on a weekend, it always meant going to Jonie's house.

The two usually rode their bicycles the three blocks from their school to Mullhalland Park, to play tennis. Jonie always had trouble with balancing her big tennis bag on the bike, so David would place it on the handle bars of his bike. But, today, due to a flat tire on Jonie's bike, they walked. Jonie called her mom from the school and promised to come right home after she and David played a set or two. "Tell Bro, he could pick us up. Save some wear and tear on his little sister," Jonie said.

"Game, set, and match Your mind must be elsewhere today, David, your game was off."

"You're just getting that much better at your game, that's all," David responded.

"I agree." David and Jonie both whirled at the sound of a third voice so close to them.

A man stood at the edge of the court. "Oh, did I scare you, David, with just my voice? I'm sorry I frightened you, and after such a poor performance on the court too," he jeered

"Bobby Dunsmore, I know who you are, you don't scare anyone. What are you doing sneaking around here anyway?" Jonie said sternly.

"I wasn't sneaking," he retorted, "I just enjoy watching you move around on the court. You look good."

The way he made it sound bothered David, and he let Bobby know it. "I'd go easy with what you imply, if I were you." David glared at Bobby.

"Oh, you would? Well, why didn't you say so, I wouldn't want to harm your innocence, little boy."

"Hey, nobody's going to hurt nobody. Let's go David we're out of here." Jonie started packing up her equipment and David followed her lead.

"Aw come on, I want to see you play some more. How about you and I play a game or two? I can show you a better game than your boyfriend here could."

"Some other time, we have to go. Let's go David."

"That's right, David, do as mommy says," taunted Bobby. David dropped his tennis bag and turned toward Bobby. Well aware that Bobby was older and bigger, he didn't like being bullied. As the two faced each other, with clinched fists, a car pulled into the park and stopped. Ralph stepped out. Unable to see Bobby clearly, he said, Mom sent me after you, Jonie, you ready?"

Jonie picked up David's bag, handed it to him and grabbing his arm, moved toward the car. "Yeah, we're ready, let's go, David. And Bobby? I'd not bother Heather any more either, her brother might not like you messing around with his little sister. You need to find someone your own age," Jonie said.

When his sister mentioned the name, Ralph sensing something had happened, recognized Bobby, but spoke to his sister, "What's going on here, Jonie?"

"Nothing now, let's go, bro." Still tugging David's sleeve the two climbed into the back seat. Ralph hesitated, took a long backward glance at Bobby, then got in the car. "Jonie . . ."

Jonie cut him off. "Not now, let's go, bro. Home James." Ralph started the car and pulled out of the park. On the way home she and David explained what had happened.

"You guys be careful, that guy is mean. Don't egg him on, you get him started and he doesn't know when to quit. You understand me, David?"

"Yeah, I understand, but I won't let him push me around either."

"Just remember, that's exactly what he wants, for you to fight back. So be smart and ignore him. He is nothing but trouble."

Ralph's tone told David the he was serious in his warning about Bobby. But David and Jonie soon forgot Ralph's warning. They were young and lived in the present. A reminder came a few days later, when Jonie, Heather, and the rest of the tennis team were practicing at the high school courts. "Take a 10 minute break and then we practice our serves," the coach announced. Grabbing a bottle of water for her and one for Heather, Jonie walked to a bench where Heather already sat. As she neared the bench a man who apparently had been in the bleachers with the small group of spectators, walked over to Heather. Jonie hollered at him. "Hey, Bobby, I thought I told you to leave her alone. She doesn't want to talk to you."

Bobby smiled at her. "Hey Jonie, where's your boyfriend, the one who scares so easy." He laughed.

"He's not scared, he just knows an idiot when he sees one. And he doesn't believe in wasting time on idiots."

Bobby grinned, and said, "You got sass, I like that in my girls. You want to be one of my girls, Jonie? You and Heather here could both be my girls. What do you say?"

"I say you better get your behind out of here before my brother shows up, and Heather's too. They might not like you hanging around girl's tennis practice, like some dorky kid."

Bobby's smile disappeared. "There's a difference between sassy and a big mouth, you're starting to sound like a mouth. I don't like mouths, girls, I get rid of mouths. I get rid of them for good. I . . ." Bobby stopped, it seemed to Jonie he looked like a person who had said more than he intended.

A whistle blew. "Okay let's go, on the service line." the coach announced.

Jonie glared one last time at Bobby and said, "Let's go, Heather." Heather quickly ran out on the court, with Jonie close behind her. Later, she glanced at the bleacher crowd. She did not see Bobby Dunsmore anywhere.

Later that evening, she related the conversation to her brother. "The way he said 'I get rid of them for good,' sounded like a threat that he had already carried out," she said. "It was weird, bro."

"I told you to stay away from him, Jonie, you're going to get yourself in trouble. If dad hears about you talking to Bobby that way, he'll have a fit and you'll find yourself grounded for life."

"Well, he won't hear it from me, so that just leaves you, Bro."

"My lips are sealed as long as you promise not to talk to Bobby Dunsmore! Deal?"

"Deal," Jonie said resignedly.

CHAPTER 20

RALPH

The next evening Ralph looked at the headline of the Robertown Gazette with interest. *COUNTY SHERIFF QUESTIONS PERSON OF INTEREST IN LAKE LAWSON DEATH* He read:

> *Woodrow County Sheriff Mike Smith informed theRobertown Gazette on the discovery of evidence in the case of the body found near Lake Lawson on November 26 by a fisherman at the lake. Sheriff Smith indicated the evidence places the victim with that person. The Sheriff refused to identify the person of interest, or the evidence uncovered. Watch the Gazette for further developments. A related story can be found in today's Gazette.*

Ralph flipped the newspaper over to the bottom half and found the article.

> *A REPORT ON THE LAKE LAWSON DEATH*
> *A recap of the story so far*

> *On November 26, a fisherman hiking along a trail near Lake Lawson, left the trail to take a more direct route to the lake. Finding a suspicious looking mound of fresh sod*

he investigated and discovered the body of a young girl. The identity of the girl has not been released by the local authorities, nor has the identity of the teen who found the body. The Gazette has learned that the body was buried in a very shallow grave, and was fully clothed. An autopsy has been ordered, and is being conducted by the county coroner. No arrests have been made in the case. However, a person of interest has been interviewed by the Woodrow County Sheriff.

"What's your take on that, son?" Ralph, startled at the sound, looked up to see his father standing in the doorway of the rec room. He had been so intent on the article, he hadn't noticed his father.

"I don't know, why isn't the Sheriff telling what he knows? Why doesn't he tell the paper what I told him?"

"I can think of two very good reasons, son. First, if he reveals his evidence, then has to go to trial, the jury might be biased. Second, and most important, if there is a killer out there, I for one, don't want him or her to decide to get rid of one of the witnesses."

"You mean me?" Ralph asked softly.

"I mean you."

"Who do you think the person of interest is?

"I haven't any idea, that's what I wondered when I asked for your take on the article. What do you think?"

"What I've been wondering from the very first, is how do you get the body there? No road, you can't drive to the grave, and it's a long way to carry anyone." Ralph thought for a second, then added, "I wouldn't want to carry Jonie that far, especially if she were awake."

"You're right, she would be a hand full if awake, but if unconscious or . . ." Del's voice trailed off.

After a few minutes of silence, Ralph said, "Even then, she would be a load. It would take a strong man to carry her that far."

"But, she could walk,." his dad interjected.

"Jonie wouldn't go without a fight."

"That's true, but most girls her age would just do what they were told."

"There's something else, dad." Del waited for his son to continue. "How do you get to the site? I mean what route do you take? The lake and campgrounds are all pretty public, how do you park, or walk though them without being noticed?"

"Maybe they were; noticed, that is"

"What do you mean dad?"

"Maybe someone noticed but didn't think it was anything unusual."

"But, would you want to take a chance? Particularly if you planned on doing something bad?"

"I see your point, but couldn't they just wait until the campground was empty?"

"Yeah . . . but, where?" Ralph asked.

"Where what? Oh, where would I wait? Well, I guess . . . I'd . . . That's a good question." Del looked puzzled and Ralph was concerned. He wondered if, on his own, he could find answers to his questions. If he had the answers, the sheriff would have to believe him. He decided to try.

The following Saturday morning, his mother was busy in the kitchen. "Mom, can I borrow your car for a few hours. I need to run some errands."

"I suppose so, as long as you're back by one. I have a meeting at the library then, and your dad may be using his car to go see Mel."

"Thanks, mom, I'll be back by noon, for sure." Ralph left the house by way of the kitchen door. The weather outside was a gloomy gray overcast December day. Ralph wore a light jacket as the temperature was mild. When he checked the forecast last night, the weatherman called for clearing skies by mid-morning.

Ralph pulled out of the driveway feeling a little guilty. His "errand" was to do some investigating on his own. He wanted to see if he could find some answers to the questions he had put to his dad. Leaving town, he traveled south on highway 10, looking for something, he wasn't sure what. Just looking. He drove at a leisurely speed, and there was little traffic. He started looking for turn-offs from the highway. He passed a little lane but ignored it. *But that could be exactly what I'm looking for,* he thought and quickly turned around and approached the lane again. It goes west and I want to go west. He turned into the lane, muttering to himself, "Nothing ventured, nothing gained."

Driving slowly he followed the meandering lane for over a mile. A bridge loomed before him. He slammed on his brakes. The bridge looked old. He got out of the car and walked to the bridge. *It is old. I can't drive over this. I might as well turn around and go back.* As he walked back to the car, he happened to glance south along the river. Suddenly it dawned on him that he knew what lay south of him. *I wonder if I can find the trail I hiked, from this end?* Punching the remote to lock the car, he set out south along the river toward Lake Lawson. At first, the trail appeared to be an animal trail, but as he traveled further south it gradually seemed to widen and become worn. Ralph started looking for signs of recent use. There were the expected deer and coyote, then, as clear as the day it was made, one boot print. Ralph carefully stepped around it, so as not to disturb it.

After finding the boot print, Ralph started walking along the edge of the trail. If he came across any more prints, he didn't want his foot prints over them. His luck held, finding two more prints, he tried to identify them. They had curved ribs on the toe and heel, with "tractor-tire" cleats on the outer sole of the boot. The tread of the boot was quite worn as if they were old. Ralph remembered seeing a pair of *Rocky* brand boots with similar markings somewhere. About 30 minutes down the trail he began to notice familiar surroundings. *I did it, I came from the north and the old trail led into the hiking trail. That could be the answer to one of my questions, How did someone get the girl down here without being seen? They walked down. But from where? They surely didn't park a car where I did. So where did they come from?* Puzzled, Ralph began to retrace his route back to his car. He took another look at the bridge, and decided it would hold him. He walked across the bridge and looked down at the foot path in front of him. There at the edge of the bridge he saw the boot print, the same boot print that he found on the trail. Ralph wondered where the foot path led, and decided to follow it for a way. It led him to a house with a few out-buildings about one hundred yards from the river. The place looked deserted. He turned and headed back to his car. When he topped the small rise just before crossing the river bridge, he saw a shadow move behind the car. Quietly he slipped across the span of the river, when he had about five yards to go, the shadow became a person as it moved to the driver side of the car. "Hey, Bobby, what are you doing, that's my car. You live around here or something?"

"Yeah, matter-of-fact I do. Now, let me ask you, what are you doing around here? I know you don't live here."

"I've never been up this road, thought I would do some exploring, being such a nice day and all." Ralph had his keys in his hand, but had not used the remote. "Whereabouts do you live?" Ralph asked, hoping he would get a straight answer.

"Across the river, where you just came from. You nosing around my place, Mr. Football Player?"

"No, I didn't go that far, I just went to the edge of the clearing. I gotta go, promised I'd be back by lunch time. See you around." Ralph moved to the driver's door, Bobby moved to the front of the vehicle, as he did so Ralph glanced at Bobby's feet. He had on a pair of well worn boots covered with dirt.

Bobby didn't move as Ralph got into the car and started backing up. He found a wider spot in the lane, but he had to back up and pull forward several times in order to turn the car around. He slowly moved down the winding lane. Glancing in the rear view mirror, he could see nothing of Bobby. Ralph pulled into his parents drive just before noon.

CHAPTER 21

SHERIFF MIKE "SNUFFY" SMITH

"I've had it up to my eyeballs with your shenanigans. I warn you, it happens again and you're outta here. You understand?" Sheriff Smith shouted at Clara, not caring that everyone on the whole first floor of the building could hear him, even though they were in his office. His face, was the color of a ripe watermelon, his eyes, like lasers, bored holes in Clara. He wanted to fire her on the spot, but, he knew better. He knew Clara would slap him with a prejudicial lawsuit so quick that he wouldn't have time to pack before the County Commissioners would have him gone. That didn't mean he couldn't make it difficult for her to come to work each day. She was vindictive and overweight, and the sheriff disliked both traits.

As if reading Smith's mind, Clara fired back, "I have documented each time you criticized my weight, you fire me and I will sue you, the department, and the county. You'll be so hog-tied with law suits, you won't have time to make fun of me. So just remember that or else your name will be plastered across the court docket under discrimination suit!"

Nancy Miller stuck her head in the office. "Sorry to interrupt, Sheriff, but you wanted to know when Randy called in. He's on line two now."

"Thanks," he growled, still glaring at Clara. "And you, get out of my office and do something constructive for a change." Clara left the office as quickly as her body would allow. The Sheriff turned his attention to the phone. "Randy? Where are you? Okay, listen, I want you to meet with unit three and the two of you go to the Dunsmore place and pick up Bobby. No, tell him he's not under arrest, unless he refuses to come in with you, then you can arrest him for obstruction, but give him a chance to come in peacefully. Yeah, do it now, unit three has already been notified and waiting your call. Okay."

The sheriff stepped to the door, "Nancy, when Randy shows, tell him to put who he has with him in the interrogation room. Then have him come to my office. Okay?"

"Will do, Sheriff." Nancy replied. The sheriff glanced at Clara, who was listening to the exchange. Clara frowned at him, he smiled back.

About an hour later, Randy knocked at the sheriff's office door. He entered the office without being asked and said, "I got Bobby in the interrogation room, he's all yours."

"Okay, thanks Randy, I'll take it from here." The sheriff stood as if to leave.

"You sure you don't want me to stick around and be a witness on what you get out of him? You ought to have a back up, Sheriff."

"I know what I'm doing, Officer Simmons, you're dismissed." Randy knew when to back off and this seemed to be one of those times. He nodded to the Sheriff and left the office. The Sheriff soon followed and opened the door to the interrogation room. "Stand up, Dunsmore, spread 'em." Bobby, who had been sitting at a table, did what he was told. The Sheriff frisked him. "Sit down," Bobby sat. "I'm going to ask you some questions, and I want straight answers. Understand?"

Bobby nodded. The sheriff's attitude and tone of voice, told Bobby that he wasn't in any mood for games. "When did you last see Lois Newman?"

"I told you once before, in Atwood, when her mother jumped me about me and her."

"When? Bobby, I asked you when?" The Sheriff appeared agitated.

"I don't know, about the first of November, I guess."

"Where, Bobby, where did you see her?"

"I told you, in Atwood, at her mother's place."

"You're lying, Bobby, I told you no games, and now, right off the bat, you lie to me. I don't like that, Bobby, I don't like that at all." Sheriff Smith paced the room, his agitation easy to see.

"Let me read something to you. Bobby. Listen closely. Victim dressed in flannel jacket, blue blouse, and Levi jeans. Undergarments in place, no socks, and only one shoe, white canvass with pink border and pink shoelace. Any idea where that came from, Bobby?"

Now Bobby looked agitated, and his nerves were on edge. He shook his head and eyed the pacing sheriff. "That came from a crime scene report, Bobby, you want to guess which one?"

"I don't know what you are talking about, you asked about the girl, and I told you. Now you read me something from something I ain't ever heard before, and ask me to guess. I don't understand?" The Sheriff could see the "tough guy" act Bobby had displayed during their last visit, was now melting away, he decided to go for the kill. "You read the newspaper don't you, Bobby? You know about the girl. Why don't you just admit to what you did, and we can be done with it. You ready to do that, Bobby? You ready to sign a paper saying what you did?" The sheriff had stopped pacing and now with both palms on the table, leaned over, putting his face only inches from Bobby's. Bobby started to pull back and the sheriff grabbed him by the front of his shirt collar and pulled him forward. "I'm through playing games, Bobby, you're in this for the long haul now. I'll have one of the girls type up something for you to sign, and you will sign, won't you, Bobby." The sheriff, his face still within inches of Bobby's, wasn't asking a question, he was making a statement. "I'll be back, you think about what's best for you, Bobby." When the sheriff released his grip on the shirt collar, Bobby dropped his head. The sheriff left the room.

"Miller," Sheriff Smith had not yet dropped his interrogation voice, "grab a pad and pencil, and come into my office." The curtness of his speech caused Nancy to jump up and follow him. She was only a step behind him when he reached the office door. After both were seated, the sheriff opened a folder on his desk, and after examining it looked up and said, "Take this down, To whom it may concern: On the day of , leave a blank space for a date, I led Lois Newman to a site near Lake Lawson." At this point the sheriff realized there was a gap in his scenario that he didn't have worked out. *How did the couple get to the lake?* "Leave a couple of blank lines here," he told Nancy. "And with malice of heart, hit her on the head with a shovel until she was dead. Then I proceeded to bury her, fully clothed, in a shallow grave." Sheriff Smith studied the folder in front of him for a few minutes. "Nancy, put all that aside for now. We'll finish it later. Have Bailey and McReynolds come in here now."

Nancy left the office, and a few minutes later, there came a knock at the open door of the office. Officer Bailey and Clara stuck their heads in the doorway. "You wanted to see us, Boss?"

Sheriff Smith slapped the folder on his desk, and growled, "Bailey! How many times have I told you, it's not Boss, it's Sheriff, you remember that, or next time, you'll be on crowd control at the next high school basketball game. Now you two take the guy in the interrogation room down, and put him in the bull pen. And don't talk to him, either of you. Now move!"

Sheriff Smith punched a button on his console. A pleasant voice came on the speaker, "Yes sir, what can I do for you, Sheriff?"

"Nancy, where is Randy?"

"He went back out on patrol, Sheriff, I think he has sector two today."

"When Clara gets back, have her call him back in, if he has nothing going on, have her tell him we need to talk."

Smith accepted the fact that Randy Simmons, having lived in Woodrow County all his life, knew the county, as well, if not better, than the sheriff. Smith needed someone who might be able to answer his question: *how do two people, neither of which drives, and at least one of them doesn't want to be seen, get to Lake Lawson? I need to be able to answer that question because someone is bound to ask.*

CHAPTER 22

BOBBY

With mixed emotions, Bobby watched Ralph drive away. Bobby was glad to see Ralph go, he didn't like/Ralph and his interference in Bobby's desire to have Jonie as a friend. But, he also felt envious of Ralph because he had a car and knew how to operate it. *I've never even been behind the wheel of a car that would run. I remember I used to sit in the driver's seat of my dad's old pick-up and pretend I was going somewhere.* Bobby also felt anger, well not necessarily anger like mad, but anger from fear. *What was he doing at the place. How long did he "explore" the place? And what was he looking for? First the sheriff, and now the Kellam boy, searching, for what?* Bobby had checked the house and nothing seemed to be disturbed, though it was hard to tell, since Bobby never cleaned or straightened up the place. *The Sheriff found a shoe. Big deal. What did that have to do with anything? One lousy shoe, and he goes bananas over it. Then the Kellam kid, he never asked any questions, he seemed to already know . . . know what?* Bobby shook his head.

The next day Bobby hitched a ride to town by using an old trick he had worked up years ago. He got the idea from his dad, who used to drive the truck to the highway and park it in the middle of the road or along one of the lanes of traffic. If someone offered to help, he explained that the truck was out of gas. He would eventually either get some money to buy gas, or usually he would get some gas offered to him. Either way, he never spent money on gas for the truck. Now Bobby did the same thing with an old bicycle. He took off the front tire and laid it beside the bicycle in the middle of the highway.

When someone stopped he would show them the torn jeans and the broken bike, and explain that he was on the way to Robertown or to Atwood to get some medicine for his sick mother. More often than not, the ruse resulted in a ride. On occasion he would get a ten or twenty shoved in his hand. Sometimes he would even scrape his leg with a rock to show injury. Today he had little difficulty in hitching a ride to Robertown. As usual, he shoved the bike into the woods, explaining he would get it later. The bike would still be there the next time he needed it.

Once in town he headed for the school. The building fascinated him. He had been inside it a few times, but that would be when the kids weren't there, after school or on weekends when he would find an open door, or break in, if he had to. He guessed his fascination probably came from the fact that he had never attended a school and he thought it appeared to be a wondrous and exciting place. Bobby wanted to be a part of it.

Today he walked over to the tennis courts. There was no one there. He knew that Jonie usually practiced late morning, and again after school. Bobby had no idea of the time, but he knew it was not yet noon. He found a secluded spot, hunkered down and waited. It wasn't long before he heard the sound of voices. One of them he could hear over the others, it sounded like Jonie. He stood up as four young teens neared the courts. He knew three of the kids, Jonie, Heather, David, and a boy he did not know. "Hi, Heather," he called out. "You guys going to practice playing tennis?" The four stopped short At the sound of Bobby's voice,, the youths stopped. Heather smiled and started to walk over to Bobby.

Jonie reached out and caught Heather's arm. "Heather, you stay here, he's not supposed to be on school grounds without an ID card." Then David spoke up. His voice was entirely different than his normal voice, it was rather gravelly, "You need to go to the office and get a visitor's pass, or else leave." David then glanced at Jonie, surprised that she was so silent.

Bobby smiled and replied, "And who's going to make me leave? You, little boy?" He glanced at Jonie, expecting her to mouth off at Bobby, she said nothing, but she glared at Bobby.

"No, I won't," said David, "but Mr. Wyatt will, when he finds out."

"Well, why don't you run and tell him, baby? In the meantime Heather and I will practice our tennis, right Heather?" Heather nodded, and once again started toward Bobby.

"Can I help you, young man?" The sound of a booming voice startled them, and Heather stopped. At the corner of the building stood a large man. "I'm Mr. Wyatt, you have business here at this school?"

"Yeah, I do," Bobby replied sarcastically.

"Then, I'm your man. I'm the one you want. You kids go on to your practice, this young man and I are going to see what we can do for each other. Run along now." Bobby was close enough to David to give him a little shove as he passed. David bristled and looked menacingly at Bobby. "That will be enough of that, young man, go on David." Mr. Wyatt instructed.

"Yeah, do as daddy says, little boy." David's face turned red with anger, and his eyes shot fire at Bobby.

Mr. Wyatt stepped to Bobby and clamped a hand on each shoulder and glared down at him, their faces only inches apart. "Son, you and I are going to have a heart to heart talk. Now you have two choices, you either do as I say, or I make a call, and you will answer to a disturbing the peace charge at the police station. What's it going to be?" Bobby, who no longer had an audience, could see the determination in the man's look, and that he meant what he said. Bobby quietly nodded his head.

Mr. Wyatt wasn't finished yet, "I want you to know something, son," he said, "I don't want a repeat performance of today. If we do, then I will not give you a choice, I will make that phone call. Do you understand?"

Later that afternoon, Bobby sat on one of the wooden benches in front of Klinger's Drug Store. A car driven by Deputy Randy Simmons, and another Woodrow County squad car pulled up at the curb in front of him. The two officers jumped out, and approached Bobby, each with one hand on the butt of the sidearm they wore.

Deputy Simmons said, "Bobby Dunsmore, we have instructions to take you to the sheriff's office for questioning in a murder case. You willing to come along peaceful, or do we do this the hard way?" Bobby stood and held out his hands for the cuffs he knew were coming.

CHAPTER 23
RALPH AND SARAH

Ralph replayed his encounter with Bobby in his mind as he sat in Mr. Grant's homeroom. It opened up several ideas for Ralph. The grave he had discovered was not that far from the river and Bobby lived on the river. Ralph wondered about the possibility that Bobby was involved in the death of the girl in the woods. Ralph had taken a corner seat since that was where the empty desks were. His assigned homeroom was Mr. Thiel, but because "Mr. T" was absent today,, his students were split between Miss Johnson's room and Mr. "old as the civil war" Grant. He was deep in thought when someone came into the room and sat down in the desk behind him. He turned to face Sarah Muncie.

"I'm surprised to see you here, I thought you were in Mr. Thiel's homeroom," Sarah said.

"Hi Sarah, Mr. Thiel is absent today and we were told to report here. I didn't know you were in Grant's room, I thought you were in Miss Johnson's homeroom."

Sarah shook her head and opened a book. She glanced at Ralph and then back to her book.

"I suppose you have work to do, but could I ask you a question?" Ralph said.

"What's you question?" she said softly.

"Do you know Bobby Dunsmore?"

"I've heard some kids talk about him but I never met him. He's not a very nice person is he?"

"I'm like you, that's what I have heard, my sister knows him."

"You have a sister?"

"Yeah, Jonie, she is in the eighth grade."

"Jonie is your sister? The one who plays tennis? I went to the middle school the other day and we talked some. She said she'd like to be a teacher. She is nice, seems very sure of herself."

"You can say that again," Ralph said, "she thinks she can do anything. "Ralph realized that they had been talking like old friends for some time and he liked to listen to the pleasant sound of her voice.

CHAPTER 24
JUDGE MARTINDALE

J udge Janis Lynn Martindale had lived a miserable childhood. One filled with frustration and sorrow. First, she was born prematurely to parents who had two children and thought their childbearing days were over. Second, she was born with an immune system deficiency that left her susceptible to any germ the came along. Third, she had poor vision, and suffered from partial hearing loss in one ear.

Her parents fitted her with glasses and a hearing aid at the age of six. Neither seemed to function well and the little girl was teased by a few other students, to the point that she refused to wear them at school. Her brother, Mickey, eight years older, ignored her as did her sister, Georgina, five years older, who had her own demons to deal with. Janis's parents accepted her difficulties with little thought to trying to meet the girl's needs for acceptance. Her school work seldom showed a level of achievement much above a passing grade.

Janis was unhappy and developed a shyness that led to her being labeled an introvert by the school counselor. The label stuck and the only joy the girl possessed came from her reading. She read every book she could, especially those that would take her far away from the present.

At first, she read for pleasure and to escape her sorrows, later she began to read to acquire knowledge and understanding. Her last two years of high school showed a dramatic change in her grade point average to the degree that she landed a scholarship at a state school.

Along with contact lens for her eyes and surgery for her ear, she decided to study law. During her second year of law school, she met a man and fell in love, only to learn that, though separated, he was still married to his second wife. She dropped him like a hot potato, but not before he introduced her to alcohol. She became a solitary drinker, one that drank just enough to tolerate life's disappointments.

After graduation she joined a law firm in Topeka that specialized in parole cases, and gained some notoriety in her skills at getting parole boards to see her clients as "reformed" and no longer a threat to society. Ten years later she won an appointment to the bench, and at the same time was given custody of her sister's twelve-year-old daughter. Janis's sister Georgina, had dealt with drugs since the seventh grade and at the age of sixteen found herself pregnant and on the streets. Georgina "kicked" the habit several times and each time moved back into her parents home. And each time she fled the "control" her parents placed on her. Her daughter, Sarah, spent most of her first twelve years living in her grandparents home. Sarah was a quiet, polite child and maintained an honor roll status in her school work. When her grandparents retired, they wanted less responsibility and time to travel. When Georgina died from an overdose, a month later, they insisted Janis take over guardianship of Sarah.

Janis accepted the duty of raising Sarah with little hesitation. She was sure that Sarah would create few problems and after all, she had the means and position to give Sarah a good life-style and a quality status in the community.

One afternoon Judge Martindale overheard a conversation at a PTA meeting that alarmed her. The mother of a girl was describing the relationship between some of the girls and their boyfriends. During the discussion, the mother mentioned Sarah and Ralph Kellam. Janis decided to take matters by the horns and invited Ralph to the Martindale home for an early dinner. Sarah protested, but to no avail. Ralph accepted and appeared promptly at six o'clock. The meal progressed and Ralph, on his best behavior, impressed his host with his manners and ability to carry on a discussion without hesitation in defending his position.

As it turned out both the aunt and the niece were equally impressed with the young man.

CHAPTER 25

THE AUTOPSY

I n the mail on Friday, Sheriff Smith received the report he had waited two weeks for. *Finally,* he thought, *we get some information and hopefully some answers.* The sheriff tore open the manila envelope and pulled out several sheets of paper stapled together. The top page contained information pertaining to identification of the subject of the autopsy:

> RESULTS OF AUTOPSY PREFORMED ON:
> LOIS LUCILLE NEWMAN
> NOVEMBER 30, 2010
> ORDERED BY:
> WOODROW COUNTY SHERIFF MIKE SMITH
> STATE OF KANSAS

Mike flipped to the second page and read;
> GENERAL FINDINGS:
> EXTERNAL EXAMINATION:

> Subject is almost 14 years of age (birth date given by parent, 12/20/1997) Body is that of a well developed, well nourished, 14 year old female with no external abnormalities. Extremities all intact. Body fully clothed,

Cabela's brand Flannel jacket, plaid, Towncraft brand light blue blouse, Levi brand blue jeans, white anklet socks, one canvass shoe, missing shoelace, white with pink border. Undergarments: white bra, white panties. All clothing properly buttoned and displayed. Subject is 5' 1" in height, weight 100 pounds, Race: white, Eye color: brown, Hair color: brunette, No tattoos, No identifying scars. EXCEPTIONS: one small mole on dorsal shoulder approximately two centimeters from spine. Also severe bruise on back of head.

On the third page he found;

INTERNAL EXAMINATION (BODY CAVITIES)

HEART: Normal size, pericardium intact, no
    abnormalities found.
AORTA: No abnormalities found.
LUNGS: Right lung weighed 500 grams, Left lung
    weighed 550 grams. Bronchi are normal. No
    abnormalities found.
GASTROINTESTINAL SYSTEM: The esophagus
    and stomach are normal in appearance. Stomach
    contains approximately 100 ml. No evidence of pills
    or other non foodstuff material. No alcohol. The
    appendix is secure. Liver shows no abnormalities.
    Gall bladder is secure, no abnormalities.
RETICULOENDOTHELIAL SYSTEM: Spleen is normal.
GENITOURINARY SYSTEM: Kidneys normal.
ENDOCRINE SYSTEM: Adrenal glands in normal
    position, weight normal, Thyroid gland weighs 12.4
    grams and normal in appearance.

CONCLUSION: EVIDENCE OF INJURY
    The body is an example of a healthy teenager of
    normal to excellent condition. No evidence of
    sexual activity. Cause of death was a blow with a
    blunt object to the posterior portion of the cranium.

The blow caused a contusion and swelling of tissue which contributed to increased fluid collecting in the cranial cavity. This in turn shut off the arterial flow to the brain, causing death by asphyxiation. Time of death is questionable but would be placed at about 8 to 10 pm on November 19, 2010. The burial of the body prohibits a more accurate time of death.

Arnold Peterson, M D

Disappointment showed on the Sheriff's face. *That's it? I waited two weeks for this? Normal this, and no abnormalities here or there? I could have guessed everything in this report.* The sheriff had hoped for something he could use to arrest a killer. *All I get is that somebody hit her over the head with a shovel? Then she was buried. I could have written that, we know the how, we need a why, and, of course, a who?*

CHAPTER 26
JONIE, DAVID, HEATHER

Jonie slammed the door hard. She stomped to her locker and swung her tennis racket at a towel laying on a changing bench. The towel went flying. "How could you be so dumb. Any idiot with half a brain would know better than to do what you thought about doing. What are you thinking? Heather, have you lost your mind?" Jonie stopped to take a breath. Heather began to cry. "Oh, come on, Heather, you know me, I'm always talking when I should be thinking. I don't believe you're an idiot and I know you're not dumb, but gee whiz, Heather, you know better than play around with Bobby Dunsmore, don't you?"

Heather managed to control the tears. She sniffed. "Jonie, you're my best friend. I know you want what is best for me. But, I can't help it, I like him, he pays attention to me. He wants what is best for me too. Why do you dislike him so? What's he ever done to you.?" This was the first opportunity the two girls had to be alone since the disturbance on the school yard near the tennis courts. "He hasn't done anything to me, and he hasn't done anything for me, either. He isn't a nice person, you saw how he tried to bait David into fighting him. And he's a lot bigger and older than David. He was just being mean."

"But you didn't say anything. I thought you would have said something, if you didn't like what was happening."

"I couldn't say anything, I promised Ralph, that I wouldn't talk to Bobby. So I didn't. Ralph thinks he's a creep."

"Why does everyone pick on him so much? He is just lonely, and doesn't know how to act any different than what he does."

Jonie thought about what Heather said. She couldn't actually disagree with her friend. Bobby never had actually done anything to her, it was just the way he acted, like he was better than anyone else. But, like Heather said, maybe he didn't know any other way to act. Maybe if people were nicer to him, he would be nicer to them. But he is so weird, he sneaks around like an animal in the dark, you never know when or where he is going to show up.

The girls showered and changed back into street clothes in silence, each lost in her own thoughts. When they were ready, they shoved the used tennis outfits into a gym bag to take with them and left the dressing room. David was waiting in the hallway.

"It took you long enough. What have you been doing in there, anyway?"

For once, Heather spoke before Jonie, "We've been talking, and we, *I* think that Bobby wouldn't be so mean if we were nicer to him."

"What?" said David. "That's the craziest thing I've heard in a long time. The guy's a creep and he needs someone to teach him a lesson. How can you be nice to a rattlesnake like him? You've got to be kidding me."

What David didn't understand about Heather's view toward Bobby was that she spoke from her own personal experience. David, nor Jonie, for that matter, were aware of the secret Heather had kept from them all these years. At home, Heather did not exist. She was a non-person in her own home. Heather had been made to understand from a very early age that she had been an accident. Her birth had not been planned nor wanted. As a baby, her needs were met with robotic treatment and her feeding time had been treated as one might treat a family pet. Food placed before her had simply been a chore completed. And whether or not it would be accepted as being provided affectionately remained irrelevant to all involved. Nothing in Heather's care had been completed because neither parent showed tenderness or compassion toward her. Even to identify it with duty would be an exaggeration of intent. Now, as a teenager, Heather did not receive recognition in any accomplishment or even as being a member of the family. No one said "Hello, dear," or "Bye, dear," or even "Where are you going, dear," or "Where have you been, dear?" Heather entered the house to silence and left in silence. No one questioned her about anything except to say, "clean your room," and "clean up your mess." She knew nothing about her parents' life, and they knew nothing about hers, and seemed not to care. Heather didn't question whether or not her parents loved her, she knew they did not.

Jonie remained silent, she still wondered if Heather might be right. *Would Bobby act differently if they acted different to him?* When Jonie didn't say anything to Heather like he expected her to, David assumed that she must agree with Heather. "Jonie, you can't believe the garbage Heather is saying. She's crazy if she thinks Bobby will change his ways. He's mean, he's always been mean, and he will always be mean, unless the creep learns that he can't treat people like he does and get away with it."

Jonie faced her two best friends, she couldn't take one side with out going against the other, but she had to be true to herself. David and Heather both waited on Jonie to say something. Jonie surprised herself. Ralph would be impressed that she actually thought before she spoke. After a few minutes of silence, Jonie finally said, "I would not say that Heather is crazy, David, but at the same time, I believe it's hard to teach an old dog new tricks, and I think that it would be hard for Bobby to change. However, I won't say it couldn't happen. But, I wouldn't want to turn my back on him."

"So, what are you really saying? Whose side are you on?"

"I'm not picking sides, I'm trying to sort it all out. No one has to be right and someone has to be wrong. Maybe you're both right. Maybe we have Bobby all wrong and maybe he **can** change. And maybe we have him all wrong and he **can't** change."

"And if he can't change, he's still dangerous and we need to be on guard." David wasn't giving up.

"I agree," said Jonie. Then she looked at Heather, "I'll not stand in your way, if you think he will change, but be careful, Heather, don't get in so deep that you can't get out." Heather beamed.

Ralph had his mother's car in the drive where he usually parked it to be washed. He had just gotten the garden hose out and about to begin hosing it down when David and Jonie came riding up the street on their bikes. He resisted the temptation to hose them down as well. Ralph turned the nozzle off and began to soap the car from a bucket of suds.

Jonie hollered, "Hey Bro, how did you get mom's car so dusty, you been on the back roads someplace?"

Ralph threw the sponge in the bucket of suds. "I want to talk to you Jonie, I thought we had an agreement about you staying away from that

Bobby Dunsmore. I heard you were fighting with him and Mr. Wyatt had to break it up."

"Wow, the rumor mill is working overtime on this one. Who you been talking to?"

"Never mind that, is it true or not?"

"Not."

"Let's hear your side of it, Jonie."

With David adding details, Jonie related to her brother the encounter with Bobby at the morning's tennis practice. "We have an idea, Bro, what has Bobby really done that is so bad? What has he actually done. We know that he is mean, but is it possible that could change? Think about it, Bro, maybe some good could come of this. Maybe we can help him become a better person. What do you think?"

"I think you got rocks in your head, sis, no way that guy's going to change. He has been the way he is for his whole life."

"That's what I tried to tell her, "David chimed in. I think the only way to get through to him is to give him some of his own medicine. He's not going to change."

Jonie looked at David with a puzzled expression. "David, why are you so down on him? Just because he challenged you at the high school this morning? You got to let it go. Remember, he is bigger and older than you."

"Jonie's right, David, you could get hurt, messing with that guy. He's bad news. Speaking of which, I heard that the sheriff called him in for questioning about the dead girl in the woods."

"How did you find that out, the same person who told you about the thing at school?"

"No, sis, Jesse, down at Ricks told me. He has a buddy in the sheriff's office. Heard it straight from him."

"Well, our deal is still on, right Bro? I didn't talk to Bobby, right David?" David nodded.

"Okay, but you be careful, and David, you too." Again, David nodded. Ralph went back to washing the car, and Jonie and David went into the house.

Later, after finishing with the car, Ralph found his sister and David playing with her wii program on the TV in the rec room. They were racing cars. "Who's winning?" he asked.

"She may beat me at tennis, but I destroy her at driving," David replied.

Jonie bopped him gently on the head. "Let's bowl a game, then we'll see who is best."

CHAPTER 27

RALPH

The following Thursday, as soon as Ralph could get away from school, he walked downtown. It was cool and damp from the passing thunderstorm that had rolled through only minutes earlier. Standing in front of the courthouse until he marshaled enough courage he entered the sheriff's office. Ralph had thought about going to the sheriff ever since his trip to the Dunsmore place. Each time he decided to go, he would think of the experience he'd had in the sheriff's patrol car. The sheriff could turn everything around and Ralph could find himself in trouble with the sheriff again. But, he knew that he had information that might help solve the case of the girl in the woods. He had also thought of asking his dad's advice on whether he should tell the sheriff or not. But, again he knew the answer his dad would give, "What do you think you should do, son?" Then he thought of asking Mel to accompany him to see the sheriff, but, then it might look like he was hiding something. So he made up his mind to go it alone.

To Ralph, the sheriff's office was institutional, and at the same time imposing. Institutional in that it had standard metal desks situated in rows with standard swivel chairs. It seemed imposing, due to its being a place of intimidation and authority, the center of power. Plus the effect of all the electronic machinery that filled every conceivable area from corner to wall to desk. As Ralph scanned the room, there was no one at some of the desks, but the one at the center was occupied by a pretty lady who smiled at Ralph. He approached her desk to ask for directions. She said, "Good afternoon, can I help you?" The name plate on her desk read: Nancy Miller.

"I would like to see Sheriff Smith," Ralph managed to say with some authority.

"Who shall I say wants to see him?"

"Ralph Kellam." This time his voice squeaked a little.

Nancy Miller smiled, "Just one moment." She punched a button on her desk. "A Mr. Ralph Kellam to see you."

From a deep place somewhere on her desk came a voice, "Send him in."

"That door there," Nancy said, still smiling. Ralph looked where she pointed and saw a door marked: Sheriff Smith. Ralph walked to the door, paused a second or two, then opened it. Sitting at a desk was Sheriff Smith, looking as menacingly as he had in the squad car. "Sit down," he barked as he motioned toward the chair in front of the desk. "What brings you here, Kellam, you come to confess?"

"I came to tell you something. Something I discovered." Ralph hesitated, he wasn't sure how to tell his story. The sheriff stared as if he considered Ralph guilty of something. "I went out to the bridge at the Dunsmore place last Saturday, and I noticed some animal trails along the river."

The sheriff held up his hand in a stop motion. He remembered looking at the same trails and what the wags at the drug store said about an old trail. "I suppose you were alone on this expedition?" Ralph nodded. "Continue."

"I decided to follow the animal trails and see if I could find the trail I was on when I found the body . . ."

"And?"

"And I did, I found the trail, it actually travels up the river quite a way."

"And why did you think I needed to know this, Mr. Kellam?"

"I, my Dad and I, were trying to figure out how a person could get to the lake without being seen. I thought this showed how, and I thought you ought to know."

"Have you ever been on this trail before, Kellam?" His look made Ralph feel guilty again.

"Only the part I hiked when I found the body," said Ralph.

The sheriff studied the boy's face. *This kid could be guilty and he knows how to hide it. The scenario is that it would be extremely clever of him to discover the body, and then provide information pertaining to the case, as a law-abiding citizen, to throw me off his trail. But he's right about getting to the lake without being seen. And he's the only one of my suspects who can drive.*

Had Ralph known what the Sheriff was thinking, he wouldn't have asked his next question.

"I understand you brought Bobby in for questioning yesterday. Did he do it?"

Aha, now he asks the question he has been waiting to ask. He wants to know if he has supplied enough evidence to convict Bobby. He hopes like I did that Bobby will confess even if he didn't do it. Clever, Mr. Kellam. But I've got you just where I want you. I just need to give you enough rope to hang yourself.

"No, we had to let him go. Not enough evidence to convict him." *There you are Mr. Smarter Than I Am, let's see what you do with that!* "So if you come up with any more ideas, you let me know, okay?" The change in the sheriff's attitude and the tone of his voice puzzled Ralph. He couldn't figure out if the sheriff meant what he said or if he might be playing some sort of game with Ralph.

"Well, I told you what I found, and that's what I came to do. So I'll be going." Ralph turned to leave, half expecting the sheriff to stop him. He didn't, and as he passed Nancy Miller's desk, she smiled, and said, "Bye now."

From the courthouse Ralph went to the library to see if he could find anything in the micro film files of the copies of the local newspaper about the Dunsmore's. He searched the papers for several hours but failed to turn up anything of value. As he walked out of the history room, he saw Sarah Muncie in the reference section. "Hi Sarah, what'cha doing?"

"I just finished trying to find something on Nat King Cole. I want to do a piece on him for the school newspaper as a, 'did you know,' article. How about yourself?"

"I was doing research myself. May I walk you home?"

The two enjoyed their time together as she and Ralph walked to Sarah's house. The two were fast becoming friends. Sarah promised to meet Ralph in the lunch room at school the next day. Later that evening as the four of them sat around thee kitchen table enjoying a blueberry pie that Wanda had prepared, Ralph told his dad what he had done at the sheriff's office, "I wanted to let the sheriff know what I found out," Ralph said.

"Way to go, Bro, maybe they will hire you on as a detective, and you can solve all their cases," his sister added.

Del frowned, "I hope it turns out to be the right thing to do, son, but I worry that the sheriff might find someway of using it against you. I think I will give Mel a heads up call, just in case."

"Oh, by the way, the sheriff did have Bobby Dunsmore in for questioning, but they let him go, sheriff said not enough evidence. I think they were stumped with the same question we had. How he got there. But now, with the information about the trail, don't you think that would shed new light on him?"

"If the sheriff listen's to you, Bro, the case is nearly solved, said Jonie.

"That would be nice, Ralph said

"Knowing something and proving it in a court of law is two different things, that's why a confession is so desirable," Del told his son. "But, I will let Mel know about that also."

CHAPTER 28

LOIS NEWMAN

That same evening, as Ralph watched his sister do her math homework and his dad shuffle papers, a thought suddenly flashed in his mind. Lois Newman, the dead girl. Had she longed for the comforts of home, that night? Did she know what was about to happen, or was she with someone she trusted? Ralph glanced at Jonie, intent on her assignment and thought of the girl in the woods. Was she frightened, did she cry?

When Lois Newman walked into the Amber Skating Arena in Atwood, it surprised no one. Lois spent so much time at the facility, she was considered a regular. Everyone knew her and her love of roller skating. Alice and Bill Elmquist, owners of the Arena, had offered her a job, checking skaters in and out. But Lois couldn't see any value in being at the rink and not skate. The Arena went on its winter schedule after Labor Day each year, which called for it to open at 5:00 pm on week days. It was a Friday night and had been open for about an hour when Lois arrived. With her homework for the weekend completed and her mother's permission, she was free to skate the evening away. She knew most of the other young people at the rink. Some of the older people were strangers to her. She was surprised when a boy she did not know approached her. "I hear you are a good skater, do you ever skate doubles?"

Puzzled, she answered, "Well, yes, of course."

"Would you skate with me? I'm not very good, but I would enjoy it."

"Okay, but where are your skates?"

"Well, that's a problem. I went off and left my money at home. Could you talk to the lady at the desk and see if she would allow me to rent a pair of skates and pay later? You know her, don't you?"

"Yes, I know her, but . . ."

"Oh, I understand, you don't know me so you don't want to be bothered with a stranger . . ."

"No, it's not that, Okay, let me see what I can do." Lois knew there would be no problem in getting Alice to give a kid a pair of skates. She did it often because several of the kids were unable to afford to skate. Within minutes, she was back to where the man stood with a pair of skates in her hands. "We guessed on the size, if they don't fit we will try another pair."

He put them on. "Hey, they fit, how about that?" He stood and made a couple of turns. Then holding out his hand to Lois, indicated he was ready to skate. She followed his lead. They were good together.

"That was fun. Thank you," Lois said sincerely, she assumed their time together was over.

"Would you like something to drink? All I can afford is water." Lois thought the young man seemed not at all ashamed of his lack of money.

"I think I'll have a coke, you want one? My treat."

"If you insist, thanks, I'll return the favor next time."

Next time? Who said anything about next time, Lois wondered, who is this guy anyway, I don't even know his name.

"Here you go, while standing in line at the counter, I realized that I don't even know your name. I'm Lois Newman."

"Glad to meet you Lois, do you live around here?"

"Yes, I just live a couple of blocks from here, on Sixth Street,"

"It sure is warm in here, let's go outside and get some air."

"It is quite warm, I guess it wouldn't hurt. But, I want to skate around the rink a couple of times first." Lois, her long dark hair flowing after her, started to make a lap around the rink. A little boy with skates on, fell, and Lois, true to her nature, skated over to him. Lois helped him up. "Here, hold on to my hand and we will try it again." The boy, about five or six, looked at his grandmother who sat in the spectator seats nearby. She watched Lois, who said, "I'll take him around once and let him see that he can do it." The boy's grandmother nodded. Taking his hand, Lois slowly maneuvered the boy around the rink. Twice she let go of his hand for a short time to show that he could stand up by himself.

By the time they made the complete circle he was beaming, with confidence. "I did it Grandma, did you see me?"

The grandmother thanked Lois, "He is so proud of himself and I certainly couldn't have skated with him. May I know your name?"

Lois introduced herself and said, "I like to see people enjoy skating as much as I do. Maybe he will let me skate with him again later."

The lady smiled and said, I'm sure he will, thank you again." The grandmother watched as Lois left the rink with a young man.

*   *   *

Lois Newman stood on the edge of the parking lot and watched the boy leave. She never did get his name and that was just as well, because she had no interest in him. For one thing he appeared much too old for her, and for another, he was kind of creepy. Pulling her jacket around her and clasping her hands around her waist, she started up the street toward her home. As she left the lighted area of the rink, the darkness swallowed her. A car pulled up behind and then along side the girl. A man hopped out and opened the back door of the vehicle. "Get in," he ordered, Lois hesitated and took a step back. The man grabbed her upper arm so tightly she knew breaking free was impossible. The man shoved her into the car and slammed the door. Lois's arm ached, she began to cry. The car pulled out and headed north to Highway 10 and the Cheyenne Cove Campground.

When Lois didn't come home Friday night, her mother called the sheriff's office Saturday morning only to be told that a person isn't considered missing until twenty-four hours had passed. She called again Monday. Later, after reading the Robertown Gazette, the little boy's grandmother, Ethel Henderson, called the sheriff's office and relayed the incident with the girl to the sheriff; Ethel Henderson would be one of the last people to see Lois Newman alive.

When Randy Simmons visited with Mrs. Henderson, he kept his questions simple. "Mrs, Henderson, would you describe the girl who helped your grandson?"

126

"Twelve to fourteen-years old, pretty, with long dark hair, dark eyes, she was wearing a light blue country style blouse, jeans, about my height, five two, weighed about one hundred pounds."

"Shoes?"

"When she helped Chuckie, she had on skates. I don't know if I saw what she wore when she left the rink."

"That's my next question. Can you describe the person she left with?"

"I only got a glimpse, he could have been about the same age, much taller than she, and broad-shoulders."

"What about what he wore, did you see . . ."

"I seem to recall he had light colored clothing, maybe khaki, I'm not sure."

"Anything else? Anything about his mannerisms, or his attitude?"

"I thought he seemed to be forceful with her, he had her by the elbow and it appeared to me, he guided her toward the door. She seemed to be reluctant to go with him. But, maybe I'm just reading more into it than what it was."

As Randy started to leave, Mrs. Henderson thoughtfully said, "There is one other thing, I don't know if it is connected with the girl's disappearance or not, but the girl arrived about the same time as I did, and there was a man standing in the shadow of a tree at the edge of the parking lot, who was watching the kids hanging out around the rink. He was wearing camouflage clothing, and took a special interest in Lois when she first arrived. He pulled what looked like a photograph out of his pocket and studied it and Lois, and seemed to know her. When she went past him, he said something to her. I was just getting Chuckie out of the car and couldn't hear what he said, but Lois hurried into the rink after he spoke to her. I think he must have had some of that black stuff on his face, I couldn't see it, so I have no idea who he was."

CHAPTER 29

BOBBY

B obby walked out the the Sheriff's office into the late Thursday afternoon air, a free man. He breathed in deeply and smelled the rain from the clouds fast approaching. The sheriff had been clear on what he expected of Bobby. "I'm letting you go, Dunsmore, but I expect you to make yourself available and don't try to leave the county. You're not under arrest, but the next thing to it." Bobby wasn't sure what had happened to change the sheriff's mind but he didn't want to stick around. Besides, the approaching rain storm would soon hit Robertown.

"Hey. Miles," he called out to a boy about to get in his car. "You headed for home?" The boy nodded. "Mind giving me a lift to my corner on the highway?"

"Naw, come on, get in, I'll drop you off at the corner." Bobby got in and they pulled away from the curb. At the corner, a few minutes later, Bobby hopped out, and thanked the boy for the ride. As he crossed the river bridge, he noticed some fishermen in boats along the river. Eying them carefully he tried to identify them, but because some had broad rim hats pulled down low against the cool wind leading the storm, he couldn't. Bobby grinned at the thought of them getting caught on the river in a rainstorm. He entered his house, shoved some stuff off an unmade bed and plopped down. He soon fell fast asleep. As Bobby slept a silent figure flitted across the room, and exited the house by a back door. The human stood near the corner of a shed only a few feet from the house. Soon a small flame crackled in the corner of the shed. The shadow disappeared into the brush near the bridge as the thunderstorm broke. When the flame broke through the roof of the shed, a downpour nearly extinguished it. But the persistent fire continued to smolder and consume much of the contents of the shed.

Bobby knew nothing until he awoke the next morning and found the shed a total loss. Suspecting that a lightening strike must have started the fire, he rummaged through the drenched contents looking for whatever trapping gear might have escaped the fire.

After an hour of searching, he gave up looking and headed for the river to wash off the soot and ash. Stepping down the side of the bridge, he gained access to the river. While he cleaned himself, his eyes caught the clear sign of bootprints that had been nearly washed out by the rain. Some one had come ashore either before or during the storm. *Now who would be messing around here during weather like last night?* Then it struck him, *maybe that fire wasn't an accident. Maybe someone . . .* He quickly climbed back to the lane, and headed toward the remnants of the shed. At first his inspection of the ground around the former shed revealed nothing, until he got to the corner close to the house. *There, a rain washed boot print. Too small to be mine, and what's this? A matchstick, either used or ignited by the fire. It looks fairly new. I haven't used any matches outside the house since last winter. Almost a year ago. And then not this close to the shed.* Puzzled, Bobby wondered; *who would want to set fire to this old shed? And why?*

Bobby glanced up at the clear sky, the cool December sun appeared directly overhead. *Noon and I haven't had anything to eat since yesterday.* Bobby thought of the lunch he ate at the jail, a slice of white bread, a hotdog, and an apple. Nothing to drink. Most of the others complained, but Bobby thought it was a good meal; especially after one of the guys gave Bobby his hotdog.

The thought of yesterday's meal made him that much hungrier now. Fortunately, he still had some leftover rabbit stew he had cooked over the make-shift fireplace constructed in one corner of the room. The stew consisted of some tomatoes and potatoes that he "borrowed" from a house on old Highway 19, and a small rabbit, he managed to trap. The stew had been in the pot for two days now, but his hunger demanded food, so he ate it, cold.

Over the years, Bobby had become accustomed to having time on his hands. But, after having been locked up for a day and a half, he needed something to occupy himself. He walked to the highway and, with the broken bike routine, managed to hitch a ride to Robertown. He asked the driver to drop him off at the drug store so he could get his mother's medicine. There were several old timers sitting on the benches in front. They stopped talking when Bobby passed by, not that they were talking about him, but because they had heard each others stories about him. And they usually believed the stories they heard.

Bobby didn't go in the store, instead, he headed up the street towards the high school. When he got to the tennis courts he was disappointed to find them empty. He headed to Mulhalland Park. Whenever he walked the town, Bobby always wondered what it would be like to live in one of the houses that lined the streets. But, foremost in his curiosity of the homes came his desire to know what people did in the houses. He had little to compare his home and that of someone else because he had never been in a home that had a family living in it. Well that wasn't exactly true. He had gone in some homes many times when nobody was there. However, that didn't give him any idea of the interaction that took place within the walls of a house. The only interaction he could remember was of a drunken father throwing things at his son, hitting him for being a nuisance,—asking a question.

When the Mulhalland courts came into view, disappointment creased Bobby's face They were empty as well. Bobby knew of only one other place to look. He turned toward the Robertown Middle School. The schools, parks, and businesses were the only places he knew to look. He didn't have an address for Heather, and wouldn't know what to do with it if he did.

Hanging around the middle school was always a hazardous thing for him as the city cops usually drove by the school once each hour when the schools were open. He didn't know the time, but he knew school hadn't dismissed for the day, yet. It wasn't long, however, when he heard the clang of bells, and kids came running out the doors. He watched for a long time, and had about decided she wasn't in the school, when suddenly there she stood, in the doorway, by herself, no Jonie. Bobby hurried over to the fence surrounding the grounds. He hollered, "Hey Heather, over here." She saw him, and walked rapidly toward him. "Hi Heather, let's go to the park, so we can talk."

"Okay." Heather smiled, and off they went. They were so involved with each other that they didn't notice the person in the shadow of the school. The shadow followed from a distance behind Bobby and Heather. When they reached Mulhalland park, the shadow still watched, undetected.

"What did you do in school, today?" Bobby asked.

"Oh, just the same old stuff," Heather replied. Bobby bristled.

"No, tell me, I want to know, start with this morning, and tell me what you did all day."

Heather's description of her day, fascinated Bobby. It all sounded like a wondrous dream to him. The interaction, the excitement of switching from one subject to another created an imaginary world he never knew existed.

But something puzzled him, so he asked, "Heather, how do you know which room to go to? There must be so many rooms, how do you know which is English and which is Science?"

Astonished, Heather looked at him, but could see the sincerity on his face. "By the numbers on the door. Here, I'll show you, I have a schedule." Unzipping a small compartment on her back pack, she withdrew a slip of paper, and handed it to him. "There, see what I mean?"

"How does this paper help you?"

"Didn't you read it? See right here, it says first hour-Science-Room 210-Mr. Thieu. Then down here is fourth hour-English-Room-118-Miss Shonholtz. But, of course, I don't use this anymore, cause I got it all memorized."

"You memorized this whole list? That must have taken forever." Heather could tell that Bobby was truly amazed. But she didn't understand why. She knew her schedule by heart, even before school started. Why would it be so difficult to understand? Unless, of course, you couldn't . . . Oh, my gosh, maybe he can't . . . but everyone can read. I could read in the first grade. She studied Bobby's face as he looked at the slip of paper. She knew she was right. "Bobby, you can't read, can you?" Her voice filled with sympathy for him. Bobby could sense the pity in her voice.

"So what! he shouted, "who needs it? I do fine as it is. I don't need your pity, Heather." Bobby seemed to become more irritated with each word he spoke. He stomped over to the swings, and flung one of them over the top bar. His anger had not yet subsided when he turned to

Heather. "I hate people who think they are better than me. Like Jonie and her boyfriend, David, they always look down on me, and now you. You have that same look. People like Jonie and David, and you, need to be taught a lesson. Someday you all will learn not to look down on other people." Bobby started walking away, but within a few steps was running at full speed, as Heather, with tears in her eyes, looked after him.

CHAPTER 30

DAVID

Mrs. Leroy Masters stood in her kitchen reading a recipe for chicken enchiladas. David came in the outside kitchen door. "You just getting home from school, dear?" she asked in a cheerful voice.

"Yeah, I had to stay and get some help with math, then I had to stop at the shelter house in the park for the rain storm to pass" He opened the refrigerator door and examined the contents. "Anything to snack on around here? He groused.

"I know I had to stand in the post office for it to pass." She added, "you sound irritated, David, did something happen at school today?"

"I'm hungry, that's what happened." He slammed the refrigerator door, as he grumbled.

Leona Masters cheerfulness disappeared at the strange sound of her son's voice. But she covered it up well. "There's some jello with mixed fruit in the fridge, and I have some chocolate chip cookies. Want me to dish you up some?"

"Yeah." He sat down at the kitchen table as his mother went to work on his snack. Leona loved to cook, and usually prepared the family evening meal. But her hours at the diner where she worked as a cook were long and tiring. The diner opened at six a m and she had to report at 5:30. If she were a minute late, Zack, the owner, started her day by yelling at her. She cooked breakfast and lunch, and her shift ended at

4:00, and the pay sat at minimum wage. To make for an even more tiring day she walked the twelve blocks to work.

"You see Jonie today?" she asked as she sat a dish of jello and a saucer of cookies in front of him. He nodded. When he offered nothing further, she added, "I am making chicken enchiladas for dinner tonight, so save your appetite."

Finishing his snack, he said, "I think I'll go out on the river, maybe do some fishing. I'll be back by six." Leona frowned, she did not like her son to go on the river alone, but she didn't want to inhibit him either. So she gritted her teeth and kept her mouth shut. She went back to reading the recipe.

When he got no response from his mother, David rose from the table and left through the same door he had used just minutes before. On the back stoop he stopped long enough to take off his sneakers and put on his boots, and grabbed his fishing hat. Then he headed for the boat tied to an anchor at the bottom of a small incline from the sloping land to the river's edge. He climbed into the boat and cast it off. He headed down stream. Mounted on the back of the aluminum boat sat an old ducktwin Evinrude outboard motor, with manual start. It had only three horsepower but that was more than enough power to move the ten foot Jon boat up stream. He had done it many times and had no reason for concern. Almost two hours later he returned. When he entered his mother's kitchen the clock on the wall read, 6:35. He heard his parents talking at the dining room table. He knew they had already started the evening meal. He took off the muddy boots, hung up a damp hat, and washed his hands. Then he walked in and took his place at the table. Leona smiled and dished up a large portion of chicken enchilada for her son.

"Sorry I'm late, it took me longer than usual because I had to set under a bridge for the rain to stop. The current of the river has increased. I think the river will rise some because they're letting water out of the Morris Reservoir in Taft County. Mr. Thiel told us about it today in science class."

His mother smiled and said, "You must be starved. Here have some peas and carrots to go with the enchilada." She dipped the vegetables onto his plate. Leroy simply harrumphed and continued eating. He had explained to David many times before that he didn't believe in talking at the table. "You go to bed to sleep, you go to the table to eat." So everyone ate.

The following morning, as usual, David woke up to an empty house. With his mother leaving at 5:15 and his father about twenty minutes later, David awoke by alarm clock, dressed, drank a glass of juice, and jumped on his bike to make it to school with less than five minutes to spare. Often the first bell rang before he reached his locker in the upstairs hallway. He rarely saw Jonie before school because her locker was at the other end of the hall. They sometimes didn't meet until fourth hour when they, and Heather, had English the same hour. Today proved to be one of those days.

"Heather," Jonie said as they filed into English, "I can't meet you after school because I have a dental appointment at 2:30. I have to leave during seventh hour."

"Where were you guys going after school anyway?" asked David, who sat between them, but one row back.

Jonie and Heather looked at each other but neither spoke. Before David could say anything further, Miss Shonholtz shushed the class and announced the days' lesson.

Much later in the afternoon, David rode his bicycle though Mullhalland Park. Heather sat in a swing, with her head down. When David stopped in front of her, she turned her head. "What's the matter, Heather? Did you hurt yourself?"

Heather wiped the tears off her face as best she could. She turned toward David, "No, I'm not hurt," *at least not physically*, she thought. "I guess I just felt sad, because I was all alone."

"Well, now that I'm here, you're not alone any more, What are you doing in the park?"

Heather took out a tissue from the small purse she carried in her back pack and tried to clean her face of the tear stains. "I don't know, I just came here cause it's quiet, I guess."

"You want to come home with me? I've got a new video game we could play."

"I don't have my bike, it's at home."

"That's okay, you can ride with me. Get on here." David pointed to the cross bar in front of him. "I can put your back pack on with mine here behind me." Again pointing, he indicated the rack across the back wheel.

"Can you balance us and the packs all at the same time?" Heather asked doubtfully.

"Sure, no problem," David said, with all the assurance of a thirteen-year-old. With everything and everybody in place, David pushed off. The front wheel of the bike wobbled a couple of times as he started, but true to his word, he handled the load with no difficulties. They arrived intact at his house several minutes later.

Heather complimented him as she dismounted. "That was easy enough," she said.

"I told you I could do it. Let's unstrap the back packs and take them inside."

Once inside, David headed for the refrigerator opened the door and inspected it like he did almost every time he came home from school. "Want something to eat or drink?"

"What's that?" Heather said peering over his shoulder.

"That's Cranapple juice, something my mom drinks."

"Can I try some of it?"

"Sure, here, let me get a glass." David poured her a glass full.

"Yum, this is good. Have you tried it?" David finished pouring himself a glass of chocolate milk.

"No way, and I'm not going to either, so don't suggest it." Heather laughed. Then she plopped her hand over her mouth.

"What's the matter?" David asked, puzzled.

"I was loud, I might disturb someone." Heather whispered.

David snickered, "There is no one to disturb, so don't worry about it."

"You mean . . ." David didn't wait to find out what Heather might have said. "Yeah, my mom has to pull a double shift at the diner, and Dad is never home on Friday's until about seven cause he goes to Jack's Place for a couple of drinks every Friday."

Heather got quiet for a moment, then said, "I didn't think . . . maybe I should go . . ."

"Why, we have the whole house to ourselves, we can do anything we want. You want to see the game-boy card I got last week? It's all set up in the front room. Come on, I'll show you." David disappeared through the doorway leading into another part of the house. Heather hesitated for a moment then followed.

CHAPTER 31

RALPH

It was Friday evening and with football season over, Ralph had time on his hands. He couldn't clear his mind of the questions that surrounded the girl in the woods. He sat in the rec room at home. Taking a blank sheet of paper off his father's desk, he drew a line down the center of the page. On one side of the line he wrote: Things I know. And on the other, Things I don't know

THINGS I KNOW	THINGS I DON'T KNOW
GIRL FOUND IN GRAVE	HOW GIRL GOT TO GRAVE
GRAVE IS LONG WAY FROM ROAD	WHERE DID GIRL DIE
GIRL WAS NOT IN GRAVE LONG TIME	DID ANYONE SEE HER AT LAKE
LAST SEEN AT ATWOOD SKATE ARENA	WHY WAS SHE KILLED
	WHERE DID SHE GO FROM ATWOOD
	WHO DID SHE LEAVE RINK WITH
	WHO KILLED HER

When Ralph finished his lists, one difference stood out. What he did know was less than what he didn't know.

He studied the lists, *what have I got here? What do I do next? What can the list tell me?* He wrote all his questions on another sheet of paper.

His dad walked into the room. "You look perplexed, with that look, I hope you aren't studying for a final or something."

"Here, take a look at this and tell me what it is that I am missing?" Ralph handed his the list. His father examined the paper. "Looks pretty thorough, You need information that you will not find in a book nor by looking at these lists. Your answers to your questions are in the land, at the grave, by the trees. Go to the site where the events took place, and then ask your questions. Maybe you will get some answers, maybe not. But you need to be there to find out."

"You really thank that will help?"

"Can't hurt, but what you have to remember is that there is a reason *she* was killed by one person, and not someone else, and there is a reason why she was buried at a certain spot and not someplace else. Find the reason why and you may find the person who did it."

"You make it seem so easy, like it is a problem in math or something. I think there's an answer but it will take some work to solve the problem."

"That's exactly what I am saying. To solve the problem you find the equation. It's all math son, 2+2 = 4, it doesn't equal 5 or 3, it equals 4. Find the equation and you can find the answer. But you must know the equation. As I said, it's all math. That's what I do all day, is math."

Ralph didn't follow his dad's reasoning, but appreciated the input. He told him so.

"I understand," his dad said, "you just be careful in what you poke around in. When you get too close to something wild, it usually fights back instead of running away. So be careful, Ralph."

Leaving his dad in the rec room reading the latest issue of Time magazine, Ralph headed for the kitchen to talk to his mother. When he stepped to the doorway leading into the kitchen, he heard his sister talking, "She's been acting weird lately. I don't know what's going on but I plan on finding out."

"Who we talking about? Acting weird isn't a crime, if it were, you would have been locked up years ago," Ralph said.

"Hey, Bro, talk about the weird and they show up. But I wasn't talking about you this time, I never said a male weirdo, those kind are hopeless, I happened to be referring to my friend, Heather, the one who thinks my brother is cute. Like I said, she's weird."

"I'll say she's weird," Ralph said, "Just look at who her friend is."

"Okay, you two, if you're just going to belittle each other, I've got things for you to do. Jonie, I think it's time you set the table, and don't get your brother's silverware out of the dirty dishes in the sink this time." Jonie giggled at the trick she played on her brother last night. Ralph ignored her and said to his mother, "Mom, can I use your car in the morning? It's Saturday and I need to go to Atwood to check on something."

"Atwood, why there?"

"Some of the guys are thinking of having a skating party and I want to check out the rink and see when we could have it."

"Oh, can I go, Bro? I've only been there once and then only for a second. Can I go with you, Bro?" Ralph hadn't thought of taking Jonie, he didn't mind taking his sister places, but not this time. He had not told the whole reason for going to Atwood, and he couldn't afford to have Jonie along. He started to say so, when his mother interrupted.

"Jonie, you already have an appointment for in the morning. You promised to go with your father to Signal Hill. He is giving a talk to the officer's of the Historical Society and you know how much he enjoys having you go with him on things like that. You have to keep your word."

Jonie's face turned into a pout. Ralph quietly let a sigh of relief escape. "You'll be careful, dear?" his mother cautioned.

At 9:15, Ralph backed his mother's car out of the garage. His father and sister had left about twenty minutes earlier, and Ralph felt as though he was late. In reality he had no time frame that he worked from. A half hour later, he pulled up in front of the Amber Skating Arena in Atwood.

Thinking he needed a cover story for the questions he hoped to find answers for, he rummaged through the map compartment. Finding a small note pad, he searched further and came up with a pencil. He shoved the other contents back into the compartment. He approached the door of the rink. The open sign was not out, but when he tried the door, it swung open. Stepping inside, he almost tripped over Mrs Elmquist as she scrapped a spot on the floor. "We're not open yet, but you can come on in," she said, as she scooted a small bucket out of the doorway. "I wish I had a nickel for every wad of gum I've scrubbed off this floor."

Ralph smiled. "I'll bet. My name's Ralph Kellam, I live in Robertown."

"Well, I won't hold that against you," she said grinning, "I'm Alice Elmquist, the owner."

"I wonder if I could talk to you about Lois Newman. You knew her?"

"Oh my, yes, I knew her, her mother, her father. Atwood's a small town, everybody gets to know everybody else. Poor girl, she didn't deserve what she got."

"I understand she spent a lot of time here, skating."

"She sure did, she would rather skate than eat, I think. She skated here the night she disappeared."

"What can you tell me about that night." Alice looked at Ralph with an appraising eye.

"Who are you, son, you're sort of young to be a detective or cop. Why are you so interested in her?"

"I am writing an article for the school newspaper, and would like to do her a good job." Ralph didn't really lie to Alice, he did belong to the newspaper staff, however his assignment consisted of articles for the sports page and editorial page. He could write an editorial.

"Well, I guess she would like that. I tried to hire her to work here. I figured since she spent so much time here, she might as well be working here. But she was afraid that she wouldn't have time to skate, so she turned me down. She wanted the money but not at the expense of skating."

"Did you talk to her that night?"

"Sure did, that night she had met a boy, I'd say more like a man, than boy, though. I usually gave her free sodas because she was so good at keeping the kids under control on the floor. If someone got a little out of line in pushing and shoving, or got to teasing someone, she would step in and explain to them that everyone was here to have a good time and ask them to help keep everybody happy. She had a knack with people. They usually did as she asked. She also enjoyed helping kids to learn to skate."

"Did she have any particular enemies or people she had trouble with?"

"Lois? No, well, a guy once got a little too possessive, and she had to set him straight. She also mentioned to me that a boy from around

Robertown kept pestering her to be his friend, like girlfriend, but she wasn't interested in being anybody's property, if you know what I mean."

"Do you have any idea who the guy might be?"

"No, I'm not sure she even knew his name, he just started talking to her and she didn't want to be unkind, so she would talk to him, but he would not take no for an answer. He must have been a very demanding person."

"Do you know a Mrs. Henderson?"

"Ethel? Everybody knows Ethel Henderson, she taught English at Atwood High School for 33 years, she retired the year they consolidated with Langton. She opposed the closing of the high school."

"Where does she live? I would like to interview her, since she's about the last person who talked to Lois."

"She lives in a three story white house down the street about two blocks. Turn left at that corner and it's the big red brick house on the left side of the street. You can't miss it, it's the only house with big native cottonwood trees in the front yard."

When Ralph pushed the doorbell button on the massive frame of the door of the mansion referred to as a home, he thought he could hear the sound waves reverberating throughout the interior of the structure. He waited for several minutes and then knocked on the door. About to give up, there came a small sound. Someone was turning a key in the door lock. Shortly, the door opened exposing a woman about eighty-five with a cane and a full head of white hair. "Ms. Henderson?" he said. "My name is Ralph Kellam, I . . ."

"Kellam, you say? I remember a Ralph Keller, nice boy, but Kellam, no, don't remember Kellam. You live in Atwood?"

"I live in Robertown, I wanted . . ."

"Robertown, nice town to shop, wouldn't want to live there because of flooding, but nice town."

"Lois Newman, you remember Lois Newman?"

"I don't think I ever had a Lois New . . . oh, the girl at the skating place, the one who was so nice to Chuckie. Yes, she went missing and found buried some place. But I didn't have her in school. She would have come after I retired."

"Yes, can you tell me about that night? The night she disappeared."

"Well, sure. She related her story.

"And the guy she left with, you remember anything special about him, anything unusual?"

"No, I told the sheriff, I didn't rem . . . wait, I do remember, the hat, he had on one of those hats, the kind fishermen wear. You know, the ones with broad rims, to keep the sun off them. I remember thinking, that he didn't need such a hat at that time of day. I forgot to tell that to the Sheriff, will you tell him?" Ralph nodded.

After visiting with the woman for a few more minutes, Ralph decided he could learn nothing further and thanked her for the time she had given him. A short time later, standing in front of the trailer house door, he introduced himself for the third time that morning.

"Yes, I'm Abigail Newman, most folks call me Abby. What can I do for you, Ralph?"

"I wondered if I might talk to you about your daughter. Would you mind doing that? I know it might be . . ."

"No, that's alright, I think it does a body good to talk about the death of a loved one. I haven't anyone except the lady next door, and she likes the beer I provide. Why don't you come in and we can talk without bothering the neighbors." Once inside, and the door closed, Abby said, "So are you one of Lois's friends?"

"No, I live in Robertown, and I wanted to do an article on her for the school newspaper."

"Oh, I guess I just assumed . . . well okay, what do you want to know?"

"Did you and your daughter get along okay, or were . . ."

Abby interrupted him. "I don't think your paper needs to know that, so if you have nothing else."

"I'm sorry, but could you tell me what kind of mood she was in that night, the night she disappeared?

"Now, that's a better question. She was herself, a happy cheerful child. So if you are thinking something happened and she ran away, then you are definitely wrong. Lois would never do that. She enjoyed her life here, no thanks to her father. We both had that to live with."

"What did her father do?"

"Got himself thrown in jail, that's what."

"May I ask what for?"

"Robbery, he and another guy robbed a store."

"You heard what Mrs. Henderson told the sheriff. Who do you think she left the rink with that night?"

"I have no idea, Lois was well liked, she had a lot of friends."

"So you think she left with a friend?"

"Well, of course, who else would she . . . you saying you think someone forced he to leave with them? Lois was a fighter, she wouldn't just go and not . . . not unless . . ."

"Unless what, Mrs. Newman, not unless?"

"Not unless the person told her something that she wanted to know about. Something that would arouse her curiosity."

"Do you know anyone who would want to do her harm?"

"In Atwood? No, she was well liked at school, she wasn't a threat to anyone."

Ralph couldn't think of anything else to ask so he thanked her, and apologized if he had intruded upon private matters, and left her standing at the door. Still wanting to satisfy himself about the questions he had and remembering what his father had said about standing at the site of the event, he turned south on Highway 10, and headed for Cheyenne Cove Campgrounds. He wanted to revisit the site of the grave. About an hour later, he approached the grave site. The yellow security tape still stood in place around the perimeter of the grave. It also appeared to have been washed by a heavy downpour of rain. Watching where he stepped, Ralph managed to approach the open pit. Less than two feet deep and three feet long, it barely seemed large enough to hold a human body.

Ralph's body shivered, not from the cold, but from what he found here that day. It now seemed like a dream. Moving around the hole, he examined it from different angles. Then stopping and looking up, he surveyed the surrounding woods. The trees were not very close together and the underbrush rather sparse. With the knowledge of having traveled the Rattlesnake trail, he could see where it ran across the ridge to the northeast. *It's not as far as it might seem. A person could cut across like I did on that day and be here in a matter of minutes.*

He then looked to the southeast and could almost make out the trail head near the lake shore. *It's only a couple of hundred yards from the trail head to the lake road. A person or persons could walk from the lake road to the grave site easy. But that person, or those people, would have to know the terrain to know that it could be done.*

143

As he visualized the idea of how a person could get to the grave site without being seen, a picture suddenly appeared in his mind, as if painted there by an artist. He saw the trail leading from the Dunsmore bridge to within yards of the grave site. *Walk in, that's it, don't drive, walk.* As Ralph replayed his exploration from the Dunsmore bridge to the trail something else came to mind. How do I get to the bridge? *If I'm Bobby, I'm already there, aren't I?*

CHAPTER 32
HEATHER AND DAVID

When Heather followed David into the living room she didn't notice anything unusual. Furnished with average American style furniture, a settee, two lazy boy recliners, and small end tables, with lamps. It also contained a kick-knack cabinet full of curios from the southwestern part of the country. In one corner of the room, sat a TV complete with a DVD/VHS recorder-player. David was nowhere in sight.

Heather, was curious where he had disappeared to, started toward a door on the far side of the room. She crossed the room to within an arm's reach of the door, when it opened and David stepped out, quickly closing the door behind him. In his hand he held a pair of Arctic White Nintendo game-boy systems with accessories. "I found them. Let me set everything up, and we'll play."

After about an hour of game-boy, they were both ready for other activity. "You want to go boating on the river?" David asked.

"Are you sure it's safe?"

"I do it all the time," answered David. "I've never had any problems I couldn't handle."

"How big a boat do you have?"

"It's a ten foot aluminum Jon boat. Come on, I'll show you." Heather had no idea what size boat that would be, and wanted to see it. David opened the kitchen back door and grabbed his fishing hat. The two walked down to the river's edge. David had the boat tied to an anchor in the ground. "You'll have to get your feet wet to get in, but the water's only up to your ankles. Hop in, and I'll shove us off." Heather looked doubtful, but David sounded like he knew what he was doing, so she got in the boat. When David got in he sat near the motor, behind her. He didn't start the motor. Heather held on.

They floated down stream at the speed of the river current. Heather began to relax and enjoy the ride. Her attention was drawn to all the wildlife along the banks of the river. For a time, she forgot about David in the boat behind her.

*   *   *

Leroy Masters came home to an empty house. There were dirty glasses and game-boy parts scattered around the TV in the living room. But none of that disturbed him because he had become accustomed to picking up after his son. Neither he nor his wife required David to clean up after himself. They wanted him to be comfortable in his own home. With a handful of game-boy apparatus , Leroy opened the door to David's room. He dumped the pieces on the desk, and glanced around. He noticed one wall that had photos of David and many more of girls that Leroy took as classmates. He smiled, *the boy has a crush on several girls, he'll learn that just one woman in a man's life is enough.*

Closing the door to the room, Leroy sat down in one of the recliners, leaned back and soon fell asleep. Some time later, feeling a hand on his shoulder, Leroy awoke in a dimly lit room, with David standing beside his chair. "Dad? You awake now? I'm hungry, can you fix something to eat?"

"Sure, son." His father slowly came awake. Mac and cheese okay with you?"

"That would be great." Leroy rose from the chair and went to the kitchen. As he worked, David sat at the table waiting for his dinner. "Will Mom be home after 8:00?" he asked.

"Yeah, did you have a friend over after school today?"

"No, why?"

"It's just that I noticed two glasses in the living room, and one of them had a little Cranapple juice left in it. I know how much you hate that drink, so I thought . . ."

146

"I tried it again, it's not too bad, I wouldn't want to drink very much of it."

David sat in silence, he waited for his dinner. After several minutes, his father announced, "It's ready to eat." He placed a large bowl of macaroni and cheese in front of his son. He had just started on the bowl when his mother came in the kitchen's back door. She looked very tired.

"Hello, dear," she said to David, and patted him on the head. Then she turned to her husband, "Hi, Honey, have you had anything to eat?"

"No, I just fixed David something."

"Well, I brought home some chicken and noodles, with mashed potatoes and mixed vegetables, and it's all still hot. Does that sound good?"

"It sounds great," Leroy answered. "I'll get a couple of plates."

"I'll take some too," said David, though he still had half a bowl of mac and cheese left.

"Oh, well okay, I'll get three plates then." Leona divided up the food as equally as she could. David ate about half of his portion and left the table to go to his room. His father cleaned his plate and then finished what David had left. Leona also cleaned her plate. "That was delicious. You outdid yourself dear," Leroy said. Leona rose from her place at the table and went to the refrigerator to get herself something to drink. She settled on a small glass of Cranapple juice.

"Did you know that our son now drinks that drink?" Leroy asked his wife. He drank some after school today, in fact."

"I can't believe that, he has always maintained that it tasted terrible and a waste of good apple juice. Are you sure, dear?"

"I cleaned up the glasses from the living room myself," he bragged. "One had chocolate milk, and the other Cranapple juice."

"That's quite a combination, I'm surprised he could eat anything after a concoction like that." Leona shook her head. "What was he doing when you got home?"

"I don't know, he wasn't here. I supposed he went down to the river, his river hat was gone."

"What time did he come back?"

"He woke me about 7:30, saying he wanted something to eat. I told him I thought he had company over, because of he two glasses. Particularly since one contained Cranapple juice."

"It is unusual that's for sure." Leona sat quietly for a few minutes, and then added, "I worry about him sometimes, he spends so much time alone."

"Oh, he's just a teenage boy, he'll work through this time of his life and move on. Probably change a lot when he goes to high school next year."

"I'm not sure he's ready for high school, he still depends on us for so much, I'm afraid he might get left behind in high school. He has so few friends, and those are mostly girls. He doesn't have any friends visit . . ." Leona stopped, her thoughts becoming private. Leona and Leroy Masters did not know that David could hear every word they said, from his room, by leaning down to put his ear to the heating duct.

CHAPTER 33
RANDY SIMMONS

A s Deputy Sheriff of Woodrow County, Randy Simmons had a serious problem. His superior, an elected official had committed criminal acts. The sheriff had falsified evidence in a criminal trial and committed perjury in false testimony in a court of law. In addition, Randy had information that a sitting judge could be guilty of suppressing evidence that she knew about the false testimony and allowed it to be entered into court records, rather than exposing the wrong-doings. Now he had to face the decision of making the information public, or ignoring it. *I don't know why I'm waiting on this, I know what I will do, what I must do. Come Monday morning, I pick up the phone and call the attorney general's office and lay my cards on the table.*

Randy stood at his desk in the outer office area. He had long been a little annoyed that the only private office space belonged to the sheriff. But that wouldn't matter in a few minutes. Randall Simmons, white, divorced, after two years of marriage, no children, twenty-nine years old, six years with Woodrow county Sheriff's Office, two years as deputy sheriff, soon to be unemployed. The phone rang once. He knew the last item he mentally listed on his resume would be true once he picked up the phone. The phone rang twice. Taking a deep breath, he picked up the receiver and spoke. "This is Deputy Simmons, how can I help you? Yes sir, yes sir, I did. I would like to speak to someone in your office that conducts internal investigations involving county law enforcement agencies, and elected officials. Thank you, I'll hold." Randy visibly checked his perimeter, no one appeared to be paying him any attention.

"This is assistant Attorney General Dustin Applegate, who am I speaking to?"

"This is Deputy Sheriff Randy Simmons of Woodrow County, and I want to report a case of fraudulent activities on the part of the Woodrow County Sheriff."

"That's a very serious charge, Deputy Simmons. You have good evidence to substantiate your charges?" Randy responded that he had the proper documents. "I'll be in your office at one o'clock this afternoon. You will have all your documents and evidence prepared for me to examine at that time?"

"Yes sir."

"Very good, I'll see you then, and, Deputy?"

"Yes sir."

"I take it that you have not discussed this with anyone else in your office?"

"That is correct."

"Good, let's keep it that way, okay?"

"Okay."

"Fine. See you at one, then, good bye."

"Bye." Randy spoke to a dead phone. He replaced the receiver, and reached for the top side drawer of his desk. Opening it, he checked the packet for the third time that morning. Seeing the string securely wrapped around it seemed to re-assure Randy that obeying the law, and honoring public trust was more valuable than worrying about being labeled a whistle-blower. *However, I know this is the end of a short career. Six years down the tube. I will be lucky to find any type of job, and certainly not in law enforcement. Oh well, as they say, "I was looking for a job when I found this one."*

Taking the packet with him, Randy headed for patrol duty. Checking to make sure he had everything, he stopped by Clara's desk. "Clara, if I get any phone calls, be sure to patch them through to me ASAP, okay?"

Clara gave him a puzzled look. "You know I would, don't you?"

"Yeah, but I might have an important call come in and I just wanted to check."

"Don't you worry, you always take care of me, I take care of you. Isn't that how it's supposed to work?"

"Yeah, but sometimes a person has to do something that is right, rather than cover another person's behind. Isn't that true also?"

"I'm not sure I know exactly what we are talking about here, Randy. You got something you want to tell me?"

"Not now, Clara, maybe later. I got to go, see you at one." Randy disappeared through the door. Leaving Clara with the perplexed look on her face.

At twelve-thirty, Randy cruised down Kansas Avenue, the main street of Robertown, about ten minutes from the Courthouse. "Dispatch, Randy here, come in."

"Randy, Dispatch, go ahead."

"Clara, what's the location of the sheriff?"

"He's upstairs in the judge's chambers. He's scheduled to be in court for testimony at one."

"I'm coming in, I have an appointment at one. I'll use the private office for a conference if the sheriff is going to be out. You sure he's in court this afternoon?"

"That's what the schedule calls for, is that a problem?"

"No, see you in a few, out."

"Dispatch out." *Somethings up, and it must have to do with the sheriff. Maybe I'll find out when Randy comes in.* Clara never missed an opportunity to nose around for secrets, particularly among staff.

Randy arrived at the office at 12:50, and stopped at Nancy's desk. "When a Mr. Applegate arrives, send him in the sheriff's office please," he told her.

She nodded and replied, "Yes sir, would you like me to bring in coffee?"

"We'll see." Randy went into the sheriff's office to wait. He didn't have to wait long. Mr. Applegate arrived at the receptionist desk at one. Nancy showed him to the door of the private office. "Shall I bring coffee? Randy looked at Mr. Applegate, who shook his head.

"Not at the moment, thank you, Nancy." She closed the door. As soon as they were alone, Randy got down to the business at hand.

"I have here sworn statements from Fred Newman, Jesse Jennings, Henry Amherst, and affidavits from defendants of two other cases. I also have the court records, plus transcripts of all three trials and all the interrogation tapes. In addition, the packet contains a list of rulings by Judge Martindale, for the past year. I think you will find everything there."

The Kansas Assistant Attorney General spent the next hour going through the material Randy had amassed. Dustin Applegate didn't miss a thing. He wanted to know how certain materials were obtained, if the were court records, were they open or closed, and if Randy had gone through proper channels in acquiring the affidavits and sworn statements. What about witnesses? Were they willing to testify to a grand jury? Only when completely satisfied, did he accept Randy's work.

"I will take all this to the Attorney General and his staff will go over it thoroughly, if it passes their evaluation of successful prosecution, we will present all this data to the sheriff and his legal advisers. At some point I think it is only fair to warn you that the source of the charges will come out. You will be identified as the person who provided the evidence for the allegations. I want you to be prepared for the backlash of people's attitude toward what is called 'whistle blower, understood?"

"Understood."

CHAPTER 34
RALPH AND MEL

R alph hurried back to the car. He rummaged through the clutter in the map compartment, looking for something he had seen earlier, the wrist watch his mother left in the car. When he found it , he checked it against the clock on the dashboard, the wristwatch was five minutes slow. Ralph figured that was close enough for his purpose. the teen ripped a couple of pages out of the notepad and checked the stub of the pencil, then shoved it all in his shirt pocket. Ralph used the speed of a linebacker to reach the trail head. Noting the time, he set off at a steady pace, first to the northwest and then as the trail fell in line along a ridge that separated the Rattlesnake and Willow Creek, the route turned to the northeast, toward the Dunsmore bridge. The marked trail stopped about an hour from the trail head, but Ralph kept moving and within another half hour had the Dunsmore bridge in sight. *About an hour and a half, not bad time, much faster than one would think, plus a person could travel the trail in street shoes. No climbing or crossing of water, not even logs to straddle. Even a city boy like me could do it.* Ralph climbed up and stood on the bridge. First looking to the southwest and then to the northeast, he saw nothing.

Then a sparkle or glint from something in the hidden recesses of an overhanging tree, attracted his attention. A small boat was tied to the tree. As Ralph watched, a shadow of a man slipped down the slight incline along the river. The boat, having been cast off, started drifting down stream until a motor came to life and the boat began moving upstream toward the bridge. Ralph anxiously awaited the passing of the boat, hoping to recognize the person in the boat. As the boat passed, Ralph looked close, the guy had on a wide brimmed hat pulled down low and hid much of his face, but Ralph knew at once who guided the boat, *David Masters, Jonie's friend.*

Ralph, though curious about David's activities on the river, had no reason to connect him with his own investigation. For Ralph, the person that aroused curiosity was Bobby. He now had evidence that allowed Bobby access to the grave site near Lake Lawson, and any link between Bobby and Lois Newman would be of significant importance. Aware of the sheriff's belief that Ralph had something to do with the death of Lois Newman, his newly uncovered evidence to the contrary, would be valuable. Just as Ralph decided to return to the trail head, his eye caught the small boat easily navigating up stream. Boom! It hit him like a rocket! *A boat! A boat would get you to the trail head in much less time and without hiking the trail. Travel the Verdi River to a spot near the mouth of the Rattlesnake, use the foot bridge there and you are at the grave site. Less than a fourth of the time and even less hassle with the trail. Wait til I tell Dad about this. First: how right he is in the "on site" concept and second; now I have three routes to the grave where before I had only one.*

*   *   *

When Ralph arrived home in the late afternoon, he found his parents in the rec room. Wanda, sat with a book in her hands, and Del was sorting genealogy records. Ralph immediately launched into a litany of ramblings and pieces of information about his day. "Whoa, easy son, calm down, if you are going to describe your day, start at the beginning. Don't start in the middle and bounce around to the end," he said fondly.

Ralph grinned and started over. He told of his visit to Alice, though leaving out the writing for the school newspaper part, then his conversation with Mrs. Henderson, and talking to Abby Newman.

"I hope you didn't upset her, Ralph, I'm sure it hurts to be reminded of her loss."

"Actually, Mom, she seemed to want to talk about it. Maybe she hadn't anyone to talk to. Well, anyway next I went to the grave site."

"Oh dear," his mother said.

"It really wasn't that bad, Mom, I did what Dad said and stood there and looked around. That's when it dawned on me. The trail head wasn't that far away, and I hiked the trail, timing myself. It didn't take as long as one might think." Ralph continued to tell the rest of his story, right up to where he realized the value of the little boat. Again, he left out the part of the story where he recognized the pilot of the small boat. "So. dad, now that I have all this information, what do I do with it? Who do I tell?"

"That's a very good question, normally I would say the nearest law enforcement agency, but with our luck there, I'm not so sure. Come to think, I know just the person who could answer that question. Mel."

Del reached for the phone, and dialed his attorney friend, "Mel, what's going on at the Crankstones? Maggie started dinner yet? No, good, cause you and the family are eating here tonight. That's right, we're cooking out tonight and you're invited. Well, Maggie can bring a salad if she wants. We have everything else. Fine, see you about six or six thirty. Okay see you in an hour or so, and don't forget to bring the twins. You bet. Bye."

"Now we have work to do, Wanda can you and Ralph run to the store and get some brats, hotdogs, a pound of hamburger, and the fixings, while I get the grill ready? I have lighter and charcoal, Maggie will bring the salad, I'll fix some baked beans and oh, you might get some soft drinks for the girls. Nothing like doing things at the last minute is there?"

"What's Mel going to think when you start pumping him for information, and he finds out this is a working dinner?" Wanda asked.

"Oh, he probably has that already figured out."

And indeed, he did. After arriving, and all the hellos and exchange of family talk were out of the way, Mel cornered Del and asked, "Okay, Del, whenever you do this last minute stuff, I end up giving free advice. So out with it, what do you want to know?"

"You think you got me all figured out, do you? Well, you're right. I do have something on my mind that's bugging me." Del proceeded to relate Ralph's escapade earlier in the day. When finished, he asked, "Mel, what do we do with this information? Do we go to the sheriff, or what?"

"That's an easy one. No, you don't go to anyone, except me. I want Ralph to type up his story and let me read it. Then I'll edit it, and only after that is completed will I take it to Snuffy. I don't want you, or especially Ralph, anywhere near the sheriff, okay?"

"Okay, whatever you say, Mel, now let's go see if that grill is ready for some brats."

Ralph completed the description of his trip to Atwood and Lake Lawson, and delivered it to Melvin Crankstone Sunday afternoon. First thing Monday morning Mel presented it to the sheriff at his courthouse office.

CHAPTER 35

SHERIFF SMITH

The door to the private office of Sheriff Smith came open with a bang, nearly separating itself from the hinges. "McReynolds, get Simmons in my office now." Sheriff Smith yelled across the room at Clara, manning the switchboard.

"Sheriff, Randy is patrol . . ." Clara didn't get to finish.

"I said now, not later, now," the sheriff roared. Clara flipped switches on her board and announced, "Randy, this is dispatch, Sheriff Smith needs you in his office ASAP."

"Copy, dispatch, be there in ten." Clara relayed the response to the sheriff via intercom.

"Tell Simmons, I want him now, not ten minutes from now!" Sheriff Smith didn't need the intercom, he just yelled. Clara ignored the request. Ten minutes later Deputy Simmons walked into the outer office. He acknowledged Clara and Nancy as he passed their desks. The sheriff's door remained open and Randy walked in.

'You wanted to see me, sheriff?" Randy had a good idea what the man wanted.

"I just received a letter from the Kansas Attorney Generals office, and I want some answers."

"Okay, what are the questions?"

Smith eyed the deputy, "don't get cute with me, you know what this letter is about and I want to know what part you played in this accusation?"

"You might as well know Sheriff, it's more than an accusation, I have court records, affidavits, and collaborating testimony, it's all in the hands of the state. I've tried to tell you in the past that we need to follow the book in interrogations, and search and seizure processes, but you wouldn't listen. So now it's payday."

"Well there will be no more paydays for you, Simmons, you're fired! Pack your things and get out."

"I would think twice before you do that, sheriff. If you try to fire me, I'll file a discriminatory suit against you under the whistle-blower act. My position is protected by Federal law. Plus I'll file an injunction to stop you from relieving me of duty before the Attorney General files a criminal case against you."

Smith realized Randy had all the answers, but he was still sheriff and as such carried some authority. "I'm still sheriff, and I can still give orders. I order you to get out of my sight and stay out of my sight, until further notice."

"Very well, sheriff, I'll be on patrol if you need me again." Randy left the office aware that the staff had heard the exchange. Nancy lost her smile, but Clara found hers. She gave Randy the thumbs up signal, and a beaming smile.

As he passed her desk she placed a hand on his arm. "Can I file a discrimination suit against him also? I have documentation of the words and comments he has made about my weight."

"Sure, but may I suggest, Clara, that you check the department requirements of fitness first to make sure you are not violating any of them."

As the deputy walked down the entrance steps of the courthouse, Melvin Crankstone walked up. Entering the outer office area, Mel noticed the Sheriff, feet apart, hands on hips, and with clinched teeth, glaring first to one side of the room and then to the other, as if he were daring anyone or anything to challenge him. When he spotted Mel walking his way, he turned and disappeared in his office leaving the door open. Mel walked in. "I have my client's statement here for you, sheriff. I think it will speak for itself."

The sheriff snatched the sheaf of papers from Mel's hand and snorted, "Will there be anything else, counselor?"

Mel smiled and shook his head. When he reached the door, he stopped and turned. "I want to remind you, that my client is a minor and as such is off limits to interrogation without counsel present."

"I will need to question the Kellam boy. You understand that, right?" The sheriff said with a smug look.

"Not without me present. You understand, right?" Mel answered sternly. "Have a good day, sheriff." Smith returned to his desk, picked up the papers Mel had left and examined them. After studying them for some time he threw the papers back on his desk.

Smith stormed around his office and continued to bellow at anyone who crossed his path. He yelled at Nancy for not having immediate access to a file he wanted. She ran to the ladies room crying. Then, later, he bellowed at her again when she couldn't provide an instant answer to a question for a telephone number. It almost destroyed her ability to function. "Well, can you at least get me the number of Judge Martindale's chambers?"

"Yes sir," she whimpered. "555-6776 Extension 34."

"Well, place the call, then, patch it through to my office. You can do that, can't you?" Sheriff Smith slammed the door to his office shut, and walked to the phone.

"Judge Martindale, how are you, fine I hope? That's great, and Sarah? How is your little niece doing? Yes, changing schools can be rough, I hope things go well for her. Good, good, Judge Martindale, I need a favor, I would like a warrant for the arrest of one Ralph Kellam, yes, that's right. I don't care what you think of him, he is a suspect and I have new evidence in his involvement in the Lois Newman case at Lake Lawson. No, I don't have time to run it by you. Just get me the warrant. What? Listen, to me, I am sheriff of this county and you are duly sworn to provide me with a warrant. You take your probable cause and chew on it, I want that warrant. Do I need to remind you that running alcohol across state lines without paying the taxes due is a federal felony? I might have a unit parked on your route from the casino you like in Oklahoma. Given your love for Wild Turkey, I bet you can't resist replenishing your supply and returning home with it. Thank you, I'll send a car for it in half an hour. You enjoy your day now, Judge."

CHAPTER 36
THE ARREST

I t seemed like a typical Monday evening at the Kellam household. With dinner over, Wanda had just finished up in the kitchen, and Jonie, with her bedtime nearing, sat busy with math homework at the kitchen table. Del, working on genealogy in the den, heard a loud knock at the front door. At home and in his room, Ralph worked on an English assignment. The last of his homework completed he was reading a chapter in the Biology text. He heard a commotion downstairs, and quickly he jumped from his desk, and opened the bedroom door. He stood face to face with a sheriff's officer. "Turn around and put your hands behind your back," said Officer Stevens.

"What?" Ralph stood still, confused.

Officer Stevens spun him around and yanked on his wrist all in one motion. "Give me your other wrist." Ralph stood still unable to grasp what was happening. Stevens then reached out and clasped Ralph's free arm and pulled it behind him. It suddenly struck Ralph that he had been handcuffed. "You have the right to remain silent, anything you say can be used against you."

"What's going on, what . . . ?"

The officer literally pushed Ralph down the hall to the stairs. "You have the right to an attorney, if you cannot afford one, one will be provided." With the officer beside him on the stairs, Ralph clumsily

160

descended them. "Do you understand these rights as I have explained them to you? Answer me, son, do you understand?"

Still dazed, and without knowing why, he answered, "I guess."

"Close enough. He's been mirandized, Sheriff." Ralph looked at the officer, trying to make some sense of what had taken place. Then the officer spun him around once more and Ralph looked directly into the face of Sheriff Smith. Now Ralph became more confused than ever. Glancing to one side he saw the anguished look on his father's face. His mother sobbed into her hands, and Jonie stood with her mouth wide open, but no words were uttered.

Sheriff Smith glanced at the officer and then looked back at Ralph. "Put him in my car, I'll take him down and book him myself. You can go back on patrol."

Del finally came to life. "Don't say a thing, Ralph, I'll call Mel, don't say anything until Mel gets there. Do you understand, Ralph?" Busy trying to keep his feet under himself as the officer pushed him out the front door, he didn't realize his father wanted an answer.

With Ralph safely tucked away in the caged back seat of his squad car, the sheriff pulled away from the curb with screeching tires, and lights flashing. After rounding a corner, the sheriff slowed his speed, and turned off the flashing lights. "Ready to tell me what really went down at the lake, son?" The sheriff looked in his rear-view mirror, with one eye on the road, and one on Ralph. "You might as well tell me now, rather than twelve hours from now. Because you're gonna tell me sooner or later."

"I don't think I'm supposed to talk to you," Ralph said meekly.

The sheriff smiled. "You know why they tell you that, don't you, son? That lawyer-friend of your fathers', bills your Dad for everything he does, every time he makes a phone call, everything, he gets money from your Dad. That's why he tells you not to talk unless he's there, he wants to be paid."

"I don't believe you." Ralph didn't sound convinced.

"Oh, believe it, my son, believe it. Now tell me why did you go back to the lake? Did you expect your girlfriend to still be there?"

"She wasn't my girlfriend, and no I didn't . . ." Ralph realized he had spoken, but what he said had been the truth.

"She thought she was too good to be your girl, is that it. She's too good for you, so you taught her a lesson, that it, son?"

"No, you got it all wrong, I went there to see if I could . . ."

"If you could do what? Plant some evidence that would lead to someone else besides you?"

"No, I couldn't do that, I wanted to . . ."

"Wanted to what? Wanted to be found out? Wanted to be caught? What/ Ralph?"

Ralph suddenly realized that the sheriff turned everything he said around and made it look like Ralph had planned the whole thing and killed the girl. "But that's not true, I didn't kill her, I only went out there to see if it could find out who did."

"Oh, Ralphie, you got to do better than that, you want me to believe you thought you could solve the crime and I could not? How much training have you got in crime solving techniques, son?"

"But, I thought that if I could only . . ." Ralph hesitated, he knew the Sheriff might think only a guilty person would return to the grave to check it out for clues.

"If you could only what, Ralph? If you could only find her alive? Is that what you wanted to happen? To make it all go away? Ralph, face it, she's dead, and you killed her. Didn't you Ralph? Didn't you kill her. Tell me Ralph, get it off your chest, you killed that girl. Didn't you Ralph? Tell me, tell me the truth Ralph, you killed her didn't you?"

"No, I didn't . . ." His voice sounded so small, even he wondered if he were telling the truth.

"When we get to the office, I want you to write it all out, just the way it happened, Ralph. I want you to tell the truth at last. You can do that for me can't you Ralph?"

"I guess." Ralph's mind was confused, did he really do it. He wasn't sure anymore.

When they arrived at his office, the Sheriff quickly hustled Ralph into an interrogation room and hooked up a recorder and called to the night clerk. "Stevens, grab a laptop and get in here. We have at job to do."

Marlon Stevens immediately appeared at the door of the room and said, "I'm not very fast on this."

Sheriff Smith frowned and said, "You just type into that thing what is said by the suspect or myself. Don't miss a word." Sheriff Smith sat down at the table, across from Ralph. "Now," he said, "let's hear it from the beginning. Who did you talk to first last Saturday? And don't lie to me, Ralph, I can tell when someone is lying."

Not sure of how to begin, Ralph said, "I wrote it all out, Mel er, Mr. Crankstone delivered it to you, didn't he?"

"I want to hear it from you, Ralph. Why did you re-visit the crime scene? What were you looking for?"

"I wanted to see if I could figure out how a person could get there without being seen. And I think that I did."

"And what did you figure out, Ralph? How did you get there without someone seeing you?"

"I believe that they came down the trail from the Dunsmore bridge. It would be a quick way to get there. But, you can get there even quicker by way of the river, if you had a boat."

"And do you have a boat Ralph? One that you could get to the river? The river isn't all that far from your house. Is it Ralph?"

"No, it's just . . ." Ralph suddenly realized that the sheriff was turning his words around again.

"Stevens, read back the question I asked about how the suspect got there."

Marlon looked over his notes and replied, "You mean the one about what he figured out?"

"Yeah, right after that."

"How did you get there without someone seeing you?" Marlon read from his computer screen.

"I asked you a question and you answered without hesitation. I think you better tell us the truth, Ralph, and you can leave out the part about how you are trying to help me solve the crime. I have it solved and the guilty person in custody. You might as well confess, Ralph. You did it and we know it. No reason to hide it any more."

The late hour and stress of the interrogation had Ralph exhausted and sleepy. He began to lose control of what he knew and what the sheriff told him. "I need a break," he said as much to himself, as to the other two people in the room.

"Tell you what I'm going to do for you Ralph, I'm going to have Stevens here, type up what really happened at the lake and when he's finished, we'll have you sign it and we can all call it a day. That sound good to you, Ralph?" Barely able to keep his eyes open, Ralph nodded his head.

CHAPTER 37

HEATHER

Jonie sat brushing her hair. The clock on the wall ticked away and Ralph still had not returned home. Well past her normal bedtime, she worried about her brother. Suddenly a light tap came from the door and her mother peeked into the room. "Jonie, I just got off the phone with Barbara Wilkes, do you know anything of the whereabouts of Heather?"

"Heather? No, I haven't talked to her since fifth hour English on Friday. Why?"

"Well . . . Her mother said she left the house Friday evening to spend the weekend with a friend and when she didn't come home tonight . . ."

Jonie interrupted her mother, "What are you saying, Mom, where's Heather?"

"That's what her mother is trying to find out. She wanted to know if you had heard from Heather. I told her I would check with you and call her back."

"Heather doesn't have that many friends. Who did she spend the weekend with?" Jonie had a pained expression on her face.

"I asked her mother that very question and she said she wasn't sure. I don't understand, how could a mother . . ." Wanda's voice trailed off into thought. Then she seemed to regain herself. "What did you and Heather talk about on Friday?"

"I asked her what she was going to do over the weekend, I thought we could go to the movies Saturday afternoon, but she said she had to help her mother clean the house on Saturday. I thought at the time that was very unusual, she seemed sort of . . . secretive, like she didn't want to tell me something, now I guess it was because she wasn't telling me the truth."

"I'll call Barbara back and tell her what we know, which isn't much." Wanda released a big sigh. "I'm sure everything will work itself out. You better try and get some sleep. Good night dear."

* * *

When Heather awoke, it took her a few minutes to arrange what she could recall in her mind. She remembered that David had told her to meet him at the tennis courts in Mulhalland Park Friday just before sundown. From there they would ride their bikes to Jonie's house for a surprise party. When the two had met, David had told her he needed to go to his house first. So they rode their bikes to David's house. "I forgot to get the new Wii game that Jonie wanted to try out," David had said. "It will only take about ten minutes for us to get it."

"I still don't understand why I couldn't say anything to Jonie about the party, David. Why are her parents keeping it a surprise? Besides, Jonie's birthday is in September, why are they having a party tonight."

"I thought I explained that to you? And it isn't a birthday party, it's a party to celebrate her winning the high school class 4-A regional. Her parents want to show their support of her tennis accomplishments. And they wanted you to spend the weekend with them. Something about going shopping tomorrow for you and Jonie; new tennis outfits I think. I explained all that to you," David said with frustration in his voice.

"Yeah, I remember that, but are you and I the only kids invited? Jonie's got lots of friends who would love to go to a party at her house. Why only you and I?"

"Look, I didn't ask her mother all these questions. You ask her when we get there, okay?" David sounded angry and Heather responded, "You don't have to get mad about it, geez, I only asked because it seems strange." When they arrived at David's house, it was dark.

"Well, come on in, let's get that Wii game." David led the way into the house and Heather followed. "You want something to drink? I, er Mom still has some of that drink you like in the fridge, want some?"

"Are you sure she doesn't mind?"

"Naw, she won't care." David said as he pulled a container of cranapple juice out of the refrigerator.

"It's about empty." Heather said eying the container. I . . ."

"She's got more here somewhere. Don't worry about it." David went to the far counter turned his back to Heather and got a glass out of the cupboard, and poured some juice. After fiddling around for something, he turned to Heather and offered her the drink. She drank it all.

"That's good," she said as she crossed to the kitchen to the sink and placed the glass in it. David walked over and ran some water into the glass and rinsed it out, dried it with a towel and put in back in the cupboard.

"I've got to check on my boat, want to go with me down to the river?" David asked.

"Don't we need to get to Jonie's?"

"We've got time, let's go." David opened the outside kitchen door and motioned to Heather. She stepped outside, and let David take the lead down to the river bank. Just as they reached the boat, Heather stumbled and fell to the ground. "Here, let me help you up. You better sit down in the boat." David said.

"I feel so dizzy all of a sudden." Heather let David help her into the boat and she sat on the front bench.

And that's the last thing I remember, Heather thought, *what happened after that? And where am I? It's so dark, I can't see anything.* Heather tried getting to her feet. Her legs didn't seem to want to work at first, but she managed to stand. Reaching out with her right hand she felt something like a pole and used it to steady herself for a minute. Slowly the strength came back and she regained control of her legs, but her head felt like a marshmallow and she was still confused.

What happened to me, and where am I? With out-stretched arms, and maintaining a connection with the pole, she groped the darkness around her for contact with something recognizable. Nothing. Heather didn't want to let go of the pole, yet knew that eventually she must. Stepping away from the pole, with both hands extended in front of her, she moved forward. After only two steps her hands touched a wall. *It feels like old boards,* Heather thought. Working her way around she found a corner and then another wall of boards. Suddenly she thought she heard a movement. She spoke, finding her voice weak and raspy.

"Is someone there? Anyone? Please . . ." Silence. She continued groping along the wall, coming to another corner. *I must be in some sort of small shed. Something old.* She pushed against the boards, *old but solid,* she thought. She started to move down the wall and then she heard the sound of movement again, clearer this time. "Who's there? Say something. Why won't you talk to me? Please, where am I?" Heather listened, nothing. "I know you're there, talk to me. Who are you?"

Then, suddenly, like an explosion, her eyes were filled with light.

CHAPTER 38
MEL AND THE SHERIFF

D el dialed the phone and got Mel's answering machine. After leaving an urgent message to call him back, Del punched some buttons on the phone again and got Mel's machine at the office. "You have reached the law firm of Hall, Hall, and Crankstone. Our office hours are nine to five Monday through Friday. If this is an urgent call, John Hall, Senior may be reached at 555-6262, John W. Hall, may be reached at 555-7845, and Melvin Crankstone may be reached at 555-7700. If you would like to leave a message . . ." Del punched a button on his phone, ending the connection. "If he isn't at the office or at home, he must be somewhere," Del muttered, as he punched the numbers 555-7700 on the phone.

"The number you have dialed is not receiving calls right now. You can leave a message after the . . ." Again, Del ended the recording.

Then on second thought, he re-dialed and left a message, "Mel, Del here, it is urgent that you call me right away, they've arrested Ralph."

Across town, at the East Wilson Community Building, Melvin Crankstone smiled as he watched the twins preform at the annual Sidney Critz Dance Recital. Before the program began Mel had followed the instructions of Miss Critz and turned off his cell phone. He thought about putting it on vibrate, *no, I came here to relax and enjoy the twins dancing. I don't want to be disturbed by the problems of the world. I can check for messages at the intermission.* And at the intermission, Maggie frowned at him when he pulled out his cell phone. Mel promptly shoved it back into his pocket with out checking it. His wife smiled and patted his arm, as they turned to acknowledge some friends.

As a result, Mel didn't get the urgent message from Del until after the recital had concluded and Maggie and the girls were getting all their paraphernalia collected and bagged. After hearing the urgent plea for help, Mel tried to hurry the girls and their mother, but their speed was based on the concept of thoroughness, not increased activity. When finally ready the trip home required a stop at Dairy Queen for a shake and a corn dog. Mel dropped the girls and Maggie off at the house. "I'll be home directly. I have to pay a visit to the local sheriff first." And that was the extent of his explanation for leaving them standing on the walk way.

When Mel arrived at the Woodrow County Courthouse, it was dark except for the wing containing the sheriff's office and the county jail.

"Sheriff Smith in?" Mel asked the officer at the first manned desk.

"I think he's back in lock-up. I'm officer Bailey, can I help you?"

"You're holding a client of mine, Ralph Kellam. I want to see him."

"The murder suspect? I'll have to clear that with the sheriff, he doesn't like for anyone to visit a murder suspect."

"Has he been charged?"

"You'll have to talk with the sheriff about that."

"Well, go get him."

"I'm the only one here, I can't leave and not have someone here. You'll have to wait til he comes out, or someone on patrol comes in."

"Well then, call someone in off patrol. Get someone here."

"I don't have the authority to do that. Not unless the sheriff . . ."

Mel took two steps toward the uniformed officer and slammed his hand down on the desk, with a loud **BANG!** "Get the sheriff in here now!" He yelled, as he towered over the much smaller Bailey.

Bailey jumped. "Okay, okay, take it easy, I'll tell him your here. You're Crankstone, right?"

"Yes," said an exasperated lawyer.

*   *   *

Sheriff Smith stepped into the cell occupied by Ralph. He was followed by Officer Marlon Stevens, who still carried a laptop in his hands. The sheriff handed Ralph a couple of sheets of paper.

"Now, Ralph, I want you to read this and then we will be finished with this little charade. Go ahead, read it." Ralph looked at the pages of material. He could tell it was an explanation of the finding of the girl's body and his part in the death of the girl. But in his tired, confused mind, the words seem to be jumbled. What he read seemed to make sense. "Doesn't that describe what happened, Ralph?" the sheriff asked.

"I guess so."

"I guess so, too, Ralph, let's get it signed and we can finish this up. Stevens, use the laptop for a table and let's get this over with." Holding out a pen, the sheriff continued, "Here, Ralph, sign the bottom of both pages and we are done." Ralph took the pen and with the help of Officer Stevens, signed the bottom of both pages.

"Can I go home now?" Exhausted, Ralph asked the question utmost on his mind. "No, but now you can lay down on the cot and sleep, Ralph, go ahead and sleep. We're finished here." Ralph did as he was told.

At the same time that Ralph laid his head down on the cot, the inner door to the four cells of the jail opened. "Bailey, what are you doing back here? I told you to watch the office. Now get . . ."

Bailey interrupted his boss, "Sorry Sheriff, but there's this lawyer up there that wants to see you now. He says it's urgent."

"Who is it, do you know?"

"His name is Crankstone." The sheriff smiled, then chuckled.

"He's too late, the game's over. I've got news for him. Stevens, first thing tomorrow, you get those two pages notarized, make three sets of copies, and then hand deliver them to the county attorney's office. That makes it all official."

As soon as the sheriff stepped into the outer office area, Mel was in his face. "I want to see my client, and I want to see him now!" Mel demanded.

"He's had a long day, Crankstone, you ought to let him sleep. But if you want to wake him, Stevens can take you back."

"You questioned him, didn't you, after I expressly warned you not to."

"Hey, he was willing to talk and he never asked for you once. We told him his rights, and did everything by the book. Isn't that right, Officer Stevens?"

Marlon Stevens never blinked, "That's right, Sheriff."

"And he gave us a full confession. All signed, and soon to be sealed and delivered."

"You better have something else, sheriff, cause that confession will never see the inside of a courtroom. You can count on that. It will be inadmissible. Ralph is a minor, and . . ."

"Save it for the judge, counselor, I'm not interested. Arraignment tomorrow morning. Bail will be set then, that is if the county attorney and the judge allows bail." Mel knew he had been bested by the sheriff, and that there was nothing to be done at that late hour.

As he reached the door, he turned and said, "I want you to know that this is going to be added to the list of charges that the State Attorney General has on his desk. Yes, Snuffy, I know about that." The sheriff kicked a nearby wastebasket toward the door as Mel exited through it.

* * *

On his way home, Mel stopped at the Kellam house and explained to Del and Wanda what had happened. "Don't worry, Ralph is safe and sleeping. I can't promise you that I'll get him out in the morning, because it will be Judge Martindale and for some reason, she usually sides with the sheriff. But I promise you the sheriff will pay for his transgressions. I'll see to that. He's pulled stunts like this long enough. It's time we reeled him in."

After Mel had left the office area, Mike Smith went back to his office and sorted through the day's mail. There were wanted posters, catalogs of equipment, resumes, and a letter from the Kansas Attorney General's office. Sheriff Smith tore the letter open and read:

Regarding Woodrow County Sheriff Mike Smith
Woodrow County Sheriff's Office
106 S. lst Street
Robertown, Ks. 66789

Attn: Office of Woodrow County Sheriff:

The office of Lynn Bower, Kansas Attorney General
has determined that sufficient evidence does exist to

> *declare Mike Smith in violation of Kansas Criminal*
> *Statutes T3759 and T4572 pursuant to handling of*
> *criminal evidence and promoting duress of a sitting judge*
> *in pursuant to bribery and concealment of evidence of*
> *a felony having been committed. Therefore the current*
> *Sheriff of Woodrow County is hereby relieved of his*
> *duties as of the receipt of this notice and is ordered to*
> *appear at a hearing to be held on January 30, 2011 at*
> *10:00 AM in Courtroom 212 of the Albert C. Landon*
> *Building, 1515 South Katy, Topeka, Kansas. Failure to*
> *appear may result in a bench warrant being issued for*
> *the arrest of said Officer.*
>
> *Assistant Attorney General Dustin Applegate*

Sheriff Smith was livid, he ripped the letter to shreds, letting the pieces scatter across the desk. *Who do they think they're dealing with anyway? I'm not some Podunk town sheriff that can be dismissed like this.* Now the letter lay in shreds around the desk of Sheriff Smith. His rage having played out and the mind of a scheming avenger had taken over. The first part of the Sheriff's plan called for him to methodically go through the files in his office and shred all documents that contained information gained by unorthodox means. That process took several hours.

Then he proceeded to make copies of the pictures he held of Judge Martindale with the bottles of Wild Turkey, and the report written by Deputy Simmons of her crossing a state line with that same untaxed liquor. As an afterthought, he enclosed a snapshot of the judge and her niece standing in front of the flagpole at the school. Only after completing his task did he go home to rest after a long day.

CHAPTER 39
HEATHER, JONIE, DAVID & THE VOICE

Heather, blinded by the bright light could not see anything of the person who held it, only a shadow loomed behind the light. Holding up one hand to shield her eyes, while the other kept in contact with the wall, she asked, "Who is it? What do you want? Please talk to me. The shadow remained silent. Heather started crying softly.

"Stop the whining," a gravelly voice commanded. "You brought this on yourself, so stop whimpering." Heather thought there seemed to be something familiar about the voice but she couldn't decide what it was.

"What did I do?" she asked the voice. "I don't know what is going on. Can't you tell me what is happening." The light kept staring at her.

"Turn around and face the wall," the voice ordered. "NOW, do it now!" The voice shouted, and Heather jumped. She did as she was told, and as she faced the wall, she felt a rush of air and a door opening and then close. When it did, the bright light disappeared. She thought she heard a click of some kind and then silence. She returned to darkness, seemingly alone.

*   *   *

When Jonie awoke Tuesday morning, two thoughts entered her mind simultaneously, that of her brother and of Heather. Quickly dressing for school, she rushed downstairs to the kitchen. There she found her mother, already dressed for work, buttering some toast, and her father sitting at the table, studying some papers. "Morning, dear," her mother said. "I have toast and juice all ready for you."

"Where's Ralph?" Jonie asked.

"He's still at the sheriff's office, dear." Wanda didn't elaborate. But Jonie wasn't to be put off.

"You mean he's in jail? Tell me, mother, I want to know what is going on."

"Okay, Jonie, yes, he's in jail, but Melvin promised to get him out this morning. There is nothing for you to worry yourself about, dear."

"I know Bro can take care of himself, but he might get beat up in there. I've seen some of those shows on TV where some guys get violent. I don't want Ralph to get hurt."

"Those shows are for shock and awe, Jonie, it's in the script, they ask guys to go off the deep end. They wouldn't have a program if they didn't." Del interjected. "In the county jail they have individual cells. I'm sure Mel has checked on that." Del was speaking more from hope than from fact.

"We better get you off to school, dear. You don't want to be late."

"Let's go, Jonie, I'm ready to go." Her dad rose from the table grabbed his jacket and headed for the door.

Jonie picked up her back pack and looked at her mother. "You'll let me know if anything happens, won't you?"

"Yes, dear, I will." Her mother sounded tired. Jonie didn't know that she had been up much of the night on the phone with Heather's mother, trying to get some idea of what was happening for herself.

*   *   *

When Heather awoke from sleep for at least the second time she could remember, she noticed light coming in from the cracks in the old boards that made up the wall where a door was located. She could now make out her surroundings. Indeed it was a cabin or shed that imprisoned her. Not more than fifteen by fifteen feet in size and six feet high, with two support poles in the middle. Her eyes fell on a door near one corner of the shed. Heather had missed locating the door when she searched the walls earlier. Slowly she approached the door and pushed on it. Nothing moved. Looking through the crack between the wall and the door, she could see some sort of iron bar or latch across it. She pushed again, this time much harder. It still didn't move.

She decided to try to attract somebody's attention. "Help!" Her voice, raspy and weak, didn't sound very loud. She cleared her throat and called again, this time with much more gusto. "HELP! HELP ME! CAN ANY ONE HEAR ME? HELP!' She listened intently but was rewarded with nothing but silence. Turning her back to the door she slid down until she was sitting. She wanted to cry, but told herself that would do no good. *What do I know? I know it is morning and this wall must be facing east, because I saw the sun first on that side of the shed. This shed or whatever it is, must be in or near some woods, from what I can see nothing but trees surrounds it. And it must be isolated, no one around.* Quickly her mind focused on the voice during the night. *Where have I heard that voice before? There was something familiar about it.*

*   *   *

When Jonie arrived at school, she was immediately surrounded by several students who wanted to know what she knew about Heather's disappearance. They didn't believe her answer, "I don't know any more than you do."

"But, Jonie, you're Heather's best friend, you have to know something," one girl urged.

"Well, I'm sorry, guys, but I'm as much in the dark as you are. Why don't you check with Mrs. Oretaga.? She's the guidance counselor, she should know." The girls looked at each other and nodded their heads, They were off and Jonie let out a sigh of relief. She really didn't have any answers to their questions. Looking across the wide walkway leading into the big front doors of the school building, she spotted David standing by himself near one of the doors. He stared directly at Jonie. She walked over to him. As she approached him, she noticed he was wearing. cameo clothes that appeared as if he had slept it them and hiking boots. He looked the part of a homeless boy. But it was his facial appearance that shook Jonie. His hair was disheveled and his face and hands were smudged with dirt or dust.

"David, what's happened to you? You look like you've been out in the jungle or something."

"I went camping this weekend and just got in. I wanted to let the office know that my parents are aware that I won't be in school, and that there will be no reason to call them. As soon as I relay that message, I'm outta here."

"That sounds pretty lame, David, Miss Taylor will never believe that, not without a note signed by your mother or father."

David glared at Jonie, then politely said, "I have a note from my father that explains everything. I gotta go."

Jonie watched David as he disappeared through the double doors leading into the school. The first bell sounded. Jonie needed to get to first hour class. It was then that she remembered David did not know about Heather. I should tell him. She started to head back to the office area when she spotted David coming out of the office. As she turned to intercept him, a hand clamped her on the shoulder. ""It's time you were getting to class isn't it, young lady?"

Jonie turned and looked up into the stern face of Mr. Wyatt. Meekly she said, "Yes sir." And hurried to class.

*　　*　　*

David quietly slipped up to the back door of his house. He listened, hearing nothing, he dropped his bike, climbed the back steps and entered the kitchen. The house appeared empty. His mother must have gone in to work early. Miss Taylor had given him first hour to get home, clean himself up, and get back to school. Otherwise he would be assigned detention and, since this wasn't the first offense, his parents would be called for a meeting with the counselor. Going to his room, he quickly undressed and got into the shower. The warm water led him to the thought of sleep. He felt as though he had had little of that in the past twelve hours. Leaving the shower, he dried himself and dressed in jeans and a plaid shirt. Slipping on a pair of loafers, he headed back to the kitchen. In the freezer compartment of the refrigerator he found some egg and sausage burritos. He placed two of them in the microwave. Going back to the refrigerator, he poured himself a glass of milk, then grabbed a banana off the counter. He ate half the banana in two bites and drank most of the milk before the buzzer on the microwave sounded. David finished his breakfast, grabbed his backpack and headed for school on his bike.

From a window, Leona Masters watched her son pedal away on his bike. She had sat quietly in her sewing room while her son readied for school and fixed his breakfast. She remained quiet, because she wanted to see if her son would take care of his own needs, rather than expect her do it. Leona knew that her husband would not want her to interfere with David making his own decisions and living his own life. But she also had concerns about his whereabouts last night. She had checked on him before going to bed herself, and found his room empty. Now she wondered what to do. *I should call Leroy, but I know what he will say, "We've got to let the boy make his own decisions. If we tell him every time what he should do, then he won't have the problem solving skills he needs when he is older." I've heard it so many times, I can recite it in my sleep.*

Leona had long felt that they were doing their son a disservice in not giving him some guidance during the difficult time of his working through the adolescent years.

*   *   *

Heather had passed the day without contact with another person. Not that she was used to contact, except at school or church. What she missed was something to drink. The little shed contained nothing, no water, no food, no bed, no bathroom. She used one corner of the shed as a bathroom, and the opposite corner, next to the door, as a bedroom. As her hunger and thirst became greater, her mind became more confused. She would catnap and awake dazed and light-headed, causing her to question herself as to how much time had passed. The sky was partially overcast blocking much of the sun and the cool air moved softly through the shed.

Shortly after dusk, she heard a noise near the door. The gravelly voice came to her from the outside. "Move away from the door. Go to the far wall," the voice commanded. Heather did as she was told. Suddenly the bright light shined into her eyes once again. She heard a clicking sound and then the door creak as it opened, and just as quickly, closed as the light blinked off. "There's a container of water next to the door," the voice said without emotion, "and an apple and orange."

"Why are you keeping me here?" Heather's voice was weak. "What do you want of me?" Heather waited for an answer, she heard nothing, but felt that the person still stood just outside the door. Heather started to whimper from frustration.

"Stop that. I don't want to hear you whine."

"Then tell me what you want. What did I do to deserve this, locked up like a criminal?"

"I don't have to answer to you. You're nothing to me. Just a person in my way," the voice sounded irritated.

"Why am I in your way? What did I do wrong?" Heather's voice became stronger as she spoke.

"You need to be taught a lesson. You need to understand you can't get in people's way. You get in my way when I am trying to get her to be more than a friend to him. I have to teach you to stay out of the way." Heather didn't say any more, she started to cry again. "I said stop that." The voice slapped the outside of the door. Heather jumped and screamed. "Shut up," the voice increased its gritty content. "You do that again and you won't live to do it a third time, I promise you that." Heather sniffled to try to stop crying. As the silence became more acute, she realized "the voice" had left the door. She would spend another night in her prison.

CHAPTER 40
WOODROW COUNTY SHERIFF

Sheriff Smith, with the help of a few shots of Jim Beam, slept through the night. He awoke on Tuesday morning with a splitting headache, and a severe pain in the neck and shoulder area. Feeling the triceps of each shoulder, he noticed a huge knot in his back muscles. After taking a handful of Aleve with a glass of orange juice, he showered and shaved. Dressed in a laundry service clean, pressed uniform, the sheriff headed for the office. Arriving some fifteen minutes later, he found Deputy Simmons in his office. "What do you think you're doing?" he growled.

Simmons picked up a sheet of paper from the recently reorganized desk top. "This says I am interim Woodrow County Sheriff until further notice. Were you not notified?"

"I am the duly elected Sheriff of Woodrow County, and I'll have you get out of my office and I ordered you to stay out of my sight until further notice. That order still stands." The sheriff's headache had returned.

"Sorry, Sheriff, but I countermanded that order. You might as well go home, Mike, you're unemployed until further notice."

Sheriff Smith took a swipe at the desk top, and in one swing of his arm, cleaned the top of the desk. Randy grabbed the offending arm and in one practiced motion, clamped a handcuff on it and with a second move had the other arm up behind the sheriff's back. Quickly, he cuffed the other wrist. "I guess we do this the hard way, Mike, you always were

179

one that had a flat learning curve. Now sit in that chair and cool off, or so help me, I'll lock you up myself." The sheriff's breathing was strained and he wheezed a few times, as he sucked air into his lungs. Randy stepped into the outer office and in a loud and authoritative voice said: "Let me have everyone's attention, I am replacing Sheriff Smith as Woodrow County Sheriff until further notice. I will post the letter authorizing my appointment on the door of this office. You are welcome to examine it. Now, everyone back to work."

Totally unexpected to the newly appointed sheriff, the gathered staff applauded. The new Woodrow County Sheriff stepped into his office. In his first act, he picked the intercom box up from the floor and flipped a switch. Nancy answered, "Yes, Sheriff?"

"Send Bailey in here. Please."

The please was not wasted on Nancy. "Right away, Sheriff, and thank you."

Within seconds, Officer Bailey appeared in the doorway. Yes, Sheriff?"

"Will you take Sheriff Smith home? And if he is polite and civil, you can remove the cuffs when you get there."

"Will do, Sheriff Simmons." Bailey helped Smith to his feet. "Let's go, former Boss, I'll give you a last free ride in a county vehicle, I hope."

Only minutes after the two left the office, Melvin Crankstone entered the outer office and bellowed, "I want to see Sheriff Smith, and I want to see him NOW!"

Clara, sitting at her radio switchboard, spoke up. "He no longer works here, Mr. Crankstone, you'll have to talk to the new sheriff, Sheriff Simmons."

"What happened to Smith?"

"He got fired." Clara beamed.

Randy appeared in the office doorway. "Come on in Melvin, we'll talk." Mel, still a little suspicious, followed the sheriff into his office. Seating himself in the sheriff's chair and motioning for Mel to take the other chair, Randy noticed Mel checking the litter on the floor. "Never mind the mess, Sheriff Smith and I have been doing some re-arranging in here this morning."

"I see, and is your occupying that chair part of the arrangement?"

"We had a changing of the guard, so to speak. Sheriff Smith has been relieved of his duties, at least for now, but, enough of that, what can I do for you?"

"You can release my client."

"And who might that be, Mel?"

"Ralph Kellam, you don't know what the sheriff . . . er former sheriff did last night?" Instead of answering the question, Randy punched a button on the intercom, which Randy had retrieved from the floor and was the only thing on the desk at the present time.

"Yes, sheriff," Nancy responded.

"Bring me yesterday's log, would you please?"

"Right away, sheriff, and thank you." Within seconds, Nancy appeared at the door with a hand full of papers. "Here you are, sheriff."

"Thanks, and what's with this 'thank you' to my requests?"

"It's nice to be recognized for a change." She smiled and left. Randy grinned to himself.

Turning to the back page of the sheaf of papers, he read in silence. After a moment, he looked at Mel and with a surprised look on his face, said, "We have Ralph Kellam locked up for murder."

"That's ridiculous, Ralph's no killer."

"It says here, that we have a signed confession." Randy re-examined the page.

"A confession acquired by the man you just replaced. Which brings to mind, why did you replace him? Did it have anything to do with the rumor going about the legal profession that the State Attorney General's Office is doing an investigation? I'll wager it has to do with acts just like this. Ralph is a minor, he cannot be questioned without counsel or guardian present. I told Snuffy that very thing myself."

"I'm afraid, counselor, that under the circumstances, we will have to go before arraignment and then maybe we can get his release. It should only amount to an hour delay. The judge will hear arraignment at nine o'clock."

"Can I at least see my client?"

"Certainly, I'll get someone to take you back." Randy again pressed a button on the intercom, got Nancy and made his request. "Nancy, if you would please, if Bailey is back from running Smith home, send him in, if not send Carla in."

Carla came to the door and Sheriff Simmons gave her the instructions. She led Mel back to the cell block.

After picking up the desk items from the floor and replacing them to the top of his desk, Sheriff Simmons consciously became aware that he needed to write or say something to the staff about how he felt the office of sheriff should be run. He needed to put his mark on the office and do it soon. In about an hour court would convene for arraignment of the prisoner, and he would need to be there. He drafted a statement of a policy based on fairness and equality, with a belief in the golden rule. Randy knew it sounded corny but he also knew that the staff would eat it up, after the recent treatment received and suffered under the leadership of Sheriff Smith.

At nine o'clock, Sheriff Simmons, Melvin Crankstone, Ralph Kellam and the county attorney, were all standing in front of Judge Martindale. Ralph's dad sat in one of the chairs nearby. "Your Honor, it has come to our attention that the confession may have been obtained through the violation of the rights of the defendant. We would ask for a continuation to give the newly appointed sheriff time to investigate the process and we further recommend that the defendant be released on his own recognizance," Randy explained, completely unaware that Judge Martindale knew exactly what he referred to; for she had just received notice to appear as a witness in the hearing regarding Mike Smith, that was to take place in Topeka on the thirtieth of January. She had replied in a positive manner to the request.

"Does the county attorney's office have any objections to the motion?"

"None, your honor, we don't think the defendant is a flight risk."

"Did Sheriff Smith obtain the confession?" the judge asked.

"Yes, your honor."

Randy barely got the words out of his mouth before Judge Martindale said, "Motion granted. Next case."

CHAPTER 41

HEATHER

The weather was turning colder, and Heather had only a light jacket. She felt the chill of the air. The night passed with Heather sitting in the bedroom corner of the shed. It seemed warmer in the corner than when she moved to the center. Light began to appear on the door side of the building, so she knew another day was beginning. Thinking she needed to keep track of the days, Heather found a small rock that she could use to scratch a line on one of the boards in her bedroom corner. There were now two lines. Also the voice had not returned since leaving the apple and orange. The empty water container lay beside her, the fruit had been consumed shortly after the voice had gone away. Her hunger and thirst were beginning to take its toll. She no longer felt like crying, instead she wanted to fight back.

Heather had noticed that there was one spot where the soil seemed to be loose and easy to scoop up with her hand. She had managed to dig a small hole along the edge of the boards. During the night she thought about how to use the water jug. The voice may have made a mistake in using a glass jar for a water container, she thought. If I could break it, maybe I could use a piece of it as a shovel. Not expecting the voice during the light of day, she moved to the center post and swung the glass jar against it. It did not break, she swung again, much harder. The jar broke, but one whole side remained intact. She had her shovel. Heather went to work, but soon needed to stop and rest. She felt warm and took

183

off her jacket. The work just made her body demand more water and something to replace the spent energy. But after resting for a spell, she went back to work. She spent the day on her digging and as the light begin to fade, she had a hole on the inside of the boards big enough for her to sit in. She was surprised at how much warmer it seemed to be. Maybe it's just because I have been working, but no matter why, I feel better.

As darkness settled in the work stopped because she couldn't see. Knowing this would be the time of the day for the voice to appear, she didn't want to take a chance that he might discover her hole. She had been wise enough to spread the dirt from the digging by scattering it along the far wall of the shed.

Leaning back against the wall, Heather suddenly realized how weak she really did feel. She became dizzy and light-headed to the point that she nearly blacked out. She believed that if she had been standing, she would have collapsed. She decided that she needed to put her jacket back on to prevent getting chilled, but she was tired and just wanted to rest. Deep in thought, Heather didn't hear the approach of a figure coming from the woods toward the shed. It wasn't until she heard the click from what she had earlier perceived to be a padlock on the door, that she became aware of a presence. The ritual remained the same. "Move to the far wall," the voice ordered, covered by the bright light in Heather's eyes. She heard the door open and close. "There is water and food, probably more than you deserve."

"I wish you would tell me what I did wrong, why do you think I need to be punished?." Heather's weak state left her in a defiant mood. Her crying days were over for now. "I think I deserve that."

"You are in the way, that's what you did wrong. You got in the way of him. I don't let people get in his way. I take care of him, by taking care of you." The gravelly voice became more irritated, the longer it spoke.

"In the way of what? What am I in the way of? I still don't understand what you are talking about. You need to be more . . ."

The figure slapped the door hard with its hand. "**Don't tell me what I need**. I don't need people like you telling me what I need."

Heather thought she detected a weakness in the way the voice whined in its reaction to her question. It seemed to her that the voice over-reacted, the anger somewhat false. Something a child would do. Maybe that is a clue to the voice's identity. Heather also noticed that the voice did not seem to be in any rush to leave like it had been the night before. *What is different about tonight? What night is this anyway? Monday night? Tuesday night? Think, Heather, Think.* Almost as if the voice had heard her thoughts it said, "This is Tuesday night. The night they first became aware of each other. Then you came along and spoiled it all. You have to pay for getting in the way of their becoming more than just friends. You'll pay just as anyone who thinks they can get away with ignoring me. As if I didn't exist. Nobody tells me what I need. NOBODY!" The voice had been pacing in front of the door. Now as it walked away, back into the woods, it still muttered to itself.

Heather's mind roamed through the possibilities: *Why is it the longer the voice talks the greater the irritation becomes? It's almost as if it is reliving the past and the past seems to become the present. And what is this about the fear of being told what it needs. Why does that upset the voice?*

Heather waited for what seemed to be an hour before moving to the door and finding the precious water container. Another glass jar. Along with the water she found two sandwiches in a brown paper sack, and also another apple and orange. Tasting one of the sandwiches, she was pleased to find they were both made of ham and cheese. She ate slowly and drank even slower. It all tasted so good, that she wanted to savor every bite and every sip. Finishing the first sandwich, she decided to save the second for morning. She also forced herself to ration the water. She ate half the apple, then put the rest back in the sack.

She returned to her digging. She had figured out that she didn't need to see, all the digging had to be done on the side of the hole that went under the boards. *Dig to the outside, girl,* she told herself. *Dig your way to freedom.* After about an hour, her energy exhausted, she had to stop. But the hole appeared almost done. *I need to break away the top two inches and crawl through to the outside.* After resting for what she took to be an hour, once again, she attacked the hole. After working a short time she broke through the top of the outside of the hole. Working to enlarge it she sat in the hole and suddenly found herself looking at the sky from outside the shed. Quickly, she slid back to the inside of the hole, slipped on her jacket, then grabbed the water jar, and brown paper sack. In a flash she stood outside the shed. She had gained her freedom.

But freedom where? Which way to home? To Robertown? To anywhere? All she knew was that the shed door faced to the east, so the side she escaped from would be north. She finally decided to go in the direction that the voice had gone. So into the woods she went. Soon she noticed that a trail of some sort had been made through the woods. She followed it, only to come upon a river, too deep to cross on foot. Knowing there were only two choices, she followed the river up stream.

Toward morning she came to a bridge across the river. *Do I cross the river, or not?* With the new day's light, she had renewed confidence. She crossed the bridge to the other side of the river. After walking only a hundred yards or so, a house appeared, it looked as if it was abandoned. A burned out shell of a shed stood beside it. She sat on the porch and ate the rest of her food, and drank most of her water. With food in her stomach and the thirst quenched, she leaned back against a pillar and closed her eyes. Half asleep, she thought she heard something move about in the house. Ignoring the sound as a probable small animal, she continued to doze. Then she heard the unmistakable sound of footsteps approaching the door from inside the house. Somebody's in the house. Quickly she slipped off the porch and quietly stepped around the corner of the house, hidden from the doorway. She listened intently as the door opened and closed. She knew someone now stood on the porch. Afraid to look around the corner, Heather pressed her body against the side of the house. The sound of more footsteps let her know that the person stepped off the porch and she could hear no more movement. Desperate to know who it might be, she peeked around the corner. A figure, she guessed it to be a man, walked toward the lane that led to the river. She couldn't make out features, but the figure seemed familiar to her. It disappeared down the lane leading to the river. Now Heather had a problem. Her exit path to the river was blocked, and she didn't know which direction she should . . . wait a minute, the river, it could be the the same one that flows through town? This might be the river that goes past David's house! Maybe if I keep following it . . .

CHAPTER 42
SHERIFF SIMMONS AND
OFFICER BAILEY

Sheriff Randy Simmons returned to his new office just as Barbara Wilkes spoke to Nancy, "I would like to talk to someone about my daughter." Nancy smiled and motioned for the Sheriff to come over to her desk.

Randy approached and nodded to the lady. "Can I help you?"

"I have a missing daughter, and I think I'm supposed to report it."

"Have you been to the Robertown Police about it?"

"No, I thought you might do that, if it's necessary."

"When did you see her last?" Randy tried to read the woman's face. He saw no evidence of worry.

"Friday about 6 o'clock. I figured she would show up." There was no change of expression.

"What is you daughter's name?"

"Heather, Heather Wilkes. I'm Barbara Wilkes."

"Address?" Perplexed by the behavior of the woman, Randy took out his note pad.

"1305 Elm Street."

"Here in town?" The woman nodded. "Do you have a picture of your daughter?"

"I've got a school picture, that's all I have."

"Where did you last see her, and what was she wearing?"

"I saw her just before she left the house, I can't remember what she had on, maybe jeans and a blouse? No, I think she was wearing a jacket, plaid I think."

"Can you describe her for me?"

"She's about 4' 4" weighs about 95 pounds, blue eyes, blond hair, shoulder length. Is that all?"

"I'm sorry, but you don't seem to be too concerned about your daughter being missing." The lady said nothing. "Was she alone when she left the house?" Randy asked. The lady nodded again.

"Where was she going?"

"To a friend's house, I think." Randy didn't like what he heard, and the lady seemed either uncaring or evasive. He wasn't sure which. "Have you checked with the friend?"

"I called Mrs. Kellam, to see if Heather had been there. She said no. I need to be going. My husband is waiting in the car for me." Randy mentally recorded the name Kellam.

"This Mrs. Kellam, she have a son by the name of Ralph?"

"I think she might." Randy made another mental note to check on the relationship of the Wilkes and the Kellams.

"Where can I reach you or your husband?"

"I guess you can call the house, 555-8987." She started toward the door and Randy didn't try to stop her.

Randy exhaled loudly. "There is one strange woman. And her husband is sitting in the car? Give me a break. Nancy, would you please get this out to the Robertown Police Department and then give it to Clara and have her send it to all patrols. Thank you."

*   *   *

Officer Jerry Bailey on patrol south of Robertown, had been parked along Old Highway 19, using his radar unit watching for speeders on Highway 10. Suddenly the radio came to life. "All units, dispatch here, be on lookout for missing person, Heather Wilkes, twelve year old female, height 4-4, weight 95, shoulder length blond hair, blue eyes, possibly wearing plaid jacket and jeans, last seen Friday evening." Bailey finished jotting down the description, then pulled out and turned on to Highway 10 headed north. As he cruised along the road he noticed a man sitting beside the roadway with a mangled bicycle nearby. He recognized Bobby Dunsmore.

Passing the location, he flipped on the emergency lights, and made a U-turn, pulling up a short distance from the bike, with lights flashing. Stepping out of the patrol car, he approached Bobby. "What's going on Bobby, you having some trouble?"

"Naw, I'm just waiting for a ride to town."

"What's with the bike?" Bailey stood with the bicycle between himself and Bobby.

"I just use it to get people to stop."

"Does it work?"

"You stopped, didn't you?" Officer Bailey had to laugh.

"You got me there. What town you headed for?"

"You offering me a ride, Sheriff?"

"I'm not the sheriff, Bobby, I'm just an officer. But, yeah, I'll give you a ride. What do we do with the bike?"

"I just shove it off in the ditch." Bobby stood and picked up the bike and tossed it back into the weeds along the road. Looking at the officer, he climbed into the passengers seat and waited for Bailey to walk around and get into the car. When Bailey had settled in behind the steering wheel, Bobby said, "Let's go to Atwood, you can drop me off at the skating rink."

Bailey shut off the lights and pulled onto the road. "You spend a lot of time there, Bobby?"

"I suppose so."

"Did you know the girl found buried in the woods, Bobby? Lois Newman?"

"Yeah, she was pretty. Her name was Lois?"

"You like pretty girls, Bobby?"

"Don't you?"

Officer Bailey grinned. "Yes , Bobby, I do. You know lots of pretty girls?"

"Some."

"You know Heather Wilkes? From Robertown?"

"I know a Heather, not sure of her last name."

"What does your Heather look like?"

"Short, thin, blond hair, she's Jonie's friend."

"Jonie who?"

"Jonie Kellam. That football player's sister."

"Ralph Kellam?" Bobby nodded. "So Ralph Kellam's sister is a friend of the missing girl?" Interesting, thought Bailey, maybe Sheriff Smith wasn't so far off base, after all.

It was shortly after one o'clock when they arrived at the skating rink. As Bobby searched for the handle of the door, Officer Bailey said, "Why are you stopping here, Bobby? Nobody here except maybe Mrs. Elmquist, the owner."

"Yeah, she usually has some left-over food to eat." Bobby found the handle and got out. The officer stayed put.

After Bobby entered the rink, Jerry put in a call to the office. "Clara, when he's free, have the sheriff call me on my cell, okay?"

"Will do, Jerry . . . er, Officer Bailey." Clara responded.

Continuing on south, the officer made a swing around the Edwards school parking lot, and headed back to Robertown. As he re-entered Atwood, his cell phone started playing "Dixie." Jerry pulled to the side of the road. "Hello? Yeah, Randy. I just received a bit of information that you might want to be aware of. The missing girl is a friend to the sister of Ralph Kellam. Oh, you did, yeah, I thought it interesting also. Okay, I'm on my way in now. See you in ten."

Sheriff Simmons had two files on his desk. Glancing at the top and thickest of the two, he read through all of it again. When he mentally removed all the "manufactured" data that Sheriff Smith had included, it left little more than suspicious possibilities. Nothing concrete. "It's all circumstantial evidence." he muttered to himself. "If I can find some real connection between the dead girl and Ralph Kellam, then I would issue my own arrest warrant." Looking through the second file he perused the information it contained. Assuming that the boy is telling the truth it rings true. However, when one puts the spin on it that Sheriff Smith did, then we have a possibility. But without evidence . . .

CHAPTER 43
HEATHER AND RALPH

Heather stood in the middle of the bridge trying to detect a familiar landmark that would tell her she had been here before. She saw nothing, except for the general appearance of the land. Nothing unusual, however she still felt she was correct in her belief that this river and the one at David's were indeed the same river. Heather crossed the bridge and started walking down the crooked lane. Suddenly she heard a noise and quickly ducked into some tall grass. "It's a car," she whispered, as if someone were beside her. "There must be a road just around the bend up ahead." Heather decided that the best thing for her would be to stay out of sight. She knew that the voice had to be nearby. She hurried back to the bridge, crossed it and slipped up on the porch of the house. She again assumed the house to be empty.

Upon entering the house by way of the front door, Heather's first reaction was to the smell. "Phew!" She said in reflex, to the odor. It wasn't an odor of decay; more of the musty smell of mold and mildew. Then came the sight of litter. Empty boxes, paper of all variety, and remnants of food. Even a pot of something over a pile of rocks in one corner of the room, that must have been used to provide a cooking fire, at one time. Heather thought about the difference at her home, where no one left a mess, everyone cleaned up after themselves. That expectation did not seem to have been practiced in this house. It appeared as Heather thought it must be: an abandoned house. She cleared an area in a side room where the clutter was sparse and laid down on the bare wood floor. She didn't intend to fall asleep, just rest, but the stress and anxiety had exhausted her more than she realized and soon fell into a sleep filled with weird images of frightful dreams. Not exactly nightmares but close to it.

*   *   *

After his release from jail, Ralph rode home with his father. Del tried to converse with his son but soon realized Ralph's mind was overwrought and he was unable to think clearly. After arriving home, Ralph spent the rest of the morning and part of the afternoon sleeping. When he awoke about three o'clock, it was to an empty house. His first order of business was to fix himself something to eat. While consuming a plateful of leftover chicken and noodles with a side dish of broccoli with cheese sauce, he thought of his problems with the sheriff's office and its criminal investigation. Ralph believed there was only one choice for him, to continue to do some investigating on his own. It made the most sense. *I am accused of a crime that I have confessed to. I have to clear the table and set the record straight. I need to explore the site of the crime and do it without the interference of the sheriff's department.* He finished the plate of food, put the dirty dishes in the sink to soak. In passing the kitchen phone, he noticed a note scrawled on a pad.

Ralph—Jonie and I went with Mrs. Wilkes to the newspaper office.

Explain when we return, Mom, 2:45.

Ralph glanced at the key rack near the phone and noticed his mother's car keys. Grabbing them he headed out the door. Stopping, he stepped back to the notepad and jotted a note to his mother.

Mom—Borrowed your car—will be back before dark, Ralph

Later, as he left Robertown, headed south on Highway 10, Ralph mulled over the events of the past two days. He had been interrogated as a criminal, forced to sign a false confession, locked-up in a jail cell, and appeared before a judge in a court of law. All because he tried to do the right thing when he found the girl's body buried in the woods.

Thinking that Bobby Dunsmore knew more about the dead girl than he let on, Ralph was determined to quiz him personally. Approaching the Dunsmore turnoff, Ralph slowed, made his turn and stopped the car a few car lengths off the highway. He shut off the engine, locked the car and walked to the river bridge. He checked to see if any fishermen were nearby, and finding none, Ralph preceded across the bridge.

Moving quietly as he neared the house, Ralph cautiously climbed the steps onto the porch and without knocking, opened the front door. Peering into the dimly lit room, all Ralph could see was clutter and debris of all manner. Slowly, he entered the house, and being careful of where he stepped, worked his way over to the far side of the room. Without so much as a hint that anyone else was in the house, he passed the doorway to a side room. There, on the floor of the room, lay a girl curled up in a fetal position. The first reaction in Ralph's mind was *another dead girl, I found another dead girl.* Suddenly the girl rolled over on her back, and opened her eyes.

Startled, Ralph jumped back a step, and Heather, seeing a human form in the back light of the doorway, screamed. Ralph, frozen to the spot for a moment, regained his senses enough to realize who he was looking at. *Heather! Jonie's friend. The girl was Heather Wilkes.* "Heather? Is that really you, Heather? It's Ralph, Jonie's brother, it's Ralph."

Heather stopped screaming as through the sleep-induced fog in her head, his words came to her. "Ralph? Is that you Ralph?"

"Yes, it's me. Are you alright, what are you doing here?"

"What do you mean? Aren't you looking for me?" Heather asked, bewildered at Ralph's apparent lack of understanding. "Isn't anyone looking for me?" Heather begin to cry softly.

"Heather, I have no idea what you are talking about. Why would anyone be looking for you?"

Heather's crying became more of a wailing. Ralph was confused, *what was Heather crying about?*

Ralph finally was able to quiet Heather enough to get her to tell him about the ordeal she had been through. She explained about being locked in the shed that must be somewhere in the area, and the voice, the person that was surly responsible for holding her captive for how many days? Three, four, five? When she ran out of story, she suddenly looked at Ralph and asked, "Why don't you know I have been missing, hasn't anyone missed me? Isn't anybody looking for me?"

Now it was Ralph's turn to explain, "Heather, I have been in jail for the last two days. I just got out today, and have talked to no one but my father since. I knew nothing about your disappearance. But your story explains the note my mom left for me today. Something about going to the newspaper office with Jonie and your mother."

Heather's crying had stopped, but a sniff escaped her as she said, "Can you take me home?"

"Of course, are you strong enough to walk to the other side of the bridge?"

"Yes, I think so, let's go, before he comes back."

Ralph looked at her. "Who?"

Heather glanced around as if someone might be listening and whispered, "The voice."

* * *

As the two teenager's made their way to the bridge, they were unaware of the presence of someone watching from the treeline at the side of the house. The figure moved as a shadow hidden within the trees and underbrush, as it followed the two young people. The figure took notice as the young man, upon arriving at the bridge, examined the river in both directions for any activity. The young man seemed to be satisfied that nothing unusual exhibited itself on the river, and the pair continued down the lane toward Highway 10. Only after the pair reached the parked car, made a U-turn and headed north on the highway, did the figure return to the bridge and descend the river bank to a boat hidden in shadows under the bridge.

Ralph had been concerned that there might be someone still in the area that could be a threat to Heather. Bobby Dunsmore must be around somewhere he reasoned. Ralph peered at the treeline near the house as they headed for the bridge, but saw nothing. At the bridge he stopped long enough to check it for any suspicious people or activity, but saw nothing. As he turned the car around on the narrow lane, he thought he saw movement in the trees. He hesitated for a second, but saw nothing further and continued back to the highway.

"Do you think you can identify the voice if you heard it again, Heather?" Ralph asked.

"I don't know, there did seem to be something familiar about it though," she answered. "I can't really say what, but something about it was whine-like and I seemed to have heard that sound before. But I can't remember where or when."

"Maybe it will come to you, when you least expect it," Ralph suggested.

"Maybe," Heather said, unconvinced

When Ralph drove into Robertown, he almost turned onto a side street to avoid going past the county courthouse. But deciding he would not be intimidated, he continued on to the 4-way stop. Because there were three cars in front of him, he pulled to a stop beside a sheriff's squad car parked in front of the courthouse. Officer Bailey was in the process of opening the car door and turned to look at Ralph and Heather. Ralph thought he seemed much too interested and as soon as the traffic in front of him cleared, Ralph moved on down the street, toward Heather's home. Ralph pulled up to the curb and glanced in his rear-view mirror to see the patrol car pull up to the curb about ten feet behind him. Heather opened the passenger side door and got out.

"Stay where you are," came a booming voice from a speaker somewhere on the squad car. Heather froze at the sound. "Put your hands on top of the car," the voice continued. After a few seconds, Heather responded by putting her hands on the car. "You, driver, get out of the car, slowly, very slowly," the speaker was loud. Slowly, Ralph did as he was told. "Put your hands on the top of the car." Ralph put his hands on the car top. Only then did Officer Bailey emerge from within the patrol car, and approach Ralph's vehicle. He carried a nightstick in one hand and the other was on the butt of the weapon on his belt.

"What's going on?" Ralph asked, without really thinking.

Bailey ignored his question and looked at Heather. "Are you Heather Wilkes, young lady?" Heather nodded, but did not speak. "Well, well, we have been looking for you, and guess who you show up with, Ralph Kellam, of all people." Ralph felt a tingle go up his spine at the way Officer Bailey said his name.

Before Ralph realized what was happening, the officer had hooked the club on his belt and had a set of handcuffs locked around Ralph's wrists. Reaching inside Ralph's car he removed the keys from the ignition, pushed the power lock button, and closed the car door. "In my car with you, son, young lady, if you will, get in the back of my car."

Heather, still in a state of shock, moved toward the curb side of the car, like a zombie. Bailey led Ralph to the driver's side. After settling them in the back seat, he climbed in behind the wheel and buckled in. "We'll let the sheriff sort this all out, but I would guess that your troubles have just begun, young man." Bailey said, talking to Ralph's reflection in the rear-view mirror. At the mention of the sheriff, Ralph suddenly felt sick to his stomach.

Later, as Ralph sat in the interrogation room alone, Heather, in another room tried to answer the questions being thrown at her by the sheriff. "Where did you go after school that first day? Who did you see or talk to after school that first day? Where did you go next? Who saw you? How did you get to the shed? Describe the shed, how big was it? How many times did the voice talk to you?" The questions just kept coming and Heather was getting confused. The sheriff then asked Heather about Ralph. "Couldn't Ralph be the voice?"

"No."

"How do you know that Ralph isn't the voice?"

"The shadow of the voice was of a much smaller person. Besides, I have never seen Ralph angry like the voice. Ralph doesn't make me scared, the voice scared me a lot." Sheriff Simmons left Heather in the care of Nancy, and walked to the interrogation room.

Ralph had been sitting in the chair for over a half hour when the door opened and Randy Simmons came in instead of Sheriff Smith. He was relieved.

When Randy asked him about the shed, Ralph could only tell the truth. "Sheriff, I don't know anything about this whole thing except what little Heather told me after I found her at the Dunsmore place." Randy asked Ralph what he was doing at the Dunsmore Place and Ralph explained he wanted to talk to Bobby.

"You a licensed investigator?" Ralph mutely shook his head. "It might serve you best to leave the police work to us. Sheriff Smith makes a strong case out of your creating answers for our questions. You understand?" Ralph nodded. After collecting statements from both teenagers, Sheriff Simmons released them.

*   *   *

Later that evening, Ralph's mother walked into the den where Del was engrossed in a stamp collecting magazine and both children were busy with homework. "Ralph, there's a phone call for you, I believe it's Sarah Muncie."

"Hey Bro, your girlfriend is calling. You better toe the line before her aunt gets after you," Jonie teased.

Ralph glared at his sister and left the room. "I'll get it in the kitchen, where it's more peaceful."

"That's fine dear, your sister and I are going to have a little talk about speaking before we think." She gave her daughter a hard look. The grin on Jonie's face disappeared.

"Hello?" Ralph said into the handset.

"Hello Ralph, this is Sarah, I have a question to ask you."

"Hi, Sarah, okay fire away."

"I just got off the phone with a friend and I want to know if it is true that you were riding around town with another girl?"

"No, I, oh wait, you mean Heather?"

"I don't care what her name is, so, is she your girlfriend?"

"Heather Wilkes? She's a friend of my sister, she's only an eighth grader."

"You didn't answer my question."

"Wha . . . ? Oh, no, she's not my girlfriend, she needed help and I helped her, that's all."

"Is she pretty?" Sarah asked.

"Who? Oh Heather? I guess, no, Sarah, let me explain, just give me a minute."

Ralph explained about finding Heather asleep in the Dunsmore house and bringing her back to town. He told her about being stopped by a sheriff's deputy and being taken to the sheriff's office. "Then I walked back to my car and came home. We weren't riding around town."

"I want to believe you Ralph, but my Aunt Janis says you were held overnight by the sheriff and they call you a suspect in the death of that Atwood girl," Sarah's voice was muffled like she was crying.

"Sarah believe me, I had nothing to do with that girl in the woods except to be the one who found her, that's all."

"And Heather?"

"Heather is my sister's friend, that's all."

"I believe you, Ralph, but my Aunt . . ."

"As long as you believe me, Sarah, that's all that matters."

In the background of Sarah's phone Ralph could hear someone call out something. "I gotta go, Ralph, see you tomorrow, bye." She hung up.

CHAPTER 44
BOBBY AND JONIE

Jonie stood out side the school building watching two girls argue. *Probably over some dumb boy,* she thought as she shook her head and looked away. Not sure what she was looking for, she scanned the area and suddenly noticed a figure standing at the corner of the south wing of the building. Something familiar about the shadow drew her attention. When the figure moved into the sunlight, she suddenly realized who it was. She tightened the straps of her book bag and hiked it further up on her shoulders. With the stealth of an army commando, she worked her way around the collage of students standing in groups from twos and threes to as many as five and six in a bunch. Soon she was within speaking distance of the figure.

"Bobby Dunsmore, what are you doing lurking around the school?"

"I'm not lurking, whatever that means. I'm waiting for someone, a friend."

"And who would that be?" Jonie then thought of something. "You mean Heather?"

"That's none of your business. You're not the boss of her. So just back off, okay? Miss Smarty Pants."

"Listen, buster, I . . ."

"What's going on here?" It was Mr. Wyatt, who apparently had been patrolling the school grounds. "Bobby, I thought I told you once, if you want to roam the school grounds, you need to enroll."

"Me? One of those zombies, walking the halls of their prison? Not me. I got more important things to do."

"Then you better be doing it and leave the school grounds. I catch you here again and I'll call the police, you got that?"

"You can tell Heather . . ."

"Keep moving, Bobby, you have nothing in common with these students, they're trying to make something of their life."

"Like Jonie here? Her brother's a jailbird, what kind of life is that?" He laughed at Jonie.

Jonie started to lunge at him, but Mr. Wyatt laid a hand on her shoulder.

"He's not worth it, Jonie, let it be."

Bobby sauntered off, his head swinging left and right as if he owned the world, but it was all an act. His true feelings were of someone who had been rejected by those he admired most. Jonie knew his outward appearance, she had seen other kids show it before. She began to feel sorry for him. She knew that he probably had few friends and no family to love him. *How sad that would be, not to have a mother or father to love you. And no brother to look out for you. That's sad Maybe that is why he acts so tough,* she thought, *he covers up for the lack of love that is missing in his life. He is not really bad, just lonely. Maybe he just wants to have a friend.* Jonie remembered her promise to Ralph, but knew that he would understand her wanting to help someone who was in need. Mr. Wyatt had hurried over to the two girls who were still arguing, so it gave Jonie an opportunity to catch up with Bobby.

"Bobby, wait! I want to talk with you!" she called out. He stopped and turned, surprised that she was hurrying after him.

"What do you want?"

"I just want to talk with you about Heather."

"Heather? I don't know anything about Heather. What makes you think I would know anything?"

"I just wanted to know what your feelings were toward her. Do you like her?"

"What's that to you?" Bobby bristled, he was standing next to an old Russian Olive tree, that looked like it had seen its fair share of wind storms. The leaves were silver on the bottom of the leaf and olive drab on the top. As they floated in the sunlight, they sparkled and gave a twinkly effect to Bobby's appearance. Jonie giggled.

"You laughing at me?"

"No, of course not. I just thought it funny with the leaves of that tree making it look like fireflies were dancing around you."

"I don't know how to dance, I never learned."

"Bobby, did you ever go to school? Did you not learn to read because you never went to school?"

"I don't need to read, I can know things without reading."

"You're right, you can, but being able to read makes things more interesting and more exciting. Like when you see a picture. Like you see a picture of a family going down the road in a car. You can read the words under the picture and find out who they are and where they are going and why. By reading you find out a lot of things about the people in the car."

"How long does it take to learn to read? How many days of school?"

"Well, that is a hard question to answer. You learn to read easy words at first and then you learn harder words. The longer you read, the more words you learn. So you never stop learning to read. You just get better at it as you keep reading."

"How long would it take to be able to read a letter your mother wrote to you when you were only eight."

"Is it in print or in cursive?" Jonie asked.

"I don't know what you just said, what is cursive?"

Jonie pulled a pad and pencil out of her book bag and wrote PEN and *Pen*

"See, the first word is in print, and the second is in cursive."

"I think it must be in print. The marks on the paper look like the first word." Bobby hesitated and then continued, "My mother left it on my pillow the morning she left us. My father was still asleep and she thought I was too." Bobby looked like he was about to cry. Then he straightened up and said, "I knew she was leaving, I saw the little bag she had packed the night before. She never told me why she left me there with him. He was mean. I thought of doing what she did but I didn't know where to go."

"Do you still have the letter, Bobby? I could read it to you, if you still have it."

Bobby stared off into space for several minutes, then said. "I have it at my place."

"I have to get home, Bobby, why don't you go get it and bring it to my house. I can read it there."

"You would do that? For me?" Bobby said, surprised.

Jonie was a little surprised at herself. She had seen Bobby as a bully and mean spirited, and thought he was a no-good person. "Whenever you're ready, just bring it to the house. I gotta get on home. See you later." Jonie glanced back and noticed that Bobby was still standing in the same place, watching her as she started down the sidewalk. After she had gone a block she looked back again and he was nowhere in sight.

When Jonie arrived home, her mother had another surprise for her. As Wanda came out of the kitchen wiping her hands or a dishtowel, she smiled and said, "Guess who I just got off the phone with? Jonie gave her a puzzled look and Wanda explained. "Heather's mother, Barbara Wilkes called. Heather's home. Ralph found her wandering around south of town. What she was doing out there no one seems to know yet."

"Is she alright?"

"Yes, she is fine. It's Ralph that I'm worried about. He is back at the sheriff"s office. Telling them what he knows."

"I don't like that sheriff, he thinks Ralph did something bad."

"Well, as I understand it, Sheriff Smith is no longer Sheriff. Randy Simmons is now sheriff, so that might be better for Ralph," her mother said.

"Is Mr. Crankstone at the jail with Ralph? I think Dad should call him about being there."

"That's a good idea, Jonie, I'll call Del right now."

"Can I go see Heather now?"

"Yes, dear, just be back in time for dinner."

Jonie was out the door in a flash, the door closed with a bang behind her. When she reached Heather's house on Elm Street and knocked on the door, there was no answer. After knocking several times and getting no response, she started to leave. Suddenly from an upstairs window, Heather called out in a weak voice, "Jonie, don't go, I need to talk to somebody."

"Heather, why didn't you open the door? I've been knocking . . ."

"My mother doesn't want anyone to hear what happened to me. She said it would disgrace the family."

"Oh, good grief, come down and open this silly door, I want to talk to you." Heather's head disappeared from the window and soon reappeared peeking out the front door. Jonie motioned for her to step back, and entered the house, closing the door behind her. "Now tell me what this is all about," she demanded.

The young girl started crying and talking at the same time and Jonie couldn't make any sense of what she was saying. Jonie stopped her and quieted the girl down. "Just start from the beginning and go slow. We're in no hurry." Composing herself, Heather told Jonie of her experience in being held captive and about the Voice.

*   *   *

Three days later, Jonie was using the backboard at Mulhalland Park tennis courts. The coach wanted her to work on her back hand and she had been at it for over an hour. She was ready to quit. As she gathered up the balls that had failed to make it over the backboard, she noticed Bobby standing by the statue of General Mulhalland for whom the park was named. Jonie motioned for Bobby to come where she was practicing. He slowly walked the twenty yards and when he neared, his pace slowed even more. Jonie knew her brother would be furious with her for talking to Bobby but she thought that their pact might no longer in effect since their last discussion.

"What's the matter with you?" She asked him. There was no response. "Cat got your tongue?" Still no response.

She was about to let him alone and had turned to leave when he said, "You still do what you said you would?

Jonie turned back and looked at him. He wore a clean shirt and was clean-shaven.

"I say a lot of things, what did I say?" She said curtly.

Bobby turned to go, "never mind," he said.

Jonie reached out and touched his arm, "I'm sorry Bobby, That was rude, what did you want?" Bobby turned to her and held out a grubby scrap of paper. Jonie hesitated; it looked like he had gotten it from the trash barrel. She started to unfold it when she noticed faint printing on the outside, barely visible was the name BOBBY. She opened it and scanned through it. "This is the letter from your mother," she said in a quiet tone Bobby nodded. Jonie motioned to a nearby bench, after they were seated, Jonie read:

203

> "Dearest Bobby:
>
> I hope you can find someone to read this to you. First let me say to you that I love you and you are in no way to blame for what I am about to do. Bobby, I am leaving, I cannot continue living the life your father has chosen. I wish I could take you with me, but I have no idea where I will end up. Remember that I love you with all my heart, and hope you will understand.
>
> Love, Your Mother

"I found it the morning she left. I knew what my name looked like."
"Wonder where she went?" mused Jonie.
"I don't think she got away," Bobby said softly.
"What do you mean?" Jonie asked.
"I think he stopped her."
"Who stopped who, Bobby?"
"My dad. I think she's in the well."
With a miserable expression covering his face, Bobby took the letter from Jonie. He slowly stood, and walked away, leaving Jonie sitting on the bench, dazed and speechless She never mentioned Bobby's secret to anyone, not even to Ralph.

CHAPTER 45

DAVID

David sat in the boat with a dazed expression. He was confused. Where had he intended to go? The last that he remembered was coming home from school and fixing something to eat. But he couldn't remember having eaten. The next thing he could recall was tying the boat up to the anchor and having no idea where he had been or knowing what he had done.

The feeling wasn't new to him. For the past six to eight months he had experienced similar times when he was confused about what was real and what he imagined. Plus he suffered from severe headaches on occasion. He gingerly climbed out of the boat and made his way to the back of his house. Entering the back door he stripped off his boots and hung up his fishing hat. The kitchen was quiet and he called out, "Mom, are you home yet?" There was no answer. He washed up in the kitchen sink and opened the refrigerator door. He knew that there was leftover fried chicken his mother brought home from the diner yesterday. He drank several mouthfuls of milk straight from the carton, set it on the counter and grabbed a drumstick and an apple and headed for his room. He flopped down on his bed and was soon asleep.

Leona Masters walked in the kitchen door at half past seven that same evening. She had a container of left over Beef Stroganoff from work in her hand and went to the fridge. She noticed the milk carton on the counter and checking it found that it was still half full. And she knew it had been out for sometime because it was warm. David must have forgotten to put it away after school, she thought, it probably isn't any good, but she put it in the fridge anyway. She then stepped to David's bedroom door and opened it slightly. She could see that he was on the bed asleep with a partially eaten apple still clutched in his hand. She closed the door.

Half awake but still with his eyes shut, David heard the door to his room open and close. David thought about his mother, she cooked all day at the diner then came home to fix meals for the family. "But that's her job, to fix family meals. She is supposed to do that," a voice in his head would say. "Women cook, men work. That's the way it's supposed to be." David listened to the voice, and eventually decided it was correct.

David rolled over and got up off the bed. Turning to his computer, he played several games before he tired of it and decided he was still hungry. Going to the kitchen, he found his mother busy making an apple pie. "I'm hungry, what's to eat?"

"I have Beef Stroganoff, peas and carrots and apple pie for desert. Your father should be here most any time, I thought we would wait on him before we had dinner." David plopped down at his place at the table. He was about to complain because his Dad was late, when they heard a car pull up to the house. "There he is now," Leona said.

After he had eaten his fill of food, David stood from the table and said, "I think I will go to the river and see if the catfish are biting. I'll be back after a while."

"It's a school night, so don't be out too late," his mother said glancing at her husband. David ignored her and left by way of the outside kitchen door. He slipped on a pair of sneakers and stepped off the porch to his bicycle. He headed for Jonie's house.

Upon arriving, David was greeted at the door by Jonie's mother. "David, what are you doing out on a school night?"

"I need to talk to Jonie for a minute. May I see her?" he said politely.

"Well, she's not here, she's . . . she's with a friend." Wanda knew she had said too much.

"Mrs. Kellam, I really need to talk to her."

"Well, I'm sorry David, but you will just have to wait until tomorrow." As she finished her statement, Wanda watched in fascination as David's facial expression changed. The face of a scared little boy became the face of a menacing thug. When he spoke again it was in an ugly gravelly voice.

"I know where she is. She's at **her** house isn't she? The two of them are plotting against him aren't they?" And with that he turned and left. Bewildered, Wanda watched as David pedaled furiously away. Wanda immediately headed for the phone.

*   *   *

Jonie listened intently to Heather's story. When Heather reached the part about coming face to face with Ralph, she shivered. "I thought sure that the voice had caught me again. The shadow was so real to me."

"Was Ralph's shadow larger or smaller than that of the voice?" Jonie asked.

"I've thought about that," said Heather, "I think the voice had a smaller shadow."

"You know, Bobby Dunsmore, could it have been him?"

"But, why would Bobby . . ." Heather fell into thought.

"I'm just trying to figure who, then worry about why." Jonie said as if thinking aloud.

Heather shivered again and Jonie said, "You're still scared aren't you?"

"Yes, do you suppose you could spend the night, Jonie?"

"I could call Mom and ask, but she would want to talk to your mom."

When Heather asked her mother about Jonie spending the night the answer at first was "No." Then Heather told her mother how scared she was to be alone and her mother gave in and agreed. When Jonie called her mother, the arrangements were made. Jonie's mother would bring over a change of clothes and p j's for Jonie. Heather felt much safer with Jonie around. About eight o' clock the girls got ready for bed. They were starting to brush their teeth when a commotion down stairs distracted then and they slipped down to see what it was.

"What's all the racket?" Jonie noticed that Heather spoke without actually addressing her mother.

"I saw someone looking in the front window. Evin has him in the kitchen now. Probably one of your friends." Jonie again was aware Mrs. Wilkes did not speak directly to Heather, at first she thought Mrs. Wilkes

207

was speaking to her. *How strange, these people don't speak to each other; they speak to the space around them.* Quietly the two girls approached the kitchen door. Heather and Jonie peeked into the room. "DAVID!" They exclaimed in unison.

CHAPTER 46
DAVID AND DARRELL

"You've got some explaining to do, boy." Evin Wilkes was definitely in control of the situation. "You might as well tell me what you were thinking, sneaking around my house in the dark of night."

"David, what is going on, what did you do?" Jonie jumped in.

"Yes, David, what happened to make my Dad so mad." Heather asked.

David's voice changed to one of vengeance. It became gravelly.

It's not David, it's Darrell, I'm Darrell, and you suckers better stay out of my way. That includes you, Heather, and this dumb family of yours."

"David, what are you talking about, it's me Jonie."

"I know who you are. You're his friend, and I aim to see that you and him become more than that. He doesn't know about me and what I do for him."

"What does this have to do with you prowling around our house? You haven't explained your actions yet." Evin asked.

"It's none of your business what I was doing. Nobody gets in my way. I have to help him and no one will stop me. He is nothing without me doing the dirty work that needs to be done."

David. You? You're crazy, I . . ." David jumped up out of the kitchen chair and lunged at Heather, but her dad forced him back into the chair In a gravelly voice and a menacing and threatening look on his face, David spoke with the conviction of a caged animal. With piercing flashing eyes, and his face beet red, he shouted,

"DON'T CALL ME CRAZY, I AM NOT CRAZY, AND I'LL TEACH YOU TO GET IN MY WAY. I'LL TEACH ANYONE WHO GETS IN MY WAY . . ."

"Just a minute young man, you don't talk that way while you're in my house." Heather was trembling and shivering with fear. Her father awkwardly patted her on the shoulder.

"What's the matter, Heather? You seem to be scared to death, you're home and safe, nothing to be frightened of." Jonie wrapped her arms around her friend and Heather begin to breathe easier. After a few seconds, while still trembling, she was able to say, "It's him, that's the voice I was telling you about Jonie, David is the voice."

"I told you I'm not David, I'm Darrell. Can't you get that through that thick head of yours? I am Darrell, I'm David's protector, I'm the one who looks after him and I take care of anyone who gets in my way." David spoke with fire in his eyes.

"We'll let the authorities deal with this mess. Heather, you and Jonie go to your room. Barbara, you call the sheriff's office and get an officer out here now. Tell them it's an emergency and we want help now. David or Darrell, whatever your name is, you sit in that chair and don't move. Now everyone do what I said. Go!"

Jonie hesitated, until Evin Wilkes said it again, "GO!" She grabbed Heather's hand and they started for the doorway. Barbara Wilkes did as she was told.

In the few seconds, all this took place David sat at the kitchen table with a menacing look. But when Evin Wilkes took charge, David's facial expression begin to change. No one except Jonie, who stopped at the kitchen doorway to look back at David, saw the change in the boy. The flashing eyes, the red face, and the veins protruding from the skin all disappeared and he became himself. When he spoke to Evin his voice was back to it's normal 13-year-old squeaky calm voice. "I don't know what you want me to do. I don't know where I am. I have never been here before. How did I get here?"

When Officer Bailey arrived at the Wilkes home, he was faced with the most unusual story he had heard during his short career as an officer in the Sheriff's Department. The tale that Mr. Wilkes related to him did not make sense and he got absolutely nothing from the boy in question. David, or Darrell, he wasn't sure from the story told which name was the real name. He did finally determine that the boy's last name was Masters and that he lived along the Verdi River. There were only three Masters in the phone book and only one in that neighborhood. He called Leroy Masters and found that a boy David's age lived there. Leona Masters answered the phone and after a brief conversation with her husband, said that she would be at the Wilkes home as soon as possible, but David's father was too ill to come.

"Your son is about to be charged with window peeking, a misdemeanor," Bailey told Leona, when she showed up at the Wilkes home, "but I want you to know that his behavior when caught was very unusual. I think you should get someone to take a look at him."

After a short discussion, Evin and Barbara Wilkes decided that they didn't want the hassle of filing charges against David and he was released into the custody of his mother. However, Officer Bailey insisted that someone with some knowledge of emotional stress should visit with David. The Masters agreed to contact Mrs. Terri Deprey, the Robertown High School guidance counselor. Leona and Terri both went to the First Methodist Church and were in the same Sunday School Class. The two ladies considered themselves friends, even though their families never interacted.

When Leona contacted Terri about David's behavior, she did so without the knowledge of her husband. Not wanting to tell Terri about the window peeking charge, her premise was that since David would be enrolling in high school the following semester, she told Teri that she was concerned about his being mature enough for the high school environment. She wanted some assurance that he would fit in with that level of social interaction. Terri agreed to visit with David outside the school environment, they would meet in David's home, where he would presumably be most comfortable. She had several tests she could administer to gauge his level of maturity. Terri told Leona that the sooner she interviewed David the better. "I would rather that as little time as possible transpire before I talk to him. Memories have a way of altering themselves. Let's set it up for tomorrow during the last class period, I can arrange it with the school counselor for David to leave early."

"Can you pick David up at school and see that he is home at 2:30? I will be right behind you." After Leona had everything set up, she told

Leroy what she was doing. At first he objected and insisted she contact Teri and call the meeting off. But eventually she convinced him of the need to be assured that David would be happy with his high school experience. When informed of the plan, David became furious with them both. He refused to cooperate and demanded that the meeting be canceled. They stood their ground, the following day the interview took place.

"I am going to record our visit, David, is that okay with you?" David didn't respond so Mrs. Deprey sat a hand-held cassette recorder in front of them. Terri and David sat at the kitchen table. Leona had excused herself to go to the market. David was angry, he had been having a bad day. Teasing from other students, who had heard that the sheriff had been called to the Wilkes home, upset him. He told everyone that he had never been to Heather's home and didn't know what they were talking about. David ignored the attempts by Mrs. Deprey to establish a non-confrontational atmosphere. She explained that she had twenty questions that she would like for him to answer. The first five questions were soft and unoffensive: his age, number of family members and his church affiliation, Then she asked questions such as, "Do you consider yourself independent? Are you confident in yourself? Do you consider yourself responsible?" He answers were the same for each of them and with one word: "Enough."

He bristled and refused to answer when she asked, "Do your parents clean up your messes? And, do you ever tell good lies?"

She then asked, "How many good friends do your have? Friends that are loyal and trustworthy?" David seemed to be stunned by the question. Then the blank look on his face turned to one of disgust and then he became angry. His facial expression became beet red. In a gravelly voice he answered, "How dare you ask such a question. That has nothing to do with maturity. That's a question of preference, not one of a person's level of emotional growth. How dare you ask him that question," David literally spat out his words. For the first time in the interview Terri felt herself fearful of the thirteen-year-old. She decided to end the evaluation.

"Okay, David, we will stop now."

Still with a deep and raspy voice he replied, "I would think so, and I'm not David, I'm Darrell. I think you have pried into my plans enough. I'm getting out of here and won't be back. And shut this thing off." As he spoke, he reached out and grabbed the recorder off the table and flung it to the floor where pieces of it flew off. When she looked up at him, his eyes were like burning embers of a fire.

Caught unawares, all Teri could think to say was, "Who is Darrell?"

With that David stood menacingly, glared at her, then stormed from the kitchen to his room. As she quickly collected her papers and the recorder off the floor, she muttered, "This is one scared little boy, and that fear turned him into one angry kid, which makes him a dangerous person."

CHAPTER 47
HEATHER AND JONIE

"I'm serious, Heather, you've got to talk to someone," Jonie said. It was a few minutes after four o'clock and Heather, who had rode home from school with Jonie and her brother, sat at the desk, in Jonie's room. Jonie sat on her bed. Heather was busy doing what she usually did when she was upset, she was sketching in a notebook.

The two girls had gone to Heather's room that night when her Dad caught David outside the house. Heather was so upset that it took Jonie an hour to get her to talk. "Now tell me, what did you mean downstairs? What did you mean about David?

Heather whispered, "David is the voice in the woods. The voice I heard when I was in the shed." Heather started trembling again. "Jonie, David is the guy that kidnapped me, the one who held me captive in the woods."

"Heather, do you know what you're saying? Are you sure? Maybe they just sound alike."

"Jonie, you must believe me, I would know that voice anywhere, it's him!"

The girls talked until sleep overtook them and the next day Heather refused to discuss it again. She didn't really want to go to school, but slowly got ready.

Now, Jonie was insistent, Heather needed to talk to someone about what happened. She repeated herself, "I'm not kidding, Heather, you need to tell the authorities. David has been my friend since forever, but if he did this to you then somebody needs to know."

"You mean like the sheriff?"

"Yes, I mean the sheriff."

"I wouldn't know where to go, or how to talk to him, you would have to go with me, Jonie."

"Hey, maybe we could get Ralph to take us, he would know who to talk to."

"Okay, let's do it, let's go talk to him now, before I chicken out." Heather finally agreed, she almost smiled.

Later, as they sat in the backseat of her mother's car, Jonie sang with excitement. "We're going to see the sheriff, we're going to see the sheriff, we're going to see the sheriff of old Robertown."

"Jonie, would you please stop that squalling, you sound like a kid," complained Ralph.

"I am a kid, Bro, isn't that what you're always telling me?"

When they arrived at the sheriff's office, Jonie told the lady at a switchboard that they needed to see the sheriff, she punched a button and the sheriff came out of his office. Ralph explained to him what Heather and Jonie wanted to tell him. Randy immediately asked Nancy to bring her notepad and follow them into his office. When everyone was settled he turned to Heather. "Since this involves you why don't you just tell me the story. Just start with when you left school and what happened. Go slow, Nancy here will be taking notes. She's good, but we don't want to test her today. Okay?"

Heather explained about meeting David after school and going to his house. She described the shed and the voice. Heather paused and Jonie elbowed her to get her going again. She told how she dug a hole under one wall and escaped. She finished her story by telling how she and Ralph were stopped by Officer Bailey. "When I heard David the other night at my house, I knew that was the voice at the shed."

"When, Heather, when did you recognize the voice?" Randy asked.

"What do you mean?"

"At what point did you know it was the voice? What was David saying?"

Heather hesitated for a moment then said, "When he said he was Darrell."

CHAPTER 48
SHERIFF SIMMONS

Randy Simmons stacked the report written by Bailey on top of the response to the Wilkes residence, which were on top of two other reports on his desk. It was obvious to him that the boy, David Masters, had a personality problem that had manifested itself and he realized one other thing: he now had three, or four depending on how you counted, suspects in the case of the girl in the woods. Ralph had not been eliminated, even though a case against him had been severely damaged by the actions of Sheriff Smith. Bobby Dunsmore was on the list, mainly because of proximity. And now David and or Darrell would be added to the list, primarily because of his apparent aggression toward Heather Wilkes and Jonie Kellam. Anyone of the four could have had access to the area where the girl was found.

The sheriff was intrigued by the file that Jerry Bailey had put together on David Masters. It included a report from the guidance counselor at the high school and the dialogue from the confrontation at the Wilkes home. Heather's testimony about the voice was weak evidence, because it could not be substantiated. But it added to the picture they were building on David.

Mrs. Deprey summed up her report with, "I am no expert but I think he needs professional help,"

Officer Bailey's report had concluded with, "At times, the kid seemed to be two different people."

Sheriff Simmons punched the "Play" button of the table top cassette player that he had to rummage through a storage cabinet to find. He listened to the tape from Mrs. Deprey again. When the tape stopped, he picked up Bailey's report and re-read it again. As he perused some of the dialogue that the officer had recalled of that night at the Wilkes, Randy suddenly got an idea. He punched a button on the intercom console on his desk.

"Yes, sheriff?"

"Nancy, get me the number for Janette Freedrock at the Mental Health Center in Topeka, please"

"Yes sir, right away, sheriff." The sheriff had the number in minutes. He placed the call, and was connected to an old friend.

"Janette, good to hear your voice again, how are you? And the family? How old is little Jason now, three? Four? Ten! Now how can someone as young as you are have a ten-year-old son? What? No, well, yes, I am going to ask a favor, isn't that what friends are for? Yeah, you got me figured out. Well, I've got this case and I'm in dire need of an expert, and I remembered that I had a friend who was an expert in mental health. Yeah, can I send you some information and you give me your opinion on it? No, no hurry, anytime, tomorrow would be fine. Yeah, I knew you would appreciate that. Yeah, and say hello to Bill for me. Okay, Bye Janette, and thanks."

The sheriff picked up the file prepared by Officer Bailey and the recorder and headed for Nancy. "When you have time today, transcribe the conversation on this tape and make copies of it and of Officer Bailey's report. Fax a copy to Janette Freedrock in Topeka. I would like for this to go out today if possible."

"I think I can get that out okay, sheriff." Nancy said sweetly.

"Thanks, I will be out of the office for the next couple of hours."

He then walked over to Clara at the dispatch desk. "I can be reached for the next couple of hours in unit number four."

"Sure thing sheriff." Clara responded cheerfully. Randy noticed she was chewing on something and in a low voice so as not to be heard by others, he said, "We need to cut back on the snacks during office hours, Clara."

Clara pulled a wad of gum out of her mouth. "Oh, this, it's a new diet gum, designed to curb the appetite between meals. I'm trying it out, maybe I can lose a few pounds now that I am not so frustrated at work."

Clara plopped the wad back in her mouth and smiled at the Sheriff. Randy grinned and headed for the front door.

As he cruised south on Highway 10, his mind reviewed the thick file that Sheriff Smith had collected on Ralph Kellam. One of the reports had described Ralph's explanation of how someone could get to the spot of the Newman girl's grave in the woods without being seen. Sheriff Simmons wanted to see for himself the lay of the land that Ralph had described. Randy knew that it could be different because Sheriff Smith was not above leaving out certain facts or including them to suit his agenda.

He pulled the squad car into an empty Cheyenne Cove Campground and shut off the motor. "Dispatch, Sheriff Simmons here, do you read?"

"Dispatch here, go ahead, sheriff."

"I'm going to be away from Unit Four. Will be in contact on the mobile. Copy? Out."

"Copy, out."

The sheriff popped the trunk lid and grabbed the ax handle carried in all squad cars. "More convincing than a Taser, and simpler use." Sheriff Smith had explained to his officers. Now Randy felt the handle might be useful for a walking stick. Closing the trunk, he turned off the radio to conserve the battery, locked the car and headed for the trail head.

When he reached the foot bridge at Willow Creek, he glanced at his wristwatch to note the time, then started up the trail until he spotted the yellow tape still visible in the woods. The recent rains had erased much of the footprint activity around the grave. "Not much to see here any more," he muttered to himself. Returning to the trail he followed it to the ridge that separated the Willow and Rattlesnake Creeks. From Ralph's description he had found in Sheriff Smith's file, he knew that the Dunsmore bridge should be about an hour to the northeast. As he traveled the trail he admitted to himself that he would have to agree with Ralph's belief that the trail, even after the marked part stopped, was easy to transverse. The sheriff beat Ralph's time by twelve minutes. *Someone familiar with the terrain could probably do it in even less time.* Randy reached the bridge that he knew was about one-hundred yards from the Dunsmore place. He decided to pay Bobby a visit. As he crossed the bridge he stopped to look out over the river. *I think Ralph was correct in his other assumption. The river would be even faster by boat than traveling the trail.* The sheriff noticed no activity on the river., "The fishing season must be over for the winter," he murmured to himself

Now that all the leaves were off the trees, the Dunsmore place was visible from the bridge, and Randy headed for it. He was amazed at its appearance. It had an abandoned look. "Hello, the house!" he called out. "Anyone at home?" No answer. Carefully he stepped up on the porch and pounded the ax handle on the wooden floor. "This is Sheriff Simmons, anyone here?" He was met with silence. Glancing around the side of the house he spotted a burned out shed. The fire looked rather recent to him. He walked back to the front door and pushed on it. It opened, not even latched, he thought. As he examined the interior of the place he couldn't believe that someone actually lived there. The odor alone was enough to cut the sheriff's time inside the house short. He decided to take a closer look at the burned out shed.

Randy had taken a course on detecting arson and this was a no-brainier. The fire started on the outside of one corner of the shed and spread to the interior. Nothing visible to ignite the fire by accident, and not a lightening strike because the burn is from the bottom up. *My guess is that someone dumped something on the wall and started the fire deliberately.* Then Randy realized something else. *The fire was started in such a way that, with the wind in the proper direction, the shed would burn without much danger of setting the house on fire. Someone planned this as a warning or as vengeance against somebody, and that somebody must be Bobby.*

Randy heard a rumble in the distance, glancing at the sky he noticed a cloud bank off in the western horizon. Realizing that he still had a hours hike back to the squad car, he quickly started for the bridge.

In his hurry, he failed to notice a shadow along the river bank under the bridge. The shadow stood frozen in place as the sheriff rushed toward the footpath he traveled earlier. The storm caught up with him about half way back down the trail. In the driving rain, he somehow lost the trail and by the time he realized it, he was surrounded by woods.

Suddenly in front of him stood the wall of a small shed half-hidden among the trees. Finding a door, he flipped the latch and stepped inside, he was out of the rain, almost, the roof of the shed leaked like an old rusty bucket. But at least it was better than nothing. In the dim light, he could tell that the shed was empty. At one of the center poles he could see broken glass on the ground. Checking the walls he found a hole dug from the inside of the shed to the outside. Then it struck him, *the Wilkes girl, this is like what Heather Wilkes described in Bailey's report. Could this be the same place?*

At the same time as his revelation, he heard a sharp snap outside the door. He knew the click of a lock when he heard it, and that snap was the same sound. He tried the door. It didn't budge. He heard a strange giggle outside the door. "I'm Sheriff Simmons of Woodrow County, you're interfering with an official investigation. Open this door now!" Again the giggle. Then silence. Whoever the person was outside the shed, they had disappeared.

CHAPTER 49
DARRELL

D arrell didn't pretend to understand what was happening to cause him to suddenly appear, he just knew that at times it became necessary for him to take over David's body and act for him. *David was too timid and didn't have the courage to do what was necessary to take care of people who got in his way. He would get angry, but he wouldn't get even. I teach them a lesson they'll never forget.*

Darrell knew David but David was not aware of Darrell. Therefore, David had no idea of what Darrell did for him. His only clue was the occasional severe headache that he would have after experiencing a period of time that he could not remember where he was or what he had been doing. A couple of hours here, an hour there, that seemed to have vanished. And the times when his mother would ask where he had gone and he had to make up a story because he couldn't remember. He was getting good at making up stuff.

Darrell was the dominating personality. Darrell was much more aware of the necessity to take matters into his own hands when it came to dealing with problems.

Like Heather, now there was a problem. She interfered with the way things should be. She was coming too close to David. That would cause problems with David's relationship with Jonie. That's the person David should be concentrating on. She was the one for David, not Heather. Heather was too weak. David needed a strong personality to help him become a person to be taken seriously in high school. A person with all the right moves and a following among the students. Someone recognized as a force to be admired. With the right girlfriend and a push in the right direction it could all come about. But first, Heather needed to be out of the picture.

That's where Darrell came in, that was **his** problem to deal with. And he could deal with it. *Oh yes, he knew what to do. He had a plan. Put her in the shed and wait for her to become completely helpless and soon she would be willing to stay away from David. But Heather surprised him, she didn't scare so easy and figured out a way out of the shed, and escaped. Now he would have to come up with a new plan in which to eliminate her.*

And also, there was Bobby Dunsmore. who thought he was so tough. David was going to get hurt if Bobby kept egging him on. But Darrell got even with him, he knew that Bobby would think twice now about threatening David. The fire took care of that. Bobby would realize that it could just as easily been the house on fire as the worthless shed. And now, today the new sheriff had come nosing around.

Darrell had watched from the riverbank below the bridge as he used that ax handle to stir around in the ashes of the fire. Later, he had followed the sheriff down the old trail to the point where he veered off the path to the shed. Darrell giggled to himself as he re-lived the sheriff walking right into the shed all by himself. All Darrell had to do was flip the latch and click the padlock. He didn't have any reason for imprisoning the sheriff, except that it was sort of funny that the sheriff was his prisoner. Darrell giggled again at the thought. Maybe he would burn the shed with the sheriff inside. Wouldn't that be a big deal in the newspaper?

CHAPTER 50
SHERIFF SIMMONS, OFFICER BAILEY AND CLARA

O fficer Jerry Bailey was on patrol in the southern half of Woodrow County. He had pulled into the campground at Cheyenne Cove and spotted the only car parked in the campground. It was a Woodrow County squad car. "Dispatch, this is unit six, my location is Cheyenne Cove, at Lake Lawson. A Woodrow County unit is parked here. Who is using vehicle number twenty-four today?"

"Unit six, this is Dispatch, Sheriff Simmons is in number twenty-four. His call sign is unit four. He is on mobile. Shall I contact him for you?" Clara was all business.

"We have experienced a rain storm here and if he is out of the unit, he must be soaked. You might check that he has found cover. 10-4?"

"Will do, dispatch out."

Officer Bailey sat in his patrol car for about ten minutes before he heard the crackle of the radio. "Unit six, this is dispatch, I am unable to reach unit four's mobile. Perhaps you should you investigate whereabouts of unit four."

"Thanks, Clara, I wanted to go for a cold swim today. Believe I'll wait till the rain ceases and all I have to worry about is the mud under foot. Suggest you run a check on my mobile. Unit six out."

Jerry waited another ten minutes before exiting his vehicle. He could only assume the direction that the Sheriff might have taken. With no other visitors to the lake in the area, he thought that the sheriff was re-visiting the grave site of the girl found in the woods. It had been some time since he had been to the trail head at Willow Creek and wasn't sure that he could find it. The wet underbrush didn't encourage him any. When he finally reached the footbridge at Willow Creek, he still had questions in his mind whether he was on the right trail. The hard pack of the trail had turned to mush from the rain and only when the marker for the trail came into view did he feel confident that he was where he wanted to be.

Looking for some sign of recent activity along the trail handicapped his rate of travel along the trail. After about forty-five minutes he had still found no evidence that he was on the sheriff's trail.

*   *   *

Clara sat in front of the switchboard, the hub of all communications between the sheriff's office and units on patrol, and between individual units. Also she controlled the traffic between the emergency 911 office and citizens of the county. She was Dispatch, and as such controlled all telephone, radio and mobile phone contact with the outside world. With the flip of a switch, she could even control the incoming calls to Nancy's desk. She set the frequencies used by the units on patrol and the channels used by the *walkies-talkies* or portable radios used when the officer was away from the radio in the vehicle. She had tried everything she could think of to raise the sheriff on the mobile unit. Nothing had worked. It had been over three-quarters of an hour since she had spoken to Jerry. She called him, and got a "no signal" response.

Usually the presence of low-lying clouds produced better reception of the mobile units, but it appeared that wasn't the case today. Then she had an idea. Maybe she could patch a call through the radio in the sheriff's vehicle and key it to his mobile unit. It was worth a try. No luck. Then it dawned on her that her idea would not work if the sheriff didn't leave the radio on when he exited the car.

Clara then tried the same tacit on Officer Bailey's radio. Bingo, she had a signal. A few seconds later, she heard, "Unit six here, go ahead dispatch."

"This is dispatch, any luck on finding unit four?"

"Dispatch, I am at the end of the trail from Willow Creek and that's a negative, repeat a negative."

*   *   *

Randy wasn't angry but he was highly irritated with himself. Not at his predicament of being locked in the shed, but at apparently having been followed without having detected it. This was his second trip around the perimeter of the shed and this time he was checking the boards of the walls for a weakness. He found the most likely one and let fly with a swing of the ax handle. He swung it like a golf club and the bottom foot of the board snapped. With a second swing coming down like a sledge hammer, the top portion of the board also snapped. He used the ax handle and jabbed at the center section. A few jabs and it separated from the cross beams. In a matter of minutes, using the handle as a pry bar, he separated the board on each side of the missing board. The rain had stopped and he stepped through the opening. The first thing he wanted to examine was the padlock on the door. After noting the make and the number on the lock, he then got his bearings and started toward the direction where he thought the trail was located. Finding the trail at about where he expected to, he set off to the southeast toward the Cheyenne Cove Campground.

As he came over a slight rise, he noticed a shadow of a man sitting on a log along the trail. Ever so stealthy, he slipped along the trail, keeping trees and brush between himself and the figure on the log. When he was within a dozen feet, he prepared himself to charge the figure, when he heard the static of a radio. "Dispatch, say again."

"Bailey, you about got your head whacked with this ax handle." As Randy spoke, Bailey jumped, dropped the mobile and reached for his weapon, all in one fluid motion. When he realized who had spoken, he relaxed his stance. He stood with a stunned look on his face.

"I've been looking for you, Sheriff, where have you been?"

"I'll explain later, right now I want to get back to the squad car and get out of these wet clothes."

The sun had set upon their arrival to his unit. Randy peeled off the wet shirt and undershirt, wrapped his torso in a dry blanket from the vehicle's trunk, and climbed into the car turning the heater on high.

Flipping the radio switch on, he called dispatch. "Dispatch, this is unit four."

"Dispatch here, go ahead four."

"I'm taking unit six with me. We're paying a visit to the Dunsmore place. I have a hunch I owe Bobby a night in the county lockup. Unit four out."

"Copy unit four. Good to have you back in communication. Dispatch out."

Officer Bailey had climbed in the front passengers seat of the sheriff's vehicle. Once Randy was off the radio he asked the same question he had asked on the trail. "Care to share what's going on, Randy?"

"Well, first close the door, you're letting all the heat out." Bailey did as asked. The sheriff filled his deputy in on what had happened, from his examination of the fire at Bobby's to his escape from the shed. "I think Bobby followed me from his place and locked me in the shed. I intend to return the favor."

"Okay, Sheriff, I'll be right behind you." As soon as Bailey left the vehicle, Randy grabbed his shirt draped over the rear-view mirror and spread it on the passenger seat to dry as much as was possible in a short time. He turned the vents toward the shirt. He flicked the switch for the flashing lights but not the siren. He noticed that Bailey did the same. The tandem was soon on Highway 10 headed north.

When they reached the winding road to the bridge, he shut down the flashers, Bailey followed suit. They both quietly exited their vehicles at the bridge. Randy quickly slipped on a still damp shirt, not bothering to tuck in the tail. He wrapped the blanket around his shoulders. Looking at his deputy he said, "Got your light?" Bailey nodded. Maintaining silence, and without the use of their flashlights, they moved toward the house.

At the door of the dark house, Randy pantomimed what he wanted Bailey to do. Randy reared back and kicked the door, As it flew off the hinges, he and Bailey flicked on their lights and bathed the interior of the place in bright light. Randy hollered, "SHERIFF'S OFFICE, DON'T MOVE, WE'VE GOT YOU COVERED!"

Nothing, there was no one in the room, then a flash of movement in an adjoining doorway, "STOP, SHERIFF'S OFFICE!" Randy called out again, He fired his weapon in the air. The figure froze. Two department issue flashlights were trained on it. "Stay where you are and don't move!

You're under arrest for interfering in a police investigation. Cuff him Bailey. Then read him his rights."

The sheriff was shocked when his light displayed the face of the figure. *David Masters! It wasn't Bobby Dunsmore they were arresting at all. What was David Masters doing in the Dunsmore home? And in rain gear too.*

Sheriff Simmons and Officer Bailey inspected the west of the house and found a broken window large enough for someone David's size to go through. "Breaking and entering," muttered Randy.

"I don't know, look at that dust on the glass, It looks like it's been there for a while," Jerry said.

"It's enough to hold him with," Randy replied.

CHAPTER 51
DAVID AND THE SHERIFF

He was confused, people were saying all kinds of things about him. His parents wanted to know why he was looking in the window at Heather Wilkes' home. Jonie had e-mailed him and asked why he was acting so weird, and wanted to know who "Darrell" was. Now the sheriff wants to know why he was at Bobby Dunsmore's place. It was all too confusing.

He couldn't understand what they were talking about. He had never been to Heather's house, nor had he ever been to the Dunsmore place. At school today he hadn't talked to Jonie because there were too many ears listening. And he certainly didn't know any Darrell.

David tried to recall what he had done after school today. He remembered being in the back of Sheriff Simmons patrol car, but that was after dark. And he remembered being taken to the sheriff's office. And being in handcuffs, and the sheriff putting him in this room and setting him down at the table. But that was all later. What he couldn't remember was where he had been or what he had done after school. And why he had been dressed in rain clothes? So many questions, with no answers.

The door opened, Sheriff Simmons, and Officer Bailey walked in. Bailey walked over to the corner behind him facing the large mirror on the wall. The sheriff dropped a folder of papers on the table and sat down in the chair in front of David, with the big mirror behind him.

"Officer Bailey, why don't we switch the cuffs from behind his back to in front of him. That will be a little more comfortable." Bailey did as asked. "Well, David," the sheriff continued, "we need some answers to our questions, and it looks like you're the person to ask. To save time, why don't you tell us about your day? Start with when you woke up today and take us to when we found you at the Dunsmore place. Don't leave anything out, nothing. Okay, David?"

"I can't do that. There are some parts that I can't remember." The sheriff eyed him suspiciously.

"Then tell us what you do remember."

David told Randy of his talk with his parents that morning. "They were pretty upset with what had happened the night before. I didn't understand what they were talking about. I have never been to Heather's house. My mother asked a lot of questions that I couldn't answer, and as I said, they got pretty upset. So I went on to school." David told the sheriff of his day at school. "It was a bad day, some of the kids had heard about the cops . . . er you guys being at Heathers' and some kids at school teased me about it. I ignored them because I didn't know what they were talking about."

The sheriff nodded, and said, "and after school, where did you go?"

David grimaced. "I remember going home and finding a note that my mother had left for me. It said that she had made arrangements for me to be interviewed by the high school guidance counselor. It made me mad and I don't remember much else until I was in the patrol car."

"Didn't you have a visit from the high school guidance counselor?" Randy asked.

"Yeah."

"How did that go?"

"Didn't amount to anything."

"Want to tell me about it?"

"Nothing much to tell. She asked some dumb questions, and that was it."

"I heard you got mad and walked out of the meeting."

"I left, yeah. She asked such dumb questions."

"Give me an example of one of her dumb questions."

David thought for a few seconds. then said, "I can't think of one right now."

"How many times have you been to the shed in the woods?"

"What church do you go to?"

"What?" The sheriff asked.

"She asked what church I went to. That was one of her dumb questions."

"Why is that a dumb question, David?"

"It's just dumb."

"How many times have you been to the shed in the woods?" The sheriff asked again.

"What?"

"You heard me, how many times have you been to the shed in the woods? The one you put the padlock on."

"I don't know nothing about no shed."

"Well, David, I think for your sake we better stop this right here. We are getting very close to you incriminating yourself. You will be charged on two counts; breaking and entering, and obstructing justice. You will be allowed to call your parents and have them come down to the office. Then we will go from there. Officer Bailey, book him as a juvenile, then take him out to a phone, but the cuffs stay on."

An hour later, Sheriff Simmons, Officer Bailey, and Mr. and Mrs. Masters were in the Sheriff's office with David. The Sheriff was explaining the evenings events to the Masters. ". . . and when we entered the Dunsmore home, we apprehended David inside the residence. We believe he may have placed the padlock on the door of the shed that I took refuge in, which would carry a charge of interfering with an official investigation."

David, still in handcuffs, spat out, "I told you, I don't know anything about no shed."

Leroy Masters held up his hand, palm out. "David, let me handle this," he said to his son, then turned to the sheriff and continued, "If the boy says he knows nothing of the shed . . ."

"If he knows nothing of the shed, then where was he earlier in the evening?"

Leroy looked at his son for an explanation. David had a pained look on his face. "I don't remember."

"David, I have to admit, that doesn't answer the question," his father said.

"Mr. Masters, this is where I stopped asking David questions earlier. We are getting close to David incriminating himself. I really think you should get the advice of council before we continue." Leroy shot a glance at his wife who stood with a look of disbelief on her face. She didn't acknowledge her husband. Leroy with head down, nodded, then said. "Can we take the handcuffs off?"

Randy also glanced at Mrs. Masters, then spoke to Leroy, "Tell you what I will do. I will release David in your custody and he is to remain at home the rest of the evening. Tomorrow he is to attend school, and then go directly home. You are to bring him here, I would suggest with council, at five o'clock." The sheriff then turned to David. "At that time, you will need to have some answers to my questions. Okay, young man?"

David glared at the Sheriff. Then said in a deep raspy voice "Okay"

The Sheriff eyed the boy closely, then said, "Officer Bailey, please remove the cuffs."

CHAPTER 52
SHERIFF SIMMONS

"Sheriff Smith, this is Randy Simmons, how are you doing?"

"As if you cared."

"Of course I care, if I didn't I wouldn't have notified the state attorney general."

"Yeah, yeah, what do you want?"

"I saw where your grand jury hearing is to convene on the 30th of this month. With your case on the docket, I thought I'd check if you are under the advice of council?"

"What's it to ya?"

"I hope you have hired a lawyer to represent you."

"That's my business."

"Okay, I'm just giving you a heads up, I'll let you get back to what you were doing." Randy hung up the phone. He suspected that the sheriff, or former sheriff would just let things ride, and take it as it came.

"Sheriff, you have a call on line one. A Mr. Giles, representing the Masters boy," Nancy said in a pleasant voice.

Jake Giles, who had recently passed the bar exam, was one of Robertown's new crop of lawyers. He had tried to find a position with one of the law firms in town, but with no success. So he had gone independent.

"Jake! How are things in your part of town? Busy, I bet."

"You stay busy, I stay busy," Jake replied.

Randy suspected that was not true. The rumor mill had it that Jake hadn't handled more than two cases since opening his door. He guessed that Jake had undercut everybody else in fees for the Masters and he probably promised something he might not be able to deliver. A clear road for his client.

"About those charges against my client, Judge Ruth Tindle of Juvenile Court, just gave us a continuance until February. So you won't have to prepare your testimony until then. The Judge allowed me twenty-four hours to visit with my client. So we won't be in today at five like you planned. We'll see you Friday instead. Sorry if that messes up your schedule, Sheriff. Well, I gotta run, anything else I need to be aware of?"

"That will give your client time to remember things then." Randy had filed charges against David yesterday because he didn't want to wait any longer. He assumed the arraignment had taken place this morning for David's charges of obstruction of justice and breaking and entering. Randy suspected that the broken window had happened some time ago, but when you have someone inside a house and a broken window, the two just naturally go together. He knew it was a weak case because he also would have a difficult time tying David to the shed unless he was able to do it with the padlock.

If I can tie David to the shed and get evidence that was also the shed which held the Wilkes girl captive, we will have a kidnapping charge to add to the case.

Randy picked up the phone and dialed the number written on a note pad on his desk. He spoke into the hand set. "This is Sheriff Simmons, is Esther in? Thanks. Hello, Esther? This is Randy, how are things at Ace this morning? Good, Esther, I have a Master brand padlock question. You folks carry those right? Yeah, Ace is the place, Esther, can you tell me if you sold the lock. Yes, I have the number from the lock. It's 137433. I understand, a couple of days will be fine. Yes, Esther, just let me know what you come up with, and thanks." He dropped the hand set in its cradle, then picked it back up and made a similar call to Hometown Lumber. He had put the play in motion, now it was wait and see whether he came up with a strike or a gutter ball. Randy pushed a button on the desk console. "Dispatch here."

"Clara, contact Officer Bailey and have him call me from a phone. Tell him no radio call,"

"Will do Sheriff, that it?"

"That's it, thanks Clara."

"Anytime, dispatch out."

A few minutes later his phone rang. It was Jerry "Jerry, do a couple of things for me. I need the padlock off that shed in the woods. Don't cut it off just use a pry bar and bring in the latch, padlock and all. And Jerry, while you are there, take some pictures of the shed. There should be a hole under one wall, get a picture of that. Plenty of pictures Jerry, plenty of pictures."

"Okay, Sheriff, plenty of pictures."

*   *   *

Later that same afternoon, Randy leaned back in his chair. *We found David at the Dunsmore place, if he was there when I arrived by way of the trail and followed me back to the shed, then he had plenty of time to make it back to Dunsmore's before Bailey and I did. And if that is the same shed where the Wilkes girl was held, then David could be responsible for that also. Does that somehow tie into the case of the dead girl in the woods that the Kellam boy found? Could David actually be guilty of hitting someone over the head and burying the body? It seems so unlikely for a kid only thirteen.*

Then there is the Kellam boy, He is much more physically capable of such an act. Could Sheriff Smith be correct in his assumption that he is the killer? And what about Bobby? Talk about a loose cannon, there is someone who . . . Randy was jolted from his thoughts by a rap on the office door. He turned in his chair and saw Nancy standing in the doorway.

"Sorry to bother you, Sheriff, but this just came in over the fax and I thought you would want to see it now."

"What is it?"

"Well, it says for your eyes only. But the cover page says it is from Janette Freedrock in Topeka." Randy jumped to his feet and held out his hand.

"Yes, I certainly do, thanks, Nancy"

"You're welcome Sheriff"

As Nancy returned to her desk, Randy glanced at the cover page. Sure enough, Janette had hand written the words, "For Sheriff Simmons eyes only," across the page. Randy dropped the cover page on his desk and started reading.

> *Randy—First I want you to understand that this is just a preliminary report and that any evaluation of the materials that you sent me would have to be accompanied with a direct examination of the people involved before it would be acceptable in a court of law. That said, here is what I perceive to be what you have to deal with. Most importantly,, I agree with Mrs. Deprey that we have a very disturbed child in regard to David. There are indications that he has a lack of self-esteem and that this stems from a feeling of being unwanted. It is not an unusual condition to find teenage insecurity manifesting itself during puberty. However, it is unusual to find this insecurity about acceptance by family and friends manifesting itself in a second personality. At this juncture I believe that is what you are dealing with in David.*
>
> *Sometimes called an alter-ego, a split-personality, or dual personality, it remains as one of the conditions of schizophrenia. I suspect that the Darrell in your materials is another personality and possibly a dangerous one at that. Also, it is not unusual, when these conditions exist, for one personality to be totally unknown to one-another.*
>
> *David may not be aware of the presence of Darrell. and therefore may have time spans in which he has no recollection or recall of actions or events. Please keep in mind that this is all an educated guess and a full evaluation would have to be completed before any attorney worth his salt would admit it into evidence at a trial. By the way, you owe me one. Take care, Janette.*

Randy re-read the evaluation. Janette was right about one thing. The presence of another personality or alter-ego or whatever it was called would fit David's complaint that he didn't remember where he was or what had happened. If the person out side the shed was David, as he suspected, then it was the personality of Darrell that he heard giggle. And the personality that he and Bailey had arrested at the Dunsmore place was "Darrell" until sometime after they put him in the squad car.

Randy reached for the report that Jerry had produced on the confrontation at the Wilkes home. Reading through it, he could believe that the idea of two personalities fit the dialogue that Jerry had recorded in his notes. He punched a button on his console. "Dispatch here," said Clara

"Clara, what is Officer Bailey's location?"

"He's running a radar check on Sixth Street at the high school."

"Have him stop by the office as soon as he is finished there. Tell him it is important, but not an emergency."

"Will do, Sheriff, is that all?"

"Yes, thanks, Clara."

"Anytime, dispatch out."

The Sheriff was still going through the files on his desk when Bailey tapped on the open doorway. "Yeah, Jerry, come in. I need to pick your brain for some insight into an idea I have about the confrontation you responded to at the Wilkes place."

"Pick away, you won't find much there. I was lost most of the time. A lot of what was said didn't make much sense to me."

"Well, that's just what I'm trying to do, is to make some sort of sense out of it."

"Okay, what do you need from me?"

"Let's close the door and I want this to stay just between us for the present, okay?"

The officer closed the door and turned to the Sheriff, looking a bit puzzled. "Okay."

Randy first asked Bailey to read Janette's report. After they discussed its implications, Randy explained to Jerry what he wanted from him.

"I want to read parts of your report and I need you to assume that there are two thirteen-year-old boys in that room. One is David and one is Darrell. Get the picture?"

Randy and Jerry played out the scene at the Wilkes. When they were finished, Jerry had an amazed look on his face. "I believe you've got some of your questions answered. At least to the extent of who knows the answers."

"Now the big question. Where do we go with this and who do we talk to for the answers. The parents, their attorney, or David-Darrell?"

CHAPTER 53
DAVID AND DARRELL

David came straight home, after school, like his mother, his father, the Sheriff, practically everyone, had told him to. He sat at the kitchen table re-reading the note his father had left for him.

> David-The appointment we had with the Sheriff for after school has been canceled.
> I suggest that you stay home until your mother or I get there.
> Dad.

He wadded up the note and threw it towards the wastebasket, missing badly. He left it lying on the floor and opened the refrigerator door. He found some leftover pizza and tossed it in the microwave, punching some numbers on the keypad. In a few seconds it dinged and he removed the warm slices and consumed them in a few bites. As his mind wandered back over the night before, he became angry. *I bet that sheriff and his deputy thinks I'm a dumb kid, not being able to remember what he had done after school. And that talk about a shed, what was that all about? And the dumb questions that the high school guidance counselor asked this morning. And now an e-mail from Jonie wanting to know what was going on and why I was acting so strange.*

As David agonized over his frustrations and the belief that people thought he was a dumb kid. The pent-up emotion caused him to tense, adding to the stress he was already under. Slowly his physical features changed. His face hardened, his mouth turned into a scowl and his voice deepened and developed a harsh tone. David didn't know it but he was no longer in control, Darrell now controlled his body.

David, you weak dummy, you'll never learn will you? You got to take control. When things get tough, you got to get tougher. Now the first thing we're going to do is fly the coop. We got to get out of here and go places.

David, now Darrell, exited the kitchen by way of the porch door. He grabbed the big fishing hat and headed for the river. Soon he was in the boat and headed down stream. He passed the Dunsmore bridge. *Maybe I'll cone back and finish the job there.* Darrell had not started the motor on the boat, letting the current of the river carry it. He spotted a familiar tree, and using a small oar, guided the boat to the tree, where he stepped out on some flat rocks, and quickly tied up the boat. He climbed the bank of the river and headed into the woods. Darrell knew exactly where he was going, having been there many times before, but he was shocked by what he found. *Someone's been here and torn the latch off the door. Look at all these foot prints, somebody's walked around and around the shed, and look here, inside too. What were they doing? Taking pictures? Hey, I bet that's right, They were taking pictures. Who? Well duh, the sheriff, that's who. He came back to get the padlock and take pictures. He's collecting evidence. Well, we'll see about that.*

The thirteen-year-old hurried back to the boat. He unhooked the gas container from the motor, and grabbed a metal box from the knapsack David always carried in the boat. He hurried back to the shed. Sprinkling some gas along the bottom of the old boards, he popped open the metal box and retrieved a book of matches. Carefully he lit the gas which flashed into a fire. He jumped back, picked up the gas can and backed up to admire his work. *Now let's see the sheriff's evidence.*

As the fire grew, the boy giggled. When the fire tore though the roof of the shed, the flames licked at the nearby branches of the Maple and Persimmon trees. Fortunately, the trees were nearly bare of leaves and only singed by the flames.

Darrell now content, his anger gone, relaxed. It seemed as if the fire burned away all the stress he felt. The boy stood, perplexed staring at the dying flames of what looked to be the remains of a wooden shed. In his hands he held a gas can, and the waterproof match box he always carried in the boat. He stood confused, *he didn't understand what had just happened. Had he burned the shed? Why? Would he have to make up another story?*

David stood and tears ran down his cheeks.

CHAPTER 54
SHERIFF SIMMONS

Nancy and the sheriff spent the following morning organizing reports to be turned over to the county attorney. There were two interviews with Heather Wilkes. One took place after she was brought in with Ralph Kellam. The other, with Jonie Kellam present, was about who the voice at the shed might be.

Also he scanned Deputy Bailey's report taken at the Wilkes home with the interrogation of David. In addition he included Mrs. Deprey's notes, but not the letter from Janette.

"I don't want to violate her trust in this office. She labeled it for my eyes only and that's the way it will stay. If the county attorney wants an evaluation, she knows how to go about getting one," he explained to Nancy, who was standing in the doorway waiting for the file. "I think we will add my report on the visit I made to the Dunsmore place and the incident at the shed, plus what I learned of the trail along Willow Creek."

And finally, they added his report of the second visit to the Dunsmore place, and Officer Bailey's statement, on the apprehension of David. As an afterthought he also inserted a selection of Officer Bailey's pictures of the shed.

Nancy typed up a cover page identifying each of the documents in the order of their occurrence, addressed the packet to the county attorney, and delivered it back to the sheriff. "I believe it is ready to go.

Oh, and I put an asterisk at the bottom of the cover page, that we are still waiting for an identification on the padlock."

"Thanks Nancy, I'll deliver this personally." Randy said. Delivering the packet was not a problem. It meant walking down the long hall that separated the judicial and law enforcement wing from the rest of the office area. Then down a flight of stairs to the basement office of County Attorney Beth Bushman.

When he entered the small outer office area, Beth was visiting with a co-worker. He caught her eye and she came to him.

"Beth, why did they move you over here? The County Attorney's Office used to be in the enforcement wing close to the Sheriff's Office."

"You might ask your predecessor, Mike Smith, that question."

"Why? What happened?"

"Let's just say we didn't see eye to eye on a couple of things. First, I am a woman, he didn't like the idea of equality, and second, he expected the county attorney to be subservient to the sheriff's office. So I asked to locate here. This office was vacant and the distance separated the two areas of law enforcement."

"I get the picture." Randy handed her the packet. "Here's some reading for your evaluation. I need to know what your office thinks about this. Is it a case, or not?"

"Who's involved?"

"It's a juvenile case."

"Judge Ruth Tindle's court. It'll have to be tight."

"Any suggestions you can make would be appreciated."

"I'll give you a call."

*   *   *

Later that day, Randy spent several hours pouring over the information they had collected on the girl in the woods. Stacked in front of him were several piles of paper. First was the report he had written up on the discovery of the body, another group was from the medical examiner and the autopsy report. There was a thick file on Ralph Kellam and a smaller file on Bobby Dunsmore. It was not a surprise to Randy that Sheriff Smith did not bother to write a report on his investigation of the crime scene. The sheriff wasn't big on paper work. Especially if it meant using a computer.

After reading through the material, Randy decided to do what Ralph had done and take another look at the crime scene, then he could write up another report so he had something official to match Ralph's report.

"I'm going to take a run out to Lake Lawson," he told Clara. "I'll do a radio check before I leave."

When he got in his cruiser, he keyed the mike. "Dispatch, four here,"

"Dispatch, go ahead four, Clara's voice came from the speaker.

"Radio check" he said.

Once he got to his destination, he notified Clara. "I'm at Cheyenne Cove Campground now, I'll be off air for an hour or so. Reach me on the cell if need be. 10-4?"

"10-4, dispatch out."

Sheriff Simmons worked his way to the footbridge and along the trail leading to the dead girl's grave site. When he went to leave the trail and cut across the woods he had some difficulty orienting himself until he noticed the rock pile that Ralph had constructed to mark the location. "Amazing how everything looks the same, in the woods, unless you know what to look for," he mumbled to himself. As soon as he hit the top of the ravine, he could see the other pile of rocks Ralph had placed near the grave when he first discovered the girl's body. As he approached the spot, something in the back of his mind started gnawing at him. He shook the feeling off and began examining the area. Finding nothing out of the ordinary, he scanned the horizon. As he did, the feeling which was chewing on him returned. From his position in the ravine every direction he looked was uphill. "This spot was well selected," he said aloud, "someone knew what they were looking for."

About to leave, Randy's eye caught the sight of a bush. It was missing a large section. Looking a little closer, he could tell that a portion of the bush had been broken off. *I wonder?* Searching the area he found what he looked for, the missing section of the bush. *Do you suppose that this was used to wipe out footprints by the person responsible for the girl's burial?* The gnawing intensified. *What's here that I am not seeing? Why do I have this feeling that I'm missing something?*

Disparagingly, Randy shook his head but the feeling remained. He took one last look around and left the burial scene, retracing his route back to the car.

When he reached the trail leading away from the lake, he decided to follow it northward. As the Dunsmore bridge came into sight, Randy checked the time and determined that Ralph had been correct in his belief that the grave site and the Dunsmore place was within easy reach of each other. *How the girl was transported to the site without attracting attention is an important part of the puzzle. And I still have no motive for either Ralph Kellam or Bobby Dunsmore. But then, where murder is concerned, I may not have a motive until I know who the murderer is.* Randy turned and followed the trail back to the campground.

CHAPTER 55

THE MOTIVE

A figure moved through the darkness with the stealth of a leopard. Quietly and without wasted motion. It remained in the shadows of the house as it stopped at a window and peered inside. After a brief minute, the cameo-clad figure moved to a side door and tried the latch.

One could almost hear the response," locked. I may have to check this out more often, they usually don't lock this door. Maybe one of them is getting smarter." The figure moved to a larger window with a bright light protruding from its transparent opening. *There she is,* the figure almost said out loud, *what are you studying, woman? You act like you know it all when you issue a decision, now we find out you have to study. I wonder where the young one is this time of night. Is she not home? And it's a school night too.*

The lady was sitting on a couch with papers scattered across it. She was dressed in a heavy white terrycloth robe and wore pink slippers on her feet. On the coffee table in front of her was an open brief case and a laptop computer straddled the case. A book lay in her lap as she held sheets of paper in her hands. Several sheets had slid to the floor as she dozed.

The figure outside moved to the door and turned the knob. It turned the full distance, and with a slight push the door freed itself from the latch. Leaving the door ajar, the intruder paused to listen. Suddenly a slight breeze moved through the house, and caught the door as it stood ajar. SNAP—The noise wasn't very loud but it was sharp and echoed through the house.

The lady on the couch jerked awake at the sound. "What . . . Who's there? Sarah, that you?" She could not see the door from where she sat but did not move from the couch The figure inside the door quickly opened the door and slipped outside, closing the door behind it.

When the woman heard the door close she stood abruptly, dumping the book on the floor and grabbed a poker from the fireplace. "Who's there?" she called out.

When no one answered she cautiously stepped to where she could see the door. There was no one there. Quietly, the door began to open and the woman grasped the weapon with both hands and prepared to strike. "Sarah! You about got walloped with a poker, did you see who opened the door about five minutes ago?"

"I saw someone walking down the sidewalk, but I couldn't see who it was. Looked like a man, but I didn't pay much attention. Why?"

Janis Martindale shook her head. "Never mind, I was just curious. Thought I heard a noise. Did you get what you needed at the library?"

"Yes, and now I'm off to bed. Goodnight."

"Night, Sweetie."

The judge locked the door then went to the couch to clean up her mess. As she passed them, she pulled the curtains across the big window. Janis raked all the papers into the briefcase, picked up the large law book and re-checked the locks on the windows and doors.

*   *   *

The intruder tried to give the impression of someone out for an evening stroll. After slowly walking half a block before entering a walkway leading to the front door of a home, he disappeared momentarily then stood in the shadows of a large oak tree.

His thoughts were on the car that pulled to a stop in front of the judge's house, *the one that that kid Sarah got out of, I think I recognized it. Del Kellam's wife drives a car just like that, what kind of connection could there be between the judge and Mrs. Kellam? Maybe I need to check this out.*

The figure moved through the adjoining lawns and made the way around to the back of Judge Martindale's house. He tested the back door. *Locked. How about the windows? Also locked. I could break in but I think I know a better way. I've got time to pick my spot. I have to teach the judge that I mean what I say.*

Just like that Atwood brat. Her father tried to threaten me. I promised him that if he ratted me out it would cost him his first born and he did and it did. When will these people learn that they can't win in a game of; "I'm a bigger threat than you" It's time to discover the missing shoe laces. It's circumstantial but good enough for the judge to allow as evidence. The shoe at the Dunsmore place will fit also. Two shoe laces and one guilty verdict. But the judge still needs a reminder of who is in charge. The figure glided toward the shed behind the house and from a jacket pocket pulled out a squeeze bottle. The arsonist flipped off the cap, and squeezed the contents onto the corner of the shed, and struck a match. In seconds the shed was ablaze, and the arsonist was gone.

An hour later the cameo-clad typist sat at his typewriter drafting a letter to Officer Bailey of the Woodrow County Sheriff's Department.

> *Dear Sir:*
>
> *It would benifit your department to search the trunk of Mrs. Delbert Kellam. You will find a match to evidence found at the Dunsmore place. That evidence was planted by Ralph Kellam. I know because he told me so. I am a law-abiding citizen who wants to help.*

As the paper was pulled from the typewriter, a police scanner setting on a shelf behind the typist locked on to a call to the fire station in Robertown. "We have a utility shed out back that is on fire, hurry before it catches the house on fire." The typist grinned as he recognized the frantic voice of Judge Martindale.

CHAPTER 56
FORMER SHERIFF SMITH

The clock on the night stand read 5:59 am and Mike Smith was still in bed. The calendar on the desk beside the clock read January 30 The hearing with Lynn Bower the state attorney general was set to begin today in Topeka at 10 o'clock. It was a two hour drive, and he had a problem. His driver's license had expired last month during the time he was battling the flu. He needed some one to drive him. "Briiinnnngggg" Mike bolted upright in the bed. The alarm sounded as the clock flipped the numbers to 6:00. Mike's head fell back on the pillow, and he closed his eyes, within seconds he dozed but a minute later, "Briiinnnngggg," the alarm sounded again. Now wide awake, Mike rolled over the edge of the bed and let his feet touch the floor. He felt the stubble on his chin, it wasn't too bad and he didn't feel like shaving. Later, dressed, he dialed the number of a retired member of the sheriff's department. "Bob! How are you? Fine I hope? Good, good, say Bob, how would you like to make fifty bucks plus mileage today? That's right, all you need do is drive me to Topeka this morning. Yeah, that's it. You will? That's great, we need to leave as soon as possible, can you be here in ten minutes? Great!"

Bob Williams had little difficulty finding the Landon building. but parking was at a premium and it took several turns around the block before they found a slot. "I'll come in for a while," Bob said, "see what is going on." The pair rode the elevator to the second floor and found room two-twelve. Taking a deep breath, former Sheriff Smith lead the way into the court room, There were less than five people in the room. It wasn't difficult to identify them. A judge sat at the bench. Two men were sitting at the prosecution table and unlike himself they were dressed in suit and tie.

Another man sat at the defense table, he looked like a kid to Mike. He stepped forward. "Hello Mr. Schmidt. Last week you contacted the public defenders office, and they called me. I'm Jeff Cramden, a local attorney, I'll be representing you, Mr. Schmidt."

"It's Smith, the name is Smith," Mike said, as he glared at the young man.

The man at the bench slammed down a book. "Order, let's have some order. I am John Tait, retired from the fourteenth judicial district. Now we are meeting in a court room, but this is a hearing, not a trial. This hearing is to determine if enough evidence exists to bring charges against a duly elected public officer, one Michael Smith, Sheriff of Woodrow County. Mr. Peterson, the prosecution may begin." Mike was dumbfounded, he had a lawyer who didn't even know his name, and hadn't been given a chance to visit with the man.

Peterson outlined all the reports prepared by Randy Simmons, and gave a summary of the charges against Mike. At the end of his delivery, Peterson said, "It is clear that this is a man who has allowed the power of his office to dominate his actions. Mr. Smith has ridden roughshod over the rights of the citizens of Woodrow County. All we ask is to be given a chance in a public court to show the despotism of the man."

John Tait called on Jeff Cramden to present the defendants case. Cramden explained to the judge his lack of time to prepare for the hearing.

"Now, Jeff, your client had as long as the prosecution had. This hearing has been set for months. Your client chose to wait until the late hours to request a public defender. His choice. You go right ahead and present your case. Let's get on with it." Tait glanced at his wristwatch.

Cramden fumbled with a sheath of papers on the table, then motioning to Mike Smith, identified his client. "This is Sheriff Smith, he has been Sheriff of Woodrow County for twenty-eight years, and in all that time, has never had so much as a patrons' complaint filed against him. He has an impeccable record. Now, there is this barrage of charges, all filed by the same person. This is obviously an act of vengeance and an attempt to discredit him. And for what purpose? The charges are contrived by an inferior officer to gain Sheriff Smith's position in Woodrow County. Deputy Simmons knows he can't win an election to the office so he fabricates charges against Sheriff Smith. We have affidavits here to show Sheriff Smith's true record and the respect that his constituents have for him. I would like to submit them to you along with a request that Sheriff Smith be excused from all charges."

"Mr. Peterson?" said Judge Tait.

"Judge Tait, we have testimony from Fred Newman and Jesse Jennings, both former citizens of Woodrow County. Their testimony contradicts what Mr. Cramden just presented." Mr. Peterson held up a folder as he spoke.

Jeff Cramden jumped to his feet. "Your Honor, both of these men are formerly of Woodrow County because they are currently serving time in Hutchinson,. They are criminals, taken off the public streets by Sheriff Smith, I might add."

"We also have testimony from a sitting judge that . . ." Peterson started to respond.

"A judge that is under question herself, you might add," said Cramden.

Retired Judge John Tait motioned for both men to sit down. "I think we have the picture. Both of you file all your affidavits and whatever else you have, and we are done. The Kansas Attorney General's office will notify all parties of the results of our deliberation. This hearing is adjourned."

Later, Bob had stopped at an Arby's in south Topeka,. Mike Smith was livid. "Why did I even bother to go?" He roared for the third time. The waitress quickly plunked the tray of sandwiches and fries down on the table and scurried away.

"Mike its been over half an hour since the judge dismissed the hearing. You need to calm down." Bob said, as he reached for a giant roast beef sandwich.

"I could have been in Tim-buck-too, and it wouldn't have made any difference," Mike grumbled.

Bob sat across from him at the little table, sipping on a straw from a large Dr. Pepper. He didn't respond to Mike's question, except to shrug his shoulders and take a huge bite of the sandwich and another sip.

"Let's get out of here and go home. I need a drink and no more of this Dr. Pepper, I need a real drink. Something that will dull the pain." He shoved the soft drink container away, grabbed the remaining sandwich and headed for the door.

"Wait a min . . ." Bob started to object, then grabbed a mouthful of fries and with a sandwich in one hand and a drink in the other, hurried after his irate passenger.

It was later that evening when he awoke from the alcohol-induced sleep that had resulted from the session he had with a bottle of Jim Beam after arriving home. He sat on the edge of the bed. Holding his head as if a grenade ready to explode at the slightest noise. "Somebody is going to pay for this and it's not going to be me, he vowed, I will see to that. I will not take this lying down, but someone's going down. I can promise that."

"Snuffy" Smith groaned and carefully lowered his throbbing head back on the pillow. He soon was snoring loudly.

CHAPTER 57
THE BREAK-IN

J udge Janis Martindale had been a member of the order of the Eastern Star for the past twenty years and had never missed a meeting in all that time. Tonight was no exception and Sarah was left to fend for herself as far as dinner was concerned. She opted for heating a chicken patty and fixing herself a small salad and adding the cut-up chicken. After eating Sarah needed to go to the library and finish her research for a paper in Social Problems Class. She had learned of a flu out break during the winter of 1918 and was trying to find information on its effects in Robertown.

At five forty-five Judge Martindale left for her meeting and Sarah left for the library at six thirty. It was a fifteen minute walk for Sarah and the teen would have almost two hours to work before the library closed at nine. Her aunt's meeting would be over at nine and was to pick Sarah up shortly after nine in front of the library.

A man dressed in a camouflage shirt and matching pants, exited Red's Place, a bar on twelfth street. It was shortly after eight-fifteen that same evening. He walked down the alley to the back yard of Judge Martindale's house. The house was dark and appeared empty. After slipping on a pair of latex gloves he tried several windows before he found a side door on the garage unlocked and entered the house through a second door leading into a utility room. He knew from previous visits that there were no pets in the home save an aquarium in a rec room off the dining area.

Besides the front foyer, the house also had a living room and a kitchen on the ground floor. Stairs led to the basement from the kitchen and to the second floor from a short hallway just off the dinning room. The upstairs consisted of a master bedroom with an office workroom off to one side of a hallway. There were two other bedrooms each with its own bathroom. From the clothing in the closets he could tell that Sarah had the use of both of the smaller bedrooms and their closets while the Judge slept in the master bedroom. He quickly went to work, first in the master bedroom, and then in the other two. When he finished the man went back downstairs to the kitchen where he completed his work. *This is going to be just a warning visit, Judge, if you don't listen, then I'll be back. But if I have to come back, I'll make it worth my time.* The intruder quietly exited the house by the kitchen's patio doors , making sure that he left them unlocked. His exit route took him past the torched shed. He smiled and disappeared down the alley.

It was shortly after nine fifteen when Janis Martindale and Sarah Muncie arrived at their home. "Why don't you put on a pot of water and we'll have a cup of tea before bed?" said Janis. "I'm going to change into more comfortable clothes." Sarah nodded and headed for the kitchen. There she picked up a pan from the stove top and going to the sink, emptied the dab of water from the pan and refilled it with fresh. Putting it on the stove, she turned the knob to heat the water. When she opened the cupboard to get a couple of tea cups, she found the cupboard full of pots and pans. She was puzzled, but before she could question what had happened, her aunt yelled from the top of the stairs, "Sarah, will you come up here now, and I mean now!" Sarah turned off the stove and went bounding up the stairs.

When she entered her aunt's bedroom, her mouth dropped and her eyes widened. She rapidly took in the disarray of the room. The bed covers had been ripped from the bed and shewn about the room. Almost every drawer in her aunt's dresser had been pulled out and dumped. Jewelry was scattered across the room and bed. Clothes from the closet were piled in a heap on top of a vanity, and lipstick scrawled across the mirror.

"What happened here?" she said.

"I was about to ask you the same thing. What do you know about this?"

"Me? You think I did this? Aunt Janis, you don't really believe . . ."

"No, of course not. I was just letting off steam, dear. But you and I are the only ones who . . ."

"Auntie, somebody must have broke in! They could still be . . ." Sarah threw herself into the arms of her aunt. Judge Martindale separated herself from Sarah and moved to where the telephone lay on the floor. She checked and found a dial tone. She dialed 911.

Officer Bailey of the Woodrow County Sheriff's Office was the first to respond. Upon learning that the intruder could still be in the vicinity, he called for backup and Clara McReynolds responded. Placing the judge and Sarah under the protection of Clara, he proceeded to clear the area. After searching the house and grounds and finding no one, he returned to the kitchen where Clara had established herself and her charges.

"The bedrooms upstairs have been ransacked, and the kitchen has been re-arranged as Sarah has already found out. I also found a side door of the garage open and the patio doors here in the kitchen are unlocked. Did you find anything missing Judge?"

"I don't think so. My jewelery was strewn about the room, but I think it is all there."

"Well," said officer Bailey, "somebody wanted your attention. You send anyone to jail lately?"

"A few," Judge Martindale answered.

"Make out a list of people you might have ticked off in the past week or so, and we'll check them out."

"Thanks for your concern."

"I'll leave Clara in a car out front for a while just in case someone comes nosing about."

Bailey nodded at Clara and she beamed at being placed in charge of something besides the dispatch board.

Jerry Bailey returned to the sheriff's office to write up an incident report for the record and for the Sheriff. Then he returned to patrol. As he passed Judge Martindale's house, he waved to Clara. They saw each other but failed to notice a shadow standing at the edge of a neighboring house, watching the exchange. "Fools." the shadow muttered.

It was after midnight when the cameo-clad typist sat down to his typewriter.

Dear Judge

You've had a hard time getting your house back in order haven't you? It would be to your benifit to heed the warning and not get involved in things that you shouldn't. Sarah seems like such a nice girl, too. It would be such a shame if____

CHAPTER 58
DAVID'S HEARING
MORNING SESSION

The Juvenile Court was held in a courtroom at the end of the third floor hallway. It was equipped with several private entrances or exits for the protection of the identity of both witnesses and those underage being charged with a violation of the law. Judge Ruth Tindle held juvenile court in Robertown on Thursday of every week provided there were cases on the docket. Usually there were no shortages of cases and today was no exception. As usual there were no juries. The judge heard the case and ruled for the court.

The first case on the docket was David Masters, brought by the Woodrow County Attorney's Office, with Beth Bushman representing Woodrow County. Jake Giles, Attorney, represented David Masters.

David entered the courtroom by way of a side door. He was neatly dressed, with a proper haircut and escorted by a bailiff without any form of shackles. He glanced quickly around the room for his parents, who were seated in the first row behind the table where he now stood. Jake Giles stood a few feet away talking to a woman in a pantsuit. The woman was Beth Bushman, as David later learned. Besides the court reporter, they were the only people in the room.

"All rise," the bailiff called out in a loud clear voice. A lady in a black robe came in through a door behind the judge's bench.

Everyone stood so David did also., "Okay, everyone take your place, and be seated."

Judge Tindle had taken over the courtroom. David sat and took a look at the Judge. She appeared to be an older person much like his grandmother Masters., except for the short cropped hair and dark rimmed glasses. Of course, his grandmother weighed a lot more. Judge Tindle looked slim and trim like she worked out,

"Baliff, are we ready to proceed?" she asked.

"Ready your honor," the bailiff answered.

"Ms Bushman, you may begin."

"Thank you, your honor," Beth hesitated, took a deep breath and then continued, "Your honor, Smith county has testimony showing that David Masters, a thirteen-year-old did willfully detain another human being by locking her up in a shed in the woods. Furthermore, we will present evidence of window peeking and malicious threats by David Masters. We believe David to be a danger not only to himself, but to those around him."

Beth decided not to go into the evidence since there was no jury to inform, only the judge. "Thank you, your honor."

"Short and to the point, I like that, Ms Bushman, perhaps Mr. Giles can do the same. Mr. Giles?"

Jake rose. "Thank you, your honor, I certainly can. Nonsense, pure nonsense, the county has nothing but circumstantial hearsay to defend its actions. This is nothing but a contrived attempt to display the authority of both the County Sheriff's Office and the County Attorney's Office, without regard to the individual rights of its citizens." Jake stood behind David and placed a hand on David's shoulder. David brushed it off. An act that didn't go unnoticed by the judge.

"Ms Bushman, you may call your first witness," said the judge.

"I call Mrs. Terri Deprey to the stand."

The bailiff walked to a side door and allowed a pretty blonde woman to enter the courtroom. He motioned for her to take the witness stand.

Judge Tindle said. "You have previously been sworn, you are under oath." The woman nodded.

"Ms Bushman, you may continue."

"Thank you, your honor. Mrs. Deprey, you are the guidance counselor at Robertown High School?"

"Yes I am, for twelve years now."

"You interviewed David Masters?"

"Yes, I did, at the request of his mother."

"And what was your conclusion?"

"Objection," Mr. Giles jumped to his feet. "No foundation."

"That's what I am trying to establish, Your Honor," Beth responded.

"Let's give it time, Mr. Giles, give it time. Overruled."

"Your conclusion, Mrs. Deprey?"

"Objection."

"Now what, Mr. Giles?" the judge asked.

"Are we to treat this witness as an expert? Or a casual observer? We have no credentials."

"Ms Bushman?" said the judge.

Beth turned to Terri. "Will you tell the counselor your credentials? Mrs. Deprey?"

"I am certified by the state of Kansas as a guidance counselor in secondary education. I have a bachelors degree from Baker University and a masters degree from Emporia State University."

"Sounds good enough for me at this juncture of the hearing. What about you, Mr. Giles?" The judge stared down at the attorney with a stern expression.

"I reserve the right to challenge at a later time, Your Honor."

"Granted Mr. Giles. You may continue, Ms Bushman."

"Your conclusion, Mrs. Deprey?"

"I found David to be a very disturbed boy who has difficulty with his own identity. He may be somewhat schizophrenic."

"To what degree?"

"He could have an alter-ego complex."

"What do you base this on, Mrs. Deprey?"

"At one point during our session together his personality changed completely and he referred to himself by the name of Darrell. When I asked who Darrell was he became belligerent and destroyed the recording devise I was using by throwing it to the floor. I immediately ceased the interview."

"Did you feel for your personal safety?"

"Yes."

"Thank you, Mrs. Deprey." Beth glanced at Jake Giles, and said, "Your witness."

"Mrs. Deprey, how many cases of schizophrenia have you worked with in your twelve years?"

"Probably more than I know."

"How many documented cases, Mrs. Deprey?"

"Documented? Probably none."

"So you have no background in working with cases of schizophrenia, your not even sure you could recognize the condition, isn't that correct?" Not waiting for an answer, he said, "nothing further."

"Redirect, your honor?"

"If it is short, Ms Bushman."

"Yes, your honor. Mrs. Deprey, in your studies are you trained to recognize abnormalities in children?"

"Yes."

"Thank you. That's all your honor. I would like to call Mrs. Janette Freedrock to the stand."

Again the bailiff opened a side door and a tall, trim brunette, about forty years of age walked in and took the witness stand. She had an air of confidence about her that was re-enforced by the power of her voice. The judge reminded her that she was under oath.

"Mrs. Freedrock, what position do you hold with the state of Kansas?"

"I am a case worker with the Kansas State Board of Mental Health. I work out of Topeka. I am certified by the United States Department of Health and Human Affairs. I have been with the Kansas Board for seven years. Before that I was with the Board of Health in Indiana for three years." Beth turned to look at Mr. Giles, who apparently was ignoring the proceedings.

"Now, Mrs. Freedrock, have you had a chance to examine Mrs. Deprey's taped recording of her interview with David?"

"Yes, I have."

"What did you conclude?"

"Objection!"

"On what grounds, Mr. Giles?" the judge asked.

"Hearsay."

"It's written testimony, Mr. Giles, how can it be hearsay?"

"It was taken from a recording that Mrs. Freedrock was not privy to."

"You have a point, objection sustained."

"Mrs. Freedrock, did you later receive a copy of the tape recording from the Woodrow County Sheriff's office for your perusal?"

"Yes, I did."

"What did you conclude?"

Janette Freedrock went on to explain the circumstances much the same as Terri had done in her report. When Beth finished, she turned the witness over to Jake, who accepted her with the question, "Did you at anytime interview David yourself?"

"Yes, I did."

"When was that?"

"About a week ago."

"After you had read Mrs. Deprey's statement?"

"Yes."

"Move to strike, Your Honor, there is no way what she read could not have affected what she observed."

"I think Mrs. Freedrock is capable of drawing her own conclusions without being influenced by someone else. Overruled. Are we done with this witness?" When no one answered, the judge nodded to Beth to call her next witness.

"I call Randal Simmons."

Randy's testimony was straight forward and without much room for challenge as he stayed strictly with facts and direct quotes. What little editorializing he did in his reports was based on actual statements.

He described the episode of his being locked in the shed, which resulted in a charge of obstruction of justice, and the resulting interview with David concerning the shed and about the breaking and entering charges which were later dropped. This led to the window peeking charge. "The evidence we have is the boy himself. He was apprehended outside the home of Heather Wilkes, and his identification by Mrs. Wilkes as the face she saw through the window of the house."

"How does this tie in to the kidnapping, or detaining charge?" Beth asked.

"That's when Heather recognized the voice she heard while being held in the shed I spoke of earlier."

"And whose voice was it?"

Before Randy could answer, Jake Gills jumped up. "Objection, your honor. Hearsay."

"Sustained"

"Did you question David about the shed?"

"Yes."

"What did you learn from the discussion?"

"That he said his name was Darrell and he protected David."

"Objection, Your Honor, order to strike."

Sustained, you know better than that, Ms Bushman." the judge admonished her sternly.

"Sorry your honor. Anything else, Sheriff?"

"Just that we finally got a report on the lock I took off the shed, it was sold at Hometown Lumber. Lock number 137433 sold for cash on October 27th of this last year. It was a local sale."

"Your honor, are we talking about something that has not been entered as evidence? If so, I move to strike," Jake said. He was only too glad to get Randy Simmons off the stand but he couldn't let the lock be connected to his client.

"So ordered," the judge said. "That will be enough for this morning. We will re-convene at 2: o'clock. Court in recess."

As the Judge finished speaking, she stood and tapped her gavel lightly. While the bailiff called "all rise" she disappeared through a door behind the bench. David was led out of the court room. There was no expression on his face. He did not look up at his parents, nor at his lawyer.

CHAPTER 59
DAVID'S HEARING
AFTERNOON SESSION

Promptly at two o'clock, the bailiff called, "All rise" Judge Tindle entered, reached the bench and took over the court room.

"Everybody in their places and ready bailiff?" she asked.

"Yes, Your Honor," he answered.

"Very well, you may continue, Ms Bushman."

"I call Mr. Evin Wilkes."

The bailiff stepped to a side door and Heather's dad entered. "Mr. Wilkes, you are under oath," reminded the judge. He nodded.

"Now, Mr. Wilkes, would you relate the events on the evening in question?"

"It was a December night, after dark, when I noticed this boy standing outside the window of the front of our house. I went out, grabbed him by the coat collar and marched him into the house. I sat him down in the kitchen at the table. I asked him what he thought he was doing looking in the window. He said he . . ."

"Objection, hearsay," said Giles.

"Sustained, just tell us what you saw, not what you heard, Mr. Wilkes," the judge said.

"Then that's it. That's what I saw."

"Your witness, Mr. Giles," said Beth. As Giles stood he started to approach the witness then stopped and suddenly announced to the court. "No questions."

"I call Heather Wilkes," said Beth. Once more the bailiff did his magic at one of the side doors and Heather appeared, small, alone and frightened. The judge reminded her "you are under oath." Heather walked nervously to the witness stand. She looked like a doll sitting in a big chair.

"Heather, can you tell us about your experience while you were locked up in the shed in the woods?" asked Beth.

Even after the bailiff adjusted the microphone closer to her face, Heather could barely be heard. With a little prompting, Heather was able to tell her story about the voice and about her escape. "I woke up and there was Ralph Kellam. He brought me back to town. We were on the way home when we were stopped by the police and they put Ralph in handcuffs and we went to jail. Later I went home, I think they kept Ralph, they didn't know that he was just trying to help me get away. I was afraid that the 'voice' would find me."

"Did you ever hear the voice again?"

"Yes, I heard it at my house. It was David, he sounded like the 'voice' when he said he was Darrell."

"Your witness, Mr. Giles," Beth said.

"You said 'he sounded like the 'voice' didn't you, Miss Wilkes?"

"Yes."

"Not it was the voice but, 'it sounded like the voice,' right?"

"Yes"

"So it sounded like the voice, the voice wasn't David?" Jake Giles said.

"Yes," said Heather then she added, "the voice was Darrell."

"Move to strike that last comment, your honor," Jake tried in an effort to correct his mistake.

"You asked the question, so you have to live with the answer," replied the judge.

When it was determined there were no other questions, Heather was excused.

"I would like to recall Janette Freedrock, Your Honor," said Beth. The judge nodded to the bailiff.

When Janette was situated on the witness stand, Beth asked, "Do you believe that David has an alter-ego?"

"I believe that Darrell is David's alter-ego and is the stronger of the two."

"What is the relationship between David and Darrell?"

"There is the possibility they are not aware of each other, but if they do know of each other, they certainly do not interact with each other. If they know of each other, they almost surely do not like what they see in the other personality. That's the whole reason for having an alter-ego in the first place. But Darrell, being the stronger, may try to protect David the weaker. It is difficult to say to what degree he may go to provide such protection."

"What would it take to find that out?"

"If we could talk to Darrell . . ."

"Objection! No foundation has been established that Darrell even exists."

"Objection sustained. You finished Ms Bushman?"

"The county rests, Your Honor."

"Mr. Giles, you wish to call any witnesses?"

"I would like to call Jonie Kellam." David jerked alert, he looked at his lawyer. Noticing, Jake whispered, "stay calm."

Jonie appeared and the judge did her thing. Jake asked Jonie a simple question, "Miss Kellam, You are probably David Masters best friend, aren't you?"

"Yes, I suppose so."

"You spend a lot of time together, right?"

"That's true."

"Miss Kellam, have you ever seen David Masters harm another person?"

Jonie thought about the question. She knew what the lawyer wanted her to say but she also knew that her answer wouldn't be the whole story. Then she remembered something her father had told her brother. Her father had said, "Knowing something and proving it in a court of law is two different things." Jonie knew the answer to Mr. Giles's question. "No," she said.

"Thank you, that's all, Miss Bushman?"

"Jonie, have you ever seen David threaten someone else?" Beth asked.

"Objection, not covered in direct testimony," said Jake.

"You opened the door, when you asked about harm, Mr. Giles, she has the legal right to follow you in that door. Please answer the question, Miss Kellam."

"Yes, I have."

"And who was that?"

"He threatened Bobby Dunsmore, when Bobby was bothering us."

"Can you remember what he said to Bobby?"

Jonie didn't want to rat out on her friend, but she was under oath to tell the truth. "He said he would give him some of his own medicine."

"Thank you."

"You're excused. Anything else, Mr. Giles?"

Jake shook his head. "No, Your Honor."

"I'll make my ruling next Thursday, 10 o' clock, until then, David, I will release you to your parents and you are confined to your home, understood? Your parents can arrange for you to be home schooled." Then with an "all rise" she was gone.

CHAPTER 60
SHERIFF SIMMONS

At ten o'clock on Friday morning Sheriff Simmons sat at his desk in the quiet of a cold blistery day. The mild weather Robertown had experienced for the early months of winter came to an end. Snow flakes swirled around the windows and a cold wind seemed to be blowing from all directions. Randy decided it was a good day to get some of the paper work completed that had been piling up on him. He had spent the previous hour and a half visiting with Beth Bushman in her office. Beth had related to Randy what had transpired in the courtroom since witnesses were barred from being in the courtroom during the proceedings. "I think we have a solid case and since the defense had little to present, our case was made that much stronger," Beth said.

"I wonder why Giles didn't try to find someone who would counter your presentation on David's schizophrenic condition?"

"He may very well have and was unsuccessful."

"I guess that's all water under the bridge now, we just wait a week and hope for the best."

"The best would be for David to get some professional help."

Beth had gone back to her office vowing to see what she could come up with in an effort to get help for the boy. "He's not a bad kid, he just needs medical treatment." She had said to Randy on her way out.

The sound of the console on his desk brought Randy back to the present. He pushed a button, "Yes Nancy?"

"Mr. Mertz to see you."

"Give me a minute and then send him in." Randy straightened up his desk and cleared his mind. *Bet I know what this is about. The death of a young girl needs answers.* The door to his office opened, and the mayor of Robertown entered.

"Hello, Adam, how's the world of insurance doing these days?"

"Never mind my business, let's talk about your business. What is happening on the Lois Newman case. Any developments?"

"We are still checking what few leads we have, it isn't an easy one to crack." Randy offered nothing further.

"I had a call from Frank French this morning and he suggested it be turned over to the Kansas Bureau of Investigation. What do you think about that?" said Adam Mertz.

"Frank never did like to solve his own problems, I remember . . ."

"Never mind changing the subject, Randy, we need some movement on the case. Something that the public can chew on for a while."

"I do the best I can, Adam, you know that."

"I hope it's enough." Mayor Mertz left the office. His parting comment wasn't a threat, for he knew Randy would do everything he could to solve the case. But sometimes you had to light fires.

Randy knew that Adam had paid him a visit so he could tell people, like Frank, that he had talked to the Sheriff about the case. Once again he pulled the pile of files on his desk toward him. *I'll go over these again and again until that gnawing in the back of my head shows itself. If only I could figure out what it is that I am missing.*

He opened the file on Ralph and read it for the second time that morning. When he got to the report Bailey had written about Ralph's visit with Sheriff Smith and his belief that someone could easily get to the grave site by way of both the trail from the Dunsmore bridge and by boat using the Verdi River, the uneasy feeling returned. *What am I missing?* he repeated to himself. Shaking his head, he picked up his own file and started reading the report he had written on Ralph's discovery of the dead girl. "I asked the Kellam boy why he was in the area and while he answered Sheriff Smith came over the rise of the ravine and when he reached the grave site he took over the investigation. He **"Bam,** it hit like a bug on the windshield of a car. *That's it! That's what has been nagging me. How did he know? He came over the rise by himself. Walked right up to the site without anyone showing him the way. Ralph and I* *were standing away from the site doing the interview, he could have seen us and assumed we were at the site, and come to us. But he didn't come to us until later, he went to the site first. And he knew nothing about the rock piles Ralph had constructed, he knew nothing about where the site was, yet he came over the rise on a direct line to the site as if he knew where he was going like . . . like he had been there before.* "He knew where it was. HE KNEW!" Randy literally shouted.

A moment later, Nancy came to the doorway and asked, "Is everything okay Sheriff?"

"Okay? No, everything is not okay, it's great, everything is great."

*   *   *

"Clara, Logan Springer just brought this by, said it was found in the night deposit box at the Wells Fargo Savings and Loan Bank downtown. They thought you might want to take a look at it," said Linda Tipton handing an envelope, to Clara.

Randy and Jerry had spent the morning going over the pile of information that had collected during a ravenous late night effort to develop a plan to trap a killer. Randy didn't want Bailey to be disturbed, "Not now, Clara, we're on the verge of breaking a case wide open and whatever you have can wait. He started to toss the envelope aside, when he noticed the address. *Officer Jerry Bailey Woodrow County Sheriff's Department.* On a whim, he tore the envelope open and took out a single sheet of paper with a short typewritten note on it.

> *Dear Sir:*
>
> *It would benifit your department to search the trunk of Mrs. Delbert Kellam. You will find a match to evidence found at the Dunsmore place. That evidence was planted by Ralph Kellam. I know because he told me so. I am a law-abiding citizen who wants to help.*

Bailey handed the sheet of paper to Randy who glanced at it and then studied it closely. "Add this to the stack of evidence, and, Nancy, get me a warrant for the Kellam car that I can have Judge Martindale sign. Bailey, I want you in front of the Kellam house in ten. Clara, you ride with him. Secure Mrs. Kellam's car, but don't touch it til I get there with a warrant. Get moving."

Sheriff Simmons made it to the Judge's house in record time. It was eight o' clock when he knocked on the door and was able to rouse the judge, who came to the door in a house coat. "Sheriff Simmons, I was just going to call your office. I have something to show you."

"Not now Judge, I need a warrant signed and I'm short on time."

"Whoa, you are beginning to sound like your predecessor, Let's see a reason for the warrant first."

The sheriff pulled out the letter to officer Bailey and held it out for her to examine. When Janis Martindale saw the contents of the letter she pulled an envelope out of the pocket of her housecoat and handed it to Randy. "You better take a look at this sheriff, I found it stuffed in the backdoor handle when I got home a few minutes ago"

> *Dear Judge*
> *You've had a hard time getting your house back in order haven't you? It would be to your benifit to heed the warning and not get involved in things that you shouldn't. Sarah seems so nice, too.*

Randy noticed the similarity of the two notes. They appeared to have come from the same typewriter. "Judge, I really need that warrant and this just adds to the need. Don't you think?"

Let me see the warrant." Randy produced the warrant and gave it to the judge. She scanned it and signed it immediately. "This is planted evidence, you know that, don"t you sheriff?"

"Yes, but that doesn't mean it isn't evidence."

Del Kellam had no choice but to allow the search of his wife's car, and why shouldn't he? There was nothing to hide. It took less than a quarter of an hour for Randy to search the vehicle and find a pair of shoelaces in the trunk. Shoelaces with pink hearts on them, pink that matched the pink of the two shoes, one found at the Dunsmore place and one worn by the victim. Now to see if he could net his fish.

CHAPTER 61
JONIE AND SARAH

"**M**om, they're here, I'm leaving. See you in a few hours," Jonie called out.

"Bye dear, good luck," her mother called back. Jonie moaned. *Doesn't her mother know that you're supposed to say "break a leg?" Do you do that on a rehearsal? Or is it just on performances? I'll have to ask Sarah.* Jonie grabbed her coat and play book and dashed out the door to the waiting car.

It was six-thirty Friday night and the temperature was dropping. What little sun had shone that day was long gone, and the darkness had descended on Robertown. It would be a cold winter's night.

Two weeks before, Jonie had asked her mother if she could go to the tryouts for the winter performance of the community theater group. The play they had selected was a comedy and the lead part called for a teen age girl. In the play the girl dressed as a boy so he/she could try out for the boy's tennis team, since the school did not have a girl's team. "I should have a chance to get the part since I already know how to play tennis," Jonie told her mother. Jonie's dad was more than happy to loan Ralph his car so he could drive his sister to the tryouts, because it meant Del could stay home.

When they arrived at the community center, both were surprised to find Sarah there also. "My aunt says that I need to get involved more, and I thought this would be fun," she explained to Ralph.

"What part are you trying out for?" asked Jonie. She hoped it wasn't the lead.

"I thought I would try for one of the girls on the tennis team. I didn't want a big part, maybe the part for 'Mary.' That would be a fun scene where 'Mary and Marty' are trying on shoes."

Ralph watched the two girls and noticed how easy it was for them to talk to each other.

"I'm going to the YMCA for a swim. I'll be back about nine to pick you up, Jonie. Do you need a ride home, Sarah?"

"No, my aunt is meeting me here about eight o'clock." Ralph frowned, he'd hoped he could take her home.

"Then I'll see you later, Jonie." The two girls watched Ralph leave.

Jonie turned to Sarah and said, "I think he likes you a lot."

"I hope so," said Sarah as the two smiled at each other and walked over to the sign-in table.

Jonie and Sarah were watching the auditions for the singing parts when Judge Martindale came in. "Aunt Janice, you are early, we haven't tried out yet," said Sarah.

"Oh dear, my meeting was cut short. I guess I will have to wait."

"If you want to go on home, I can give her a ride home, my brother is picking me up at nine."

"That would be great, do you mind Sarah?"

"Not at all, thanks, Jonie, I'll see you about nine-nine thirty Auntie," Sarah said cheerfully.

The two girls finished their auditions and were told the cast for the play would be announced in a few days. They had been waiting outside the community center for almost an hour and Jonie was getting antsy,

"It's nine-thirty and Ralph 's not here yet. Let's go on down to the Sonic and get something to drink. It's only two blocks and I'm tired of sitting," Jonie said and off she went, with Sarah right behind her.

After getting a smoothie they were on the way back to where Ralph was to pick them up when a man wearing a Ronald Reagan mask and camouflage shirt and pants, stepped out of the shadows and threw a Styrofoam cup full of liquid on Sarah's face and chest. "That's just lemonade," he said. Then with the other hand he threw a second cup of liquid on her. "That's paint, but it could have been most anything, tell your aunt that, and tell her I . . ."

He never got to finish his sentence because he had Jonie's raspberry smoothie all over the front of his clothes and mask which failed to protect his mouth, nose and eyes. Jonie then stomped on his foot and kicked him in the shin with the point of her boot. The man, definitely in pain disappeared into the bushes. She turned to a shocked and crying Sarah. "Are you alright Sarah?" she asked her friend. "Here, let me help you . . . Your hair is a mess, sorry, you already knew that, didn't you? Hey here's Ralph, maybe he has a towel or something in the car."

Sarah was crying, but the paint had splattered on to her coat, which Ralph helped her remove.

Fortunately they found not only a couple of old blankets to use as towels, but a half dozen bottles of water that they found washed off much of the paint. "It must be latex paint," said Ralph,

"You look a lot better, Sarah.," said Jonie.

Ralph handed her his coat, "Here put this on, I'm sorry for being late, I had to change a flat tire, and the spare was low so I couldn't drive very fast on it."

Judge Martindale had begun to worry about the kids when they didn't show up by nine-thirty. When they did arrive and she heard their story, she worried even more. *Who would do such a thing to a sixteen-year-old girl? Someone has a warped mind.*

Realizing the danger that the man in the mask posed, she did what any parent would do, she called the sheriff's office and informed them of the incident.

A similar scene took place at the Kellam household when Jonie told her father of the confrontation with the masked man. Del was upset that his daughter retaliated instead of getting Sarah out of harms' way, he also was aware of the danger that existed as long as the man was loose on the streets. He called the sheriff's office, and reported the threats made by the disturbed man. In response to both calls, the Woodrow Sheriff's Office promised to have extra patrols of the area.

Meanwhile the man had departed the area and the "typist" went to work. On a blank sheet of paper, he typed out a note.

> *Dear Little Sister*
> *You are too big for your britches. Some one needs to punish you. I think you would benifit from a good spanking. Watch for it.*

He would place the note in Wanda Kellam's car a few hours later. "First I have to get this raspberry smell off me," he muttered, as he started changing out of the cameo clothes.

CHAPTER 62
SHERIFF SIMMONS AND SHERIFF SMITH

On a normal Saturday, Sheriff Simmons didn't arrive at the office until sometime in the afternoon, basically because his Saturday on duty often lasted well into the night. But this Saturday would be different. First, he was in the office by eight o'clock, and a barrage of people were in his face by nine. Judge Martindale called at eight-fifteen, and Del Kellam stopped by at eight-thirty, bringing with him a third note threatening Jonie and wanting to know if a report had been filed on the incident involving their children. Also Judge Martindale asked if an investigation had been started. Both parents were adamant concerning the danger the man posed for their children.

The sheriff confiscated the third note and promised Del he would do everything he could to protect the girls. At eight-forty five, Adam Mertz and Frank French appeared at his office door with a request that the sheriff should place a notice in the newspaper that the violence was under control. "To quell the rising discontent among the town folks," as the Mayor put it.

"Mayor, you know I can't release everything we have in the case. If, and that's a big if, we get a break in the case, then I would consider what you are suggesting, but not before." He finally convinced them to leave shortly after nine. Jerry Bailey came into the office from patrol about nine-thirty and Randy corralled him so that they could continue their work on organizing the information they had in the files. Only after a thorough review of the evidence did he look at Bailey and say, "Let's bring him in."

Within the hour a disgruntled man wearing a white tee-shirt, and khaki pants sat in the interrogation room of the sheriff's wing of the courthouse. He needed a shave and a haircut.

He also needed a lawyer. Jerry Bailey had the tape recorder going and he turned to Randy and nodded. Randy Simmons stood over the former sheriff and said, "Mike, you have been mirandized, and I strongly urge you to ask for an attorney to be present. Do you want an attorney present?"

"Who do you think your messing with, boy? You play with me and you'll get burned. You let me go and all is forgiven, but you carry this charade out any further and you'll pay, boy. You hear me, you'll pay big time."

"I take that to be a no, is that right?"

"Are you listening to me, boy?" Mike Smith hissed.

"Am I correct, no attorney?" Randy hissed back.

"No attorney."

"Okay, now anytime that changes, you say so, understand?" Mike sat at a table in the center of the room. Jerry Bailey had the recorder on the table and stood at the table's end. Randy stood across the table from where Mike sat. There was no answer to Randy's question. "I'll take your silence as a yes, said Randy. "Now then, why did you kill Lois Newman?"

Sheriff Smith exploded in laughter. After a time he quieted down and said, "I have to hand it to you, boy, you put your cards on the table right away. That's what I would do."

"Just answer the question." Randy was all business.

"I can't, because I didn't kill anyone."

"Would you describe what you did when you got the call about a body being found in the woods near Lake Lawson?"

"What do you mean? I responded, of course."

"No, no, I want you to walk us through it. Take it step by step, and tell us what you did." Randy checked to see that the recorder was going.

"I was in my office when the call came from . . . from you, that a body had been found near Cheyenne Cove Campground out at the lake.

I got in a unit and drove out to the campground. Then I hiked to the grave site."

"You were alone?"

"Of course, I don't need anyone to babysit me."

"Tell me about the hike to the grave site. Describe it to me."

"What do you mean? I hiked along the trail til I came to . . ."

"To what? Sheriff, what did you come to."

"I don't remember."

"Isn't it, til you came to the spot where you leave the trail and head to the ravine?"

"No, it's where I saw a bunch of people and guessed that was the grave site."

"But Ralph Kellam and I were the only ones there and you could see us in the ravine, but you didn't come to us, did you? You went to another spot didn't you?"

"I . . ."

"Where did you go Mike, where did you go."

"I went to . . . to . . ."

"You knew where the grave site was, didn't you? You knew because you had been there. You drove her out there in a squad car. No one would take notice of a squad car in the campground. You're the sheriff, it would be easy to control her. You led her to the spot. What did you use, Mike? The shovel? You used the shovel to kill Lois didn't you? You killed her, didn't you?"

"No, I . . . why would I?"

"That's my next question, Mike, why, why did you kill her? Do you even know?"

"I . . ."

"I doubt that you do. You probably never really thought about it, right sheriff?"

"I . . . You don't know anything. You don't understand."

"Oh, but I do, I have been studying you for several days and I understand you better than you understand yourself. You hit the weak spots, the weakest people. Fred Newman got in your way, so you struck Lois. Del Kellam and his lawyer-friend Mel got in your way and you lashed out at Ralph. Judge Martindale got in your way and you attacked Sarah. You are a sick man Mike, a sick man."

'You can't prove anything. All you got is guess work."

275

Randy had been so intent on his interrogation that when he straightened up he realized how tight his neck muscles were. He nodded to Jerry and the officer left the room. When he returned, he had an old typewriter which he sat in front of Mike Smith.

"What's going on here? What's that for?"

"We know how much you dislike computers Mike, so we will use your typewriter."

"Hope you had a warrant for that," Mike said.

"We did, Mike, now we're going to do a little exercise Mike, here's a sheet of paper, put it in the typewriter for me."

"What kind of kids game are you playing? I don't have time for this."

"Just do it, Mike and we can all get out of here." Mike put the paper in the machine.

"Now, type this for me, I cannot benefit from this. Go ahead, type I cannot benefit from this."

Mike did as he was told, and leaned back and started to stand. "Now can I go?" With one hand placed on Mike's shoulder to keep him in the chair, Randy used the other to pull the sheet of paper from the typewriter and lay it on the table. Bailey took a small camera from his pocket and took a close-up of the paper. "What's going on here? What are you two up to?"

"You just proved your own case, Mike. First of all we found this typewriter in the basement of your house, The whole department knows of your dislike of computers, and few people use typewriters any more. Now, look what you typed." Randy showed him the paper. *I cannot benifit from this.* "You misspelled benefit the same way you misspelled it on all three of the threats you sent. Mike 'Snuffy' Smith, you are under arrest for the murder of Lois Newman and two counts of making terrorist threats to do bodily harm, and breaking and entering, vandalism, and whatever else I can think of."

Mike made an attempt to grab the sheet of paper, "I'll get you for this, you think your so smart, I'll teach you," Mike lunged forward but Randy was too quick for him. He grabbed the former sheriff's wrist in mid-air and twisted it behind his back while slamming him down on the table, his head against the typewriter. In one fluid motion the handcuffs appeared and were clamped in place upon his wrists. "Jerry, you take care of the evidence and be sure to include the typewriter. I will take this sick-o back and personally place him in a cell. We'll book him later, when he calms down."

CHAPTER 63
TWO YEARS LATER

I t was graduation night and Ralph posed once again so his mother could take a picture. "Now Sarah, I want you in this one." Sarah shook her head.

"Come on Sarah, she won't quit till she gets her picture," said Jonie standing nearby. Sarah relented and moved to stand beside Ralph.

"Okay, Jonie, now one of the three of you," her mother ordered.

"You sure that camera can handle the three of us at once?" Jonie quipped.

It was a time of celebration, Ralph and Sarah had graduated with honors. Jonie had just won the district 4A tennis tournament, and was bound for the state competition. Heather and Jonie placed second in district 4A doubles division and would also compete in the State Championships.

Judge Ruth Tindle made her ruling on David Masters the week after the close of the hearing. She assigned David to the Lake Mary Center for Disturbed Children located in Paola, Kansas. An evaluation was made at the end of one year to determine what progress the thirteen-year-old had made. When the evaluation was submitted the review board decided that the child be retained for another year. He was due for another evaluation in two weeks. The staff at Lake Mary Center hold little hope for a good report.

"Darrell" apparently continued to manifest himself on occasion.

Mr. and Mrs. Leroy Masters sold their home in Robertown and moved to Paola to be near their son. However, David, due to his behavior had to earn visitation rights through credit gained by cooperation with the staff at Lake Mary. He seldom earned any credits. When visits were allowed, he refused to attend the visitation. Leroy and Leona had seen their son twice in the two years and both times from a distance.

The murder trial for former Sheriff Mike Smith was in its second week and the prosecution, under the leadership of Beth Bushman, had rested its case against him. The case was expected to go to the jury in the next day or two. The trial against him for terrorist threats was to begin in three weeks. In an article published in the Robertown Gazette, a retired judge predicted that if found guilty in the murder trial, Mr. Smith would plead guilty to the terrorist charges. He further stated that a civil suit brought by Mrs. Newman, would be likely.

An investigation by the Judicial Watch, a public interest organization, found Judge Janis Martindale guilty of misconduct and abuse of the public trust, and was removed from the bench. She did not lose her certification to practice law, and established a private law firm in Topeka.

The relationship between Ralph and Sarah continued to grow and in the fall began classes together at Washburn University with the goal of a law degree. Their plan was to join the Martindale Law Firm upon completion of passing the bar exam.

With the financial help of Jonie's parents, Bobby was encouraged to enroll in the GED classes at the YMCA during the following winter. He completed the course in one year. Delbert Kellam negotiated an agreement with a tax client, Bill Tolman, for Bobby to work in Bill's Motorcycle Repair Shop as a mechanic's apprentice at a minimum wage salary. The Methodist Men Church Group accepted Bobby's home as a mission project and cleaned and renovated the Dunsmore place. Bobby began to work eight hours in the evenings at the Methodist Church cleaning and dusting in exchange for his food distributions from the church food pantry. Heather Wilkes taught Bobby Dunsmore to read. That success and the faith and trust people placed on him had an effect on Bobby and he became a part of the community.

Heather and Bobby are often seen together at the YMCA, the Methodist Church, or at the movie house and on occasion at a school function. A few of the town folk who knew Bobby's father doubt the change in the man to be genuine, "you know what his father was like . . . the acorn doesn't fall far . . ."

\

OTHER WORKS BY JAMES WHALEY

VISION QUEST: A TIME TO LIVE
THE NEGOTIABLE LIFE OF STELLA BELLE

AND—TINA'S DREAM—A COLLABERATION WITH MARVIN
BICKNELL, DOROTHY HUSH, AND JOANNE HUTCHISON